T0355934

Dear Reader,

My favorite part of being a publisher is connecting readers to groundbreaking authors and their books. Today, I am especially delighted to introduce an evocative new voice in literary fiction.

Elba Iris Pérez's debut novel, *The Things We Didn't Know*, is at once a heartfelt coming-of-age story and a finely wrought portrait of a life across cultures in 1960s America. Pérez, a native of Aguas Buenas, Puerto Rico, spent her early childhood in the company town of Woronoco, Massachusetts, where the book is partially set. Elba is the inaugural winner of the Books Like Us First Novel Contest, which was founded to provide greater accessibility to underrepresented writers and celebrate the diversity of readers across the United States. Launched by Gallery Books in June 2021, the contest now rotates among Simon & Schuster's adult imprints.

As you join Andrea on her journey in *The Things We Didn't Know*, I hope you fall in love with her and her colliding worlds of Puerto Rico and small-town America, just as we have.

Sincerely,

Jen Bergsh

Senior Vice President and Publisher,
Gallery Books

The Things We Didn't Know

The Things We Didn't Know

Elba Iris Pérez

G

GALLERY BOOKS

New York   London   Toronto   Sydney   New Delhi

G

Gallery Books
An Imprint of Simon & Schuster, LLC
1230 Avenue of the Americas
New York, NY 10020

First Gallery Books trade paperback edition January 2025

GALLERY BOOKS and colophon are registered trademarks of Simon & Schuster, LLC

For information about special discounts for bulk purchases,
please contact Simon & Schuster Special Sales at 1-866-506-1949
or business@simonandschuster.com.

The Simon & Schuster Speakers Bureau can bring authors to your live event. For
more information or to book an event, contact the Simon & Schuster Speakers
Bureau at 1-866-248-3049 or visit our website at www.simonspeakers.com.

Interior design by *Yvonne Taylor*

Manufactured in the United States of America

10   9   8   7   6   5   4   3   2   1

Library of Congress Control Number: 2023937122

ISBN 978-1-6680-1206-2
ISBN 978-1-6680-1207-9 (pbk)
ISBN 978-1-6680-1208-6 (ebook)

To my beloved sister,
Elizabeth

one

I was half asleep when Mamá dressed my brother, Pablo, and me, hurried the two of us into the car, and cranked the starter. She backed out of the garage and hit the pedal, and minutes later the whole front end of the car dangled off a cliff.

Pablo got out of the back seat, screaming in Spanish so that our mother could understand. "Get out, it's going down!"

I stumbled out, dazed and seeking solid ground, pebbles slipping under my feet all the way down a ravine layered in massive white mica slates. We stood at the ledge, speechless, a river gushing over boulders below as hawks pierced the clear morning air with their screeches. The front of the car balanced over the edge, clumps of soil falling from the right wheel.

Pablo panted. "We just made it, Ma."

My mother sighed the way you do when everything goes wrong. "*Dios mío*, I don't know how that happened," she said in Spanish.

"Aren't you going to back it out?"

Mamá looked bewildered.

"Where were we going, anyway?" I asked.

Mamá's black eyebrows drew in. She slammed the car doors shut, grumbling as if my brother and I had had no reason to leave them open in the first place. She opened the trunk, hauled out a brown leather suitcase that had been in the closet for the four years we'd lived in Woronoco, and tossed it to the ground. "Well, we're not going anywhere now, that's for sure. Andrea, help your brother take this upstairs." She slammed the trunk lid as if she wanted to send the car tumbling down.

She'd never wanted my father to buy that car, anyway.

I watched my mother inch her way back to the street, a black leather box purse she never took out of the closet dangling from her elbow. I was only seven years old and knew she'd had it with the Beehive.

She brushed off the musty white linen suit she hadn't worn since the day we came from Puerto Rico in 1954, when I was three years old. Of course, I couldn't remember the trip to the United States, but she'd told me about it many times.

The story always began with the day she received the plane fares Papá had sent from Massachusetts, and then she told me about the moment she first walked into our apartment and said, "This is it? This is where we're going to live?" There was always a heavy sigh.

She looked stunning in that suit as she tiptoed over new summer weeds. She stomped on the asphalt pavement, knocking mud off her patent leather heels. "*Qué remedio.* Might as well put all these clothes back in the closet."

And she was right, there was no place for her Puerto Rican city fashion in the Woronoco company town. No need for the cute black curls she'd sprayed in place earlier that morning, the heavy makeup and dark red lipstick, the nylons and heels she wore as she'd hurried us through breakfast after Papá left for the paper mill. That wasn't necessary in the Massachusetts wilderness.

"Nothing happened here, now let's go. And when he comes home, anything he asks, just say you don't know."

Pablo and I grabbed the overstuffed suitcase and lugged it across the two rows of houses on Tekoa Avenue, the street we lived on, known as the Beehive. The cul-de-sac, shaded by dense forests, was one of four streets in the Woronoco company town, which no longer exists but was home to workers of Strathmore Paper Company, like my father, for decades.

One row of apartments faced south, overlooking the cliff, with Old Woronoco Road in the distance. From their windows at night, you could see car lights moving between the trees in the forests on the other side of the Westfield River. But there wasn't anything romantic about the apartments across the cul-de-sac facing north, where we lived.

Our back porch overlooked the railroad tracks. With every passing train, our windows rattled, from daybreak to four o'clock in the afternoon, when the last caboose left.

The fragrance of peach blossoms in our backyard followed us while Pablo and I took turns bumping the suitcase up the rickety stairs to our second-floor back porch. Pablo covered his mouth to hide his words from our mother.

"Papá's gonna be really, really mad."

Mad was putting it lightly. *Encabrona'o* was more like it. Anyone who knew my father could tell you how he bragged about that car. You'd think it was the only Oldsmobile in the world and he was the only Puerto Rican who'd ever bought a new car.

The ground reverberated with the rumbles of an approaching train. Mamá used her key to the apartment and slammed the door.

It had been four years since our father, Luis José Rodríguez, brought us from Puerto Rico to Massachusetts. He had come to New Jersey as a seasonal farmworker, leaving us behind in Puerto Rico until he had a home for us. When the farming season ended, he accepted an invitation from an acquaintance who lived in Northampton, Massachusetts. A few weeks later, he found a job at the H.B. Smith Foundry in Westfield and took a room in a house owned by a woman from Spain. When he complained about the hard work the foundry required, she introduced him to a man who had been to Strathmore Paper Company in Woronoco, a company that rented homes for its employees at low rates, only seven miles away.

Papá often bragged about how he got the job at Strathmore and saved money to send for us in only a few months. His plan was to live in Woronoco only long enough to save up for a car and then rent a house in the nearby town of Westfield, where a small Hispanic community gathered at church on Sundays with a *gringo* priest who said Mass in Spanish. After he bought the new Oldsmobile, my parents set out looking for a house.

But he had a problem with every house she liked. It was too old, or not in the best neighborhood, or too expensive, or too far for him to drive back and forth to the paper mill. Papá was spoiled. He walked to work. We lived next to the mill, which is why our street was called the Beehive.

From the day we arrived, Mamá complained that Woronoco was too isolated. Sure, her husband had a secure job and provided us with a home, but there were no stores, no restaurants, no public transportation. The only place you could walk to was a small post office on Old Woronoco Road. The closest towns were Westfield on one side and Russell on the other, and you needed a car to get to either. Mamá didn't know how to drive, and Papá didn't want to teach her or allow her to use his car.

She argued that if we weren't moving to Westfield, she wanted to return to Puerto Rico. But as far as our father was concerned, we already had a perfect life. She didn't have to talk to anyone or go anywhere, anyway. Women were meant for the house, and houses were meant for women, and she already had a house, and that was that, he'd say.

After dinner on weekends, he did what hardworking men deserved to do, according to him. He took off in that shiny new car wearing a freshly starched shirt, his black hair greased to one side, smelling of aftershave.

Strathmore gave him a life he couldn't have in Puerto Rico, and he wasn't planning on leaving that job and lifestyle. He'd grown up on a tobacco farm in Utuado. When he married my mother, they moved to Caguas, where he worked in construction. But the jobs were few and temporary and the pay miserable. He liked the fact that work in a paper mill wasn't dirty like work on a farm. "I don't have to take a shower before I kiss my kids every night," he said.

The foreman at Strathmore had offered to hire his entire family—the men, of course. And there were plenty of empty apartments on Tekoa Avenue in the company town known as the Beehive for Papá's whole family to rent.

Gone were the days when he drove home with his brother Felipe in a jeep full of *plátanos* they couldn't sell. Papá and his family believed farming no longer had a future in the Puerto Rico of the 1950s. His entire family accepted the offer to work at Strathmore, and in a few years' time, they would all arrive in the Woronoco Beehive.

Pablo and I had no recollection of the island we had come from. We knew our life in Woronoco wasn't the same as it was for the kids around us, but we wanted to blend in. All of our family conversations at home were in Spanish. My father spoke very little English, and my mother didn't speak it, nor did she want to learn.

Pablo and I didn't know anything about living in Russell or Westfield. We knew nothing of Puerto Rico and Utuado or Juncos, where our parents were from. We didn't know that we were Americans. We only knew that we were Puerto Rican and wanted to be considered American like everyone else around us, to be accepted by the kids in our neighborhood. But we had a huge problem. Our mother prohibited us from staying out after school. She said the American women made fun of her. So, because of her refusal to connect with anyone in the neighborhood, our time after school was spent kneeling on the living room sofa, watching the other kids play outdoors. It was torture.

The summer of 1958 would be different, though. Our father had bought us two new bikes: a blue one for Pablo, a pink one for me. More than anything in the world, we wanted to ride our bikes up and down the street. But as soon as we started summer vacation, Mamá said, "Why waste time making friends? We're not going to be here long. You don't need to practice your English; you've learned enough at school. You won't need it in Puerto Rico, anyway." And I remember thinking, *Papá says we're never going back, doesn't she get it?*

~~~~~~

After Mamá drove the car to the cliff, we heard dresser drawers, windows, doors going *bam, bam, bam!* The train chugged by as I hung up the frilly yellow dress she'd laid out for me that morning, a dress I didn't want any of the neighborhood kids to see me wearing, because what second grader going on third wore princess-style dresses?

Pablo folded his dress pants and dropped onto his bed, across from mine. "Why's she so mad?"

I dressed in pedal pushers.

He swung his feet, bumping the foot of the bed. "Do you think she'll let us take our bikes outside? Papá said we could ride them on summer vacation."

Dishes rattled in the kitchen and the stove ignited. My brother was right. But our father wasn't there to make his point.

"Let's go get them from the garage, Andrea, come on."

"We have to ask," I said.

Outside our bedroom window, a solitary dog barked. It was too early for Sally and Mark to be outdoors, everyone was sleeping in. I dreaded another summer day of waiting for nothing to happen. We had no choice but to ask our mother's permission.

"Well, go on," Pablo said.

We sat at the red Formica table while she prepared Café Bustelo. She had changed into a light-pink, button-down housedress and had a cigarette dangling out the side of her mouth. She poured coffee through a cloth colander she'd used hundreds of times, the one she'd bought at the Plaza del Mercado in Caguas just before we moved to Woronoco. "Want coffee?"

"No," I said.

Pablo fake-coughed and urged me forward with his eyes.

She sat next to me with a cup of coffee, and I was about to speak when she lowered her head into her hands. At first I thought she was coughing, but then she whimpered, her body heaving. Pablo looked stunned. Her grief ripped into my chest.

I went over and embraced her. *"¿Qué te pasa, Mamá?"*

An approaching train whistled. "That *maldito* train," she screamed in Spanish, her eyes on the window. "You can't even talk in here. Why do they have to tell everyone they're coming? We can hear you, we can hear you."

All I wanted was to see her smile, like when we came home from school and she greeted us with glasses of chocolate milk. I stroked her hair, the rumbling wheels reverberating in my chest as the train took its time, hissing by our house until it stopped at the docks.

Mamá wiped her face on her flowered half apron and lit another Pall Mall cigarette. "Go make yourself some toast."

Soothing bird songs from the breezy forests of Tekoa Mountain came in through the pantry window. I opened a jar of peanut butter.

Pablo came in behind me. "When are you going to ask?"

"Why don't you ask? Nobody's out there, anyway."

We prepared peanut butter and jelly sandwiches and returned to the table. I felt sorry for my mother, but was tired of her negativity. Why couldn't she be like all the mothers around us who allowed their kids to go play?

She flicked her cigarette on the ashtray, her fingers shaking. "Luis is going to be so mad when he comes home and finds that damned car over there. Ever since he bought that thing, he doesn't want us to leave this hole in the world. But of course, he has no problem going wherever he wants."

"I thought you didn't know how to drive," Pablo said.

She went back to the table, put her head down, and whimpered again. "I thought I could but . . . *los nervios* . . . I hit the brakes and it . . ." She wailed. "The devil pushed the car. *Dios mío* . . . I can still hear you screaming."

The memory of what had happened in the car struck me as funny in a way and I didn't want her to see me holding back laughter, so I cleaned up the table and carried the breakfast dishes to the sink—the white porcelain sink with two buckets underneath to catch the leaks that she complained about every day. Pablo wiped off the table.

"I don't know why he bought those bicycles. You can't take those to Puerto Rico. That's money down the drain. I'm not going outside to watch you. Those *gringas* are always talking about me. You're not going to be out there all by yourselves either."

"They're not talking about you, Ma," Pablo said.

"You don't have to watch us," I said.

"Sure I do. Anything happens to you, he blames me."

"But he said we could ride the bikes on summer vacation, and summer vacation started today," Pablo said.

I chimed in with my brother. "Nothing's going to hap—"

"You're the last one that should be talking. That day you fell on the sidewalk and scraped your knees, who did he yell at?"

"But Mamá, that was years ago."

"You're not going. *Señor Jesucristo*, I thought he'd slap me that day. One problem is enough for today."

She put her cigarette out and stood up.

"Now go watch TV and forget about those bicycles."

Pablo ran to the living room and knelt on the sofa, facing the window. Kids had come out. Their voices drifted in through the windows. Tears rolled down his cheeks.

I knelt on the sofa next to him.

"That's Kevin," he mumbled.

I couldn't bear to watch the kids playing. "I know."

Kevin Martin, his older brother David, Sally Nowak, and Mark Abbot. They took the school bus and walked home with us every day. They were free to be whatever they wanted to be. Free to be outdoors without an adult watching, commenting, criticizing, scolding, ordering, or stopping them from doing anything.

There we sat, staring out the window again, looking away from the stale, limiting world behind us. The green jungle leaves on the wallpaper, the pink flamingos on the upholstery, brown squares on the linoleum floor, and a television. Our home was no match for the vast outdoors, for the smiles and laughter of our friends, for the excitement of a game. The nicotine stench in our kitchen would never compare to the splendor of the woods, air so crisp you wanted to be out there forever.

"He's in my grade. That's the new family, the one with those two big kids," Pablo said.

I heard my brother, but I wasn't listening. I wanted to open the door to the front hall, grab his hand, run downstairs, and never return. I wanted to roll down the grassy little hill under the elm trees, sleep under the tower-ing maple tree at the bottom of the railroad tracks, and play on the Tarzan swing, listening to the train go by, staring into the sun.

I'd had enough of Captain Kangaroo, Roy Rogers, and Mamá's bad moods. When she wasn't sniffling and tearing up, she was dancing cha-cha to records on her Victrola.

I hated my mother's records from Puerto Rico. They had songs nobody else had ever heard. That Felipe Rodríguez always sounded like he was cry-ing about something. Why couldn't she listen to the music on the radio instead? Why couldn't she say hello and be polite to our neighbors?

She came into the living room and sighed, the kind of sigh that says you're tired of being alive, the kind that doesn't go over well with a seven-year-old going on eight with enough energy to explode out into the world.

"Why are you two always talking in English now?" she asked.

"Mamá, we've always talked to each other in English," I said.

"Well, stop it. I don't want you speaking English in this house."

Pablo shook his head and then yelled in Spanish, "First you won't let us go play, now you don't want us to speak in English? Mami, I don't under-stand you."

"You're both too young to understand," she said.

Pablo ran to our bedroom and slammed the door. She was darn right. We sure as hell didn't understand. She didn't understand either. The Wor-onoco company town was the only home my brother and I knew, and we loved everything about it, including the trains. Our father, who every-one called Louie, was the only Puerto Rican at the mill, but that wasn't a problem for him. The neighborhood kids were always asking us how to say things in Spanish. They seemed to think it was cool that we spoke an-other language. All the men worked at the paper mill. All the women stayed home. And all the kids in the Beehive played in the cul-de-sac. The only one who had problems with the Woronoco Beehive was my mother.

Pablo was the first one to see our father coming down the hill with some
workers that evening, the shiny black curl on his head in sharp contrast to
the blond crew cuts the other guys wore. They saw the car.

My brother grabbed the car keys and took off down the back staircase,
and I followed as fast as I could.

Faint rays of sunlight took their last peeks between the trees while the
perplexed men, all dressed in dark-blue uniforms and steel-toe boots, inspected the Oldsmobile. Papá stood there with his mouth open. Before taking the keys from Pablo's hands, he was asking questions.

"What happen to my car? Who move my car?"

He handed me his black metallic lunch box. His bright-green eyes met
mine, expecting an answer. He always wanted explanations from me because I was the eldest. And I always told him what he wanted to know, but
that day I was torn. Our mother had warned us not to say anything. Luckily,
with all the men talking to him at the same time, he didn't wait for a response. But I knew my father. He was perfectly aware that we were holding
back what had happened, and later, when all the men were gone, we'd have
to respond.

How to back up a car with half its wheels dangling in midair, that's all
they cared about. Some of the guys thought an attempt to back it up could
be dangerous. The wheels could wear off the ledge just enough to send it
down the cliff. Someone suggested calling a tow truck. But my father insisted he could back it out.

He started the car, and the back wheels skidded. We all watched him
shake his head. Then he gave it another go. The wheels skidded again. The
car roared, grabbed onto the ground, and rolled backward, over the weeds
and onto the street. The guys cheered as he backed into the garage.

Neighbors, mainly the wives, had come out by then, asking how the car
had gotten to the edge of the cliff to begin with, and it was the new kids'
mom who pointed to us and said she saw us with our mother in the car.

Papá nodded and thanked her, then he called my brother and me over
and pointed to the cliff. "How'd this car get over there?" he asked in Spanish.

My stomach knotted. People didn't have to speak Spanish to under-stand his question. Pablo faced the tracks, dug his hands into his dungarees, kicked up dirt, and never lifted his eyes from the ground.

"Stop getting those shoes dirty," Papá said. Then he zeroed in on me.

"That's not where I left my car when I went to work this morning at the break of dawn. I left it In. My. Garage. Where I leave it Every. Single. Day. Who moved it?"

Everyone looked at me for an answer, even though none of them under-stood Spanish. The pit of my stomach became a huge hole.

"Answer the goddamned question."

He wasn't camouflaging his body language. Anyone who saw him could tell he was pissed as hell, and I didn't want the big kids to see him scolding me. Our father had never placed a finger on us, but I wasn't sure what he was capable of doing on account of that car.

His shoulders fell, he let out a sarcastic smirk, and went back to his bro-ken English. "Nobady know anyting now. The vehicle drove ober der to dat *precipicio* all alone."

His coworkers chuckled.

Luckily, as soon as the guys saw Mamá approaching us, they shook hands with our father and took off with their wives.

Mamá walked with her head high, wearing a cotton dress, old slippers, and a scarf wrapped around bobby-pinned ringlets. Pablo and I leaned against the Cyclone fence in the front lawn. All the big kids passed by on their way home. Some smiled, others called Pablo and me the usual funny names, "Andrew and Pah-blee-toe," trying to add humor to the situation. Most of them avoided eye contact, to spare us the embarrassment, I guess.

Mamá scrubbed her nervous fingers on her apron.

"Are you almost done? Dinner is ready and waiting. Close that garage and let's go warm up your stomach."

Papá let go of the garage door, spun around, and spoke in Spanish.

"Before we go anywhere, I want you to tell me what the hell happened to my car today."

"All you had to do was back it out, right?"

Papá shifted the weight of his body to another boot, cocked his head to one side, and bore his eyes into her. "What kind of an answer is that? How did this car go from here to that abyss?"

"I wanted to surprise you—"

"Answer my question. How did this car move from this garage to that cliff?"

The fire coming out of my father's eyes could've fueled ten of those Oldsmobiles all the way across the United States. I wanted to run inside but didn't dare.

My father stared at Pablo for a while. Then he glared into my eyes, his head bobbing up and down.

"What do you think of that?" he asked me. "'Surprise me,' she says."

His eyes made direct contact with mine, and he leaned toward me as if I was his accomplice.

"I've given her one driving practice and she thinks it's enough to drive an automobile."

He pointed at my brother. "Were you with these two?"

Then he pointed at me. "What the hell is wrong? Why aren't you answering my questions?"

Pablo stared at the ground. I clung to the chain-link fence and stared at the forest on the opposite side of the cul-de-sac, where the car had stopped just shy of the cliff. And that was a big mistake, because all the images of our pathetic morning drive resurfaced.

I remembered my excitement going out with Mamá so early. When she chose the frilly dress, I thought we were headed somewhere special. I remembered her foot going up and down on the brakes as she drove it out of the garage, the car jerking and springing forward like a mountain lion.

And now, I couldn't help myself from cracking up in front of my father. I bit my lips, and some of the impulse to laugh relaxed. But more images swamped me. How the car came to a powerful stop, the three of us bumped around, I banged into the dashboard, fell to the floor, grabbed onto the door anticipating we'd flip down the precipice. Then I remembered her face, the color drained, her wide eyes fixed on the cliff, her nostrils flared.

It was awful. And it was hilarious. I shied away from my father's eyes and covered my mouth, but quivering laughter blurted out.

My mother turned to me. "Stop that laughing, I'm telling you . . . his belt stings like a bee. *Mija, cálmate.*"

And I did calm down. But before I could catch my breath, Papá's eyes fumed at me. He was on fire, and I was out of control. Everything inside of me poured out in laughter.

Every time I glanced at Pablo, he dismissed me with his hand and covered his face, trying to maintain control, until he too exploded. I whirled around and pushed my face into the chain-link fence, sucked on my lips and cheeks, took in deep breaths.

"Tell those kids to shut up," Papá said.

"Don't pay attention to her," Mamá said. "You know that *mal de risa* attacks when the devil gets into her. And the other one. It doesn't take much to get him started."

Papá looked at her with angry eyes. He was not done. "Why did you tell the kids not to tell me anything?"

Mamá locked eyes with me. "*Cucha,* I didn't tell you to hide anything from your father, did I? Tell him." She spun around and pounded up the staircase.

For a moment, my brother and I stood there, frozen. Then, Pablo ran after her. This was one of the things that most bothered me about my mother. She strayed from the truth, and I was caught in the middle, not knowing which direction to take. I suppose this was her way of dealing with a toxic relationship, but it sure spread the heat on my brother and me.

Papá bolted the garage door and returned to the back of the house. "That woman told you not to say anything, right? I'll find out where she was going."

Later that evening, my brother and I gobbled down supper without lifting our eyes from the plates, then exited the kitchen while our parents ate in silence. Pablo had just finished adjusting the television antenna when Mamá screamed, "Hit me! Go ahead, *cabrón!*"

I ran over in time to see my father standing next to the kitchen sink, struggling with her. His shoes shuffled on the floor as he braced himself, his face an angry grimace. He grabbed her hair and she flinched, screaming, "Let me go!" He wound her hair around his knuckles and brought her head up close to his face. Her torso twisted, and she let out a high-pitched wail and banged her fists into his body wherever she could reach him.

Even though my parents argued on many occasions, I had never seen aggression like this. That night, my father didn't even resemble himself, his eyes protruding, his pale skin sweaty and red.

Pablo walked in behind me and ran up to our parents. "Papá, Papá, you're hurting her!"

"Let go of her, Papá!" I yelled.

But I don't think they heard us.

His body tensed, he stared into her eyes and spoke through his teeth. "I know what you're doing, but you're not making a *pendejo* out of me, understand?"

I thought he was going to slap her or spit in her face, yet all he did was hold her there, staring into her eyes, breathing into her face, his muscles quivering with the weight of her body, just long enough to show his dominance. Seconds later, she broke away screaming insults I had never heard before, words sounding so bad I had no desire to know their meaning. She pushed my brother and me out of the kitchen, ran to her bedroom, and slammed the door.

Our father pointed to us with piercing eyes and a voice that bolted through the walls. "Don't look at me like that, I haven't done anything. And let me tell you something. The next time she says she's taking you somewhere in that car, you don't have my permission to go. Understand? You do. Not. Have. My permission. That woman doesn't know how to drive. *Cristiano.* It's a miracle you're alive. She's gone crazy."

We listened obediently with our eyes on the floor, and as soon as he finished, we squirmed along the wall into our bedroom, watching our backs. I didn't think our father would hit us, but I wasn't sure. We took our shoes off, turned off the light, and crept into my bed, the one that had a view of the kitchen.

I stared at the dirty dishes, still in their places at the table under the yellowish light of the overhead bulb. The kitchen curtain fluttered in a warm breeze, and I could smell the lard Mama had fried pork chops with.

"Does he love the car more than Mamá?" Pablo whispered.

I didn't have an answer.

Papá's feet shuffled in the shower room, the door opened, he turned the bathroom light off, and I got a whiff of his cologne. Keys jingled. Then the screen door banged against the porch wall, his steps creaked down the back staircase, and the Oldsmobile rumbled.

We heard Mamá clear the table and bang dishes against the enameled sink. Then all went quiet. We peered into the kitchen. She sat at the table in her robe, crying.

"Did he know it was there?" Pablo whispered.

"What?"

"The suitcase."

The image of the brown leather bag struck me like the blinding flash of a camera. My brother was only six years old, yet he noticed things that surprised me. When had my mother placed that suitcase in the car?

"No, I don't think he knows about the suitcase."

"Well, we were going somewhere. Somewhere with a suitcase."

After a while, my brother fell asleep next to me. Where had we been going with her in that car?

two

From then on, my father took the car to work every day, even though the paper mill was less than five minutes away. It felt like the fight just never ended. If she wasn't complaining about him going out at night and coming home late, he was complaining about her cooking, which, according to him, was worse than American food. The pork chops were too greasy, the soup had too much oil on top, the rice was too sticky.

But our father gave us permission to ride our bikes. We were to be home at four-fifteen, when he came home. And we had no problem following that rule. As soon as we saw his car coming down the hill, we stopped our bikes and waved, he slowed down until we caught up with him, then we tagged onto the car and glided all the way to the garage. He'd give us smacking kisses and store the bikes along the wall, next to the car. Then we followed him upstairs.

He walked through the door and kissed our mother, but she always leaned away. She wanted nothing to do with him, and it became normal to see the distance between them. We watched television after dinner, went to bed after a warm bath, and got up to ride our bikes again the next day.

Almost every day, I played with Sally Nowak, who was in my classroom and lived two homes away. Her parents spoiled her with toys, but she enjoyed sharing it all with me. She had Barbies and their doll clothes, houses, and cars. She also had a Hula-Hoop, yo-yos, and Play-Doh. But the best thing she had was her mother.

Mrs. Nowak routinely gave us lemonade and cookies. She squeezed and kissed Sally often, making cooing sounds. My father told me Mr. Nowak could afford all those toys because he was one of the big shots at the mill. They were the only family in the Beehive who had a big, plastic swimming pool and a pitch-black dial-up telephone that rang so loudly you could hear it throughout the cul-de-sac.

When we weren't on her porch, Sally and I rode our bikes to a secret place we discovered away from the raucous baseball games in the cul-de-sac. Up the little hill, short of the dump, we hid our bikes behind the bushes on the side of the road. We ran into the forest until we reached an opening just before the riverbank.

Birds, grasshoppers, and butterflies welcomed us. The sun's luminosity surrounded us. We named it Faeries Meadow. To the right, there was a field of pussy willows. And later that summer, we discovered bushes loaded with wild blackberries behind them.

Pablo and Mark Abbot played with Kevin Martin, the new kid, and they became inseparable. Pockets stuffed with marbles, running around with long sticks in their hands looking for snakes and frogs to kill—although I don't think they ever killed any frogs or found a single snake.

That fall, I started third grade and my brother second. But our mother closed herself in and never walked us to the school bus again. We became two more kids who walked, skipped, and ran with all the others through rain, sleet, or sunshine, across two hills to get from the Beehive to the bus stop on Valley View Avenue.

As we entered Russell Elementary School, walls covered with banners and teachers standing in doorways greeted us. Our school was a wonderland where everyone had a polite smile, followed the leader, and waited their turn in line. We came home to rake leaves into huge mounds and took turns jumping into them from the Tarzan swing. On Halloween, we trick-or-treated all the way to Valley View Avenue and Hill Street, the big kids watching out for us and sometimes stealing pieces of our candy too. In winter, we slid down snowy hills all the way from the railroad tracks to the cul-de-sac on sleds and toboggans.

While life was perfect for Pablo and me, an unstoppable war rumbled between my parents. We didn't see much of our father anymore. Mamá rejected affection from all of us. She only smiled once a week, when she took a stroll with us to the Woronoco Post Office. Pablo was too shy, and she might as well have had no voice, so I was in charge of asking the postmaster for the mail for box one-hundred-seventy-two.

When Mamá received mail, she beamed. She couldn't wait to reach our apartment to open her letters, so we tumbled onto the Strathmore Paper Company lawn, while she sat next to us reading letters in silence, the aroma of red rose bushes behind us, the smokestack shooting black clouds into the sky, and trains chugging along behind the blue-and-white company buildings. Then she folded her letters into her bra and spoke about her sisters— Cecilia the *negrita machúa* and Florencia the eldest—all the way back to the Beehive. When she didn't get any mail, she stood at a window staring into the distance and lit one cigarette after another. "Go watch Roy Rogers," she'd say, even when Roy Rogers wasn't on.

It was 1959 and I was about to turn nine years old when Mamá came into the kitchen wearing the same white suit and black patent leather heels she'd worn the day she drove Papá's car to the edge of the cliff. She dragged the old suitcase across the linoleum floor and plopped it in the middle of the living room. "Get dressed and help me carry this downstairs."

Pablo and I looked at the suitcase, then at each other. *What now?* Mamá hurried us into dress clothes, opened the hallway door, and told my brother to carry the bag downstairs.

A short, stout man I'd never seen before, with half a can of pomade in his hair, stepped out of a black car with white wheels, threw the suitcase in the trunk, and hurried us into the back seat. Mamá ducked under the dashboard, clutching her purse, and told us to crouch down on the floor. By the time I figured out what she wanted us to do, the car had swerved out of the cul-de-sac, my brother and I flopping over each other on the floor, asking why we were hiding, where we were going.

The driver headed up Tekoa Avenue, passed the smokestack, and crossed Woronoco Bridge. "You can sit up now," he said, heading toward Westfield. Mamá, my brother, and I climbed onto our seats.

Mamá smoothed out her skirt. *"Aleluya, Dios mío,* I'm finally leaving this hole in the mountains." She lit a Pall Mall.

"Mamá? Where are we going?" I asked.

"¡Puerto Rico!" Mamá cheered.

"We're going to Puerto Rico? Is Papá coming too?" Pablo asked.

"I don't know about that."

I hated everything I knew about Puerto Rico. Papá's stories about mosquitos and bugs in his bed, about only having one pair of shoes, no water, no electricity, and fighting with another kid over a piece of bread. Why would anyone want to return to such a place?

Pablo whined, "What about our bicycles, Mamá? We can't leave our bikes."

"Ay, mijo, there's plenty of bicycles in Puerto Rico," she said. "We can buy whatever you want over there. Let's get there first."

I was nauseated by the smell of my mother's cologne, cigarette smoke, the plastic seat covers, and the driver's cigar. Pablo didn't make eye contact with me.

Hours later, we arrived at an airport in New York and the driver took our suitcase to a counter. Mamá fumbled through her purse and paid him, her eyes dancing with renewed sparkle.

"Can I sit at the window?" Pablo asked.

"I don't know if they're going to give us a window seat, *mijo,* let's wait until we're on the airplane," Mamá said. Then she laughed. "The one that didn't want to go, now wants the window. And wait until you see Puerto Rico."

My stomach grumbled. "Can we eat on the airplane?"

"I don't know, but I think sometimes they give you food. We'll only know when we get there." Then Mama's voice turned soft and assuring. *"Ay, mis hijos,* you're going to like it so much you won't ever want to come back here. We have family we can visit whenever we want to—one day one house, another day another house, always someone we can go see. And you can always play outside. There's no snow over there—"

"You mean it doesn't get cold?" I asked.

"Never."

Pablo groaned. "But I like the snow."

"Well, you're going to have to come all the way back here all by yourself if you want to see snow."

Pablo frowned but soon perked up with excitement as we boarded the Pan Am flight with our mother. He took a window seat and I plopped into the seat next to him, fearing what awaited us. I didn't know where Puerto Rico was, but I did know we were leaving my father. I thought of the way he always said, "*¿Cómo está mi santa familia?*" the moment he came home.

What would he do that night when he realized we weren't there? He'd search the house, going from one room to another, turning lights on, calling *Raquel, Andrea, Pablo*. But no one would answer. There would be no dinner plates on the table. No coffee brewing. He'd slam the hallway door open and run down the stairs, leaving the door banging against the wall. He would call us, his unsteady voice escalating as he reached the front of the house. He wouldn't see us in the cul-de-sac, under the magnificent maple tree, or on the Tarzan swing. He'd see our bikes along the wall in the garage. Maybe Kevin's mother would say she'd seen us. Would he run back into our apartment and search our closet? Would he notice the old suitcase missing? That's when he'd go to the sofa, running his hands through his hair the way he did when he was worried, until, exhausted, he'd throw himself in bed with his clothes on, knowing he should have seen this coming.

We flew through turbulence, the captain's voice came in through a speaker, and I fumbled to strap my seat belt. Mamá spoke in Spanish in the seat behind me. A woman asked my mother if she was going to look for a job, and I was surprised at the joyous sound of her voice when she responded.

"That's the first thing I'm going to do. As soon as I can, I'm taking a *carro público* and going to Caguas."

"My husband is from Caguas," a woman said.

"Well, I'm from Juncos, but my sister lives in Gurabo. My family tells me there are a lot of factories in Caguas where I can work as a seamstress and . . . I live near . . . *el cinco* if I find something affordable . . . my sister."

Even though I didn't understand what my mother was talking about, I was surprised to hear the tone of her voice. She sounded like another person. A happy, positive person who I couldn't remember having met before. With her new attitude and so many Spanish speakers around me, I felt as if I'd entered someone else's world, one I could understand but that was not my own.

I didn't know what my mother expected of me. Was I supposed to be excited about leaving my father behind? Was it okay to cry because I already missed Sally? I knew Mamá was unhappy in Woronoco, but why did Pablo and I have to be sucked into her problem?

I wanted my father to carry me off the airplane in his strong arms and set me on the ground next to the birch trees under the railroad tracks. With each breath, I fell further into suffocating darkness until I exploded into sobs and dug my face into my knees.

Pablo turned away from the window and rubbed my arm.

I imagined my father watching us in his white, sleeveless undershirt, telling us not to be afraid. He'd rub his shaving brush on a bar of Ivory soap and cover his face in thick suds, staring into the mirror, his chin stretched upward as he slid a razor up and down his face. I knew my father. He'd brush the dark-gray wool suit that hung next to the empty hanger Mamá's white suit had left. His key would turn in the Oldsmobile, the engine would roar, and he'd pull his *máquina* out of the garage, rage in his eyes. He wouldn't rest until he found us.

Muggy heat smacked us in the face the moment we stepped into the San Juan airport. The place was jammed. Mamá carried our suitcase as we followed passengers into the lobby, her eyes searching the crowd for someone.

"Watch the suitcase. I need to find Cecilia."

Mamá had often spoken to us about her two sisters, especially Cecilia, as well as her father. And now we were finally to meet Titi Cecilia.

"Is she older or younger?" Pablo asked.

"She's the youngest," Mamá said.

"Does she look like you?"

"She has a different *papá* than me. After my *papá* died, my *mamá* married a Black man called Erasmo, a wonderful man. Right away she had Cecilia."

"Did you take care of her sometimes?"

"Of course," Mamá said. "But me and my sister Florencia knew she was different. All Cecilia wanted was to hike through the field with her father, chop down *plátanos*, and ride horses. Wearing pants just like a boy."

Mamá told us she hadn't seen either of her sisters since their mother's death seven years before, when Cecilia was a teenager.

In the airport, a pudgy Black man held his arms up high on the other side of the arrival gate. He called out to someone as a line of passengers pushed through. Mamá didn't go very far before she made an about-face. "Let's wait for the line to go down. *Ay, Señor,* what are we going to do if Cecilia doesn't show up?"

The man followed Mamá with his eyes and called her again, a huge grin on his face. "Raquel, Raquel, over here."

My mother looked the other way.

"*Ay, Virgen*, he's calling some Raquel."

The man's eyes widened and he called louder, his arms above the crowd. When he couldn't attract my mother's attention, he waved to me with such insistence that I avoided making eye contact with him, until he called my name. "Andrea Inés, tell your mother I'm over here."

How can you ignore someone who knows even your middle name? I tugged at Mamá's elbow.

She pushed me away. "*Ay Dios*, don't pay attention. Why won't he leave me alone?"

But the man's eyes demanded attention. "Raquel, Andrea, it's Cecilia!"

Mamá spun around and gasped. "¿Ceciliaaaa?"

The man gave her a shy smile, his hands on his head.

"*Virgen santísima*. That is her. Grab the suitcase."

The man didn't strike me as a Cecilia, but Mamá rushed us into the line.

"That's Titi?" Pablo asked. "I thought our aunt was a girl."

Mamá mumbled, "*Ay, Señor Jesucristo*, that's her all right. How was I supposed to recognize her looking like that? *Qué ridícula*. I knew she liked pants, but she's unrecognizable."

"But why's he have a girl's name?" Pablo asked.

"No, no, it's not a he, I tell you. That's Cecilia, my sister. I don't know why the hell she's dressed like . . . so embarrassing. *Vámonos*."

The man called Cecilia followed us with affectionate eyes, laughing and yelling out to us the whole time.

"Stay close," Mamá said. We moved through the crowd, following our mother, who didn't stop mumbling until we reached her sister.

"*Dios*, listen to that, can't she wait for us to get there? You can hear her ruckus all the way over here. *Qué bochorno*. I wouldn't have asked her to come if I'd known she was going to show up in those clothes, *ay, Señor*. Don't stare!"

Cecilia met us with open arms. She tussled my hair with a grin that took up her entire face. "*¡Canita!* Well, you must be about nine years old now, is that right? Still have that golden hair on your head!"

I smiled as she stomped her feet, twirled, her laughter so exuberant people stared.

She sized all of us up. "You're all *jinchos*, you need some sun." She jumped back and forth like a boxer, taking Pablo by surprise with soft punches, her huge chest bobbing up and down.

"Wait a minute. This is Pablo? The man. Gimme a punch. How old are you now?"

Pablo dug his hands into his pockets. "Seven."

Cecilia extended her arms to my mother, and when they pulled away, her face was covered in tears.

"Always the sentimental one," Mamá said, drawing her into another hug.

Cecilia wiped her face. "I don't know if your mother told you, but we don't have the same father." She rolled up her sleeve and placed her arm next to my mother's to dramatize the difference in their skin tones. "See? I'm the *negrita* in the family."

Mamá pushed Cecilia's arm away. "*¡Ay!* Stop it. We're all *puertorriqueñas*, a rainbow of colors."

Cecilia hugged her again. "I know, I know."

Mamá grabbed us by the shoulders and guided us away from the crowd. "You were one difficult kid. *Traviesa*, always getting into trouble."

Cecilia laughed and focused on me. "But then she met your father, Don Luis, and you know how that goes. They moved to Utuado, and I didn't see her again until Mamita passed away. That's the way it happened, am I right, Raquel? What has it been now, six years?" She took a handkerchief out of her pocket, one just like my father's, wiped her eyes, and forced a smile.

"Seven," Mamá said.

Cecila patted my mother's shoulder. "I'm glad you're living *allá afuera*. I was sad when Florencia told me you had left, but happy for you and Don Luis. Hey, I'd go with you if it weren't for my father. I just can't leave him alone here." We walked toward the parking lot.

My mother waved her hand. "No, no, you don't want to go over there. Let me tell you, there isn't one place I'd change for Puerto Rico. Now tell me, how is Don Erasmo? Still making cigars?"

"Not the same since our mother passed, but his cigars are still the best in Aguas Buenas."

"Good," Mamá said. "I couldn't wait to come home, and you won't find me over there again." She grabbed the suitcase and jerked her head. "*Vámonos.*"

"*Oye, mi hermana,* you mean you're staying here?" Cecilia asked.

Mamá held a finger to her lips and picked up our suitcase. "We have a lot to talk about. Where's the car?"

Cecilia stepped in. "Here, I'll take that. Follow me. Lots of people. Make sure the kids don't get lost." She took long, broad strides, leading us to the parking lot.

A light shower glittered in the sun and turned into steam the moment it hit the ground. Ahead of me, Pablo held onto Mamá's skirt, his jet-black hair shining. I had a hard time keeping up with them, mulling over Mamá's words. She was never going back? Did that mean *we* were never going back?

Pablo slowed his pace to catch up with me.

"A guy with huge tits," he mumbled, covering his mouth. He peered out of the corners of his eyes, making sure Cecilia didn't see him, and then placed his hands over his chest, imitating the size of her breasts, and chuckled.

I held back a snicker. I didn't want my brother to hurt her feelings. "Shut up." I'd never seen a woman dressed like a man, other than costumes on Halloween. But still, something about her was familiar and loving.

"He's really a girl with boy clothes, right?" Pablo asked.

"Yes, a girl."

Cecilia stopped at an old jeep and placed the suitcase in the back. "*Mi hermana*, you gave me such short notice. I couldn't borrow a car."

Pablo and I climbed in the back, giggling with the excitement of riding in a jeep for the first time.

"No problem at all," Mamá said, "as long as it takes us to your house, that's all we need. You don't know how much I appreciate this. I knew you'd be the one person who'd be here no matter what, *llueve, truene, o ventee*, or like the *gringos* say, rain or shine."

Cecilia pulled the keys out of her pocket. "You got that right. I'd go to the end of the world for you. Welcome back to the rain, heat, and hurricanes. They say a big one is coming this year."

"They say that every year. Give me a thousand hurricanes over snow."

Cecilia grabbed a paper bag from the windshield, took out a loaf of bread, stuffed it with ham, tore it into three, and handed each one of us a sandwich. "*Pan de bollo con* mortadella. *Buen provecho.*" She started the jeep.

Mamá bit into her sandwich. "All we had was a little breakfast. You haven't changed, *mija*, taking care of everyone around you."

A warm breeze tainted with car fumes blew in my face as I bit into the soft, delicious bread.

"*Gracias, mi amor.*" Mamá rubbed her hand against Cecilia's cheek. "Your face is scratchy. Why are you shaving?" Mamá asked with a mouthful. "Those hairs are going to grow back hard, and you won't be able to turn back if you want to. Your cheeks used to be so soft. And why are you so black? That's not your natural color. You've been in the sun too long."

Cecilia put her hands up on the wheel with the jeep running. She stared at the parking lot for a few minutes, and I didn't know if she was angry or trying to come up with a response. "I'm never turning back, Raquel."

"But I didn't recognize you at the airport."

"You haven't seen me since I was fourteen. I'm almost twenty-two now. I like the way I look, dark skin and all. I work on a farm, remember?"

Mamá bit into her sandwich and spoke with her mouth full. "Why don't you wear a hat for the sun? And why don't you dress normal, like a woman?"

"I don't mind being darker. And my clothes, well, this is normal—"

"I mean, normal the way God made you."

"God made me the way I am. The way I look right now."

"*Cucha eso*, you're born a woman or a man. Nobody gets to choose that."

Cecilia turned the jeep off.

"You're *machúa, marimacha*, we've always known that. How many times did I have to go to school to complain about the bullies? But you're not just a tomboy now. I don't want to offend you, but you look completely like *un macho*."

Cecilia chuckled. "You're not offending me. But I'd like you to understand that this isn't about the clothes. Even if I dress like a girl, my mind doesn't see me as a girl."

"*Marimachas* can still dress as women, get married, have kids. Not very feminine, but still a woman."

"But I wouldn't be happy saying I'm a tomboy. That's not me. I'm not trying to cover the whole sky with one hand anymore."

Mamá looked away. A car stopped and waited for us to move out of the parking space, and she signaled him to move on. "I remember how good you looked in dresses, and one day I told Florencia, 'When she grows up and puts heels on, she'll have some legs.' Show those legs off."

A long silence ensued, and I wondered if Cecilia was angry. Cars honked, people around us talked and yelled. The heat was unbearable, and I hoped we'd get going wherever we were headed. Cecilia wiped sweat off her temples just above her shaved beard and leaned her head on the steering wheel. Why was my mother questioning her? She wasn't your typical girl, it was obvious.

"Are you ashamed of me?" Cecilia asked.

Mamá brushed crumbs off her lap. "No, of course not. I'm just worried about your happiness. You're the little one in the family."

"Well, it's a little late for that. You haven't been around."

"I know, but I couldn't—"

"Don't feel bad, we're good. But this is the thing. I wouldn't have been any different if you had been here all these years."

"Why don't we forget about this and leave now?"

"I need to know that you understand. If we're going to have a good relationship, we have to accept each other."

She spoke with her heart in her hands, and I understood her as plain as daylight. I couldn't imagine her being any other way. Pablo chewed on his last bite and looked at me out of the corner of his eye. I knew he too was concerned.

"Start the jeep," Mamá said. "If you're happy like this, then let's leave it at that. It's getting hot in here, let's go."

"No. I don't want to leave until I know you understand that I can't change who I am. And yes, I'm happy."

Mamá shook her head and raised her arms. "Okay, so what more is there to understand?" She reached out, hugged her sister, and leaned on her chest. "There's nothing more to talk about." Mamá looked at me and rolled her eyes. "If you're happy, I'm happy."

Pablo and I looked at each other. I knew Cecilia had not altered my mother's opinions, and I empathized with my aunt.

Cecilia held onto her for a while, wiped her eyes, and started the jeep. "Help me read the signs, *mai*. I don't come here often."

Mamá shouted out directions as Cecilia headed out of the airport onto Avenida Campo Rico, which was the picture of paradise, outlined with mounds of red hibiscus, pink bougainvillea, and golden trumpets. By the time the evening cooled off, we were on Carretera Número Uno toward Caguas. Pablo and I rested on each other's shoulders as we rode through the night.

When I woke up the next morning, thick Caribbean monsoon drops pelted the zinc roof. Pablo slept next to me. Gusts of wind circled the house. Branches scraped against the cement walls. Storm shutters rattled as I stepped out of the bedroom in my underwear.

Rocking chairs creaked on the porch where Mamá and Cecilia spoke in subdued voices. Across from the bedroom there was a small couch with yellow plastic-covered cushions and rusty metal legs. A set of keys, an old black wallet, a bottle of rubbing Alcoholado Superior—green from the herbs added to the bottle—cluttered a side table. Two old rocking chairs were strategically placed to take in the view beyond the porch.

To my right, a red-checkered plastic tablecloth covered a small metal dining table with four matching chairs, one of them missing a cross rail on the back. On the kitchen table, a square tin can of Sultana soda crackers with an image of a woman dressed in a red belly dancer outfit. A bottle of *pique*, salt, and other spices were bunched up in a corner.

Behind the chairs, an open window with an outdoor sink and faucet attached to a windowsill showed off a dense forest. Leaves whispered in the rain. Next to the door, an old, rusty refrigerator hummed. On top there were bottles and a flyswatter. A rusty machete covered in dried clumps of reddish soil leaned on the side of the refrigerator.

The entire home smelled of coffee and burning wood. Smoke came through the door that led to a shady area outside with a *fogón*, the wood-burning fire pit where Cecilia cooked.

It didn't take long for me to figure out that Cecilia and my mother were speaking about my father, and I wanted to listen in. When would he arrive? What was my mother's plan?

"I don't think it was a good idea for you to just disappear like that," Cecilia said.

"I left him a letter. What was I supposed to do, stay there forever? Waiting for nothing?"

Cecilia held an old metal cup of coffee between her knees. "Don Luis isn't going to sit around as if nothing happened."

Mamá stared at the river for a while. "Everything is so much easier here. You cross the river and the *carros públicos* are right there. *Mija,* you have no idea what you have here. There's no way out of Woronoco unless you have a car. No *carros públicos*, no buses, nothing. You don't need a car here. You can go wherever you want without waiting on anyone. That's what I want. To come and go freely."

I stood on the porch and slithered along the balusters.

The moment Cecilia saw me she beamed. "*Hola,* how was your first night in Puerto Rico? Look at her, *tan linda*. Come, sit with me." She pointed to her lap. "How did you sleep, were you warm?"

"Go sit with your *titi*," Mamá said.

I sat on Cecilia's lap. She kissed my forehead and stroked my hair. "This blonde hair. They say our grandmother had blonde hair and blue eyes." She pointed to the trail. "That winds all the way up the mountain. Lots of kids your age live around here."

There were voices of people walking down the mountain trail. "They're going to the *carros públicos*," Mamá said.

"What's a *carro público*?" I asked.

"It's the same as a taxi, you pay for a ride, and some of them carry five or six passengers. Didn't you have those in Owroroco?" Cecilia asked.

Mamá laughed. "No, *mija*. It's Woronoco. And we lived in a hole deep in the mountains where there was nothing but the factory where Luis works and no way out of there but driving. And I don't drive, so we were stuck there all the time."

Cecilia gave her sister a gentle nod as if she was giving her words some thought. Then she patted my back. "Just started raining when we crossed the river last night. I carried you and Pablo to bed. I bet you don't remember. No way to get back across in that jeep now."

I stood at the balusters. Below us, a muddy trail ended at a rumbling river that gushed with intensity past the house. Fresh, earthy scents surrounded us. As far as I could see, mounds of giant bamboo bent in the wind and red *flamboyán* trees spread their flowers onto the riverbanks.

Pablo came out, dragging his feet, and went to the right side of the porch, where the river sounded almost as deafening as a train. "Aren't those people over there getting wet?"

"Soaking wet," Cecilia said. "Even though there's a *parada* on the side of the road. And how'd you sleep, *pai*?"

Cars honked before they came around a sharp curve. Mamá sipped on a mug of espresso. "That's the bus stop, where the *carros* pick up passengers. This is what I wanted."

Cecilia stood up in a long, black linen dress. "You must be starving, let's fill you up." Then she turned to Mamá. "Everyone has a right to seek happiness. I do it my way, you do it yours. I don't have to tell you that you can stay here as long as you need. What's mine is yours. Papito will be happy to see you."

Cecilia offered to watch over my brother and me so that our mother could go job hunting. They agreed Mamá would go out on the days when Cecilia wasn't working at the gasoline station on the road to Cidra.

"You're going to love it here," she told Pablo and me. "I can already see both of you climbing trees, getting all dirty, having a blast with the other kids."

Mamá thanked her and they went out to the *fogón*. Pablo and I sat in the rockers, fascinated by the wilderness around us, the quiet song of coquí frogs and the river. Minutes later, Cecilia came out with a supersize bowl, called us to the table, and fed us *yautías majadas*, a concoction of mashed taro root with butter and milk.

Mamá served herself more coffee. She laughed and we all stared at her, wondering what was so funny. "Do you remember when they called you Macha in school?" she asked Cecilia. "They called her Macha the Macho, and boy did that make her angry. Oh God, she'd beat up kids and then run home crying."

"Everyone calls me that now."

"Really?"

"Well, not Macha, they call me Machi. Ask anyone in Aguas Buenas, and they don't even know my name is Cecilia unless they went to school with me."

"Machi? *Cucha eso*, where did that come from?"

Cecilia snickered. "Someone very dear to my heart called me 'Machito' and then shortened it to 'Machi.'" She fed Pablo, scraped the bowl, and held a spoonful in front of my face. "I'm going to fatten these kids up."

Pablo snorted. I could tell he liked Cecilia as much as I did. She was lovable, fascinating. The twinkle in her eyes, the perfect white teeth, the curly black hair against ebony skin, the deep dimples punctuating a splendid smile that revealed a good-natured heart. She was a character I'd never seen before, and I loved her.

The next day, Mamá left at sunrise. When my brother woke up he called for her, and when she didn't show up, he cried.

Cecilia came into the room. "Your mother will be home in a few hours. The rain stopped. Get dressed and let's go."

Soon we were being fed a bowl of *maicena*, a delicious cornstarch pudding with egg yolks, butter, and milk. We spent the day exploring the farm with Cecilia. There were women working in a tobacco shed, workers in a field, neighbors walking down the trail, all of them calling Cecilia "Machi." It only seemed natural for us to call her Titi Machi from then on. There were chicken pens, goats, and horses. There were tobacco fields, orange trees, plantains, bananas, breadfruit trees, mango trees, guavas, passion fruit vines, and squash vines covering a valley and a hillside.

Just before sunset, bathed and fed, my brother and I waited on the porch for our mother, until we saw the last *carro público* and watched her cross the river. We called out to her with excitement, jumped and waved from the porch, but she inched her way along with dispirited eyes, her shoes and a loaf of bread in her hands.

The same story went on for weeks. Machi would place a cup of coffee in her hands before asking how the job search had gone, and they'd go to the rocking chairs on the porch. Every day Mamá told a story more depressing than the last. Prices of *públicos* were higher than she expected, she couldn't afford lunch, and none of the factories were hiring.

Machi took time off from the gasoline station to take care of us for a few days. But when she returned to work, we were on our own all morning in the empty house. We poured ourselves coffee, helped ourselves to the can of Sultana crackers, and waited on the porch until she showed up at noon and prepared lunch.

It was the last week of June when Mamá told us she'd visited her older sister, Florencia, in Gurabo, who suggested she move there to try her luck in neighboring towns. "I've never thought of working as far as Humacao," she said. "But if I have to, I'm ready and willing. What else can I do? I can't go much longer without making money."

"When are we leaving?" Pablo asked.

"Florencia doesn't have an extra bed, and she's too old to watch over you. Cecilia has room for you here."

Pablo clung to her waist, whining. "You're going for a whole week?"

Mamá raised her arms over her head. "*Ay, mijo,* don't be silly, I'm not leaving forever."

"It doesn't change anything," Machi told Pablo. "We're just going to continue having fun on the farm every day, right Andrea? I need you, *pai,* you're *el jefe* now. Help me dig up *yautías.* Sack is empty." Machi faced my mother, "He's a great helper."

My mother brushed her off with her hand. "They think life is all fun and play."

"That's what kids are supposed to do," Machi said.

The next day the door creaked at the break of dawn, and I ran to the porch. I was disheartened when I saw Mamá on the trail carrying the suitcase. Pablo showed up next to me and called out to her, but she didn't respond. A neighbor took the suitcase from her, and she crossed the river, which had become a trickling stream. Pablo screamed, "Mamá, take me with you! Mamá, please, don't leave us here!"

She reached the other side and continued up the riverbank, talking with the guy who carried the suitcase. When they reached the top of the road, he set it down. Pablo whimpered. The middle of my chest grew hollow. My brother called out to her, his voice desperate. I knew she had to hear him, and I couldn't understand why she didn't turn around and wave to us, just one last time. Why didn't she take us with her? We didn't care if there wasn't an extra bed, as long as we were together. Sure, Machi was nice, but she wasn't our mother.

I noticed she wasn't taking a *carro público.* Someone waited for her in an old red car. A huge gap opened up inside of me and tears filled my eyes. Who was in the car? Through the woods I saw the door open and a man step out. She put her shoes back on. They embraced. He took the suitcase and placed it in the trunk. The old car screeched when he turned it on. And just before it whizzed away, my mother's hand came out of the window and she waved. My heart broke as I recognized the skinny hand with long nails painted in her favorite shade of bright coral, a hand I could distinguish from anyone else's, anywhere in the world.

Pablo screamed, "Why didn't you stop her? Why didn't we run with her?" I huddled into a corner and grabbed my knees.

Machi's strong arms surrounded me and lifted me from the floor. She lifted Pablo into her other arm, set us on her lap, sat with us in a rocking chair, and squeezed us into her bosom. "Hey, hey, *ay, madre mía*. My princess, *mi jefe*, what happened here?"

She whispered calming sounds, her strong heavy hand gliding over our heads in long, gentle strokes. Her soft cologne warmed up a cold place inside of me as my father's had done before. I breathed into the comfort of her embrace, mistrust breaking away like dust.

After a while, my brother quieted down and all I heard was her heartbeat, her breathing, and the soft rumble of the river where life continued untouched by anything but the calls of the coquí. Pablo perked up and stared at the river.

"Are we doing good now?" Machi asked.

He sniffled.

"Why didn't she take us?"

"There's no room for you in Gurabo. Florencia has a tiny house. But you have a nice bed here, and you can wait for her here, with me."

I rested my head on her shoulder, her strong hand stroking my hair.

"We've gotta check on the tobacco *ranchón* and I'll need the two of you. Tobacco leaves are way up high, strung together in *ensartas*. I'll need you to climb a ladder and take them down so the workers can tear the vines out." She held us close to her bosom. "Come on, *jefe*. She'll be back before you know it, and I'll bet when she comes for you, you won't want to go."

Machi's embrace momentarily soothed my pain. But nothing changed the feeling of being left with a stranger, and that the sounds of the river, the forest, the animals, were all alien and even scary at times. Nothing shook off my sense of abandonment, and I knew my brother felt the same.

   Late at night, when everyone slept, I remembered the stairs in the back of our house in Woronoco where I waited for Sally to come out and ride bikes with me, where Papá met us every day. We had lost our home, our father, our friends. It didn't matter what explanation anyone gave, I had now lost my mother as well. All I had left was my brother and Titi Machi, the man called Cecilia.

three

There was something magical about finding Machi in the outdoor kitchen every morning wearing her long black dress, the bare ground under her feet. Without saying a word, she would sit me on a bench next to the doorway and brush my hair into a braid. Nebulous heat arose from the ground as the sun evaporated morning dew. The aroma of coffee brewing on her *fogón* greeted rays of light that snuck through holes in the walls. Trails of smoke from the burning wood dissipated through the windows, followed by the deep fragrance of coffee that threw wisps of toasted nuts and chocolate into the air.

Along the trail to the *carros público's* stop, everyone wore muddy shoes and villagers' voices interrupted sounds of morning critters. Machi's dark, silent silhouette contrasted against sparks flickering throughout the dimly lit room as she turned coals with a long stick.

One afternoon, she told us someone was coming to watch over us the next day. "I don't want to leave you two alone, but I can't miss more days at work."

"Aww," Pablo said. "I don't want anyone watching me."

Machi chuckled. "I get it, but when this person comes, you'll be able to go out and play."

The next day, we heard a rare bird chirping and ran to the porch hoping to find it. Then we opened the door and there he was, eating an orange in the tree above the driveway. A skinny brown kid, not much taller than Pablo. He jumped to the ground, his curly black hair flopping around; his jolly laughter so contagious that we had to laugh with him. He'd pulled our leg with the bird call. "I'm Tito," he said. "And you're the kids Machi wants me to watch."

Tito was one hell of a kid. He taught us how to knock down oranges from the trees using a stick. We scooped them up as they bounced to the ground. Pablo started the slow process of peeling an orange with his index finger. Tito laughed and pulled out a knife for his own, taking off the peel in one long swirl.

We climbed Machi's mango trees to experience the world from above. Mothers knuckled their kids' heads and rushed them into *públicos*. When the trail was muddy, we watched people switch to old shoes and carry their good ones in bags. People argued, not knowing we watched, and one morning, we saw a guy take a piss on the side of the road.

Tito showed us how to bring *ensartas* down from the walls of the tobacco barn. He used a long pole with a fork on the end, grabbed onto the cord full of dried tobacco leaves, and lifted them from the hooks they hung from. Then he lowered the pole and we took the dry leaves off the cords. We placed the leaves in bushels at the foot of a table where three women cut the center stems out with round knives. Three guys Machi called *peones* came around the house at noon, dropped off the machetes and pickets they'd used in the field, and set down all sorts of tools next to the shed with the *fogón* pit. If Machi wasn't home, they stood around and waited for her until she came and paid them.

When the *peones* told her about the work we'd done with Tito in the tobacco barn, she put on a big smile, went into her bedroom, and brought out a jar of change. "Here you go, *pai*," she said, and gave each of us three cents. Tito jumped up and down with excitement and headed out the door, but she stopped him.

"Nah, nah, nah," she said. "You know how that goes here, *mi jefe*. You have to eat lunch first." And then she cooked and served us *viandas con bacalao*, a codfish stew with root vegetables that filled us up. After the last bite, Tito led us up the trail.

Pablo ran ahead of me, shouting at Tito in Spanish, "Where we going?"

"*Ventorrillo*," Tito responded.

"What's a *ventorillo*?" Pablo asked.

"To buy candy."

We stopped at an old shack on the side of a house and Tito banged his fist on a window shutter. "Doña Carmen!"

Two shutters opened, and a woman with more lines on her face than I'd ever seen on one person smiled at us. "I have *limber de coco* today. Made it this morning, but it must be frozen by now."

Pablo whispered at me. "What's a *limber*?"

The woman must have noticed that we didn't know what she was talking about and handed me a freezing plastic cup with something solid inside. "Eat it," she said in Spanish. Then she looked at Tito. "*¿No hablan español?*"

I told her we spoke Spanish but had never eaten this. When I bit into the frozen cup it was similar to a snow cone, and I smiled.

The woman's eyes twinkled. "That one's on me," she said. "How many do you want? Two more?"

Pablo didn't look too happy. "Is that coconut? I don't like coconut."

"I have grape and pineapple," she said.

The boys each paid her one cent, and we ran back to Machi's house to eat our *limbers* on the porch.

Tito sat in Machi's rocking chair. "We still have two cents left for more later. We can get *marrallos*."

"What are *marrallos*?" Pablo asked.

Tito squeezed his lips together. "Ah, I guess you won't like them, they have coconut, but you can get *gofio* or *pilones* or *dulce de ajonjolí*."

I stared at him, wondering what all these candies were and why I'd never heard of them before.

"You'll like them," Tito said.

We couldn't get enough of Tito. He taught us how to harvest *yautías*, *malangas*, and other tubers that grew on Machi's farm. We cut down plantains and bananas and picked lemons and mangoes. He taught us how to find eggs in the chicken coops, and how to grab a chicken for dinner. After he caught the bird, Machi came home and wrung its neck while Pablo and I watched, our eyes popping out of our heads as it shook on the dirt floor of the shack.

Tito laughed at our horrified faces until the chicken stopped shaking. "Now it's ready for the pot. You can't eat it alive."

Machi dipped the whole chicken into a pot of boiling water, pulled out all the feathers, cracked the breast open with a huge knife, and showed us the gizzards in her bloodied hands. At first, I found the reality of it all repulsive. When you're on a farm long enough, you learn the value of preparing wholesome foods, but I didn't see ever getting to the point where I helped her wash parts of a chicken.

Tito didn't know a lot of things. We were on the porch one day and he asked questions.

"What is snow like?"

"It's cold," Pablo said.

"I know that, but what's it like? Is it hard like *un limber* or soft like rain?"

"It's like a frozen cotton or a feather," I said.

"But the size of raindrops," Pablo said.

Tito looked across the river. "You mean it's really soft."

"But when you take a bunch of it and squeeze it together, you can make a hard ball and throw it at someone," Pablo said.

"Or make a snowman," I said.

"Maybe someday I'll see it," Tito said.

"Have you seen a . . . I don't know the name in Spanish. A sled or a toboggan?" I asked.

"I don't know," he said.

"You use them to glide on the snow," Pablo said.

"You mean a *trineo*?" Tito asked.

Pablo and I didn't know what that was either, so we discussed all the ways you could slide down a snowy hill.

"I miss Woronoco," Pablo said. "I wish we could go with Tito to the Tarzan swing and watch a train go by."

"I've only seen trains on television," he said.

"Yeah, and in October, all the leaves on the trees turn colors and then fall off, and if you pick one up from the ground it's brown and crispy."

"Brownies are my favorite dessert," I said. "Pablo, why'd you remind me of brownies? Now I miss them more. And chocolate ice cream."

"You can get ice cream here at the plaza. Tell Machi to take you. They're really good. My favorite one is mango."

"Yeah. Machi took us one day and they're not good," Pablo said. "No chocolate. No strawberry. Just the Puerto Rico flavors."

Another day we were sitting on the porch eating *pilones*, red lollipops with sesame seeds.

"You don't have a lot of things here," Pablo said.

Tito looked confused.

"Like what? Puerto Rico has everything."

"You don't have Bosco for my milk."

"You don't have Corn Flakes or M&M'S," I said.

Tito looked perplexed.

"I never heard of those. Ask Machi. She can probably find all that in the *mercado*."

"She already looked. They don't have them."

Tito's eyes crinkled. "What do you need them for?"

Pablo laughed. "They're just good. I like milk with chocolate."

"She can get a Chocolate Cortés bar," Tito said. "She knows how to make that. Grates it. She made hot chocolate for me one day when there was a storm."

"But Bosco isn't like that," I said. "It's in a bottle."

"I guess we don't have it here. Gotta use what you have." Tito grabbed his burlap sack, the one he took everywhere. "This is all I need." He pulled out a long rusty knife, and a blue metal cup.

When we worked on the farm, Machi handed him fruits and vegetables throughout the day. "*Llévatelo, pai*," she'd say. And he'd stuff his sack. One day, Pablo and I were fussing over our dinner when Machi served *arroz con calamares*. I took a few bites and pushed my plate aside.

Machi looked surprised. "Aren't you hungry?"

I shook my head. I was hungry but couldn't stand the smell of the calamari.

"Okay then, have some coffee and crackers and I'll save this for Tito. He'll eat it."

Pablo pushed his plate away.

"How come he eats everything?"

"Tito? Necessity is the mother of invention, they say. When you're in need, you do whatever you have to do to survive."

I was confused. Tito didn't seem to have any problems.

"What does he need?"

Machi frowned.

"Tito doesn't have parents. He never met his father and his mother died when he was a toddler. His only family is an aunt who has four kids and is also a single parent. Tito is just an extra in that house. He only gets a roof over his head and an occasional bowl of food."

I couldn't believe that happy, confident boy had such a sad story.

"But does his aunt love him?"

"In her own way she probably does, but when you don't have money, there isn't much you can do for a person even when you love them."

Pablo and I were silent for a long while, and then he pulled back his bowl of rice with calamari and ate a few spoonfuls. I tried to eat some of mine but felt queasy and stopped.

Machi noticed my struggle and pushed my plate away.

"It's okay if you don't like it. I just want both of you to know not to be wasteful with food."

Pablo looked worried.

"So, does Tito not have enough food?"

"Everyone in the neighborhood helps him in one way or the other. He knows where to go when he's in need."

"Is that why he comes here all the time?" I asked.

"He's here every day because I asked him to watch you two. But normally he comes around to help with chores on the farm, around the house. He gives much more than he takes."

From that moment on, Tito became my hero. He didn't look much older than me, yet he worked for a few coins and seemed so happy with so little. He told my brother and me there wasn't a television in his house. He had no idea who Captain Kangaroo was. He had never owned a box of crayons. Tito accepted his life like an adult in an eleven-year-old body.

There always came a time when he slipped away, and we never realized he'd left until we saw him running toward the river.

One day Pablo caught up to him before he could disappear.

"Why do you leave when nobody is calling you home?

"*El río* and the *guaraguao* call me," he responded. We had no idea what he meant, so the next time he ran toward the river, we followed him.

Instead of crossing to the other side, he turned left at the end of the trail going upstream along the riverbank. We jumped over rocks and crawled over boulders on a steep incline behind him. The river split into gentle streams, and when I heard the overpowering sound of a waterfall, Tito's head disappeared ahead of us.

Beads of water splashed my face as my brother and I struggled to keep up with him. When I caught up with Pablo, I saw Tito up ahead, nestled in the crease of a massive boulder on the side of a blue-gray pool under the thunderous thrust of a magnificent waterfall, his palms up, shielding his eyes from the sun. A pair of brown-and-white–striped hawks circled above him, close enough that it looked like they danced for him.

Pablo and I moved closer, but the hawks flew over us, and they didn't look friendly. Their raspy screeches punctured the soft rumble of the falls. They looked angry, their long claws visible from below. Tito signaled us to keep still and quiet. We squatted. The birds circled above Tito again, their flaming red tails as bright as a sunset. I watched the splendid birds in awe. Tito was with the *guaraguao*, and they were with him. Then they flew to the *flamboyán* tree and made a commotion, chirping and flapping their wings.

Tito rested his back on his burlap sack, the birds making scolding calls from the tree. "They're nesting over there." He contemplated the *flamboyán* branches above, content painted on his face. After a while, I located what he was so involved with. The *guaraguao* nested on a branch between fernlike leaves and clusters of red-orange flowers. Suddenly my heart expanded with joy. I thought I could hear tiny chirps, but I wasn't sure. All I wanted was silence so that I could hear them again.

Watching the *guaraguo* became my most prized moment of the day. From then on, after getting chores done, we disappeared into the river, distanced from humanity, right under the road. Soon I identified voices of neighbors crossing the river as I watched them from a distance. The mother that smacked her kids. An old man with a cigar that stunk up the world for miles. The teenagers who came from the plaza acting as if they owned the world, smoked cigarettes, and pissed behind trees. Some of them lived along the trail above our house. Many had a long way to go ahead of them, up the steep hills.

Some days Tito was talkative and told stories about all these people. He told us about the two sisters who married twin brothers and built houses next to each other. One day he pointed out an old man with gray hair.

"He used to own all these lands, but he was an alcoholic and spent all the money he made and had to sell all of this, and even lost some to the government. That's when Don Erasmo bought the farm where you live now."

Pablo and I listened, not understanding a lot of what Tito said, because often, he spoke like an adult. The old man crossed the river, pausing often to keep his balance.

"And where does he live now?" I asked.

"He lives in a little shack just past the *ventorrillo*. Even when the river is high, he won't let me help him cross. He's really stubborn."

He told us about how Machi was as generous as her mother, when she gave out produce from her farm.

"Why did she give it away?" Pablo asked.

"That's what she learned from her mother. Your grandmother."

"Did you ever meet her?" I asked.

"No. Maybe she was here when I came, but I don't remember. Still, people here talk about how good she was, and they say Machi is just the same."

"So how come people don't have their own food here? Don't they have their own farms?" I asked.

"Yeah, and how come there isn't a factory here like where our father works?"

"Some people here only have the plot where their house is. There are only two more houses that have as much land as your aunt's. And they're smaller. I know because I help them pick oranges sometimes."

"So why can't they buy food?"

"They don't have jobs. They can't sell their produce."

"Why?" Pablo asked. "Machi sold her *plátanos*."

"I don't know why, but that's the way it is. My aunt gets food from La PRERA. A lot of people here get it. Sometimes I go get it for them."

My brother and I asked him what that was.

"You go past the school and there's a building there that looks like the school but is a lot smaller. And inside you get groceries. They give you a whole chicken in a can—"

Pablo made a sour face. "Yuck! A chicken in a can?"

Tito smiled. "It's good. My aunt makes a stew with it. We get a can of peanut butter, a can of butter, rice, lentils. Lots of stuff. I get it once a month. It's like a *mercado*, but it's free."

"Can we go over there and get some for Machi?" Pablo asked.

"No. I think you have to fill out papers and things. I don't know. And I don't think they give it to people who don't have kids."

"But now she has two kids," I said.

"Yeah, but you're not her kids."

"Yeah, but you're not your aunt's kid either," Pablo said.

Tito shrugged. "I don't know how it works. You could ask her. If she could get it, someone would've already told her, I think. People here love Machi. There was one lady in the neighborhood who used to call her 'that fresh *pata'* until neighbors told her she couldn't be talking about Machi that way and put an end to the name-calling."

"Where is that woman now?"

"She moved into town."

Tito told us that his mother died in a car accident when he was two years old. Another day he told us his cousins were mean to him. "When Alfredo, the one who's two years older than me, is at the house, *se arma la de San Quintín.*"

"What's that mean?" I asked.

"We have a big fight. He always starts fights with me. I don't go home when he's there."

"So, where do you go?" I asked.

"Pa'l río."

"Even at night?" Pablo asked.

"Anytime."

"Isn't it scary to be here at night?" I asked.

"No. Not at all. It's just me and the river and the moon."

I wished I was as brave as Tito, but as soon as it got dark and all the sounds of crickets and frogs came out, I wanted to be indoors. We were never outside when it was dark because Machi called us in after she returned from the tobacco farm in the evenings.

"¿Están ejmallaos?" she'd ask. And of course, she knew the answer to that question. We were always hungry, and often, Tito stuck around for dinner. She fed us *serenata* (stewed codfish with tubers), *arroz con leche* (creamy, warm rice with milk), or *funche* (a delicious glob of cornmeal with warm milk and butter).

After Tito left, she heated a pot of water on her *fogón* and poured it into a round metal basin. I was the first one to bathe, and she always had a tender smile when she wrapped me in a towel and carried me to the bedroom, where I changed into clean pajamas, the ones she'd bought and then paid a neighbor to wash in the river.

Sometimes she had a beer while my brother and I sipped on hot chocolate she made from a bar of Chocolate Cortés after we told her how much we missed Bosco.

At my aunt's house that summer, we lost our sense of time. It must have been the end of July and we had just taken our bath when Pablo asked me, "Was it already Fourth of July?"

"I think so," I said.

"So how long have we been here?"

"We came in June."

"Yeah. The first day of summer vacation, remember?"

Then he asked our aunt: "When's our mother coming back, wasn't it a week a long time ago?"

"How long have we been here? Two months already?" I asked.

"You came here on June fifteenth. It's only been a month. She'll be back when she's ready, and you'll be here as long as you need to be," Machi said.

One night I woke up to the sounds of a woman's voice and thought my mother and Machi were on the porch. But when I went out there, I didn't find anything but moths fluttering around the porch light. The sounds I'd heard came from Machi's bedroom. Bottles of beer sat on the living room table. I was stunned to realize that Machi had a friend in her bedroom. I'd never seen anyone but Tito and Machi's father, Don Erasmo, around my aunt.

I tiptoed back to the bedroom and it was a good thing I closed the door, because seconds later, I heard them in the living room.

"*Mai*, I just can't do what you're asking of me right now," Machi said.

"Tell their mother to come get them," a woman responded.

"I don't know where she is, *la pendeja*."

"Why don't you visit Florencia and find out?"

"I went there three days ago. She doesn't know where Raquel is either."

"You mean, she left the kids here and got lost?"

"I have an idea who she's with. I could find her if I needed to."

"*Mi amor*, I never see you anymore. Go find her and tell her to take her kids."

"I know, I know. But please try to understand the situation. It's not that

I don't care . . . but they have to be a priority now, until I resolve this. Can you understand that?"

Don Erasmo's hut was next to a tree behind Machi's house, and we went there often. Sometimes we stood at a window and talked to him while he made cigars, or we sat on a bench just outside his door, eating oranges, mangoes, or Cuca crackers. But we were not allowed in his hut because he had all kinds of knives on the table.

It was August, and Tito hadn't come around for days. Day after day we waited, restless and hopeful that he'd show up, but he didn't. Monsoon rains were upon us, and the trees swayed in cool winds that swirled as thick rain pounded the ground for a week. From Machi's porch we could see the river ran high, higher than we'd ever seen, and every day, Machi had to leave her jeep on the other side of the riverbank.

One morning we were with Don Erasmo, sitting on the bench outside his hut, but all we wanted was to see Tito. Same people as usual scurried down the dark-orange clay mud trail, the weather so extreme I was glad we weren't going anywhere.

Erasmo wiped the humidity off his ebony face with a handkerchief, his white shirt drenched in sweat. "Your friend didn't show up again today, huh?"

Pablo kept his eyes on the trail. Half a dozen children wearing navy-blue skirts and pants with white tops rushed by, hovering from the rain.

"Why're they all wearing the same clothes?" Pablo asked.

Erasmo stepped onto the ground next to us. "*Ah, Dios,* that's the school uniform. Didn't you wear that *allá afuera*?"

I crinkled my nose. "Where?"

Erasmo grabbed his coffee cup from the windowsill, a cup he'd been sipping on for a hundred years. "Over there in Machachuchet where your father lives. *Allá afuera.*"

Pablo and I looked at each other and shook our heads.

"When are we going to school?" Pablo asked.

"Don't know what to say about that. Your mother's word is the only answer to that question."

It felt like I hadn't seen her in years. "But we don't know when she's coming back."

A few more kids passed by, and I ran through Machi's house to get to the porch, but the grass was so high I couldn't see them crossing the river.

Pablo sat on one of the rockers. "They're all going to school, and we're stuck here."

"That's why Tito isn't coming."

"Why didn't anyone tell us?" Pablo asked.

"Because we're supposed to be in Woronoco, I guess."

"But we're not."

"That's okay, it hasn't started over there yet. Maybe we're going back home in September."

I had not thought about school, Papá, Faeries Meadow, and how Sally's cheeks made tiny dimples when she bit into a sour apple. Soon, the forests in Woronoco would change to orange and yellow. All the kids would walk together past the fiery red poison sumac flowers along Tekoa Avenue to reach the bus stop on Valley View Avenue, just before Woronoco Bridge. I had been away all summer. Fourth grade would start without me, and I wanted nothing more than to take the bus to school with all the kids from the Beehive. I wanted to be there to pick bushels of McIntosh apples before October. I nestled into a rocking chair, heartbroken and confused.

"And what about Mamá? *¿Se perdió?* Is she ever coming back?" Pablo asked.

I whispered, not knowing what to think or say, "Yeah, she sure got lost. I don't know."

"I don't get it, do you?"

"No."

"Maybe we should tell Machi we want to go back with Papá."

"I think he forgot about us too."

"He'll never forget us. He just thinks we're okay over here, don't you think? And we're okay, but I want to go back to school. Do you think that's where Tito is?"

That afternoon, we hounded Titi Machi with questions. At first, she responded with a simple, dismissive answer. "*Ay, mi madre, cálmense.*"

"But I'm supposed to be going to fourth grade," I said.

"Yeah, and me to the third," Pablo said. "And where did Tito go? I think he's in school."

"We're the only ones not going."

Machi stared at us as if we'd said something strange. Then she whispered, "I guess you're right; I saw them in uniforms today. *Ya sé, ya sé.* Let me think about this."

That night she bathed us quietly, sent us to our room, and closed the door. Soon after, I heard Don Erasmo's voice in the kitchen.

"Cecilia, this cannot continue, them here all day. If Florencia doesn't know where to find her, you have to put them in school over here."

"But Papito, *la pendeja* didn't say anything about enrolling them in school. I can't decide for her, they're not my kids."

Erasmo sounded angry. "It doesn't occur to her . . . in her head? . . . and . . . gone for months. *Esgaritá.* Doesn't even . . . they're dead . . . you took him to that doctor when the boy was sick, and now . . ."

"What am I to do?" Machi asked.

"All I can tell you is she's over there focused on her things. But her kids are in this house. We have to do the right thing. Go talk to . . . and do what you need to. They're not supposed to be in this house . . . are in school."

"Erasmo doesn't want us here," Pablo whispered with a pained face.

"No, that's not it. He just wants us in school."

A chair moved and Erasmo's voice trailed off. "You'll have *la policía* right here asking questions if you don't resolve this situation. Let me know how much money you need. They're going to need uniforms and books. Two of everything."

"You're right, you're right, Papá. *Yo resolveré esto.* I'll take care of this."

four

A few days later, Machi woke us up earlier than usual. She had an ironing board set up in the middle of the living room and placed my dress on it.

"Eat that breakfast while I figure this out without burning your dress," she said with a chuckle. She slid the iron over the dress, dispelling the aroma of fresh starch.

Pablo and I giggled with anticipation while she hung the pink dress on a doorknob and ironed one of his shirts. We were definitely going somewhere. "Where? Machi, tell us where we're going."

She grinned. "You know I keep my word."

"Can't be school, we don't have uniforms," I said.

"Aha! I got that taken care of."

I jumped out of my chair.

"The uniforms are coming today? We're going to school?"

"Tito will be here any minute. Finish eating."

I returned to the table to eat a boiled egg with cheese and coffee as fast as I could. "Tito hasn't been coming over because he was in school? And he's the one taking us?"

"Yes. School started this week, so you haven't missed anything, really. He's taking you today. Uniforms come later. Now let's go."

We both screamed and jumped until she scolded us. But I wanted to go to school with a uniform. I wanted to look just like all the other girls I saw on their morning walk.

Erasmo came in with a big grin, set down his cup of coffee, and buttoned Pablo's shirt. Machi brushed my hair into a ponytail and surprised me with a new bow and barrette.

"Did you tell them I'm going to the fourth grade and Pablo, the third?" I asked.

"I sure did. And we need to get in touch with your father to get a letter from your school, but we can do that later."

"And what grade is Tito in?"

"Sixth grade."

When I looked in the mirror, I was happy with myself even though I didn't have a uniform.

Tito showed up in his uniform, and Machi served him a cup of *café con leche* with cheese and bread that he gobbled down in a few gulps and told us we had to leave, or we'd all be late.

"Where's your uniforms?" Tito asked.

"Don't have any," Machi said. "It's okay, get going, *mi madre*, you're all going to be late." She placed a few coins in our pockets and kissed our heads. "*Pa' la merienda*."

"*¿Merienda?*" I asked.

"Something to eat in between classes."

The river rumbled as Tito veered downstream to a log laid from one side of the riverbank to the other. Pablo and I looked at each other shocked as Tito stepped on the log, grabbed on to a rope, and scurried across.

When I saw him on the other side, my chest quivered. Kids got around us and crossed to the other side. When we were the only ones left, Pablo stepped on the log and grabbed onto the rope. "I'll be the leader."

I stepped on the log behind him, but with every step he took, I swayed. My legs grew numb. I was afraid I'd fall in the river and jumped back off.

Everyone had moved on. Pablo called out to me, and I tried again, but the tighter I held the rope, the more it stretched away, threatening to throw me off balance. A big kid came running behind me and pounced on the log, startling me. I scrambled to stay on, inching my way forward, but I could barely move, squeezing the rope so hard my fingers were pale.

"Forget the rope and run," Pablo yelled.

I don't know how I gained the courage to loosen my grip, but the rope slid under my fingers just enough for me to keep my balance, and I sprinted to the other side. We followed Tito along the side of the road until we reached a fence covered in red hibiscus, children running everywhere. Tito ran through the playground and pointed to a classroom door. He waved goodbye and ran off with Pablo.

A few doors ahead, he dropped my brother off, continued down a corridor, and disappeared among bigger kids. Children in navy blue and white uniforms kissed mothers, dashed around, called out to each other, played games. Everyone knew where to go and who to talk to. And everyone spoke in Spanish. Pablo disappeared into a classroom with a teacher's guiding hand on his head. But there wasn't anyone there for me; all the doors looked the same, and I wasn't sure which one Tito had pointed to.

My breath paused when I noticed a girl watching me. With wavy, long black hair, a white blouse trimmed with lace, and a white bow in her hair, she was so gorgeous that the moment I saw her, I wanted my blonde hair to turn black.

She scrutinized me. "Are you *la americanita*?" she asked in Spanish.

I didn't know; was I?

She giggled. "Well, you're a *canita* with no uniform. Is your name Andrea?"

"Yes. Andrea Inés Rodríguez."

She snickered and placed her hands on her waist. "You came from *allá afuera*, right?"

Out there. This was the same phrase Erasmo had used. What did it mean?

"Well, where did you come from?"

"Massachusetts."

She covered her smile with both hands and giggled. "Machu what?" She burst into laughter. "That must be *allá afuera*. You must be *la americanita*."

I smiled, confused. Why was she calling me *americanita*? At school in the US, I had always been called "the Puertorrican." Now I wasn't sure what that meant either. This was the first time in my life my identity had been questioned, and it became obvious that I didn't know how to name who I was.

"It has to be you. I'm María Elena. *Mucho gusto.*"

She grabbed my hand and pulled me through the crowd. We dashed onto a sidewalk around the edge of the playground to the back of the school. A fragile white statue stood before us, centered in a modest courtyard. María knelt on the floor next to me and pulled on my skirt. I had been to Mass many times with my parents, so I knew to kneel before a religious statue even though my knees were uncomfortable on the cement, but I was filled with nervous anticipation. What if things were different here?

Through the corner of my eye, I watched her make the sign of the cross, exactly as the priest and churchgoers did in Westfield. It was strange to see such a young person taking on this role.

"That's *la Virgencita,*" she whispered. "And my name is María, like hers."

All I saw was an old, beat-up statue of a simple woman wearing robes, yet there was pride in María's delicate face. She led me as we tiptoed backward into the schoolyard without our backs ever facing the statue.

Once in the classroom, María made sure I sat next to her. The day progressed in a haze. The teacher pronounced Spanish differently from how I'd heard it before, and it took me a while to catch on. It was like listening to someone speak in British English when you're accustomed to American English. After a while, there were too many words flying around for me to keep up with her. Math class was the worst. Words my parents never used, like *descifrar, calcular, denominador.* Words I could figure out as soon as I placed them in context, but I was slow. During reading class, I watched people's lips move. I listened. But by the time I figured out what the person had said, I'd missed the point.

That night as Machi bathed me, I asked why I couldn't understand everything my teacher said.

"She pronounces every *r*, every *s*, and every *t*, right? She's speaking the same Spanish you are but pronounces it more properly, that's all."

"What Spanish do I speak?"

"Most of us speak like you speak, informal Spanish. And remember, your parents only went to second grade. Their Spanish is more *jíbaro*."

"Second grade? But I'm in fourth grade."

"Correct. So you have two years education more than they do. Think of that."

"But Papá knows how to divide and multiply."

"He probably taught himself. Don Luis is a very smart man."

"Do you know how to divide and multiply? What grade did you go to?"

"I finished high school two years ago, but I didn't like school. Now, don't follow in my footsteps, though. I should've gone on to learn something. I wanted to be an electrician, and maybe I can still do that one day."

Even though I was nine years old, Titi wrapped me in a towel and carried me to bed. Then she dressed me, combed my hair, tucked me in, and went after Pablo.

◦⌒⌒⌒

It was the end of September when Miss Rivera called me to her desk at the front of the room as everyone in my classroom packed their books, closed their desks, and prepared to leave for the day.

"I saw you in town on Saturday," she said, wiping chalk off her dark-blue uniform.

I smiled and tried to remember what I had done on Saturday.

"Standing on the sidewalk on Calle José Sánchez?" She cleaned off her hands.

Then I recalled we'd gone into town with Titi Machi.

"Your brother was with you. I saw you talking to . . . I don't know her name. That Black woman who wears men's clothes. What were you doing with her?"

From the tone of her voice, I gathered she didn't think I should be around Machi. My face burned with embarrassment, and all I wanted was to get away from her glaring eyes.

"I don't want to see you anywhere near that woman again, *mija*. I can't imagine your parents would approve either."

I nodded. But how was I going to avoid my aunt? Maybe I wasn't supposed to like her so much. Maybe she was supposed to act more like a girl whether she liked it or not. Maybe it really was a bad thing that she dressed like a guy.

"You're old enough to exercise more common sense, you hear? Please tell your mother to come see me. We should speak about your progress and your uniforms too."

I was afraid everyone thought my family was dirty, unacceptable, and for the first time in a long time, I yearned for my father. Didn't he remember us? I stepped out of the classroom in tears and found Pablo at the door.

"What did she want?"

"To talk to Mom."

Pablo ran toward the gate. "Let's get going." A man closed the school gates behind us as we reached the road.

"Tell me what happened."

"She doesn't want to see me with Machi."

"What? How does she know Machi?"

The street was quiet as we followed the curb under the *flamboyán*, the river running low. Pablo kept his head down and I struggled with my conscience. Why hadn't I told her Machi was my aunt? I could've told her what a wonderful *titi* she was, how she gave food away, how she cared for her father and everyone on her farm.

Pablo ran down the trail to the riverbank. But when he reached the river, he didn't cross to the other side. Instead, he headed upstream and sat on a boulder. "Are you going to tell me everything?"

I told him what Miss Rivera had said.

"Why didn't you tell her Titi is our aunt?"

"I'm afraid to. She doesn't want me around Titi."

Pablo shrugged. "Then Machi can go and tell her she's our mom."

"But she's not."

"I wish you didn't have to tell Machi anything. It's going to hurt her feelings."

From a distance, I spotted Machi on the porch waiting for us with worried eyes. As soon as we walked in, she barraged us with questions, like she knew something was wrong. "What were you doing alone in the river? Why didn't you come straight home?"

"Andrea had a bad experience at school," Pablo said. Then he went to the porch.

Machi crouched down and looked into my eyes. "What happened? Did someone hurt you?"

I rubbed my hands together. "No. It was my teacher. She said she doesn't want to see me around you and wants to talk to my mother."

Machi stared at me, but her eyes were glassy, like her mind had gone somewhere else. She stood up and paused. Then she realized I was staring at her and she took a deep breath. "Don't worry about this," she said. "I'll pick you up at school and talk to her tomorrow."

The next day, all the kids had left, and Miss Rivera was at her desk with one of the mothers when Machi's voice blared at the doorway, her aftershave so strong it filled the room. *"Buenas tardes."*

She took a puff on her cigarette from the side of her mouth, threw it on the floor, stepped on it, and strolled in. A woman closing the windows stared at her with apprehension. I couldn't have felt more out of place when Machi grabbed my arm and ushered me to the front of the room. The mother speaking to Miss Rivera stepped aside with startled eyes.

"Hola, Misi. I'm Cecilia Vélez Martínez."

The teacher stood back and gave me a *what are you doing with her in my classroom* kind of look. "How can I help you?"

"Misi, Andrea told me you want to speak with her mother, but her

mother is out of town. I'm her aunt, she's living with me temporarily, and I'm here on behalf of my sister."

Miss Rivera didn't blink. She chewed her lips. "I see. I told Andrea I wanted to discuss a few things with her parent."

Machi let go of me. "My father and I live on the tobacco farm beyond the *flamboyán* tree. Everyone knows Don Erasmo Vélez, the *negrito* who's been making cigars here for over thirty years. I attended this school when I was a child and I've never had a problem here with anyone. Now I came back in here for the first time when I enrolled my niece and nephew a couple weeks ago and I spoke to the principal. She never told me they couldn't come to this school because I'm *pata*. And you know why? Because if I'm *pata* or *puta* it's no business of anyone in this school, because it has nothing to do with their education."

Miss Rivera stepped back with her mouth wide open, shaking her head and looking at me like, *Why did you tell her?*

"Misi, let me say something to you. You have no right telling my niece not to be around me, as if I'm not good, as if I've done something wrong. Your job is to teach, not to judge your students' relatives."

Miss Rivera took a deep breath and leaned on the chalkboard, gripping her *Virgen María* gold medal and chain. "*Dios querido*, I have not said anyth—"

"Oh, yes, you have. You told her to stay away from me and she came home crying. Now I understand I'm not the likely person you'd find in here with two kids. *Pero te equivocaste*." She pointed a finger straight at the teacher's face. "What you've done without knowing me is uncalled for, Misi." Machi now looked double in size, her cotton shirt bursting at the seams. "You'd better watch your words."

Miss Rivera fidgeted with the bottom of her blazer.

Machi walked up closer to her. "Now you do what you're being paid to do and wash out that filthy mouth, *bochinchera*. And if there's a next time, I'm gonna be in your face!"

As we stepped out, we ran into Pablo. A group of mothers at the door sneered and stepped aside.

"What're you looking at?" Machi said. "*Váyanse al carajo* and mind your own business."

They rushed past us into the classroom. Machi pulled my brother and me by our arms and whisked us into the jeep.

Pablo's eyes were as sharp as darts. "Nobody will want to play with us anymore."

"Pablo, I hear you and I understand how you feel. Do you remember what it was like when you first came here and you felt nobody liked you because you were different?"

Pablo nodded.

"And now how do you feel? You've worked hard to learn and integrate with everyone here, right?"

"Yeah," Pablo said. "Even with Tito."

"So that's the same thing I've had to do. I've had to do my part so that people accept me. If I hadn't put that teacher in her place, she would've continued making comments about me, maybe in front of others. And tell me something, do you think it's okay for people to talk bad about any of us because we are, in any way, different?"

"No, Titi."

"You need to man up. Can't be afraid to go and put an end to it, *pai*, or the world will trample over you."

At bedtime, Pablo was quiet, faced the wall, and wrapped himself in his blanket.

"Are you mad at me?" I asked.

"No."

"Then what's the matter?"

"I wish we were with Dad."

"I do too, but I don't think he knows where we are."

"Machi is good to us, but she's not our mother and she's not our father and this isn't where we're supposed to be." Pablo sat up in bed. "And other people don't think she's normal. I don't like that. I don't want to have to argue with people. I want to go with Dad."

"Well, we can't go with Dad. And I don't like it either, but it's not Machi's fault."

I had a hard time falling asleep that night. Words in Spanish and English darted through my mind, a war between languages raging inside of me.

It must have been a Saturday morning in October when Machi left us with Erasmo and pulled out in the jeep. He pulled out a chair and surprised us with a piece of gooey coconut *marrayo* candy.

"When I was your age, I had already worked on my father's farm for over two years carrying water," he said.

"After school?" I asked.

Erasmo mulled his chewing tobacco around his mouth and spit in the same spot next to the doorstep. "No. I was taken out in first grade."

"Papá went to second grade," Pablo said.

Erasmo smiled with a new mouthful. "You've already had two and three times more schooling than all of us. The worst thing that can happen to a person is to not have an understanding of letters. The only letters I know are the ones in my name."

"Do you know how to add and subtract?" I asked.

"Oh, I know the numbers. That I learned. You don't learn numbers, you can't do anything in life."

Erasmo went back to his cigar making while Pablo and I played a game of cards on the bench. When Machi's jeep rumbled up the road to the side of the house, we ran, eager to see what she had brought from town. A fresh loaf of bread? *¿Pastelillos de guayaba?* Mortadella?

As soon as I stepped into the house, she held up a white linen blouse and a white shirt. Then she held up a navy blue trouser and a pleated skirt from another bag. "You have two of each, *mis amores*. They'll look better when they're starched and ironed." She hung them on the doorknob.

I couldn't contain my excitement. Everything in my life was marvelous. I could finally look like María and all the other girls in Puerto Rico. Oh, the white blouses, their lace dainty and soft, their buttons like pearls, the most beautiful pieces of clothing I had ever owned. I couldn't wait to wear them to school.

Machi beamed with happiness.

"Try on these shoes, *mi vida*," she said.

"Shoes?" Pablo and I asked in unison.

"Oh, wow, we don't have to wear the mud shoes to school anymore?" I asked.

Machi opened up a pair of shoes. "No, you don't. You're going to look just like everyone else now, from head to toe."

She set two pairs of brown leather shoes on the floor. "You like them?"

Pablo and I ran to her and clutched onto her legs as hard as we could. We didn't calm down until we'd tried everything on.

Erasmo came to the door. "You see? That's how you go to school in Puerto Rico. Marvelous, marvelous. Was it sufficient?" he asked.

"Enough and more," she said.

The hours couldn't go by fast enough. All I could think of was wearing my uniform on Monday. Life was the best it had ever been.

Hours later, Erasmo smoked a cigar on the porch, as Machi fed us a *serenata*. He stared out across the river in silence. Then he came into the doorway and pointed to the river. "*Ay Dios, mira*. I think that's Raquel crossing."

We raced to the porch, and there she was, on the other side of the river with a polka-dot halter that showed off her shoulders, her shoes in her hands. She reached the trail, pulled her shoes on, and waved. Pablo ran and screamed as if the world was ending. As soon as he reached her, he grabbed onto her A-line skirt and wailed. I waited for them to reach the front of the house and hugged her.

Nearing the house, she crouched and pulled our heads in. "You've grown so much. And look at your chubby cheeks, you look healthy."

We wept together. But there was something different about her, a new detachment in her embrace that left me empty. She had been away for almost four months, yet every move she made came across as rushed, when all we wanted was to cry and rejoice because she had returned. "*Ya, ya, cálmense,*" she said, and I couldn't understand how she expected us to calm down.

We went in the house, and she embraced Machi. "I'm sorry I couldn't come sooner. I started working and was going to come on a weekend and then I lost that job and didn't want to use up my money on *carros públicos.*"

"*No hay problema, mi hermana*, we've been doing good," Machi said.

Mamá brushed off her skirt and sounded nervous as she spoke. "I have another job pending now." Then she pointed to my brother and me. "I'm taking them with me. Go pack your clothes."

Behind her, my new white linen blouses that meant the world to me hung from my bedroom doorknob. I wanted to say, *Where the hell have you been?*

But I was nine years old and knew my mother. Confrontation wasn't going to work. She had come for us, and nothing would stop her. Did it matter to her that we missed our father, friends, school, our bikes?

The dismay on Machi's face didn't encourage me.

"You're starting a job?"

"I have, you know, something pending."

"Then why are you taking them today? They're doing very well in school."

"I can put them in school in Gurabo."

"You're taking them to Gurabo? I don't think it's a good idea to move them in the middle of the semester. It hasn't been easy for them to adapt to school in Spanish. They almost got put back a grade. But we weren't going to let that happen, right Pablo? You're getting a B in Spanish now and Andrea has an A."

"That's good and I thank you, but there's a *carro público* waiting for us."

"A *público*? Tell him to leave, I'll pay him, how much is it? I'll take you to Gurabo."

I ran to the door and picked up my uniforms. "Mamá, look. My new uniforms Titi bought. And look, these are for Pablo. We're wearing them on Monday."

"Let me give you some money to pay that driver," Machi said.

Mamá glanced at the uniforms and turned to Machi. "Never mind. He's a friend, he's not going to take money. The uniforms are nice, but I'll get them uniforms in Gurabo. We have to go now."

And with that I knew there wasn't anything we could do to change her mind. Something new was in her life and it ruled her. Its presence glared at me.

Machi walked up close to Mamá and spoke in a soft tone. "*¿Qué te pasa, chica?* Why are you doing this? Florencia doesn't have space, why would you take them over there?" Machi grabbed our uniforms. "I just picked these up. Let them finish the semester here. It's only a few weeks. I'll take them to Gurabo the day after the last day of school."

Erasmo went to the porch, and I ran after him.

"Do we have to go?"

He tightened his lips and lifted his eyes. "That woman in there is your mother and you will do whatever she says. That's what is correct."

I returned to the living room. Mamá and Machi were in the middle of a conversation about my father and a lawyer.

" . . . if they're not living with me," she said.

Machi set a box of matches on the table. "You can explain to the lawyer that they're in school. You can show him their report cards."

Mamá looked exasperated. "All right, I understand you took care of them and put them in school, but anyone listening to you might think there aren't any schools in Gurabo. *Por Dios.* Florencia lives right in the middle of town. Andrea, go stick your clothes in a bag and let's go. Pablo, help your sister. We have to leave. That man is out there waiting. I appreciate what you've done, and I thank you, but no, you're not keeping my kids."

"I'm not trying to keep your kids. I have my own life. But it's October. You left them here in June. It's been four months since we last saw you, and they're in school."

Erasmo came in from the porch. "Raquel, please. I know you need child support and all that, but please don't take them over there. Your sister can't even provide for herself. And you don't have a job yet. These children will suffer. They require a place where they're cared for, meals, clothing, school. Cecilia and I have provided. And we've done it *con gusto*."

My mother placed her hands on her hips. "I appreciate what you've done, but I've made my decision. Andrea, your clothes. In. A bag. I'm not telling you again. Hurry up, Pablo. Go with your sister and bring. Your. Clothes."

Machi stepped out to the balcony and slumped onto a rocker. My white blouses blew in the breeze behind her. I had a strong urge to scream at my mother. But I couldn't bring myself to disobey.

Erasmo ushered my brother and me into our bedroom and gave us two paper bags.

Pablo hugged him and whimpered.

"You do as your mother says and don't worry. We'll see each other again."

Pablo and I gathered our belongings, swallowing tears. Why did she have to interrupt everything that was important to us?

In the living room, Mamá spoke in a low voice.

"Unfair of you . . . I do appreciate . . ."

Machi mumbled in what sounded like a disagreement.

"I know that," Mamá said. "But he's a good man."

"He didn't care for you then, why would he care now that you have two kids and no money? You're making a mistake."

Someone shoved a chair. Then my mother yelled, "I'm not asking you to advise me on what to do with my life."

Machi's voice shot through the house. "But you're not being truthful. I went out there, and Florencia told me she hadn't seen you in weeks. You're taking them to a slum just to be with that married bum who has nothing to offer you."

Mamá came into the bedroom.

"Your things. Hurry up, *nos vamos*."

We each had a bag in our hands. She grabbed me by one hand, Pablo by the other, and headed for the front door.

Machi had her back to us, facing the sink at the window, and I could tell she was crying.

Mamá called out to her.

"Cecilia, you're nobody to question what I'm doing. Take a look in the mirror. I may not be the best mother in the world, but you're no model of perfection. Carry a kid for nine months the way the rest of us do, then maybe you can talk about what somebody else is doing right or wrong with their kids."

She stopped in front of Erasmo. "*Lo siento.* Thank you for everything." Then she led us out the door.

When we stepped outside, we bumped into Tito. "Where you going?" he asked.

Our mother shoved us. "*Vámonos.*"

Pablo mumbled, "With our mother."

Mamá ignored Tito, not knowing how much we had learned from that child and how much we loved him. As we crossed the river, he stood in the middle of the trail in his oversize cotton shirt and tan rolled-up pants that exposed his skinny legs, his whole body looking like a question mark. He probably knew we'd never see each other again. He didn't have his burlap sack with him, which meant we would have spent the day at the river. But that would never happen again. My whole face trembled and tears surfaced. I waved goodbye to Tito, knowing that I was saying goodbye to a whole world that I loved.

When we reached the other side, Pablo screamed out Tito's name and waved. Tito raised a hand and left it there, without waving. Mamá yanked my shoulder, insisting that I move faster. Pablo swung around and waved again, but I couldn't. No matter what happened to me for the rest of my life, I would always see Tito standing on that trail with that hand up in the air.

Minutes later, we were immersed in the hot smell of an old red car that had a rabbit tail dangling from the rearview mirror. Thick cigarette smoke made me squeamish. As we sped off, our mother explained to the driver what had taken so long: "She thought she was keeping my kids. I had to fight for them, can you believe that?"

The man chewed gum, cracking tiny bubbles in between puffs of cigarette smoke. Pablo stared at me. Even though he had missed our mother for all those months, I knew this wasn't what he wanted either. I knew I would never see my mother in the same way, and that the woman from Woronoco was gone.

five

The driver maneuvered around pedestrians on the busy streets of Gurabo and parked in front of a small, dilapidated house at the end of a street. There were people on the street with beers in their hands, faces oily from the sweltering heat.

"They're waiting to see you," Mamá said.

But I didn't see one person in the crowd whom I could possibly be interested in meeting.

The group grew silent as we stepped out of the car. A small, thin, elderly woman laid eyes on me, and I knew at once she was my aunt Florencia. She looked identical to my mother, only much older, with deep furrows around her eyes and mouth. Florencia limped with a hand on her back. Her oily gray hair and shabby housedress added to her worn-out appearance, even when she smiled.

She stroked my hair. "She doesn't remember me. No hair dye here. Takes after our great-grandmother, used to have blue eyes and blonde hair just like this. And the *muchachito*, he takes after Don Luis."

Pablo and I looked around with apprehension while Mamá greeted everyone. Then she excused herself and made her way around them to the doorstep. "Let me get a *cafecito*."

Florencia kissed my head. "Last time I saw you, you were taking your first steps, and look at you now, *una señorita*." She smiled, showing the few yellow teeth left in her mouth.

I followed my mother into the tiny living space that could hardly be called a house.

"Mamá, when are we having lunch?" I asked.

She opened the refrigerator. "Let me see what I can find here."

Florencia came in. "Here's some bread." She grabbed a bag from the top of the refrigerator.

"*Pan sobao. ¿Quieres?*"

She broke off a piece of hard, stale bread and gave it to me. "I thought you were going to leave them with Cecilia."

"The lawyer said to get the benefits they have to live with me."

"Were they in school?" Florencia asked.

"I can put them in school here."

"Who's going to take them? You're never here."

"Don't get started. I have opportunities. Teodoro is helping me."

"You left a good man and everything you had over there for this bum? He's not leaving his wife for you."

"*¡Deja el tema!* When I get full child support, you won't recognize me."

"I thought Don Luis was already sending you money."

"It's not enough. The court will make him give me more if I have the kids."

"Where are they going to sleep? Teodoro's mother has an extra room, take them over there."

"No. They're staying here in the living room. I can't take them over there."

Mamá put sugar in a cup of coffee. "Let me take this to him."

"They're better off with you over there," Aunt Florencia said. "Put them in the San Lorenzo school. A bus goes right by Teodoro's house." She looked into my eyes and smiled. "I don't even have enough for myself."

"I can't do that. Gonzalo comes next week, doesn't he? He gives you enough for a few weeks. You'll be fine until I get back. They don't need anything. Let me get to that lawyer in Caguas and then we can talk."

"Gonzalo is no Don Luis. He barely gives me enough to buy a loaf of bread."

"You don't know what you're saying. A good *hijo de la gran puta* is what Luis is. I'll come by every day if I have to."

Why was my mother calling Papá a son of a bitch?

Florencia looked at me and pointed to my mother. "*No sé como*. Your mother doesn't have a car. *Carros públicos* cost money. How's she going to get here every day?" Then she turned to my mother. "Don't make promises you can't keep."

Mamá looked enraged. "Stop. I'm doing the best I can."

Mamá gave me another piece of bread. "Go give this to your brother."

As I approached the door, my aunt's angry voice cracked.

"I told you, I can't take care of them. This backache is killing me. I can't even take care of myself."

I handed Pablo the bread and he leaned against the side of the house, his face as white as a bone.

"I'm starving. What's for dinner?"

"I dunno."

"Is this where we're staying?"

Under the dim light of streetlamps everyone glowed, and the smoke from cigarettes and cigars gave the place a mysterious aura. A jukebox at a corner store a few houses away played a song by the incomparable Felipe Rodríguez. I recognized his voice from hearing my mother's records in Woronoco.

Mamá brought me a cup of coffee and told me to share it with my brother. Pablo took a few sips and gave me the rest. I watched Teodoro and the way he looked at my mother. He was skinny, with tight dress pants and a long-sleeved shirt. When he didn't have a cigarette dangling off the side of his mouth, he was chewing bubble gum. He grabbed my mother often, embraced her, ran his hands through her hair, and pulled her close. She pushed him away as soon as she noticed my stare, but I had seen enough to know that Teodoro was the man Machi and Florencia called the married bum. He was the reason why we were in Gurabo.

I couldn't help but feel shame and embarrassment. Was he her boyfriend? But how could she have a boyfriend if she was married to my father? I was nine years old and didn't know how to interpret what I was seeing. I didn't know the rules of this new reality.

All I wanted was to be with my *titi* Machi, or in Woronoco with my father, but I couldn't imagine how I would see either one of them again. I sat
on the curb. The only thing my mother paid attention to was this Teodoro.
The only thing everyone else wanted was the bottles in their hands. Pablo
and I sat there watching everyone, hungry.

"I hate that guy."

"I hate everything."

"Are we going to sleep in that house?"

"That's what she told Florencia."

Later that night, Teodoro took a mattress that was leaning up against
a wall in the bedroom and placed it on the floor in the middle of the living
room. It didn't leave much space for my aunt to walk between the front door
and kitchen. Pablo and I took off our shoes and hopped in bed with our
clothes on. With the door open, we were so close to the street that anyone
could walk in and sit next to us.

"See? They already like it," Mamá told Florencia. "Kids are kids."

A guy crouched down in the doorway, right next to me. His breath made
me sick. I didn't want to fall asleep surrounded by a crowd of drunks.

Mamá sat on the mattress. "When I find a job and we have our own
home, you'll have your own room, just like before. But this is what we have
for now, so go to sleep. I'll be back in the morning."

My brother sat up straight. "Mamá, I want you to sleep with us."

"Don't start with the crying," she said, and walked out of the house.

We watched as she joined Teodoro. They got in his old red car, the motor
revved, and then it disappeared down the street.

"Do you think she really is coming back tomorrow?" Pablo asked.

"I don't know." Unfamiliar songs played on the *vellonera* alongside
laughter washed out by alcohol coming from the people in the street. Stars
in the night sky moved through holes in the zinc ceiling, and I cried for my
titi Machi and my father as my brother drifted into dreamland.

When I woke up the next morning, the doors and windows were closed,
and I was damp from morning dew, or perhaps from a light rainfall that had

come in through the holes in the roof. Florencia stood at the back door with a cup of coffee in her hands, staring at a river that ran along the backyard.

⌒

She smiled. "You're awake."

I stared at the floor, shying away from her eyes.

She handed me a cup covered in stains.

"*¿Quieres café?*"

I took the cup to the sink and scrubbed it with my bare hands rather than with the dish rag that must've been there since the day she was born. The whole sink was gray from never being scrubbed, and a foul odor in the air made me queasy.

"Where's my mother?"

Florencia gazed at the river.

"Over at El Cinco."

"Is that far?"

"A *barrio* between San Lorenzo and Caguas."

There was a long silence. My aunt filled my cup with black coffee and offered me sugar. "Your mother is looking for a job, but I don't think there are any. Things are difficult for her, and I don't have room here for all of you."

I looked around. There was a chair near the door where my aunt had sat the night before while all the neighbors hung out drinking. The mattress on the floor where my brother and I slept took up most of the room and entryway. Toward the back of the room was a small table with two chairs and a wall hanging of *The Last Supper*. I presumed my aunt slept behind a flower-print curtain that hung in a doorway on one side of the kitchen. She was right, there wasn't much space.

Every corner of Florencia's face creased as if it were gathered by thread.

"I don't know what she's going to do."

She stepped out to the backyard and wobbled over a slimy stone pathway leading to a hut. When she opened the door, it creaked like it might fall off and the malodor smelled as if a toilet had never been flushed. It was an outhouse.

In an effort to avoid the smell, I went in her bedroom. On top of her dresser there were candles burning in tall bottles, a bust of a Native American wearing a headdress, images of Jesus, and a small bowl of water full of pennies. Her bed's yellowish wrinkled sheets looked like they'd never been washed. A pan of urine under her bed burned my nose all the way up to my brains. I dashed out of the room, bumped into her, and screamed. She laughed. "I'll give you my *palangana* if you want it. I'm too old to walk out there at night."

I hated everything in that house. Her spooky laughter, her outhouse, her piss pot. She went into the living room and opened the double-paned front doors. A breeze came through, and what a relief it was to breathe clean air. Pablo moved around but continued sleeping. Someone on the street yelped, "*¡Hola!*"

My aunt dragged the same chair as the night before to the doorway and sat with her old cup of coffee in her hands. I sat on the mattress next to my brother, with my cup of coffee.

"You're intelligent," she said. "How old are you now, eight?"

"Nine."

There was a long silence.

"Your mother has known Teodoro since they were kids. No sooner she's in town he finds her, or she finds him. You understand, *mija*, don't you? She was too young when our father died. Mamá married *el viejo* Erasmo, moved to Aguas Buenas, and had Cecilia. I was busy raising my son, dealing with problems of my own. Your mother spent her childhood between our mother over there in that mountain in Aguas Buenas and over here with me. Over there, over here, know what I mean?"

A few big kids wearing wine-colored uniforms walked by and waved.

My aunt waved and smiled at them. "Everyone knows me here. I've lived in this house for over thirty years. Same house, same husband, good or bad but in one place. When Raquel married your father, I thought she'd settled down too, but I guess it's an unstable spirit that follows her."

For days, my brother and I moped around with little food and nothing to do. My aunt had chickens in the backyard, and she gave us hard-boiled eggs with bread and coffee in the mornings. But we didn't have anything to eat again until late in the evenings, when she gave us a fried plantain with another egg. We were always hungry.

Around midday, we washed under an outdoor faucet on the side of her house that you could see from the street. Because of this, I washed fully dressed, then shivered in the sun until my clothes dried, refusing to use an old grungy towel my aunt offered. We only had what we were wearing, and never found the two bags of clothes we'd brought from Machi's house. Throughout the day we sat at the doorstep next to Aunt Florencia and watched neighbors walk by on their way to and from the town center. Then the drunks arrived one by one and started their daily imbibing. At nightfall, we slept with our clothes on, tossing and turning until late into the night when she closed the doors.

Her husband, Gonzalo, showed up late one night, a thin old guy with tan rolled-up pants. He worked in sugarcane fields throughout the island, following the *zafra* seasons.

When he first walked in, he stared at the mattress on the living room floor with a surprised look on his face. Florencia told him who we were, and he smiled. He hadn't seen us since we were infants.

For a few days, his brothers came by to pick him up before sunrise in an old green pickup that you could hear approaching a mile away. They returned late in the afternoons, their catch in plastic buckets next to them in the back of the truck. They knocked down *panas* from the breadfruit trees in the backyard and fried fish, and we had a feast. But I longed for a peanut butter and jelly sandwich.

It must have been two weeks later when Pablo and I were on the doorstep having coffee and saw our mother at the corner store. Pablo screamed, ran, and grabbed on to her waist. Minutes later, they came out of the store with bags of groceries. I helped carry them to the dining table.

Pablo clung to Mamá. "Mamá, oh, Mamita, you came to get us. Mamá, I want to go with you and sleep where you sleep."

Mamá stood in the middle of the living room and gave me a long, hard stare.

"Aren't you going to hug me?"

I walked up to her and leaned my body into her embrace. That was all I had left.

"Mamá, are we going with you today?" Pablo asked.

Mamá smiled at Florencia. "I brought some things for you and the kids."

Florencia took bottles and cans out of the bags.

"*Qué bueno.* We need this. She's upset because she's not in school. And you never brought them any clothes."

Mamá lit a cigarette.

"You mean, they've been wearing the same clothes for two weeks? *¡Ay bendito!* Andrea, what did you do with the bags of clothes?"

I didn't move from the doorstep.

Florencia carried groceries into the kitchen. "Thank God I have good neighbors, and someone gave them a spoonful of food."

Mama puffed on her cigarette.

"I got a check from Luis today. I'll be back every week with groceries."

"And where's—"

"Waiting in the car."

"Should've told him to come in. You're not hiding anything. They know what's going on."

"He's going to set me up in an apartment."

"If he hasn't left his wife by now, he's not leaving her. You're wasting your time. When are you putting them in school? They're going to lose the year if you keep waiting for that apartment. They could be eating free lunch every day. You have money from Luis now, why don't you get it yourself?"

Mamá grabbed her purse.

"I can't give you an exact date."

"Your kids should come first, *mija*."

"I brought food. See you next week."

Pablo clung to her.

"Don't leave us Mamá, *por favor*, take us with you, Mamita."

Mamá kissed him.

"I'll find a place for us, Pablito, don't cry." She headed out the door. "Andrea, aren't you going to kiss me? I'm your mother, *sabes*?"

Pablo sobbed and ran after her as she walked away from the house. I noticed a neighbor watching from her porch. Mamá knelt on the street, hugged Pablo, and wept.

"I don't want to be away from you either, *mijo*, but it will be a short time. Andrea, come get your brother."

I embraced Pablo as she walked away, and we heard Teodoro's car start up around the corner. Pablo pushed me away and disappeared down a stairway at the end of the street. I ran after him.

There was a river at the bottom of the stairway, but it wasn't like the one in Aguas Buenas. Murky suds in stinky puddles lined the riverbank, and there was a burnt car on our side of the river.

Pablo wiped his nose. "I came here the other day. You were washing under that faucet. There's rotting fish in those puddles."

I didn't respond.

"Tito's probably over there in the river. Why can't we go back with Titi Machi? Or maybe we can find Papá. We have to do something, Andrea."

"Find him? But he's not even in Puerto Rico."

After Gonzalo's visit, Aunt Florencia had money to send us to the corner store every few days. Sometimes she added a *marrayo* candy to the list. But when her money ran out, we went back to stale bread and boiled eggs. Weeks passed, and we didn't see our mother.

Every so often Aunt Florencia complained. "Your mother said she was coming every week to bring us groceries, and see that? Where is she? I knew she'd do this. You know that saying 'where one eats, three eat'? That's not true."

The days we were hungry were when I most wondered why she wouldn't visit more often or take us with her. There were houses along the street between my aunt's house and the corner store. Wood huts with paint peeling off and rusty, flat zinc roofs crisscrossed by electric wires in every direction. The few cement homes were nicer. Their paint seemed to hold on better. They had front porches surrounded by iron grates my aunt called *rejas*, and you could tell they had bathrooms because people showed up on their porches with hair dripping, drying themselves with a towel, looking refreshed, the smell of shampoo filling the air.

Pablo and I sat on the curb in front of the corner store and gazed down a street. Engines accelerated, cars honked, buses filled the hot streets with diesel fumes. People scurried from one sidewalk to another between traffic, some carrying packages, others getting in and out of cars.

The first few times we went to the corner store, Aunt Florencia's next-door neighbor, a woman called Doña Nereida, waved from a rocking chair on her porch. I'd seen her speaking with my aunt many times before. One day, she called us over and asked if we could do her a favor. She sent us around the corner to the local *panadería* for a loaf of *pan de agua* and mortadella. When we returned, she gave us each a penny. From then on, she sent us to the pharmacy, the shoe repair, and the *mercado* to buy things like green plantains, cilantro, and *recao*, and always gave each of us a penny.

One day, she invited us inside for a bowl of food. My brother and I stepped back onto the sidewalk.

"No, that's okay," Pablo said, and nudged me to leave.

Nereida smiled. "Go ask permission and I'll wait right here."

Pablo ran to our aunt's house. Nereida invited me to sit on a chair, but I smiled and waited for my brother on the street.

"How long has it been since Raquel has come around?"

I shrugged.

"Raquel and I used to play right on this street when we were little girls. I couldn't wait to see her on Sundays when she came to visit Florencia with your grandmother. That was a long, long time ago, when my mother was alive and owned this house." She pointed to Pablo. "Here he comes."

My brother yelled from the street. "She gave us permission." As soon as he reached me, we ran up the stairs and sat on the porch.

Nereida always wore a black A-line skirt with a white linen blouse, and sometimes she wore a *mantilla* veil over her shoulders on her way home from church. Florencia told me she wore *medio luto*, which meant that she no longer wore all black clothing since her husband had passed away a year ago, but still wore dark colors. She sat on her big porch with four wrought iron chairs all by herself most of the day.

When we stepped onto the porch of her cement home with its light-green *criollo* tile floor, she locked a padlock behind us and slipped the key into her apron pocket. All of her windows and the porch had iron grates.

"They'll take the food out of your mouth here if you're not careful. You have to watch out for thieves."

She went into her house and left us with the aromas of refried *sofrito*, pork skins, and all the delicious spices of Puerto Rican cuisine. I heard her banging a metal spoon against the rim of a *caldero*, the way Puerto Rican women do when they stir rice, and imagined her serving big spoonfuls into two bowls.

When Doña Nereida came out with two bowls of rice, bean stew, and fried chicken, I choked up. She surely knew we had not eaten like this since we moved in with our aunt Florencia a month before. As we ate, I thought of my poor aunt drinking coffee out of an old cup at the back door and was relieved when Nereida told us she was sending a bowl with us for our aunt.

"Eat whatever she gives you," Aunt Florencia said when we returned. "She's a good person, just a little nosy, poor woman, doesn't have anyone to talk to."

A few days later Doña Nereida invited us into her home for a warm bath and gave us each a set of new clothes, which I hated because the pants were baggy, but still, they were something new and clean to wear. From then on, she often fed us such meals.

We usually ran her errands in the morning when the town was bustling. There were vendors selling all kinds of things and services on the streets, some of them announcing over speakers: "*Amolao. Se amuelan cuchillos grandes y pequeños, tijeras y machetes. Amolao.*" That was definitely the guy to call if you needed to sharpen anything. Right behind him another one sold vegetables and fruits: "*Vendo piña, batata, cilantro, repollo y maíz.*"

A man sold doughnuts from a red glass cart that filled the street with the aroma of warm sugar. One day, he called us over and gave us each a doughnut. They were delicious, but afterward, we always waved from a distance so he wouldn't think we were beggars.

On one occasion, our aunt sent us to the *panadería* at about three o'clock in the afternoon. Her husband, Gonzalo, had just left, she had money again, and she wanted *pan sobao*. That was our favorite bread, a slightly sweet, butter-soft loaf. We had just bought the bread when the sound of a group of kids startled me. I panicked. I wanted to leave before they saw me in my homely clothes. I'd seen my reflection in a store window and noticed my curly bangs had grown out and stuck up like horns on both sides of my head. I'd seen the way my shorts bunched up around my thighs. It hadn't mattered if my aunt and her alcoholic neighbors saw my dirty, ugly clothes. But the thought of being seen by kids dressed in beautiful uniforms was unbearable.

I wanted to hide my shame and ran to my aunt's street.

Pablo caught up with me.

"Where you going, what's the matter?"

I sat on the curb in front of the corner store and sobbed into my knees. "We don't have clothes, Pablo. We don't have uniforms. Don't even have a toothbrush. We're not in school."

Pablo grabbed a pebble from the street and threw it. "Yeah, I know. We look pretty stupid, don't we?"

"I don't want to go anywhere ever again. Why doesn't Mamá just come get us? I don't understand her. She said she'd be back every week, every single week. But she never comes."

Pablo crouched down in front of me and looked off into the distance. "How about we try to find our way back to Titi Machi? She's closer to us than Papá."

"I don't know."

I wanted to do something to change our situation, but what?

"Papá is going to find us, you know," Pablo said.

"He doesn't even know where we are."

Florencia came out with a limp, her hand on her back. "Why she crying on the floor? *¿Qué te pasa, mija?*"

I didn't lift my head from between my knees. I had nothing to say and didn't care what anyone thought anymore.

"We saw kids going to school," Pablo said.

Florencia let out the sigh of one carrying a load too heavy for her shoulders. "Aha, yes. Your mother doesn't make up her mind, you know what I mean?"

She took the loaf of bread.

"*Ven*, Andrea, get off the street, *mi amor*. I'll make *un cafecito*. Let's have this nice warm *pan sobao* with butter."

We followed her to the front of the house and settled on the doorstep. An old guy, one of the ones that came in the evenings, stopped by with a bottle of beer and stood there, staring at me until he fell over. My aunt told me she felt bad for him. She said he was a good man who never married and cared for his sick mother until she died. I felt bad to see him fumbling with his beer can on the floor, but I didn't want to be near him. I wanted to be strong for Pablo, but I was broken. I didn't care if these people saw what I was going through. Pablo looked helpless as I wiped my face with my hands, but I couldn't control myself. *If only Papá could see me right here, right now,* I thought.

six

It was a few weeks before Thanksgiving, and we hadn't seen our mother since mid-October. Several times a week, someone in the neighborhood sent us to the *panadería* for fresh bread, and with the coins we earned we bought ourselves treats to keep us going. I only went in the morning to avoid seeing the school kids.

One day, our aunt sent us out early. On impulse, we walked past the bread maker and followed the sound of a church bell. We crossed several streets until we came to the town plaza, facing the church. I was fascinated by the height of the steeple atop a structure that reminded me of a ship, and the sound of the bell. Pablo nudged my elbow and ran ahead of me to another street, where we were flabbergasted by a steep cement staircase the size of a road going up a hill. It was lined with colorful houses, trees, and flower baskets hanging on porches.

A boy who looked our age jumped around, while all sorts of people walked up and down the staircase. When an elderly woman approached him, he ran to her and took her bags. He jumped up a few steps and waited for her to catch up with him. She wobbled up a few more steps. He jumped up two or three more. They continued climbing the staircase until they reached a house slightly above the middle. She leaned on the porch of a yellow home with orange shutters, and he placed the bags next to the door while she searched her purse.

I remembered Tito helping people cross the river and couldn't bear to look at the staircase any longer. I told Pablo we should leave before our aunt worried, and we headed home. But when we were halfway down a street, we both turned around and asked each other where we were going.

"I thought you knew where we were," I said.

"I was following you."

We decided on a street we thought we'd come from and walked for about two blocks when Pablo turned around and said we were going the wrong way. Then he gasped, his eyes focused behind me. When I turned around and didn't see anything in particular, I thought he'd played a joke on me, but he continued to stare like he'd seen a ghost.

"What's the matter?" I asked.

"It says Post Office."

The words *United States Post Office* written across the building behind me looked so out of place in the middle of Gurabo, Puerto Rico. I had only seen that sign in Woronoco.

"What was our mailbox number?"

My jaw dropped. "We just need to save money for a stamp and an envelope," I said.

Pablo pulled two dimes out of his pocket. "No, we don't. You were the one that asked for the mail every day. Remember the number? Papá checks the mail every day."

"One hundred seventy-two."

We tripped on the steps at the door as we ran into the post office. The postmaster looked like he was about to throw us out. I had never sent anyone a letter, but my third-grade spelling teacher had dedicated a whole project to the post office. I knew exactly what to do. We found a piece of paper on a counter, a pen attached to a long string, and argued about what to say.

"You write it. Hurry up," Pablo said.

Daddy, We're in Gurabo with Titi Florencia. We don't have clothes, we're not going to school, and sometimes we get hungry. Can you come get us?

We signed our names on the note and went to buy an envelope, but when I wrote the address, I had a problem. We didn't know the number of our aunt's house. I asked the postmaster if it was necessary since it was a return address.

"Let me see," he said, taking the envelope and the note and surveying us with suspicion.

"Where are you from, don't you know your address?"

I told the postmaster our mother had recently taken us to live with our aunt Florencia but I didn't know the number of the house.

The postmaster read the card with a serious face. I was afraid he was going to scold us or call a police officer when his demeanor softened.

"So this is your father you're writing to in, what does it say here, Woronoco, Massachusetts, United States?"

I nodded. Pablo rubbed his lower lip and looked away.

"I think I know where your aunt lives. Is there a *riachuelo* in the back? Not a big river."

Pablo blurted out, "Yes. In a wood house right at the end of the street."

"On the other side there's a street that goes to the plaza. She lives on the side of the street where there's a staircase going down there to that river, right? I think I know the house you're saying. Let me look that up."

He went through a pamphlet on a shelf and returned.

A customer walked in and stood behind us.

"The number is fifty-seven."

He wrote the address on the envelope and didn't charge us for the stamp. "This should be there in three days," he said. "If you don't get a response in a week, come back and we'll see what we can do."

Pablo and I thanked him and left. As soon as we were outside, he grabbed me by the shoulders.

"Andrea. This is a secret, right?"

"Yes."

"What about when Mamá comes back?"

"Don't tell."

"Okay. But I feel bad, you know?"

"I know."

"Papá is gonna come here and fight with Mamá, and it's going to be our fault."

We sat on a curb.

"But I'm always hungry, aren't you?" Pablo asked.

"Yeah. And Mamá's with that guy and she's not coming here like she said."

"It's November and we're supposed to be in school. He's going to be really mad when he finds that out. He'll come get us."

In my heart, I knew my brother was right, but I lacked his confidence. We hurried down the street to our aunt's house. A group of people were gathered there, as usual, and we pushed our way around them into the home.

On Sunday, Pablo was with my aunt in the kitchen. They stared off into the distance, while I stayed as far as I could from the outhouse stench. Streams of light snuck into the house through the holes in the zinc roof, and I admired how they danced on the dust in the air, like fireflies under the trees in Woronoco when my father played dominoes with friends from Westfield. His voice was alive in my mind. How he called me his *adorada canita,* how his cologne filled the room, the sound of his smacks when he kissed my forehead.

Every day that week, when the mailman delivered my aunt's mail, I hoped to receive a letter from my father, and when none came, I wondered if he'd respond. Was it too soon? Or would my mother show up in a fit of anger, blaming us for having lied to our father? Pablo and I wondered what Florencia would do if a letter came in for us. Would she give it to us? Would she open it? Would she ask how he knew we were with her? Sometimes Pablo and I worried, felt guilty, and regretted having sent the letter.

But we were always hungry, and that's when we most agreed it was a good idea we wrote to our father. It was fall. I was supposed to be in the fourth grade. That raised another host of questions and worries. What would it be like to go back to Russell Elementary School and not know any of what everyone else had read or learned in science and math? The thought was terrifying.

When the front door creaked open that morning, I expected Doña Nereida, who occasionally came over on Sundays with meals. But instead, a polite, distinctly male voice said, "*¡Buenos días!*" He sounded like the postman, and I was confused because there were no mail deliveries on Sundays.

I went to the door, but the midday sun blared in my face, and all I saw was a dark silhouette. Then he repeated the same two words. By the time he reached the end of the last one, every muscle in my body froze, my chin trembled, and tears welled in my eyes.

It was my father. I stood there incredulous, unsure if I was imagining things. He came closer, squinting between the light and the shadows, and when I saw his charcoal gray wool suit and hat and no longer doubted who he was, I burrowed my head in his chest, my heart pounding. He had seen me the whole time and got on one knee with open arms. "*Mi hija, mi hija.*" He smiled, his lower lip trembling. Like a miracle standing before me, Papá had found us.

He stretched his arms out and Pablo let out a sharp, piercing cry, running at us so hard, he knocked us backward. "*Llegó Papá, sagrado hijo. I never forgot my children.*" He kissed our heads, his eyes misty, and we held on to each other. With each word he uttered I found it more difficult to breathe or speak, his voice coming through his suit, his chest, his neck. I knew he wasn't angry. I knew the hunger, the stench, the boredom, the longing was over. His raspy face brushed against my cheeks. The rest of the world disappeared.

He took our faces in his hands and inspected us.

"*Santo Dios*, why are you so thin? When was the last time you ate, are you hungry?"

Aunt Florencia watched from the kitchen door with a smile.

Papá stood up and extended his hand.

"*Buenos días,* Doña Florencia, *Dios la bendiga.*"

"*Gracias,* Don Luis, may God bless you too. What a surprise to see you."

"When are you expecting Raquel?"

Florencia frowned, shook her head, and mumbled. "*Este . . .* I can't tell you—"

"So, my children are living with you and she's living in Caguas. That's the way it is, right? These two *criatura*s are supposed to be in school in Caguas. Is that correct?"

Florencia squeezed her lips together. "I don't know her plans."

"Are you in school?"

Pablo and I shook our heads.

"And all this time, I've been thinking my children are fine. Doing well in school. I send money for them. But now I see that she dropped them off here, and they look like they're starving. *¡Dios mio!* There's absolutely no need for them to suffer any of this. They have a refrigerator full of food over there in my house. Their home."

Florencia avoided eye contact with him. "She comes when she can, but—"

"I can't believe this woman has done this to me. To our children. How long have they been here?"

My aunt frowned. "Andrea, would you say, about a month, right?"

I nodded.

"I think it's been about two years," Pablo said.

"They're leaving with me right now. And when your sister comes to this house, you tell her that I came and took them *personalmente.* She doesn't have anything at all to do with me from here on. I've filed for divorce."

Florencia gasped.

"*Ay, señor. ¿Divorcio?* Don Luis, that soon?"

"I'm not a millionaire. I have a job to get back to in Estrasmoar, in

Masachuse. And when a person disappears for months with two children the way she did, that person is going to have a hard time with a judge. These kids have a father. Understand?"

"*Ay, Virgen Santa*, I know my sister loves her children—"

"There's no need for you to explain anything. She can do her explaining to the judge. God forgive her. Thank you for what you've done for my children, but there's no need for them to be here any longer."

"*Ay, Dios mío*, you're taking them now? But she isn't here to say goodbye."

He thanked and hugged Aunt Florencia, swept us into his arms, and placed us in the back seat of a *carro público* parked outside. Florencia stuck her hand through the back window and ruffled Pablo's hair. "Take care of yourselves," she said. "I'm sorry it wasn't better for you, but please remember your aunt, *pobrecita* with a big heart." She came over to my window and kissed my head. "You don't have to be afraid of seeing the kids from school anymore."

Papá climbed into the front seat. Pablo and I knelt on the back seat, waving until we passed the corner and our aunt was no longer in sight. I remember feeling sadness in the midst of the joy of being reunited with my father. I knew I was leaving my mother behind, probably forever. My poor aunt Florencia had done the best she could to care for us and would be lonely without us. And would I ever see Titi Machi again?

Papá startled me when he reached out from the front seat and gave my brother and me soft pats on our legs.

"We're getting you something to eat right now."

Minutes later, we ate a delicious meal at a *fonda criolla* in Las Piedras and told him all about Machi, school in Aguas Buenas, and how our mother had brought us to Gurabo.

"Did you get our letter?" Pablo asked.

Papá yelped with joy, smacked his knees, and tousled our hair. People in the restaurant stared at him.

"Oh, I loved that letter. That letter was incredible! How did you think of sending me that letter?"

He pulled the letter out of his jacket and stared at it as we told him the story.

"God bless that postman," he said. He hung his head low.

"*Caramba*. When this letter came in, I already had plane tickets to come resolve things with your mother once and for all, but I didn't know you were in such a bad situation. We're going to have to go visit that other aunt of yours and get your school records. Then we'll go home and trust in God."

"We're going to see Machi?" Pablo said.

"Who? I'm talking about Cecilia. Your aunt in Aguas Buenas. We have to get your school records." He gave each one of us a smacking kiss. "And I have to thank her, *personalmente*."

We spent a few days in Vega Alta with our young cousin Evaristo, a blond-haired, short guy who giggled and tried to tickle my brother and me whenever we weren't watching. His father was Papá's oldest brother, Bartolo, who lived in Utuado, about three hours away.

Evaristo and his wife, Rosaura, a freckle-faced redhead, owned a small store that sold cigarettes, penny candy, and basics like eggs, milk, and the newspaper, on Carretera Número Dos, toward Vega Baja.

Every day, Papá and Evaristo left for Caguas at daybreak, while my brother and I spent the morning in the store with Rosaura. The first day Pablo woke up and didn't see our father, he cried. But Rosaura came into the bedroom with a smile full of teeth.

"Evaristo took him to Caguas to meet with a lawyer," she said. "They'll be back in a few hours."

She fed us a bowl of cornmeal. I too was getting a little nervous about my father, so she distracted us by showing us how to play dominoes. Soon after, Papá returned, and Pablo ran to him.

"He was afraid you weren't coming back," Rosaura said.

Papá placed his big hands around my brother's shoulders. "Let me tell you something. When I make a promise, I keep my word. Now let's go buy you some clothes."

Evaristo took all of us into the town of Vega Alta, where Papá bought my brother and me a few outfits. Then my father invited all of us to a *fonda*-style restaurant where we ate while he drank beer with his nephew.

Papá didn't speak to us about the divorce, but we overheard his conversations with adults and knew it meant we'd return to Woronoco without our mother. Pablo and I never spoke about her either. It had been over a month since we'd seen her and that had been only a brief visit. I'd grown accustomed to not having her around and I suppose my brother had as well.

It was on the third day when Evaristo and Papá came home from Caguas that my father said he was done with the divorce, and he planned to visit Evaristo's father, Bartolo, in Utuado and our aunt Cecilia in Aguas Buenas before leaving for the United States.

The next day, Evaristo drove us across the northern coast, where Pablo and I counted every glimpse we caught of the aqua-blue Atlantic Ocean. Just before we reached Arecibo we stopped along the coast and ate delicious fritters filled with *chapín* fish, shrimp, and chicken. Papá and his nephew had a couple beers while Pablo and I ran across the sandy beach, our toes gliding across the water.

"Let's go," Papá called after a second beer. "We don't want to get there and find him sleeping."

When we reached Arecibo, Evaristo veered toward the mountains of Utuado. We drove through winding roads for what felt like hours before he parked the car at the end of a road in Barrio Ángeles. When we stepped out, I was nauseated and felt like I was floating.

"Get the *jacho*," Papá said.

Evaristo opened the trunk of the car and took out an empty Coca-Cola bottle stuffed with a rag soaked in a combustible fuel that made me even more nauseous. Then he turned off the car. It was pitch-black darkness outside. They lit the *jacho*, their big smiles illuminated, and we were on our way, following a grassy, worn-out trail exposing hardened, red, claylike soil that smelled like the trail leading to the flowing river beneath Titi Machi's house.

"Do you think we might see your sister, Socorro?" Papá asked Evaristo.

"No. Last I heard, she's working in Aguadilla."

"You mean she lives over there? Does she have a boyfriend yet?"

"She's renting a room in a house. But, Tío, I don't know where she's going to find a man to put up with her. She doesn't take anything from anyone, and men don't like women like that."

Their laughter echoed through hills we couldn't see.

There was no moonlight, but Papá's *jacho* lit our way, leaving a billowing trail of dark smoke behind us. A cool mountain breeze came out of the forests as we passed tiny wooden homes, their candlelight and kerosene lanterns a sign that they were awake. People came out and waved from their porches.

At the bottom of a hill, a small house with a tin roof and streams of light flowing out through the cracks of the windows and doors came into view.

Dad sounded joyous as he called out his brother's name. "Is this the home of *mi hermano*, Bartolo Rodríguez Cabrera?"

"You made it!" someone said from inside the house.

An unpainted wood door rattled open, and our uncle appeared with laughter that filled the night.

"Oh, my brother!" he shouted, embracing my father.

He was tall and lanky, his head to one side, his big nose and broad smile inviting us into his humble home. As soon as we walked in my nausea worsened.

My father took me on his lap. "*¡Ay, Dios,* we've come this far and now you're sick?"

Minutes later, my uncle placed a cup of warm ginger tea in my hands. The warmth of the cup, the scent of cinnamon and cloves, and every sip eased my stomach. Then I fell asleep on a mat on the floor next to my brother, with the familiar laughter of my father and his family in the background.

The next day, we walked around Bartolo's farm at daybreak, and had fresh bread with cheese for breakfast.

Bartolo patted my father's arm. "That girl of mine, Socorro, didn't finish school. She's working in a factory in Aguadilla and told me she's quitting. I don't know where she's going. I don't have anything to offer her here. Sometimes I think she'd be better off going over there with you."

"I was just asking Evaristo about his sister. When you see her, you tell her that she's welcome to come to Woronoco anytime she wants. We can get her back to school or find her a job. All she has to do is get on that airplane."

The two brothers agreed that my cousin would move to Woronoco under my father's tutelage, and we left just after noon.

It must have been three or four in the afternoon, the next day, when Evaristo parked the car on the side of the road under a *flamboyán* tree. The river was low, and from a distance we could see Machi's jeep parked next to her house.

Pablo ran ahead of us, down the riverbank, calling, "Titi Machi, Titi Machi!"

I followed behind. My aunt came out to the porch and waved, then she ran toward us.

"Who is that man?" my father asked.

"That's Cecilia, Papá. Our aunt!" I said.

Papá looked perplexed and spoke with Evaristo. "Cecilia? I knew she was, you know, a tomboy, *marimacha*. But that looks like a man."

I could see Machi's excitement as she ran toward us, barefoot, Pablo calling out to her from the other side of the river. My heart banging in my chest, we jumped over stones in the river and ran up the trail to her embrace.

Machi rubbed our heads. "Look at you! Look at you! I didn't know if I'd ever see you again. My God, I missed you!" She picked us up and twirled with both of us in her arms.

Papá extended his hand to her. "Thank you for everything you've done for my kids and for contacting me."

"Oh, *fue un placer, un placer*, Don Luis. It was fortunate that I had met Evaristo before, and remembered where he lived. He gave me your address, and here we are."

"These two children wrote to me too," Papá said. "Look at them. They were starving over there and your sister, well, I don't want to say anything in front of them."

"Don Luis, you did the right thing. When she prohibited me from seeing them, I told her I would contact you. I guess she thought I wouldn't do it, but I couldn't sleep knowing they couldn't be well over there. My poor sister Florencia—"

"Oh, it broke my heart to see the conditions she still lives in. And my kids, there is no need for them to go through that, no need. Were you able to get the school papers?"

"Yes. I have everything you need."

Machi invited us in and didn't even ask if we were hungry before she put bowls of *yautía* in front of Pablo and me and urged us to eat.

"*Dios mío*, look at how skinny you are after I had fattened you up. You have to eat everything on your plate from here on, understand?"

"Where's Tito?" I asked.

"Oh, please, let's go find Tito," Pablo said.

My father shook his head. "No, we must leave as soon as we've eaten. Evaristo has to get home, and we have our trip tomorrow."

I saw sadness in Machi's eyes as we walked toward the door and wished I could take her with me. How many times had her warm embrace kept my spirits high?

Papá thanked her and hugged her. "I have no way of paying you for what you've done for my children. All I can offer you is my humble home. If for any reason you ever think of moving to the United States, you are welcome to stay at my house until you get your feet on the ground."

Machi nodded. "Thank you. Maybe someday, but I have my *viejito* here and I can't leave him behind. He must be at the plaza right now selling his cigars."

My father smiled. "Give him my regards."

Machi wrapped her arms around Pablo and me, tears in her eyes. "I know you will be well so at least I'll be able to sleep at night. And you promise me you won't forget me, and you will be good, good in school and good with your father."

We made our promise and left, waving until the house was no longer in view.

seven

Things had changed in the Woronoco Beehive while we were gone. We were no longer the only Puerto Ricans in the village. Half a dozen of Papá's relatives and friends had been hired at Strathmore and moved into the community with their families.

While we were in Puerto Rico, he'd turned in our apartment and rented one on the other side of the street, facing the cliff, with his brother Felipe, who looked identical to my father, except thinner and with an unsightly long nose. Shortly after, Felipe sent away for his wife, and Papá was on a waiting list for an apartment of his own.

The day after Pablo and I returned from Puerto Rico, Uncle Felipe's wife, Caridad, served a *sancocho* stew that filled the house with the aroma of cilantro. She watched us eating at her aqua-blue Formica table, her dreamy black eyes adding to her friendly smile. "Are you glad to be back?"

We nodded. She pushed her long, wavy black hair back and pulled a sweater over her dainty summer blouse.

"I can see why your mother didn't like it here. Isn't even a store close by. You can't say 'I'm going to buy myself some clothes, or a lemonade.' There's nowhere to go. I used to take *carros públicos* and buses in Puerto Rico. None of that here. Why didn't you stay with her in Puerto Rico?"

I just smiled, not knowing where to begin.

Caridad sighed.

"You don't make those decisions, I know. You must miss her."

I hadn't had a chance to even think of my mother after we left Aunt Florencia's house. I didn't miss the person Mamá had become, because that person didn't care about my brother and me. I was happy to be with my father again, and excited to meet the relatives who'd arrived from Puerto Rico while we were away.

Relatives were coming into the small home, and as they arrived, my father introduced my brother and me. Everyone was friendly, some of them commenting on how they'd seen us when we were infants in Puerto Rico and how much we'd grown. Uncle Felipe, who looked about the same age as my cousin Evaristo, was just as playful, punching Pablo and pinching my cheeks. Another one of my father's brothers, Epifanio, who everyone called Epi, came in with his wife, Amanda, a young woman who'd grown up in New York. They had a two-year-old son called Oscar and lived in Springfield. I was playing with him when Papá called me into the living room to meet another relative. A middle-aged woman with an elderly man and a teenage girl were taking their coats off.

"This is your aunt Perfecta, my sister, and the sister of Bartolo, the one you met in Utuado."

Pablo and I looked at her with bashful smiles, and I expected her to say something, but she looked away and told her daughter to go sit on the sofa. Her husband sat too.

Papá grabbed my brother and me and took us over there. "Bautista, Angela, these are my children, Pablo and Andrea."

Bautista had a pleasant smile. "They've grown, they've grown."

Angela smiled but seemed otherwise uninterested in us, her eyes on the television.

Perfecta walked up to Papá. "So, tell us how you found them and how that divorce went."

Everyone came into the living room and stood around my father. He spoke highly of Evaristo for taking us everywhere we needed to go and then spoke of the divorce. "I didn't have a single problem. When I showed the judge the letter she left me, which clearly states that she's taking the children without my approval, and showed him my salary stubs, and that she had nothing to show, no job, no place to live with the kids, there was no argument. He granted me custody."

Amanda looked shocked. "She didn't argue?"

Papá shook his head and kept his silence.

Amanda shook her head with sadness. "What I don't understand is why she did this. What kind of a mother does that?"

"I didn't ask her that question, and at this point, I don't care. I'm a man who works to support his kids, and that's what the judge saw. And maybe she thought they were better off with me after all," Papá said.

Bautista lit a cigar and stood up. "Well, thank God you got them and you're here."

Everyone had something to say.

"When Raquel first took these two to Puerto Rico, she left them with her sister Cecilia in Aguas Buenas," Papá said. "Cecilia adores these kids. She put them in school and bought them everything they needed. And then one day Raquel showed up and took them, for no reason, to that slum in Gurabo where her sister Florencia lives. Cecilia is the one who wrote to me."

Perfecta shook her head in disapproval. "What kind of a sister does that? Maybe she wanted something with you."

Papá laughed like he'd heard a joke. "Oh no, no, that's not why she did that at all. I went over there to her house in Aguas Buenas with the kids, to visit Cecilia, to thank her, and to get the report cards of the school where they went for two months, and I had the surprise of my life. The best person in the world, loves these kids to death, but she's a *pata* that is beyond *pata*. She looks like a man, dresses like a man, even smells like a man. That's who that Cecilia is."

Everyone in the room gasped.

Caridad looked confused. "But is that some mental illness she was born with? I've heard some women have a beard just like a man, but it's something abnormal that happens to them."

"No, no, there isn't anything in her natural body that isn't normal, she wasn't like that when she was a child. No. She was always a little too dark, you know? Her father is Black, completely Black. But that's not a sickness either. What I'm talking about is something she has chosen to do now that she's an adult," Papá said.

Amanda brushed him off with her hand. "Well, let me tell you, there are a lot of people like that in New York. Men who dress like women and women who dress like men. Some of them hide it more than others, but it's not as strange as you may think."

Papá shook his head. "I don't like it. A woman is a woman, and a man is a man. I know she was good to my kids, but I'm glad they're not over there anymore. That's not how God created us."

Caridad looked sad. "But you're a good Christian. You have to appreciate what she did for your kids."

"He hasn't said he's not grateful," Epifanio said. "He's just saying he'd rather his kids not be around those kinds of people. And I agree. Our parents were poor, but they taught us to be decent, that's all."

Papá nodded. "Exactly. My brother understands."

I didn't know how to process this conversation, with my father both praising and ridiculing Machi. He'd overshadowed her heart, her love for Pablo and me. None of these people, including my father, had any idea what Pablo and I had been through and how Machi had saved us.

Papá continued his story. "Any way you look at this, I have a debt with that woman now."

Aunt Perfecta pushed her head back and scrunched her lips together. "You don't have a debt with anyone. The *pata* is their aunt, you say? Well, she did what she was supposed to do."

Aunt Perfecta sized me up, her straight, mouse-colored hair gathered in a bun, a black leather belt tied around her fat belly.

"And where was your mother, all this time?"

"They don't know anything," Papá said.

"Send Andrea up to me. I'll teach her to tend to a house."

Caridad and Amanda, who had returned to the kitchen, came out.

"The girl has to focus on school now," Caridad said, her voice showing nervousness at confronting an authoritarian sister-in-law.

Amanda chimed in. "Tend to a house? But she's a child."

Perfecta placed her hands on her waist. "She's old enough to help her father. Sooner she learns, the better."

"In this country, girls her age are in school," Amanda insisted.

Perfecta turned her back on us and sat on the sofa next to her husband, Bautista, whose brown skin tone and straight black hair contrasted with his wife's. He bit down on a cigar and pulled on the sides of his shirt to stretch it over his belly.

I had wanted to return home for so long. But with this new aunt, Woronoco wasn't the same. Despite being thankful for the support from the others, I knew I was staring a new reality in the face.

Later that night, Papá came to say good night to us. He was sleeping in another bedroom and we were on the couch. That would be our bed for the next few days, until he was assigned an apartment.

"I don't like the way you talk about Cecilia, Papá."

"I don't either," Pablo said. "Yeah, she's Black, but she's a good person."

My father was half drunk and stared at us like we had a problem. "I didn't say anything bad about her. Everything I said is true. She's a little too Black and she's *pata*. We can't deny that. Go to sleep."

Caridad laid out pillows and a blanket for my brother and me to sleep on.

"Your father is a *jíbaro*. They think they're the whitest people on earth and everyone else is a little too dark. *Racistas.* This whole family. Just ignore it." She brushed her hair into a bun and spread Pond's cold cream over her face. "But remember, the only person who can tell you what to do is your father, *¿está claro?*"

I felt enormous relief that an adult in my family saw what I'd seen in Aunt Perfecta. After Caridad left, Pablo and I couldn't sleep. Intricate crystals accumulated on the outer edges of the windowpanes. We were on the opposite side of the street where we'd lived with our mother. Our old apartment showed off its snowy rooftop under Tekoa Mountain, and a light was on in a room.

"Someone moved in," I said.

"That was our bedroom."

Bare trees held cakes of snow on their branches and cars lost their shape under the glittery, white mass that clung to their curves. Even though the

Tekoa Avenue cul-de-sac was covered with snow, I knew exactly where everything was beneath the soft lamplights that shimmered in the mesmerizing moonlit dreamscape.

"I don't like the old lady," Pablo said, snuggling into the blanket. "She already talks like she owns you, and you know what? She doesn't."

⌒

The next morning, Papá served us hot cups of Maxwell House coffee over *queso de bola* and crumbled Premium saltine crackers. It was November. We hadn't seen any of our neighborhood friends since June and couldn't wait to go to school.

"I'm taking you to school today in case there's any problem, but from then on, you take the bus every day."

We dressed in new clothes he'd bought for us in Puerto Rico, but the only outerwear we had were old garments he found in a box in the basement. Spring jackets, a pair of lace Easter gloves for me, my old red rubber boots that hardly fit over my summer patent leather Mary Jane shoes, and Pablo's old white cowboy hat. As we walked into the school and I saw my reflection in the glass doors, I couldn't understand why we didn't leave the outerwear in the car because really, rain boots and a cowboy hat?

We waited with Papá in the principal's office until two teachers came— one for me, the other for Pablo.

Mrs. Palmer led me to the fourth-grade classroom. I took my jacket off and followed her to a bookshelf.

She pulled out a book.

"Have you read this?"

"No."

She picked up another book and, even before she asked, I knew I hadn't read that one either.

"No," I said.

"What about this one?"

I couldn't bear to look at her.

She presented me with more books, concern growing in her voice.

"No. No. No."

She frowned.

"Have you been in school?"

I stared at the floor and nodded. Was this a test that I had flunked? Would I get scolded in the principal's office? Would I be sent home? Uneasiness kneaded my stomach.

"Oh dear," she said, and left.

I heard my father's voice coming out of the principal's office saying, "Dat's okay, dat's okay, thank you, thank you." Then he saw me, waved, and left.

I feared the worst until Mrs. Palmer returned and led me to another classroom. I spotted Pablo with Mrs. Anderson, the second-grade teacher. We had both been placed in a lower grade. For a moment, I was disappointed. But I knew that kids would soon pour into the classrooms and all I wanted was to settle into a desk and act as if I'd been there the whole time.

I knew that all my previous friends would be in another grade and looked forward to finding them and seeing Sally at recess, but my teacher kept me in the classroom. She showed me third-grade books and workbooks, and I knew all of them. I'd worked through them the previous year.

When the kids came into the classroom, I was surprised to see all of Pablo's former classmates, and Kevin, from the Beehive. Some of them waved to me as they took their seats. Kevin looked at me like, *What are you doing here? Where's Pablo?* That's when it hit me that I was now in what had been Pablo's grade, and all the kids around me looked like little kids. There was no way for me to catch up with my classmates.

Pablo and Kevin slammed into each other with arms wide open at the bus line. I heard Pablo telling Kevin that we'd been put back a grade.

Charles Stolas, an older kid who'd never come anywhere near us, shook hands with Pablo, hugged me, and then said, "Hey, good to see you guys again." He called his little sister over. "Hey, Stephanie, Stef, look who's here!"

Stephanie, who was a year older than me and never played outdoors, ran over to me as if she'd been my best friend forever. "Oh my God! Where were you guys? When did you get back?"

"We were in Puerto Rico with our mother," I said.

"Are you staying here now?"

"Yeah."

"Did you like it over there?"

"Some places were nice, but in one place we weren't in school, so we got put back."

"Oh, gee, I'm so sorry. You'll be fine, though. Hey, have you met Emily?" Stephanie called a skinny redheaded girl over and introduced us.

"You two are about the same age," Stephanie said. Then she looked over at me. "Remember Sally? She moved out. Now Emily lives where Sally lived."

I was dying inside and trying to hold myself together when I smiled at Emily.

"My brother Jessie, who's eleven, and my brother Richard, who's fourteen, live with us too. And by the way, you're in my class," Emily said.

"Yeah, and they're still the only house in the Beehive that has a phone."

They laughed, but I couldn't. Teachers told us to get in line, and Stephanie went back to her place with the fifth graders.

Then I heard Kevin tell Pablo that Mark Abbot was home with the measles, Sally Nowak had moved out, and new kids had moved into the neighborhood. It was true. Sally was gone.

I was short of breath when I stepped onto the bus and sat in the first seat available. Emily was saying something about other kids that had moved to the Beehive, but I wasn't paying attention. The Stewarts, she said, but I sat in the bus next to someone I'd never seen before.

Emily walked past me. "Talk to you later."

Stephanie smiled as she walked past me with older girls from Valley View Avenue. A huge gap opened inside of me, and I didn't want the bus driver or any of the kids to notice and ask what was wrong. Pablo waved on his way to the back with Kevin.

In Aguas Buenas, I'd dreamed of returning to Faeries Meadow with Sally. In Gurabo, I'd missed María. I'd wanted to come home for so long, but with that old witch of an aunt and without Sally, home was empty, lonely. I wished I was in Puerto Rico again, and for the first time, I understood why my father always said he wanted to return there to retire.

The boy next to me moved to another seat and the bus pulled out of the schoolyard. Someone patted me on the back and I heard a girl behind me say, "Hi, we're in the same class." She moved into the empty seat next to me. I couldn't remember having seen her anywhere, nor was I interested, but I didn't want to be nasty. I faked a smile. But with her chubby cheeks, as pink as apples, and eyes as blue as the Woronoco sky, she was not letting me be. I turned away, annoyed with her bubbly personality. She wasn't Sally. She wasn't María. Just a girl like any other girl in the world.

"I know who you are," she said, and I wanted her to zip it, but she continued. "You're Andrea. I'm Hannah. Hannah Stewart. I sit two seats behind you."

Her smile and excitement were too much for me to handle at that moment, but I felt obliged to give her another empty smile before staring out the window.

"Do you remember Sally?" she asked. "I was friends with her before she moved out. She used to talk about you a lot."

My eyes sprang wide open. "You knew her?"

"She was my best friend."

A pang of jealousy hit me, but I wanted to know more. "Do you know where she lives?"

"New Hampshire. Her Dad got a job over there. Hey, you know what? Have you met Emily? She lives where Sally lived, and I live where you lived. Stephanie says I'm in your bedroom. Which is your house now?"

I tried to be polite.

"We don't have a house yet. I met Emily today."

"I know you're sad. Sally remembered you. She used to get sad. You guys left all of a sudden, didn't you?" Her voice dropped to a mumble. "She left all of a sudden too."

It became obvious to me that Hannah was going through the same loss that I was, and my attitude toward her changed. "Have you been to Faeries Meadow?"

"No."

"Maybe we can go together."

C

A few days before Thanksgiving break, Mr. Maloney, the art teacher, instructed us to draw a holiday scene using pencils and crayons. I stared at the blank paper, not knowing where to begin. I had never been to a Thanksgiving dinner and had only eaten turkey on the seasonal lunch plate the school cafeteria served every year.

Mr. Maloney held up pictures of families seated at Thanksgiving tables, pilgrims, Indians, pumpkins, turkeys. The images were cartoonish, but the turkeys reminded me of the chickens on Titi Machi's farm. I decided to draw her preparing a turkey.

I was anxious to catch up with everyone around me and worked fast. I drew a house with a door and four windows. A gray tin roof next to the house with a *fogón* and a black pot over orange, red, and yellow flames. I imagined the turkey with colorful feathers, a bright red head and large claws fighting back as Machi struggled to wring its neck, just like she did with the chickens she made for dinner.

I had watched from the doorway, aghast, so many times as she pulled on the chicken's neck and held it forcefully until it became long, elastic, and limp in her hands. She'd set it on the dirt floor and place a huge black pot of water on the *fogón* to boil. The dying bird convulsed and warbled while she gathered handfuls of *cilantrillo*, *recao*, and *ajicitos* from the herb gardens around the house. It was my job to remove the seeds from the *ajicitos*. And as we worked, their aromas dispersing throughout the home, I wondered where the chicken's spirit had gone.

I had a hard time deciding which part of the process to draw. I started with Machi in her black dress, on the dirt floor next to the house, showing off her chicken, which I switched out for a turkey. She held him up, his neck cut off and still bleeding, his colorful head on the ground.

I imagined his soul floating above the *fogón*, soaring above the clouds on its way to heaven. Then I drew the cooked turkey on the table but didn't have time to add the family members. I finished it off with a tiny, gray, turkey-shaped cloud floating above the roof, representing the turkey's soul.

Mr. Maloney strolled between our desks, collected our works, and commented on the pumpkins, pilgrims, and autumn leaves the students drew. When he stopped at my desk, though, he didn't say anything. He hovered above me, his eyes on my drawing, and I knew I had a problem.

"Why is there another turkey on the roof?"

"It's the spirit of the turkey on the way to heaven."

"The spirit of the turkey? Oh. I see. Tell me more. Who's the cook?"

I told him it was Aunt Machi at the *fogón*.

"Interesting. Is there a fire pit where the pot is?"

"Yes."

"And why did you give her a beard?"

"Because she has one."

The face he made was enough for me to know that something was off, and I wished I had drawn a turkey and a family as everyone else had, but it was too late. The class was over, and he had my drawing in his hands.

When we arrived at school the next day, our drawings were tacked onto a bulletin board at the school entrance. Kids showed them off to parents and friends on their way to their classrooms. Mine was pinned at the top left side.

"That's a Puerto Rican turkey that just got killed," a girl told her mother. "That's why it has blood."

"I see," the mother said, eyes bulging. "Oh, look at these marvelous pilgrims over here! And you painted a luscious pumpkin pie. How yummy!"

Frankie Ross, the cutest boy in my class, stood next to me and pointed out his drawing to his father.

Then he showed him mine.

"Graphic," the father said.

"Mine's just plain. No blood," Frankie said.

When the whispers continued, I headed into the classroom and regretted having included anything from Puerto Rico in my drawing. No one in school had any way of knowing I was recalling a real-life, common experience on a farm. I feared everything I did or said at school was going to be scrutinized, and I had to be more selective with my actions if I didn't want to be seen as a weirdo. But how was I to know which parts of me to hide?

I sought out my brother at recess, anxious to tell him how embarrassed I was. He was the only person who would understand. But I didn't see him with Kevin or Mark.

"Where's Pablo?" I asked them.

"The door to the gym," Mark said.

I went around the school and found him sitting on a doorstep that led to the gym. Even before I reached him, I knew he was bothered by my drawing.

"What's the matter?" I asked.

"You know. Did you have to draw that?"

Footsteps pounded the ground and Hannah's voice sounded in the distance as she came closer, running toward us with Emily Belanger.

"What're you doin' over here?" Hannah asked, catching her breath.

I looked the other way, assuming both had seen the drawing and were convinced I was a total idiot.

Pablo rolled his eyes. "She even drew the blood."

My mouth stiffened. "Everyone making fun of me now?"

Hannah looked surprised. "Nobody's making fun of you. Right, Emily?"

Emily shook her head and shrugged.

"They probably think we're stupid," Pablo said. "Why can't you be like everyone else?"

I wanted to run into the hallway and tear the drawing off the wall.

There was ice under our feet and snow on the grass, but the sun warmed our faces and we all squinted at each other. What would it take for me to think the same as everyone around me in time to do things right?

Hannah raised her shoulders and dropped them as if they weighed a ton. "Come on, Pablo. Nobody cares. My parents are from Canada, and who cares?"

Emily faked a smile. "Next time, just do something, you know, normal."

"See? That's what I mean. Normal. Forget that Puerto Rico stuff," Pablo said. "We're not over there anymore."

"Yeah. You live here now," Hannah said. "With us."

"What did you draw?" I asked.

"Pumpkins," Hannah said.

"I draw a pumpkin every year," Emily said. "It's easy."

Pablo jumped up. "See? That's what I mean. I made a pumpkin too. No blood. No spirits."

"Oh, stop it," Hannah said.

Emily pulled on my arm. "She'll draw a pumpkin next year, right Andrea?"

I wanted to be like my brother, to figure things out the way he did, before creating a problem. What would it take for me to be like everyone else at Russell Elementary?

That weekend, we moved into the apartment on the first floor below Uncle Felipe and Caridad. We had been in Woronoco for two weeks, and now we had our own home. Pablo and I were ecstatic. Especially because Papá bought us a television.

After he finished setting the furniture in place, he told us to change into dress clothes. Then he drove us to a diner in Westfield, guided us into a booth, and called the waitress.

"Do you have a Thanksgiving dinner for me and my children?"

"We most certainly do, sir."

Minutes later, she served us traditional Thanksgiving dinner plates.

Papá beamed. "This is the same meal that the first Americans prepared to thank God when they came to America."

Pablo and I smiled, wondering what his point was.

"And now we have to thank God that we came here too." He pounded a finger on the table, emphasizing his words. "And today we thank God for being here. We thank *nuestro Señor Jesuscristo* for the opportunity he gives me to use these two hands to work every day to put food on our table. And we thank him for the opportunity he gives you, my children, to have good food, and learn English. I want us to have this same dinner every year from now on, like Americans."

Papá smiled with pride. For him, adapting to life in the United States was as simple as eating turkey on Thanksgiving and as complicated as choosing between pecan or pumpkin pie. He was happy to provide us with a home, food, and the opportunity to be in an American school where we could learn English so that we could have more opportunities than he'd had when he was our age. That was his part in fulfilling our American dream.

For my brother and me, however, accomplishing that dream was more complicated. Papá barely related to Americans. He had plenty of Puerto Rican friends and relatives in Westfield and at the paper mill. He never had to watch what he was saying or doing. Pablo and I lived among Puerto Ricans, but the moment we stepped out the door, we were in the United States. And that meant not only speaking English, but participating in a completely foreign culture. It didn't matter that we had grown up in Woronoco. The Puerto Ricans in Woronoco lived as if they were still in Puerto Rico. Our life in America wasn't as easy as celebrating a holiday by eating the same thing as everybody else.

eight

It was the second week of school in January 1960 when Miss Abbey, the music teacher, gave me a part to sing in front of the class. Right in the middle of a song, she glanced at me for a second, held one hand flat in the air, directing the rest of the class to quiet their voices, and pointed the ruler at me. I sang and she smiled with a stiff lip and a slight tilt of her head, continuing to move her hand up and down to the rhythm of my voice.

She waved, directing me to stand, and I rose to my feet rather confused, still singing, pronouncing every letter of every word, pushing my voice with a force that came from the middle of my chest until I reached the highest possible pitch and held it, motionless. Miss Abbey, also motionless, watched as I allowed my voice to soar for as long as I could. Seconds before I ran out of air, she gave me the most delightful smile, her eyes half closed as she switched hands, directing the entire class to join me with vivid impetus.

When the bell rang, signaling the end of music class, it was like waking up from a dream you don't want to end. Even Frankie stopped to tell me how much he liked my voice. Hannah and Emily couldn't stop talking about it on the bus. I was the one who could sing.

Soon after Pablo and I came home from school, the sun went down, and it was too cold to be outdoors. Every afternoon, we changed into play clothes, had a snack, and did chores. Pablo emptied the rubbish and swept the floor. I cleaned the breakfast dishes, sorted and rinsed a cup of rice, and left it in a bowl on the counter, ready for Papá to cook for dinner. Other times, I peeled potatoes and soaked them in a bowl of salted water.

A few weeks into January, my father added a new chore. He told me to put a pinch of salt in a cup of water in the *caldero*, the steel pot he used to make rice. When he came home, he turned the burner on before taking off his coat. Then he'd smack kisses on our foreheads and pour the rice into the pot of boiling water.

A few weeks later, he taught me to turn the stove on so that by the time he came home, the water was boiling. We followed that simple routine for a long time, and I looked forward to the signs of approval in his face when he arrived.

Pablo, of course, never missed a minute of television, but he was the boy, and boys were not taught to do "feminine" chores like cooking.

One evening, I did my chores and waited at the window, but when the water boiled and my father didn't show up, I wasn't sure what to do next. Let it boil the heck off? Turn the burner off?

"He's gonna be here any minute," Pablo said, without taking his eyes off the television.

I went from the window to the kitchen several times, water boiling over on the stove, and still, no sign of my father. I thought of turning it off, but would that delay dinner? Water spattered on the floor. I ran for the mop, but when I went to dry the floor, the spattering water burned me. I wanted to turn it off but couldn't reach the knob without getting burned.

I wondered what would happen if a fire broke out in our home. What if the fire trucks didn't arrive on time and we died, like the three little kids from Springfield?

With sirens vivid in my mind, I ran to the kitchen and decided that I had to get that pot under control. Pablo ran in behind me. I grabbed the bowl of rice and held it over the splattering pot, letting globs of rice slide into the boiling water. A few drops burned me, but the bubbling subsided.

I was afraid of Papá's reaction. Maybe he'd say that I should've waited for him, or that I should've added the rice sooner, or that I got the stove dirty, or that the rice wasn't going to taste good. But none of that happened.

Papá walked through the door just as I placed the empty bowl on the table. He grabbed a spoon, stirred the rice with one hand, lowered the heat with the other, threw in some lard, and put a lid on the pot all while still wearing his coat. Then, he turned his head around in slow motion and stared at me.

I froze with nervousness.

"It bubbled and bubbled and bubbled, Papá, so I threw in the rice."

The surprised look on his face turned into a clownish grin, and I was startled when his high-pitched yelp turned into wild laughter. Like a maniac, he picked me up in his arms and ran around the kitchen, jumping up and down, tossing me in the air. When he calmed down, he put me on the floor and took his coat off.

"*Caramba*," he said. "We have a cook in the family!"

It must have been March or April when progress reports came in. Papá shook his head as he read mine.

"A note here says you're talking in class. It looks like that mouth has words coming out all the time. You have to shut that mouth up and pay attention, *¿entiendes?* Look at this. C in mathematics. C in science. C in conduct. *Mija*, you're wasting your time in school. Wasting the teachers' time."

He picked up Pablo's report card. "Look at this. A in mathematics, A in science, A in social studies. See the difference? A in reading. You see what I'm saying? He has A in everything. *Eso sí que está bueno*."

"But I have A's too."

He looked at my report card again. "No, *mija*. These aren't any good. A in art, A in music, A in English, B in social studies, B in reading. You're right, you have some A's, but those aren't any good. Those have no importance."

"No importance?"

"Yes, *mija*, the ones you need to become someone important someday. Pablo can be anything he wants to be with those grades. He can be a lawyer. He can be a doctor. But if you want to be anyone of importance, like a nurse, a teacher, a secretary, you know, a person that can earn enough money to survive in this world, to make it worth the sacrifice of going to school all those years, you have to get better grades than what you brought home today. Haven't you thought about what you want to do in life in the future? Do you want to spend the rest of your life cooking and cleaning a house?"

"No, Papá, I want to be a teacher."

"Well, every teacher in your school will tell you that to be a teacher, a person has to know mathematics and science. A teacher that can't add and subtract, *no sirve*. Not any good, *mija*." He dropped my report card on the table. "Anybody can sing. And that art stuff, you don't need to go to school to learn to scribble. You need to have A's up and down this card, understand? Up and down this card like Pablo, all the way up and all the way down."

Papá had only been to second grade. He never came to the school, never attended parent activities. He didn't know how well I did in music class, how I looked forward to that class every week. He didn't know how difficult it was to get Miss Abbey's attention, yet I'd managed to do that early in the semester.

My father had never had a music teacher. He didn't know how Miss Abbey drilled us on the musical scale, or how difficult her tests were. And what about reading? He had never read a whole book in his entire life. He knew nothing about spelling bees, surprise quizzes in social studies, or reading comprehension tests.

He didn't understand the difficulties I had with learning in English either. He had no idea what it was like to say "a ship drowned" instead of "a ship sank" in front of a whole classroom. Even when the teacher excused me because I was "from Puerto Rico," the kids laughed.

All I wanted was for people to forget that I was from Puerto Rico, to forget that I was different. Papá had no idea what it took for me to get the grades I had, and the grades he wanted from me were no easy feat, unless you were my brother, and I was no Pablo.

I raised my arms and looked at my father. "What is it going to take for me to see pride in your eyes when you look at me? The only thing you're proud of is the way I make our rice. But you want me to be Pablo and that's not who I am."

That night, I asked Pablo how he got good grades.

He chuckled. "I don't know. Don't worry about it. It'll be summer soon, we're going to be riding our bikes and he's going to forget about it. Maybe just pay more attention in school next year, you know? Like he said."

He was definitely right about summer, and I couldn't wait to ride my bike for long hours with all the kids in the neighborhood every single day.

nine

P ablo and I spent the first part of vacation sleeping late. It was our first summer without our mother or an adult watching over us, and I remember a feeling of liberation. Pablo had turned eight in December, I would be turning ten in July, and all I wanted was to play outdoors with our friends.

We watched the morning cartoons while drinking cups of coffee with crackers mushed into the mug, and then had bowls of cereal on the back porch facing the forest, which had come alive. As soon as we heard the other kids outside, we got dressed and joined them with our bikes.

We played marbles in the driveway for hours. We sat on one another's porches and gobbled down peaches from the trees in our backyards. We picked wild raspberries, swung as hard as we could on the Tarzan swing below the railroad tracks, played baseball in the cul-de-sac, and went for walks through the forest.

Pablo insisted we ride our bikes to Valley View Avenue even though we both knew our father didn't want us straying from the Beehive. But the reality was, there wasn't anyone at home who'd notice if we left.

We were curious about other streets in Woronoco where we had never gone except on Halloween, which didn't count because we were following a whole gang of kids and didn't even know where we were most of the time. We hopped on our bikes and reached the stop sign at Tekoa Avenue and took a right past Strathmore onto Valley View Avenue.

I was afraid our father might see us through one of the huge windows in the mill, but we took the chance anyway. The road was smooth, better than down in the Beehive. The houses were bigger than the ones in our community. They were two-family homes instead of four, with rock foundations and flower beds all around the front. Some had big orange lilies with dark brown anthers in the center, others had delicate white lily of the valley flowers.

A group of women sat on a stoop at the front porch of a house and spoke vivaciously. One had curlers in her hair, another had an apron, little kids running around. One woman was wearing madras-print shorts with a white button-down sleeveless shirt and penny loafers. Her hair curled up at the ends and she wore soft pink lipstick. I wanted to look like her when I grew up.

Behind the next house, teenage girls wearing bathing suits sat in folding outdoor chaise loungers, a scene out of a magazine. We slowed down and watched them. One of them came out of a humongous aboveground swimming pool wearing a white swim cap. She grabbed a towel from a chair. A Connie Francis song played on the radio.

I wanted to grow up to be like them. Carefree. A simple life, full of all the things I dreamed of having. Nice clothes, beautiful haircuts, a normal family. One of them poured soda into a plastic cup. Another one, wearing a big hat with sunglasses, browsed through a book. I wondered why she had a book if it was summer. Why would anyone read on vacation?

Pablo zipped past me and lifted the front end of his bike so it bounced, and we headed back. Someone had opened the clubhouse in front of Strathmore, and we stopped and peeked in from a distance. A group of boys in shorts played basketball, while other kids with an instructor jumped on a trampoline. We didn't recognize anyone.

"Let's go," Pablo said.

I thought we were going home, but when we reached the stop sign on the corner of Tekoa Avenue, he pedaled straight toward Woronoco Bridge. We stopped in the middle of the bridge, looking down at Salmon Falls.

"Remember Tito in the river?" I asked.

"We have our own river here. There's a lot of people up here we don't know."

He hit the pedals, crossed the bridge, and turned left onto Woronoco

Road. We stayed on the left-hand side, passing three houses. Kitty, a girl from my class, yelled out my name from one of the porches. I didn't know her but had seen kids making fun of her at school for being overweight. We passed the post office on the right side of the road and a feeling of freedom, uncertainty, and a little nervousness hit me as we pedaled through unknown territory. That was the farthest we'd ever gone, when we walked to the post office with our mother.

We passed the last house on Woronoco Road and continued through all the curves that lead to Route 20, staying close to the left curb until we reached the intersection. There wasn't any traffic coming either way. Pablo signaled with his hand, hit the pedals hard, and we merged onto Route 20.

After a while, I could see the Massachusetts Turnpike ahead and thought we'd gone too far. My brother looked back out of the side of his eye and yelled, "The horses are coming up. Want to keep going?"

I flew past him. "Yeah!"

We kept going, not a car in sight, and rode under the overpass. Sometimes Pablo led the way, sometimes I did. Sometimes the river was right next to us, sometimes it hid behind the trees. A field opened up to the right, and I knew we were getting closer to the white fence with horses. We approached the horses we'd seen from Papá's car dozens of times on our way to St. Mary's Church and the Hispanic meeting house in Westfield. But this was different. Scents drew us into their immediacy. I took the lead, crossed the road, and pedaled toward them.

We jumped off our bikes and stood at the fence. There wasn't anything to say. A red barn in the distance. A ranch-style white home lined with pine trees. In the front yard, a girl smaller than us, blonde hair combed into pigtails and big yellow bows, running around with a cocker spaniel. A handsome young man sitting like a king on top of a muscular, sure-footed horse, prancing past more white fences. All I could hear was Pablo breathing, an occasional car passing, the girl's giggles, the dog's bark floating toward us in a breeze.

A woman came out of the house carrying a tray. She called out to the man, who got off the horse and walked to her. She handed him a glass and he drank. The little girl didn't want any and ran with the dog. The couple turned to us, arms around each other, and stared.

Pablo and I looked at each other, acknowledging that we'd just been found. Two intruders in a world of beauty so removed from anything we had ever experienced. Beauty I thought I'd never touch. They looked like they had everything in the world. I fell in love with the life they had behind those white fences, beyond the Beehive, and the thought that one day I'd have a home of my own, a husband and a child.

Pablo hopped on his bike.

"Let's go, they're still looking at us. We're almost there."

"Almost where?"

"Westfield. Come on, we can do it."

"No. Let's turn around."

"You tired?"

"We need to go home."

A few cars whizzed by. One passed another and honked several times.

"Andrea, you're not going to tell Papá, right?"

"A course not."

We pedaled as fast as we could until we returned to Bridge Street, crossed the bridge into Woronoco, and stopped at the bus stop. Pablo threw his bike and rolled in the grass in front of the Strathmore rose bushes. I stood with my hands on the handlebars, surprised at how far we'd gone, how easy it had been to get away from the Beehive, and how fast we'd made it back. The aroma from the rose gardens filled the air, hawks circled above, and mechanical clangs coming from the mill reverberated through the forests. No one noticed we'd gotten away. Nothing had changed. We had been *out there*.

Pablo sat up. "Let's go back tomorrow."

"The horses?"

"Westfield. We almost made it."

But what would we do in Westfield? There really wasn't anything there of interest to me. What I loved was the exhilaration of being free, the nervousness of not knowing where we were going, the green aromas of moist soil and pine trees. Westfield was a town. Roads full of cars, stores, people everywhere, big sidewalks.

I got back up on my bike. "Let's go start supper."

At home, Pablo was fiddling with the television and I was putting breakfast dishes in the sink when footsteps pounded down the stairs. There was a loud knock. I opened the door and found Uncle Felipe behind the screen with a dead serious look on his face.

"Didn't you hear me honking?"

Pablo ran into the kitchen looking like a ghost and jammed his hands in his pockets.

Uncle Felipe stepped into the kitchen. "I was waiting for you to come home. I honked at you, and you two didn't even look. What were you doing *esgaritaos por allá*? Getting lost?"

Uncomfortable heat flushed my face, and I didn't know what to do with my hands. I bit a nail off.

"Do you realize how angry your father is going to be when he finds out you were in Westfield?"

Pablo looked at me, then he stared at the floor, looking as obedient as he could.

"We weren't in Westfield, Tío."

"Well, you didn't have much to go to get there."

My brother and I both stared at the floor. We were doomed.

Pablo's chest rose and fell in huge deep breaths. "Tío, we won't do it again, I promise, Tío, please don't tell Papá."

"I won't, but you have to promise you won't ride your bikes on that road again, you hear?"

❧

I had a small, impromptu birthday party when Caridad baked a cake for my tenth birthday in July, and we invited our best friends in the neighborhood. It was my first birthday party.

Soon after, I was in the fourth grade. It was the fall of 1960 and we were getting ready to go home when Miss Abbey, the music teacher, brought me to her office, which I'd never seen before. She had instruments everywhere. Bells in mesh bags along a wall, black flutes in boxes on a shelf, harmonicas in a basket, trays with triangles and tambourines.

She sat at her desk and patted a chair next to her.

"Come sit."

She picked up a bag from the floor and placed it on her lap. "I have a niece a year older than you. She outgrew these, so I brought them for you."

She smiled and winked. Then she pulled out five gorgeous winter dresses and laid them on the desk. "Think you might like these?"

The dresses were stunning, like nothing my father had ever bought for me. Luxurious fabrics, buttons, ribbons. I didn't know how to react.

"Come," she said, and took my arm.

I stared at her soft, pink mohair sweater.

"Let's see if they fit." She held a dress up to my shoulders. "You know what? I think they will. Oh, and these colors look so pretty with your blonde hair."

I smiled, hardly able to contain my excitement, enamored by her aura, the glow in her cheeks, the soft sheen of her tiny pearl earrings, her silky blonde hair, and eyes like crystal balls that held an entire universe. I wanted nothing more than to grow up to be a teacher like Miss Abbey, to wear her beautiful clothes, to pronounce every word with such perfection, to know exactly what to say and when.

"Would you like them?"

Of course I wanted them, but I didn't want to seem desperate. I lifted my shoulders and tilted my head.

She whispered, "You don't want them?"

I did, but words escaped me. I nodded, wanting her to see my desire but at the same time hoping she couldn't tell how much I wanted them.

"You do want them. Well, good. You'll look lovely. You think your mom will let you wear them?"

"She doesn't live in our house."

"Who do you live with?"

"Papá and my brother."

"Yes, Pablo. He's my student too. So, who cooks?"

"Me and Pablo and Papá."

"Really? Well, that's remarkable. And who checks your homework?"

I bit my lips. I never did homework. And I never knew someone was supposed to do it with me, but I didn't want to get my father in trouble.

"You do homework, don't you?"

I shrugged.

"Oh dear, you must do homework and study for tests, otherwise you won't pass. This is an especially hard grade."

She finished folding the dresses and placed them in the bag. "Do you think your father will like them?"

I nodded, but I wasn't sure how my father would react.

"Okay, all packed up. I'm happy they fit." She patted my shoulder.

On the bus next to Pablo, I thought about her advice and wondered what my brother would have to say.

"How come you never have homework?"

"I do it at school."

"You do?"

"I thought you did too. Don't you do your homework?"

I couldn't respond.

"Andrea, you're in fourth grade and you don't do your homework? No wonder you're always flunking. You have to do your homework."

My throat grew stiff.

"I'm not flunking. But I'm not smart like you."

"Andrea, listen. Home. Work. Get it? You don't have to be so smart, just have to do it."

Then he looked at the bag on the floor next to me. "Where'd you get that bag?"

"Clothes from Miss Abbey," I whispered.

The bus reached the Tekoa Avenue stop sign, and all the kids jumped off and headed down the hill to the Beehive. I carried my bag with both hands and ran ahead of them.

Hannah and Emily ran behind me. "What's in the bag?"

"Nothing," I said. "See you tomorrow."

I knew I'd cut them off, but I didn't want to show them the dresses.

Pablo caught up with me. "What's the rush? Wait for me!"

"Hurry up," I yelled. "I have homework to do!"

My brother cut brown paper bags open for Papá to drain fried chicken on while I peeled potatoes.

Perfecta walked in. "Is that one of the dresses?"

Papá lifted his eyes from the table and nodded.

"*Qué belleza*. You have to be rich to buy dresses like that."

Papá gave me an up-and-down look. "Go change into house clothes."

I ran into the bedroom and changed as fast as I could, my father's voice in the background.

"You're correct. I don't have money to buy dresses like those. But I don't like my daughter wearing anything another kid wore, no matter how good they are. They're used clothes."

Uneasiness hit me. I had no idea my father didn't like me wearing the dresses from Miss Abbey. Who cared if they were used? No one knew that but us. When I returned to the kitchen, he was cutting up potatoes for french fries while Pablo and Perfecta stared at him in silence.

"I don't like people giving me charity. I can pay for my own things for me and my kids. It might not be something fancy like that teacher gave her, but it would be new, and something I bought her myself. With *my* money."

His face grew somber as he placed a frying pan on the stove.

"Are you going to have her take them back?" Perfecta asked.

Papá pointed at me with a spoonful of lard in his hands.

"Of course not. She wants to look good at school, and you can't return a gift."

He placed the lard into the frying pan and lit the stove. I glared at the blue flame melting the lard.

Papá stepped back from the stove and sighed. "*Carajo.* I know the woman has good intentions. The problem is I should have thought of getting my daughter clothes months ago. Before winter."

My aunt pointed at me. "You shouldn't have accepted those dresses." She got closer and shook a finger in my face. "That's not a gift. They're hand-me-downs. The next time someone gives you something used, you tell them your father has the money to buy you new clothes."

I peeled and cut potatoes without looking up.

Papá took a few, threw them into the pan, and stepped back from the spattering lard. "It's not her fault. What does she know at her age? The teachers see these kids wearing the same old clothes every day, and they're doing something about it because I haven't."

"You need a deeper pan."

"I know. I need a bigger frying pan. I need to get clothes for these kids. I need to cook every day, clean this house, do the laundry. I need a lot of things. The most important thing I need is a wife to help with all of this."

Perfecta glanced at us with pressed lips, her eyebrows raised. "Raquel should be the one raising them."

Papá stared at the frying pan and sighed. "Stop peeling potatoes, *mija.* We have enough."

"You're not going to find anyone. Not with these two. Send the girl to her mother."

I had suspected this woman disliked me, but after that day I was convinced. I looked at her with horror in my eyes. Then I looked at my father. My lips trembled. "¿Papá? Are you sending me back to Puerto Rico?"

My father turned the potatoes in the frying pan, taking deep breaths that sounded like he was lifting something heavy, and I wasn't sure if he was having a hard time telling me that he was sending me away or if he was trying to quell his anger after what Perfecta had said.

Tears welled in my eyes, and I ran to the living room. Pablo ran in and sat next to me on the sofa. "Andrea, don't listen to her, of course Papá isn't sending you away."

Then we heard our father's voice coming through the walls like thunder over a roof. "I'm not sending my kids anywhere. Not the girl. Not the boy. *¿Está claro?* My kids stay with me. And if there comes a day when I can't take care of them, Raquel would be the last person in the world I would send them to."

"See? I told you," Pablo said. "Now let's go help him some more. Don't pay attention to her."

Papá took the last batches of potatoes out and placed them on paper bags next to the chicken. Pablo moved them to the table while I grabbed plates.

"We'll be fine until the right woman comes along," Papá said. He wiped his hands on his apron and smiled at my brother and me.

"Right? Look at all the food we just made."

We both nodded with timid smiles, and I still remember the relief and reassurance that came over me as he spoke.

Perfecta watched in silence as we set the table.

"And what is Andrea doing after school?"

My father looked annoyed.

"Would you like to eat with us? Fried chicken and potatoes?"

"She needs supervision. A *señorita* shouldn't be here all by herself."

"She's not by herself," Pablo mumbled.

"Well, she should come upstairs with me until Luis comes home."

I felt light-headed, like someone had sucked oxygen out of the room. What on earth did she want me up there for? She had Angela, the dreadful cousin of mine who was sixteen years old and wouldn't go to school. She sat around all day making crochet dresses for decorative dolls and doilies for the furniture. That's not what I wanted to turn into.

All I wanted was to be a teacher like Miss Abbey. I had school, friends, my brother. I had made a choice. I had stopped going out to play after school until I did my homework. Then I helped my father make dinner. Every single day. Sometimes I never made it outdoors while Pablo went out on his bike and had a great time, because I knew my place, the place of a girl. I looked at my father for a response, but Pablo spoke up.

"Pa, she can't go—"

Aunt Perfecta wasn't about to let an eight-year-old oppose her.

"And what do you know? She's wasting her time in school. At least she could learn to be useful."

I couldn't keep my feet still. "My report card is better, right, Papá?"

Pablo jumped in front of me like he was protecting me from an attacker.

"Yeah, it is," said Pablo. "And she can't go up there with you. She has homework. She's a fourth grader, you know."

Our father nodded, and I knew in this moment he was proud of Pablo for defending me.

"You're right, *mijo*. She has to study for school."

Perfecta reached for the door. "Can't do anything after she gets in trouble."

Before she left, she gave me a cynical smile.

No sooner did Papá close the door than he said, "*Vieja estúpida*. Who the hell does that old lady think I am? Why doesn't she give her daughter away? I'm regretting the day I brought her here."

It felt good to see both my father and brother stand up for me, but I knew I hadn't seen the last of Perfecta's interventions.

ten

I helped Caridad bake a cake for Pablo on his ninth birthday in December, and because it was on a Sunday, Kevin and Mark came over and watched television with him for hours. That Christmas, Papá brought home a Christmas tree that was a tad taller than Pablo. We loved being in the house at night just to watch the bubble lights go up and down.

On Christmas Eve, we had a party at Aunt Caridad's house. She cooked with other Puerto Rican women who'd moved into the neighborhood, women whose husbands also worked at the paper mill.

My father sat in the living room playing guitar while the men stood around having cigarettes and beers. From the living room, I could see Angela at Caridad's bedroom dresser applying makeup while Pablo and I knelt on the sofa watching the snowstorm. Uncle Felipe had gone to the airport in New York to pick up our cousin, Uncle Bartolo's daughter, who'd arrived from Puerto Rico.

We told everyone as soon as we saw the aura of glitter the car's headlights cast on the snow.

When the door opened, the most striking young woman I had ever seen walked into the living room. No sooner had she seen us than she was all over my brother and me with *my you've grown* and *oh, you're so beautiful.* Everyone hugged her and wiped joyful tears as she moved from Caridad to Perfecta to Angela.

It could have been her black high heels that gave her footsteps the sound of solid brick and projected a self-confidence that I knew Perfecta considered inappropriate, or maybe it was her stunning beauty that made you feel as if you were in the presence of a movie star, but I knew from the moment I laid eyes on Socorro Rodríguez that Perfecta's ways would be tested.

A vibrant and exciting person had just entered our drab daily existence.

With her radiant tan skin and short, wavy black hair, a curl purposefully placed slightly above her left eye, red lipstick, and a penciled-in beauty mark above her top lip, not to mention her determination and vivacity, she resembled the sensational Puerto Rican actress Marta Romero.

We ate *sancocho, pasteles, arroz con dulce.* Meanwhile, in the living room, Socorro pulled a 78 record of Cortijo y su Combo from her suitcase and stood up. "I want to teach all of you to dance to this."

She searched her suitcase until she found a package of tiny pink paper umbrellas and a bottle of Puerto Rican rum. The men roared, "*¡Palo Viejo!*" while Perfecta scrunched her lips and shook her head.

"Who wants Cuba libres?" Socorro giggled and ran into the kitchen with her goodies, followed by Felipe, who winked at me as he passed by.

"Turn the Victrola on," she called out to the women in the living room, while the men prepared drinks on the sink's drainboard and topped them with pink umbrellas.

I couldn't keep track of all the people there, given how many had just moved to Woronoco. Of course, I knew Caridad, but there was Matilde, Sonia, Esther, Elisa, Nayda, Sylvia, Delia, and Migdalia. There was also Cathy, a white American woman who was married to a Puerto Rican and spoke perfect Spanish. A whole bunch of kids younger than us ran around and I couldn't figure out who was whose parents. And who were all these husbands working at Strathmore? Carmelo, Rafa, Alberto, Rogelio, and some I hadn't even seen before. Our side of the Beehive had become a Puerto Rican neighborhood. Then Epifanio and Amanda arrived with little Oscar, who ran around like he owned the place.

Socorro swayed to the middle of the living room, where she danced to "El Negro Bembón." The men poured in from the kitchen, drinks in hand, and Socorro dragged relatives, men and women, to dance. One by one they imitated her, starting with Tío Felipe, who complained about how tired he was from all the driving, and how the rum was just what he needed. He stood in one place with a drink in his hands and jokingly re-created his niece's dance steps.

Everyone played along with Socorro except for my father, who wouldn't budge when she tugged on his arm like a child wanting to play.

"No, I don't like that music, go ahead and dance with someone else. Those are bums, all those singers and musicians. I like *música jíbara*. That's my music."

Bautista smiled. *"Drogistas, bones."*

Socorro stared at Bautista. "What does *bones* mean?"

"Bums, *mija*, bums. Cheap Black people. I don't like that dancing either," Papá said.

Socorro looked disappointed. "Tío, we're just having a little fun here, stop criticizing so much."

When the song ended, Papá hopped around like a chicken, making fun of the dancers. Everyone in the room laughed at his clowning.

Socorro grinned.

"Aha, don't learn the dance so you make fun of it. I know you, Tío."

Soon after New Year's, my father took us to Mass at St. Mary's Catholic Church in Westfield for the first time since my mother had left. Afterward, we attended a social gathering at Casa Hispana, a house that Puerto Ricans rented to hold activities. Angela and Socorro came along, and boy, were they dolled up.

The house had a back porch where Pablo and I watched kids playing in the backyard. Papá fit right in with the men playing dominoes in the living room. But Angela sat pouting on the porch, while Socorro blended in with the women serving a potluck.

Thereafter, my father took us to Casa Hispana every Sunday, often skipping Mass. It wasn't the church that had attracted him in the first place. A guy with two kids would not have missed those potlucks. There was Puerto Rican food, American food, and everything in between. After Mass, the *gringo* priest came for dinner and even had a glass of wine.

Pablo played with the boys in the backyard, but I wasn't so lucky. All the girls my age were *Hijas de María* and never invited me to join them. They walked around like virginal models in a beauty pageant, wearing light-blue skirts, white blouses, a celestial blue sash across their chests with an image of Mary, and rosary beads hanging from their waist. All I wanted was to get back to Woronoco, where life was simple.

Socorro quickly made friends at Casa Hispana. She had visitors from Westfield and found a job at a place everyone called Labrek out in Springfield—the Breck Shampoo factory. She took a ride with women who worked in Westfield, and then someone from church gave her a ride to Springfield. But Angela was another story. She moped around looking bored until a guy came into the room, and then she turned into another person.

Around boys her physique became clownish, and oh, how I vowed not to be like her. Angela posed, swayed her hair, stared at nothing, tossed her head to one side then to the other, and when she crossed from one side of the porch to the other, she wiggled her ass like her back had gone into spasms.

The more I watched Angela, the more I thought no one in the world would be interested in her, until one afternoon when I saw her talking to a guy on the porch. The following week they were sitting together. I couldn't understand what the guy saw in her. She had lived in Woronoco for more than a year and had never spoken a word to me. Did she have anything to say?

I walked around in the kitchen and munched on appetizers and when I returned, they were making out. I knew Aunt Perfecta was in for the surprise of her life and wondered how she'd react when she found out that her daughter was kissing a guy.

One Sunday, I was watching my father play dominoes with Ramón, the guy that had kissed Angela. A young, delicate woman walked up to Ramón and whispered something in his ear.

"Let me finish this game and we'll leave," he said. Then he introduced her to my father. And that's how my father met Ramón's sister, Damaris.

After meeting Damaris, my father changed so much he seemed like another person. On Saturday nights, he prepared for church on Sunday by shining his shoes, ironing his shirts, and even our clothes. He made sure Socorro or Angela brushed my hair into a ponytail fixed with a nice barrette before leaving on Sunday morning. He wanted us to look spick-and-span to show Damaris what a good father and a good catch he was.

When Damaris was around, Papá pronounced every *s* and every *t*, and rolled his *r*'s like he had an engine in his throat. When he spoke with Damaris, it was always *mi amor* this, and *mi vida* that, and *corazón* this, that, or the other, and Pablo and I hated how ridiculously fake our father sounded.

Then he stopped taking us to Casa Hispana and took off by himself on Sunday mornings. We knew he was pursuing Damaris. He even spoke about her to Aunt Perfecta, and of course she told the whole family that Papá was in love with a woman in Westfield. Pablo and I didn't think much of it and preferred to stay at home playing in the neighborhood anyway.

The kids in the Beehive weren't out as early or as late as we were. Their mothers didn't allow them to go out before breakfast, called them in for lunch, called them for dinner, called them for baths, and called them at bedtime.

It was the spring of 1961, and when Pablo and I didn't have anyone else to play with, we took long bike rides. At first, we went up and down the hills in the Beehive, but by summer we were on the Massachusetts Turnpike, no hands, gliding, taking in the panoramic view of the forests, our chests swelling with the cool air, stopping at Woronoco Bridge on the way home.

Sometimes we found big kids diving in Salmon Falls and crawled under the bridge to watch them from the boulders next to the poison sumac trees. Then we rode our bikes down the big hill, dandelion puffs circling in our faces, birds chirping, the smell of hot tar baking in the sun, and the train crackling along the tracks.

It was around that time that a group of Puerto Rican women walked past us on their way to the post office. We'd come across them at the big hill or sitting on the grass in front of the Strathmore rose bushes where they read their mail, just like our mother had. On one occasion, we saw Angela walking up the big hill on her way to the post office, all by herself.

"She's seeing that guy over there," Pablo said.

"What guy?"

We glided down the big hill.

"You know, the one from Casa Hispana. Damaris's brother," he yelled.

He pedaled really hard, and I struggled to keep up with him. "You mean Ramón?"

"Yeah."

Pablo continued pedaling hard and reached the top of the little hill. He got off his bike and waited for me.

I panted and parked next to him in the middle of the road.

"He comes from Westfield to see her?"

"On his motorcycle. They take off with her on the back."

We parked our bikes behind bushes, and I led him through shrubs until we came across an open meadow.

"You been here before? How come I've never been here?"

"Sally called it Faeries Meadow."

Pablo walked to the middle of the meadow.

"Wow, another world in here."

An intense floral aroma flooded the area, and we walked around until we found lilac bushes taller than us.

Pablo sat on the grass.

"Have you seen the clothes Ramón wears?"

I sat in front of him. "Not really."

"He wears Puerto Rican pants like the stupid ones Papá makes me wear to church."

I had never thought about those pants, but yes, I had always thought there was something off about the way Puerto Rican men dressed, and Pablo hit it on the head. They all wore dress pants everywhere.

"Like the stupid dresses I have to wear. Princess dresses."

"I hate that," Pablo said. "None of the kids wear those. They always wear dungarees. They dress up only when it's a big deal, like Christmas or Easter. Ramón always wears a white T-shirt with the sleeves rolled and dress pants. Thinks it makes him look like a beatnik. But he ain't no cool teenager. He's got the boots, the bike, and then you see those pants."

The river below echoed between shades of light that filtered through the trees. Pablo spread out his legs and reclined on the grass.

"In honor roll, they were talking about college. I want to go. Do you?"

"I don't know, should I?"

"You said you wanted to be a teacher."

"I do. I mean, do you think I can?"

"Course you can. You already had better grades before classes ended. See? I told you all you had to do was do your homework. I think I'm going to be a lawyer."

"Like Perry Mason?"

We laughed.

"Frankie looks at you sometimes in the bus line, you know?"

My heart stopped. I had never noticed Frankie looking at me.

"I can tell he likes you. When your class came into mine with Miss Abbey, you and him singing that song, he looked like he was in love."

"At recess, he told me he wanted to be my friend."

"Because we're just kids. But one day he's going to say girlfriend instead." He paused. "You've gotta keep up the better grades this year. Perfecta keeps telling Pops to send you back."

"Do you defend me?"

"Yeah. She says girls should be in the house all the time and cook and serve the men, and school isn't necessary 'cause they're going to get pregnant and have to stay home taking care of the kids anyway. Dumbbell Angela doesn't even go to school, so what do you expect?"

"And what does Papá say? Does he want to get rid of me?"

"Course not. Pops understands us. He says women can work and still come home to cook. You just need to get those better grades, that's all. Don't get any C's. Try to get A's and B's."

"I know, I know. I'm working on it."

⁓

When Papa found out that Socorro was riding home from Labrek with a guy, he threatened to put her on the next plane to Puerto Rico. "My brother Bartolo is going to lay the blame on me for whatever happens to you."

Tío Felipe chimed in, "She needs to *quitear* that job tomorrow. Get something closer."

Socorro rubbed her hands and cried. "*¿Quitear?* I came all the way from Puerto Rico for a job. No, I'm not quitting."

Papá's eyes flashed in disapproval. "What are the neighbors going to say about you, a *señorita* alone with a man in a car? That has to stop. Labrek is too far."

Caridad hugged Socorro, then turned to Felipe.

"Who says she's doing anything wrong?"

Felipe's eyebrows gathered.

"I'm not saying she is, but what are people going to say?"

Socorro broke away from Caridad.

"I'm not living my life based on what others say. I'm working to support myself. I won't be needing anything from you very soon, anyway. I didn't come to the Unites States to depend on any of you."

"And who is *ese hombre*?" Papa asked.

Socorro stood tall and pushed her chest forward.

"Let me tell you who *el hombre* is. He works in Labrek. I've known him for more than three months now. He's a hard worker, he likes me, and I like him. That's who he is."

Felipe laughed with cynicism.

"See? Just what I suspected. It's not an innocent, friendly ride."

Caridad stood in the middle of the kitchen.

"What do you expect? She's not going to be single forever."

"No, she isn't," Papá said. "But if she's going to live here, she has to do things the right way. *Con respeto. El hombre* must come here, speak with me, tell me what his intentions are, and if I give permission, he sees her. And for me to give permission, I need to speak with my brother Bartolo."

Socorro wiped her eyes. "You don't have to waste time and money making a long-distance phone call to my father. I'll speak with him. I haven't told him because I'm still getting to know the man. But you're not even giving me a chance to get to know him before you've married me off."

Pablo and I were on the porch listening to them. Papá stepped out of the house and stomped down the stairs like he was making thunder with every footstep. We followed. When we walked into our apartment, he was waiting for us in the kitchen.

"Let me tell you something," he said, pointing at me.

I stared at him while Pablo closed the door.

"The day you find yourself a man that you're interested in, you bring him here. Am I clear? I don't care if he's Black with *bembas* down to his chin, all I want is that you bring me a Hard. Working. Man. And you bring him here. *A mi casa*. Before anyone else has to dirty their mouth talking. *¿Entiendes?*"

I wanted to say, *Don't worry, no one is going to be interested in me, anyway, and where have you seen someone who has lips like that?* But I stood there in obedience, eyes on the ground and quiet.

Papá was angry for days. A few nights later, there was a knock on the door. When he opened, Socorro stepped in with a guy and introduced him. The guy, named Taylor, put his hand out, but Papa didn't respond. Taylor had the most genuine smile, huge blue eyes, and a respectful attitude. *What's Papá's problem?* I thought.

When Taylor told my father he wanted to marry Socorro and asked if he could put in a word for him at the paper mill, Papá changed. He loved getting people jobs at the mill. Before Taylor left, my father was welcoming him to the family, they were making jokes and laughing their heads off, and Papá was promising to recommend him for an apartment in the company town.

That night, I realized how easily my father could change his mind about something, and how important it was to stand your ground like Socorro had.

It was a few months later, toward the end of summer, when Socorro and Taylor moved into an apartment on our side of the street. Uncle Felipe stopped speaking to her and prohibited Caridad from seeing her.

Papá and Perfecta constantly confronted Socorro about getting married. My cousin was so bothered by the remarks, the questioning, and the talk behind her back that she avoided the family. But she wasn't the only one being criticized in Woronoco.

eleven

As soon as the ground warmed up in spring, Papá worked on clearing soil to plant a garden behind the houses at the end of the cul-de-sac. Throughout the summer, that garden yielded vegetables for the whole community.

The neighborhood women did most of the weeding, early in the morning after the men left for the paper mill. Their children played around in the dirt as they worked, and it naturally happened that I kept an eye on the small ones. Soon, all the little Puerto Rican kids knew me and looked up to me.

The women chatted, and I often overheard conversations in which I had no interest. They spoke about the foods they cooked and complained that they couldn't find *recao* or *ajicitos dulces* at the bodegas in Springfield. They spoke about missing their relatives and friends in Puerto Rico, and their yearning to return to their homeland.

Often, they sounded like my mother when she'd lived in Woronoco. They didn't like the *gringos*. Their main criticism was toward parents like Hannah's mother, who allowed her teenage daughter Claire to go out on dates and wear pants. In our culture, they said, girls were to be kept indoors and never left alone with males, young or old, a chaperone required at all outings.

Their comments didn't surprise me and reinforced what I already suspected: Puerto Rican women didn't like American culture. But their customs were too limiting for me. I had spent too many hours, even whole days, folding clothes that were already neatly folded in drawers just to kill time.

The only *gringos* the women liked were Kevin Martin's parents.

"Oh, *ese señor*, now that is gold."

"He's what you call *un caballero*."

Since the Martins lived above Emily Belanger's apartment, they also had a phone. On one occasion they'd allowed my father to make a phone call when someone became ill on a cold winter night. I didn't know the whole story, probably because I'd slept through it, but these women remembered.

It was in midsummer when Emily came to the garden one morning with a few Barbie dolls. We sat under towering corn plants when I overheard the neighbors talking in Spanish about my family and motioned for Emily to keep quiet.

Doña Delia said my cousin Angela was pregnant.

"I was thinking the same. She looks like she has a *barriguita*," Sylvia said.

"Well, it wouldn't surprise me. I've seen her up on Hill Street with that guy from Westfield," said another woman.

"Yes, his name is Ramón. And Luis is courting his sister. But that Ramón only works part-time at the bicycle factory in Westfield. He's just a lazy kid," Delia said.

The women laughed, but I couldn't tell who was who and how many were there.

"Perfecta has a glass ceiling over her head. So demanding with everyone but doesn't see how fragile her own roof is."

"And that Taylor isn't marrying Socorro."

"Why should he? He already has what he wanted."

Then they laid in on my father.

"Damaris better watch what she's getting into. That man doesn't care about anyone," Delia said.

"Well, she doesn't have much of a choice. She's a *jamona* in her thirties."

"That man doesn't even buy clothes for those kids."

"Buys himself plenty. Always well dressed."

"Have you seen the way the boy goes to school in the morning? One arm ironed, the other wrinkled. *Pobrecito.*"

"I think the girl does the ironing."

"They're the only kids in the neighborhood that don't have a dime for a popsicle. You have to be really cheap to not give a kid a dime."

At this point, I choked up. Emily stroked my hair as a train whistled. "What's the matter? Are you okay?" she whispered.

I waited for the train to pass and ran out of the garden with the rumble of the train's wheels on the ground below me. Emily followed. We ran to her house, the last one in the cul-de-sac, and sat on her steps. I hung my head between my knees.

"Why are you so upset? What did they say?"

"They're saying Angela, my cousin, is pregnant, and her boyfriend isn't any good, and my cousin Socorro's boyfriend isn't any good either, and my fa . . . father isn't a good father."

"Andrea, don't cry. Jesus. Don't they have anything good to say? Don't pay attention to them. Your father is a great father. Everyone knows that."

I wanted to hide from everyone. Me, the girl abandoned by her mother, the one who doesn't get good grades, the one who doesn't do enough at home, and now also the one with a bad father?

I wiped my nose. "I know my father is doing the best he can, and they said Pablo's shirts aren't ironed right but . . . that's not my dad's fault, I'm supposed to iron them . . . it's my fault."

True, my brother and I had yearnings for things like better clothes or a dime for ice cream, but in my short eleven years of life, I had learned to distinguish the insignificant and petty from my father's love.

"Andrea, I wouldn't know how to iron a shirt. Jesus, if they care so much, why don't they come help you do it right? I've never seen anything wrong with Pablo's shirts. And let me tell you, my parents admire your father. Everyone does."

"You think so?"

Emily caressed my hair.

"My mom says so all the time. And my dad says everyone at the paper mill likes Louie. Don't listen to those ladies. They're just stupid, that's all."

"I don't want to be Puerto Rican. I'm always doing the wrong thing everywhere—"

Emily tilted her head back.

"You are not. There's nothing wrong with being Puerto Rican. There are Americans that gossip too. But I know how you feel, because my mother is French Canadian and she didn't like being French when she first came here, and she told me that she learned, always be proud of who you are."

Emily was right. Being Puerto Rican was not the problem.

"I'm sure some of the Puerto Ricans here are really good people. I can tell they are. The way they smile, that's enough for me to tell sometimes."

"You're right. Last winter our heater broke down during the holidays, remember? We were freezing and couldn't use the stove and Matilde came over one morning and invited me and Pablo for breakfast."

I stared at the railroad tracks and laughed. "Nayda gave me and Pablo Christmas gifts."

"And who was the one who bought you a popsicle? I was there. That was really nice of her."

"Elisa. Yeah, she's sweet. I don't think any of them were at the garden today, or I would've recognized their voices."

"See? My mom says you can't let one rotten apple ruin the bushel."

From then on, I decided to observe the garden from a distance and identified the gossipers. When they were around, I stayed away, but one thing became clear. There were only a few bad apples in that bushel, but they were rotten to the core.

⁓

It was the following Saturday when Pablo and I sat on the steps in front of our house and saw a few teenagers, Hannah's sister, Claire, and Charles Stolas returning from the clubhouse. Hannah and Emily were with them.

Hannah ran over to us. "You guys should come."

"For what?" Pablo asked.

"Playing chess."

Emily ran past us on her way home. "Richard is still over there. I'm having lunch and going back. Are you coming?"

I had a secret crush on Emily's brother, Richard. He was tall with black hair and blue eyes and was starting high school in the fall. I knew he was too old for me, but I could stare at him forever. He was a model of the guy I wanted to date when I was older, what Frankie Ross would look like in a few years.

Pablo, Hannah, Stephanie, and I decided to wait for Emily to have lunch, then we'd all go to the clubhouse together. I would've joined the crowd if my tía Perfecta hadn't called me to her house.

"Go see what she wants and then come over," Pablo said.

But when I went to my aunt's apartment, she just looked at me. I had a feeling my summer would be different from my brother's.

Socorro and Caridad were on the sofa making *capias*. These small, handmade decorations are pinned on the lapels and collars of guests at Puerto Rican weddings. There was a whole production laid out, all over the living room. Socorro and Caridad, who was pregnant, threaded strips of lace that gathered into round circles.

Angela cut strips of satin ribbon that had the names of Angela and Ramón and their wedding date printed in gold. Then she made bows out of the strips and glued them onto the lace circles. My job was to glue two tiny plastic wedding rings into the center of each bow. There were fifty of the little beauties.

Angela, who hardly ever said a word, was busy giving orders.

"I don't want to see any glue on the edges, just enough so it sticks."

Socorro looked at her out of the corner of her eyes. "Okay, *mija*, we're doing the best we can."

"Did I tell you Ramón rented an apartment for us in Westfield? He bought a red Formica table with four chairs for the dining room, and a television for the living room. He is so special!"

Socorro didn't lift her head from her needlework. "Well, that's the least he can do if you're getting married. You've got to have furniture."

Caridad nodded. "I hope he's good to you. That's the most important."

I didn't fully understand what getting pregnant was about and wondered if Angela was, in fact, pregnant as the neighbors had said. She didn't look any different. And if what the kids at school had told me about sex was true, how could she have done that somewhere outdoors?

A motorcycle revved on the street and Angela ran to the window, screaming, "Ramón! Ramón! *¡Mi amor!*" and went flying down the stairs. Before she left, her mother said, "Fifteen minutes and I want you back in here, you're not married yet."

But she was out there for more than an hour, and my aunt didn't say a word.

Every day I had to go up there to work on wedding decorations, and every night Pablo came home talking about the kids at the clubhouse. He was getting good at chess, sometimes beating Kevin Martin, who already was an expert because he had learned from his father.

While we made *capias*, my aunt sat at her sewing machine working on the wedding gown. Every so often Angela stood up, and she'd measure the dress against her. When we finished the capias, we sewed pearls onto pieces of floral-shaped lace that Perfecta applied to the bodice and veil. We decorated two champagne glasses, a garter, a knife, a tablecloth. We made bows for the church pews.

During this time, Caridad gave birth to baby Vivian, and as soon as she returned home, she came back to help with the wedding preparations. When she fed her baby, I saw a glimmer of happiness in her eyes, but otherwise, she looked depressed.

One day Perfecta shook out the dress, which was almost finished, from under the sewing machine.

"I haven't seen Felipe for days."

Caridad smiled. "He comes every day, just doesn't stay."

Socorro, who only came to help on Saturdays when she wasn't working at Labrek, didn't lift her head from the garter she was decorating with lace and pearls. "Forgive me, *mija*, but that's unacceptable. You pregnant and practically alone, and now with Vivi."

Perfecta shook her head. "It's not as bad as you make it sound. The whole family is here. All she has to do is call any one of us if she needs anything. She's not alone—"

"She didn't get married to call on his family when she needs something. What does she have a husband for?" Socorro asked.

Caridad sighed with sadness. "Comes for lunch and dinner every day. Brings me and the baby everything we need."

Socorro looked like she was ready to bite someone's head off. "And what about weekends? You sit here alone while the rest of us are out having a good time. *Ay, mija*, you left your whole family in Puerto Rico for this? No, *mijita*. Tell him to go get lunch and dinner wherever he's spending his nights."

I admired Socorro for standing up to our aunt.

Caridad spoke in a soft whisper. "I thought he'd return when Vivi was born."

Perfecta filled the spool pin. "Men don't stay around when a woman is pregnant. And they don't care about kids either. Time and patience, *mija*."

Socorro smirked. "You do that to me, and I pull your eyes out. Taylor already knows he better walk a straight line with me. *Derechito*."

Perfecta threaded the sewing machine. "Socorro, women who think like you end up with nothing. *Ni la soga ni la cabra*. If he's not talking about divorce, she has nothing to worry about." She hit the wheel and pedaled. "He's fixated. He'll get over it. He knows where his home is."

Caridad sighed. "I hope your words are the truth."

"If he's showing up, you haven't lost yet. Men know the difference between all their little churches and their cathedral."

Socorro's forehead wrinkled and her breathing grew heavy. "Hot food, whatever he wants just waiting for him. *¡Qué chévere!* No man on earth will get that from me."

"She's married to him. Her place is to be his wife," Perfecta said.

"And she has to sleep with him too, right? While my uncle is with another woman. You place the responsibility on *her* to keep the marriage together. How comfortable for him and cruel for her."

"It's always been that way, *mija*. Men belong to the street, women to the house. I didn't invent that. You'll never keep a marriage together if you don't understand that."

"I'm not dealing with any of that. That's why I'm marrying an American. I would've already grabbed Vivian and left, if I were you, Caridad. My uncles? Neither one is worth anything. That's why the other one is alone."

Perfecta stared at Socorro. "You talking about Luis? Luis isn't anything like Felipe. That's a completely different situation, and you have no right talking about him like that. Raquel, she's the one who left with another man, like a whore, and left him stuck with two kids. That's why we have to watch this one, so she doesn't turn out like her mother."

My mouth fell open.

Socorro knelt by my side. "Do not pay attention to this *vieja bruta*," she whispered. Then she stood up. "Tell me something, if Raquel is so bad, then why are you constantly telling Tío Luis to send this child over there?"

Perfecta stared at Socorro. "It doesn't matter what she's like. She is their mother. She's the one who should be going through all the hardships of raising kids, not him. A man raising kids. Who ever heard of that?"

It wasn't me she saw. I was invisible. Every time she looked at me, it was my mother she saw.

Caridad opened her eyes wide. "You shouldn't talk like that in front of the child."

Perfecta straightened her back out in her chair. "I'm only saying the truth, I'm not saying anything bad. Everyone knows. This isn't a secret."

"Andrea doesn't have anything at all to do with what Raquel did." Socorro lifted my face by the chin. "This is a beautiful, obedient child and she's going to be a professional one day. Right, Andrea?"

I nodded.

Socorro stood up and walked over to our aunt. "You are *bruta* and heartless. Whatever happened in your childhood doesn't give you the right to limit our future. Yes, I say *ours*, because if it was up to you, I'd be sitting here doing crochet instead of working and making a life for myself."

Perfecta hit the sewing machine wheel hard. "Don't start on that. We've talked about that many times already, and you don't listen. You're living in sin, *mija*. And that's the end of it. And I don't see why she's crying. I'm not stupid either. The saying goes: *de tal palo, tal astilla*. Like father, like son. My poor brother is what concerns me. They have a mother. But who does he have? I worry about him. He's never going to find a good woman. No one is going to take him with those two kids."

"People with kids marry all the time," Caridad said.

Perfecta shook her head. "Well, it's not going to be Damaris. She didn't accept his ring."

Socorro and Caridad looked at each other with suspicion.

"What ring?" Socorro asked.

"*Ah, Dios*, he bought a beautiful ring with a diamond for her, and she didn't want it. She told Ramón it's because of the kids. And these kids will grow up and have lives of their own, but he's getting older. Do you want him to be an old man all by himself?"

Caridad took a deep breath. "Well, that just tells you what kind of a person she is, because there's nothing wrong with his two kids."

Socorro was about to say something, and I was about to leave when Angela, who had been silent and did not look well, ran to the bathroom.

Perfecta dropped the wedding dress. "Are you okay, *mija*?" She ran in behind her daughter and closed the bathroom door. We heard Angela throwing up and Perfecta offering to make her a chamomile tea.

Caridad shook her head. "She would even hurt these kids to protect Luis. What a warped love that is. If she loves her brother so much, why not give him a hand? He loves his kids. Everybody can see that."

Socorro looked furious. "She has the nerve to criticize me and not recognize the faults in her own daughter. The hypocrisy."

Socorro grabbed my arm, her eyes on the bathroom door. "Go on home now. I know you have your own chores. You concern yourself with living the best life you can and don't pay attention to this ignorant *vieja*. Her daughter is no saint, what is she talking about? Stop coming up here to help her, and if she bothers you, come to my house. You hear me?"

Caridad looked concerned. "Don't tell her to stop coming here. Look at all the work we have left. You're working all week; I need Andrea here to help. Don't worry, I'll take care of you, Andrea. Anything *la vieja* says doesn't matter anyway. Nobody listens to her."

But I was afraid Caridad was mistaken. What if my father did listen to her? Later that night, I told my brother how Perfecta spoke of our mother.

"Papá isn't sending you up there with that witch, so why do you go? Just stop going up there."

"But she calls me every day and Caridad needs my help."

"Help with what?"

"Decorations for Angela's wedding, and sometimes I take care of Vivi."

"Really? See? I told you about Angela. All the kids have seen her up on Hill Street. The kids are hanging out at the club in front of Strathmore. They have that trampoline we saw in the gym, and summer arts and crafts for all the kids whose fathers work in Strathmore."

"So that's pretty much everyone who lives here."

"Yeah. We can go there every day, you know. You're missing out. Kids ask about you all the time."

"They ask for me?"

"Yeah. This is the summer when we could make friends like everyone else, Andrea. And you're never there. Even Frankie Ross asked. I know you like him. It's not like their life is going to end if they don't see you. But people like us now. They treat me like I'm just like them now. It's what we've always wanted, Andrea."

I sighed.

"So, when are you going to stop going up there with that dumb lady?"

"After the wedding," I said. And I meant it.

Angela and Ramón were married at St. Mary's Catholic Church in West-field. Cars honked their horns all the way to Woronoco. The reception was, of course, under the trees, the men drinking *ron pitorro*, the women *coquito*. My father and a few other guys played guitar and we even had a traditional pig roast. Socorro, Caridad, and Amanda served cauldrons of foods they had cooked over the coals, with plates brought by other relatives who came from Westfield and Springfield. There were long tables Papá, Epifanio, and Felipe made from wood planks, covered in paper they brought from Strath-more, topped with the lace table spread we'd helped my aunt decorate.

Angela and Ramón headed off on their honeymoon, but not before she opened the front door of the car and vomited in front of everyone a few feet beyond the big maple tree. Neighbors waved from the cul-de-sac and snick-ered. "She better loosen that dress up."

Of course, Damaris was at the wedding, and at one point I saw my father speaking with her, distanced from the crowd. It looked like he was insisting on something, and she was saying no, no, no. I felt sad for my father. Long after my brother had fallen asleep, Papá played guitar under the trees with a few guys who finished off the night with whatever was left of the *pitorro*.

twelve

Once the wedding was over, Pablo and I joined the other kids at the club, and we rode our bikes and played marbles, doing things I hadn't had a chance to do for practically the whole month of July when I was helping my aunt.

Summer was nearly over when Hannah and I were in the cul-de-sac together, and an older neighbor we barely knew, Mr. Carter, pointed to some packages in the back of his truck. "Could you help me put these away?" he asked us.

He had always made me feel a little uncomfortable, but Hannah said, "Of course."

He handed us some of the packages. "Where do you want these?" I asked.

Mr. Carter pulled out a key and took his time leading us around the house and unlocking his back door, which faced the forest. I followed him into the living room. Then he turned on the television and told me to put the packages on a shelf while he went to the truck to get something else. He took Hannah with him. "Just wait here. We'll be right back."

Streaks of light came in between the shades, and I pushed one aside. Across the cul-de-sac, a train rumbled on the tracks. Stephanie's brother, Charles; Hannah's brother, Brian, and Emily's brother, Richard, sat in the shade on the hill under the Tarzan swing, talking like no one else existed in the world. I wondered if Hannah was back from the truck and peeked into the kitchen. She wasn't there. Then I noticed the back door was closed. Had they left me alone in here? Where was Hannah? The train squealed, huffed, and braked. I thought I heard a sound coming out of the bathroom but wasn't sure if it was the train and stood at the kitchen doorway, listening over the sounds of the television. I waited for the train to stop.

Then I heard a muffled gag. My chest pounded so hard I grew faint.

Shaking, with my heart beating so fast I felt it throbbing in my head, I pulled the bathroom door open. "Hannah?"

Hannah was in the bathtub with her clothes on, her mouth covered with duct tape, her face bludgeoned, pleading eyes swollen, blood everywhere. What had he done to her?

When Mr. Carter saw me, he looked at me as if I were the devil. "I told you to wait."

I ran for the front door. It had an extra bolt at the top, locked and too high for me to reach. I turned to run to the living room. *Maybe I could force open a window?*

Before I got to one, he pounded my shoulder like a boulder smashing me from behind. I fell against the coffee table and screamed in unbearable pain, holding my arm. Then I screamed as hard as I could, "Brian, Charles, Richard, help!" I don't know if I passed out from pain or fear, but the next thing I remember, I was on the floor of the back porch and Mr. Carter was carrying Hannah down the steps, squirming and kicking. I was out of breath, and he had the back door open. I tried to stand up.

Hannah was fighting him, lights going off in my head, the train's whistle moving farther away. I knew I had to continue screaming even if it killed me. Finally, I saw Brian and Charles walking the other way, and Richard coming toward me. I cried their names, my hoarse voice muffled by the sound of the train whistling in the distance.

At first, the boys looked at us with horror in their eyes as Mr. Carter sprinted to his truck and sped off. Then they knelt next to us and pulled the tape from Hannah's mouth. Brian carried his sister home in his arms, screaming for their mother. Charles walked me home.

"Andrea, what happened?" Pablo said. I dug my face into his chest and sobbed, my body one massive pain. The entire neighborhood was in the cul-de-sac when the police car came down the hill, and I remember Stephanie standing in front of me with horror in her eyes.

Perfecta said, "Take her to my house, and don't let *la policía* up there. Let's wait for her father to come home."

Socorro placed a warm towel over my face and when she took it off, I told her the whole story. Caridad walked in.

"Can she move everything? Did you check her down there? Does she have anything broken?"

Socorro shook her head and sobbed. Perfecta paced back and forth between the kitchen and living room. "Her father needs to send her to her mother, that's what he needs to do. You two never agree with me, but look what happened. She was fine when she was coming here every day. No sooner she gets out and look what she does."

Caridad's eyes welled with tears as she spoke to Socorro. "She's an old brute from the country with a mind from two centuries ago. Don't argue with her anymore, *mija*, it's a waste of time."

I sat on the sofa. This was it. My father would send me back. I'd end up with Florencia, walking the streets of Gurabo with no shoes, not going to school, hiding from other kids again. Something had to be done. My father had to know that this was not my fault.

As soon as he came home, he was surrounded by neighbors. People pointed to me at my aunt's second-floor window while the police spoke with my father. My whole body shook. I was so afraid of his reaction, of the consequences this would have, that I felt faint, my knees shaking. When my father headed for my aunt's house, my heart stopped.

My aunt and the others went to meet him in the hallway. "This is exactly what I didn't want to happen. You have to send her home to her mother," Perfecta said.

"*¡Ay, Virgen Santísima!* She's obsessed with getting rid of the little girl," Socorro said. "And you have yet to ask how she is, Perfecta."

"And you are blind with that girl. You don't see the reality of what is happening, the problems she's causing. Look what happened," Perfecta said. "How's he going to take care of her if he's working?"

I could smell Bautista's cigar coming up the staircase. "It's not Luis's fault, the man has to work. But this isn't Puerto Rico. If *la policía* says that girl wasn't being watched over, they can put her in a reformatory."

"How many times have I told him she shouldn't be alone?" Perfecta said.

My father's voice was a low, angry rumble I couldn't decipher. Then the front door slammed open, and my aunt stormed into the kitchen.

Pablo walked in, his eyes wide. "Sounds like Dad just pissed off the old lady."

I whimpered. "You think so?"

"Well, she just stomped off."

I snuck toward the front door to listen to my father in the hallway.

Caridad wailed, "Luis, you can always count on me for anything you need. I'm home all day with Vivi, I can watch over her, but don't listen to your sister. Don't send her back with that woman who doesn't love her."

"I give my life for my kids. *Cristiano*. That *vieja* thinks it's so easy to just get rid of them when you have a problem. You solve problems. That's what you do. I regret the day I brought her here. If I'd known she was going to be like this, she'd still be up in *las sínsoras* in the mountains of Utuado." Finally, my father came up to the door and saw me. He rushed in and swept me into a tight hug. "I'm not sending you away now or ever. Wherever I am is where you and your brother are going to be until you don't need me anymore. I don't get rid of my children." Then we all went home.

The next day, my father woke me up before leaving for work and told me I had to go with my aunt Perfecta after breakfast. "I'm not sending you anywhere, but you can't be here alone anymore."

"Okay, Papá."

Pablo walked into the kitchen. "She's not alone. I can take care of her."

But my father had made up his mind. "You're a minor, *mijo*. If *la policía* comes here and finds two minors alone, I don't know what they'll do. Maybe they would take both of you and put you in a home. Those homes they call *foster*. I don't want that for my children."

Despite how much I dreaded my aunt, I obeyed my father.

Aunt Perfecta didn't lift her eyes from the sewing machine when I walked in. "Games are over for you, *mijita*. You're too old to waste time when there's so much to do in a house."

I sat on the sofa in front of her and watched her sewing a seam. She took her foot off the pedal, lifted the presser foot off the garment, and slid it off the sewing machine. As she shook it out, I noticed it was a maternity blouse. She got up and told me to follow her into the pantry and pointed to a metal box full of detergents and rags. I picked up the box and she led me to the bathroom.

She took out a rag and held it up for me to see. "This is to clean the toilet. You clean it with soap. Then you pour Clorox on the rag and swoosh it around. You flush it, and you call me to check on how you did."

Cleaning the toilet wasn't new to me. Pablo and I took turns cleaning ours. But I had never used Clorox. I did as I was told, rinsed my hands, and called my aunt. As she inspected the toilet, my hands felt like I had tight gloves on and grew red. She gave me another rag for the rest of the bathroom. I scrubbed the sink and the ring around the bathtub with Ajax.

Again, she inspected. "And what about this dust on the windowsill?" She dug her nails into my ear.

Then she took me to her bedroom, pulled off the sheets and bedspread, and told me to make her bed. I wasn't sure how to cover the pillows into one long roll, like she did, but tried my best.

"Look at that. You're almost a *señorita* and you don't know how to make a bed yet. See? That's not any good."

I stood with my head down.

"Do those pillows look the way they were when we came in here?" She walked around the bed. "And the bedspread. Longer on one side than the other."

She pulled my ear. Then she grabbed me by my ponytail and pulled me to the dresser. "Did you even think of dusting this? Ha?" She pulled on my ponytail again.

I wanted to tell her to fuck off. I wanted to run out of her house right there, but what would happen if I wasn't with my aunt? What if the police came, as Papá said, and took me away to a foster home?

Every day I had different chores and endured different forms of aggression. Whenever I saw Caridad or Socorro I wanted to tell them how unhappy I was, how badly my aunt treated me. I knew Socorro was working at Labrek, but Caridad had offered to watch over me. Why couldn't I go with her instead? I loved playing with little Vivian. But I was afraid to create more problems for my father and kept my feelings to myself. I didn't even tell Pablo.

It was mid-August, and I couldn't wait to be back in school, when this nightmare my life had turned into would be over.

Some days, I cleaned the floors. When she made *guanimes*, I stirred the cornmeal. When she made *rellenos de papa*, I peeled the potatoes. After cooking together a few times, my aunt started talking. At first, it was a strange experience to hear her voice speaking without authority and anger.

"You went to Utuado and visited Bartolo with Luis, didn't you?"

I mashed potatoes in a big bowl while she turned crackers into crumbs. "Yes."

"Well, that little house, that's where all of us were born. Did anyone tell you?"

"No. You were born there? Did you play there and live there every day?"

"I certainly did. I remember my mother like it was yesterday, how she bathed me and combed my hair."

"That's my grandmother, right?"

"She had blonde hair just like yours, same blue eyes. Her father came from Spain. And her mother was like an Indian, straight black hair, really small. That's why some of us are tall and others small, blondes and black hair. They say her hair came down to her waist."

I finished mashing the potatoes. "Are these good?"

"You have to put those eggs in there now and whip them really hard."

A breeze came in through the screen door and I heard the kids outside yelling at each other.

"Those American girls waste their lives away out there running around like boys. Then they get married and don't know how to do anything and feed their husbands cans and hamburgers. Americans solve everything with a hot dog."

Perfecta rambled on and I listened, sometimes not knowing how to react. Americans ate a lot more than hamburgers and hot dogs. I knew because we had American food at the school cafeteria, and it was much more than my aunt said. I loved macaroni and cheese and meatloaf and spaghetti and meatballs. Those were the things I never ate at home.

"When Mamita started coughing, I was twelve years old. 'Make her some good hot teas,' Papá said. And he came in from the field and asked how she had been every day. I made teas from herbs I collected in the garden, always trying to find the healthiest, best ones. I made *caldo* from chickens I caught in our backyard."

I knew what she was describing, having watched Machi make chicken broth for soups and stews all the time, and I listened to her quietly. She wiped her hands covered in flour from kneading dough for *pastelillos de carne*, sat in a chair at the table, and wiped her face.

"When I carried that tea in, brimming in the cup, nice and hot, I prayed to God that it would heal my mother. But every day she was worse, until she was coughing blood and boiling with fever. Then one day Papá took me to Bartolo's house. He's the eldest. He's Socorro's father, but she wasn't born yet. She's from his second wife, Amparo. I was at my brother's house for a few days, and I don't know where Epifanio, Luis, and Felipe were. They were the babies and my father took us all to relatives. But when we all returned home, there wasn't a single trace left of my mother anywhere."

She wept. I sat next to her in silence.

"You don't do that to a child. I never said goodbye."

I got up and placed my hand on her shoulder as a train went by. Her tears and the rumbling of the train reminded me of my mother.

Perfecta told me how she was taken out of school to care for her brothers. How she cooked for the household at the age of twelve and never spoke with a boy until she was in her late teens, nor had any friends, nor played outdoors. "By the time I was old enough to marry, all the boys had been taken. And then everyone called me *jamona*."

"What does ham have to do with not being married, Titi?"

My aunt wiped sweat off her forehead and rolled out the dough. "I can't explain things like that to someone your age, but I prayed to my dead mother to send me a good prospect, and she did."

She was in her late twenties when Bautista, a widower, visited, seeking a tailor. "It was my cooking and my ability to make and alter garments that won his heart. You have to make yourself useful, *mija*. The way to a man's heart is through his stomach."

I had a hard time seeing how any of this was important for me. I didn't want to believe cooking was a way of moving forward in life. I couldn't imagine Miss Abbey cooking, except for maybe baking a cake. There was a huge difference between my aunt's view of the world and the world around me, and I liked Miss Abbey's world better. Hers seemed full of happiness and bright smiles.

The day Perfecta sent me home to clean our house, I walked through the door, and a curtain billowed in the breeze of our kitchen window. Pablo wasn't home. The television wasn't on. I couldn't remember the last time I'd been in our apartment by myself. Light filtered through the trees shading our kitchen window as I dusted, wiped, swept, and mopped.

I heard the neighborhood kids outside and ran to our living room window. Pablo pushed Kevin as hard as he could on the Tarzan swing. Kevin screamed with joy. But Hannah was nowhere in sight, and I couldn't look in the direction of Mr. Carter's house without remembering the horror we'd experienced that day. Maybe it was better that I was with my aunt, hidden from the memory.

I had never paid attention to a dusty RCA Victrola suitcase record player my father had in a corner of the living room. But that day, I cleaned it off and found a 78 record inside with *Salón México* on the label. The music transformed our half-empty living room into a stage. Theater lights appeared out of nowhere, the glow engulfed me, and I moved around like a ballet dancer, my chest up high to the trumpets. I jumped, one leg brushing the air while my arms reached for the sky as my head turned with delicate movements. Then I heard my aunt's footsteps pounding on the staircase and ran to my father's bedroom.

The screen door banged open. "What's that music?"

I yelled, "I'm over here," and rushed to wipe a windowsill.

Perfecta walked in. "You don't need all eternity to clean a house."

All the work I did in our apartment was worth my effort when my father came home to a clean house for the first time. "Wow! *Esto está bueno*," he said, his face beaming. But one thing became clear in my mind: I was not going to be a stay-at-home woman. My aunt had it all wrong. I wanted something more. I would be a teacher like Miss Abbey one day, even if it meant going against my family.

Every Saturday morning, my father went to Westfield with Pablo to buy groceries. One of those mornings, my aunt dumped all our socks into a metal basin on a table under the trees and filled it with water. She handed me a washboard and a bar of blue soap. "Scrub," she said, "and I want them hanging on the clothesline, bright and white before your father comes home."

I scrubbed every sock on the washboard for hours. Uncle Felipe ran down the stairs and jumped in his car. A woman in the house next to us walked around the block with her three preschoolers. The community was bustling, and I was washing socks in plain view.

Perfecta inspected every sock and made me rewash the ones that weren't white enough. Pablo's socks were always the worst. Mud dripped into the water, and I had to empty the basin and refill it several times. When my aunt said the socks were clean enough, I helped her hang clothes on an outdoor line.

My hands chapped and burned from the detergents and scrubbing. I was at home in the kitchen one afternoon when I heard Socorro's voice through the screen door. She was with Caridad in Perfecta's apartment, upstairs.

"He didn't tell you to turn her into your slave, *Dios mío, qué cruel*," Socorro said.

"No, I'm sure that was not what he had in mind," Caridad said.

"You have no business telling me what to do," Perfecta said.

"I'm not telling you what to do with your life," Socorro said.

"It's the child we're talking about," Caridad said.

"What do you expect me to do? At least she's good for something now. I was cooking for a whole family when I was her age."

"Tell me," Socorro said, "why is it we never saw Angela out there in the sun scrubbing socks until her hands bled?"

The door slammed so hard the building shook. Socorro and Caridad walked down the stairs and opened our screen door.

"*¿Cómo estas?*" Socorro asked, as if I hadn't just heard what she'd said to Perfecta.

I smiled, glad to see them.

"Let me see your hands," Caridad said.

I kept my hands from them.

"I don't want to see you out there scrubbing socks like a slave ever again, *¿me entiendes?*"

I nodded.

Caridad sat at the table. "If the old lady tells you to do that again, you say no. Period. *Jesucristo. Qué abuso.* And, let me tell you something. You're getting older now. You have to take care of yourself, *mija.* The old lady, a *viejo fresco*, whoever it is, you have to stand up for yourself."

My aunt never told me to wash socks again.

⌒⌒⌒

When school started in the fall, I still went to my aunt's house every day. I grew angry and conflicted. Our linoleum floor had a noticeable sheen, the entire house was spotless, our beds made up like hotel rooms, but she snapped at me and dug her knuckles into my head more often than she spoke. I understood the hardships she'd endured as a child, how her cooking helped her find a husband, but I missed playing with my brother and friends. I wanted to belong somewhere.

My aunt sent me home one evening in time to start dinner and I rushed to get a pot of rice on the stove.

Pablo came in, turned on the television, and sat at the kitchen table. "When are you going to stop seeing the witch?"

"She can be cruel, but she's not a witch. She went through a really hard life when she was our age."

"I don't care why she turned out this way. She doesn't have to treat you the way she does, Andrea. What the hell is wrong with you?"

"I know. It's just . . . I kinda feel sorry for her because sometimes she's nice, but not all the time. When do you think Papá will let me stay home after school?"

"Stop feeling sorry for her. He didn't say you had to go up there forever. Just stop."

"What if he gets mad?"

"He won't even notice. And if he gets mad, he's not going to kill you, you know?" Pablo took his eyes off the television. "We played the bottle game yesterday."

"What bottle game?"

"You spin a bottle, and whoever it lands on, that's who you kiss."

I placed a frying pan on the stove. "Can you give me the chicken? You mean you really kissed someone?"

"Yeah." Pablo looked so proud of himself, and laughed almost in a whisper.

"Who? Where were you?"

"In Papá's garage. All these kids you don't know come down from Valley View Avenue and Laurel Road. It's not kisses like you're in love or something. It's like a peck on the lips. But you can tell when someone likes you."

"And does someone like you?"

Pablo laughed like he couldn't believe what he'd just said. "Yeah."

"What? Who? Tell me."

"They all do."

I was shocked. He looked confident.

He grabbed a container of chicken from the refrigerator and gave it to me. "I was scared the first time, but then it was a cinch. That's why you should come with me. I want to show you all the normal teenager things I'm learning."

"To kiss boys? I don't—"

"Andrea, don't be a sissy. Nobody's going to do anything to you. And don't forget, I'm with you. But you have to learn too. You go through the scary moment and then, all of a sudden, you turn into a big kid, and you realize it's no big deal."

Even though I wanted the same experiences as my brother, I couldn't bring myself to disobey my father. But it was becoming clear to me that while I was locked up with my aunt, Pablo's life was moving forward. There were things about him that I didn't know, and I feared we'd become strangers.

We all walked to the bus stop together every day. Everyone but Hannah, who walked to the bus stop with her mother and stood apart from the rest of us. I wanted to ask how she was, but her mother wasn't welcoming. Hannah never made eye contact with me or anyone. I knew whatever was keeping her away was deeper than I could understand, and also that I had done everything I could to protect her, to free both of us, and that she had too. It hurt that after a struggle to survive together, she'd reject me.

We were in homeroom one morning when two policemen walked into the classroom. Mr. Grant, our sixth-grade teacher, spoke with them in whispers. Then he called Hannah and me to his desk. Hannah approached me with tears in her eyes and stretched out her hand. I grabbed on to her.

The policemen led us into the hallway, and we trembled, holding on to each other all the way to the principal's office. When we got there, the principal told us we hadn't done anything wrong. When they asked questions about the day of the week and time of day when the incident took place, and I couldn't remember a few details, Hannah sobbed, reminding me. "Andrea, don't you remember?"

One of the policemen told us they were there to protect us, not to blame us for anything. But we were already traumatized. Hannah wept and clung to me. The nurse took us to her office and laid her on the bed. "How about you both stay here for a little while?"

I sat in a chair next to Hannah and stroked her hand. Hannah breathed in and exhaled, and all I could hear was the humming of the radiators.

"Are you still my best friend?" she asked.

"Course I am. Are you mine?"

She nodded, her eyes on the ceiling. "I didn't think you'd find me."

"Oh, Hannah, really? I waited and waited, and then I heard you and opened the door."

Hannah sobbed. "He tried but he couldn't, you know. I didn't let him. I didn't." She sat up. "No matter what anyone says, you believe me, don't you?"

"Course I do. You had your clothes on."

The recess bell rang, and the nurse returned. "Would you girls want to go out for some fresh air?"

Hannah smiled, stood up, and grabbed my arm. "Let's find Emily."

Pablo, Emily, Stephanie, and Mark ran over to us as soon as we stepped outside.

Emily held on to Hannah as we told them what happened. Stephanie brushed my hair with her hands. I soon noticed that some kids at school stared at us, and no one spoke to us, aside from kids from the Beehive. Maybe they didn't know what to say. Maybe they didn't know anything at all, but on that day, it became clear to me that the damage Mr. Carter had done had not ended.

Arguments between my relatives became common after my father received a letter in the mail citing us to court. Bautista argued that I could be sent to a foster home. Perfecta argued that I should lie and say that I didn't see Mr. Carter do anything wrong. Socorro argued that I should do no such thing and say nothing but the truth.

When the day of the hearing arrived, I stood at a podium shaking before a judge. Mr. Carter sat in the first row in front of me. He stared at me with sad eyes and shook his head every time I was asked a question.

I was twelve years old, afraid of the judge, confused, misinformed. I was afraid of what Mr. Carter would do if I told the truth. I was afraid policemen would take me away if I admitted to what had happened. I said he didn't hurt me. When he smiled, I realized my mistake.

A few seats away in the courtroom, Hannah's parents looked at me with shock. I had just lied. Which meant Hannah's true story was a lie. I was ashamed of myself as my father grabbed my hand and led me out of the courtroom.

The rest of that semester is full of holes in my memory. Hannah wanted nothing to do with me, and I felt so guilty I never tried to go near her. My father told me he didn't want me outdoors. Not even on Halloween.

"Not even on Halloween?" Pablo asked in English, his shoulders curled upward. "Dad, this is ridiculous. It's over. You went to court."

Pablo couldn't wait for Christmas vacation, but I preferred to be in school, where I could see Emily and Stephanie, rather than to spend weeks with my aunt again. I didn't look forward to seeing anyone from Westfield, because I didn't have anything in common with the kids, for whom I was too Puerto Rican. Emily had already told everyone that she would spend most of the holidays with her grandparents in Connecticut. Hannah didn't want to see me, so the only one left was Stephanie, who was older than me and spent most of her time with friends from Valley View Avenue. I had nothing to look forward to.

thirteen

One of the coldest nights of February 1963 blew through the Beehive as Pablo and I waited for our father way past dinnertime. I had left my aunt's home early to cook dinner, and the food was getting cold.

Pablo came in from the living room. "He say anything about overtime?"

I placed all the lids on the pots. "No."

"Well, I'm starving."

Pablo served himself some rice and fried chicken, but I was too worried to eat and ran to the living room window every now and then, hoping I'd see his car coming down the hill. When a car finally stopped at our front doorstep, it wasn't our father's. Pablo ran to the porch.

Our father was in the back seat, and not the way we expected to see him. Two men wearing the paper mill uniform wrapped his arms around their necks and lifted him out. His head hung to one side, as if he was asleep, and he had on a pair of pajama shorts I'd never seen before. Beneath the shorts, a bandage covered his entire right thigh, down to his knee. In the freezing cold, the two men threw his coat over his shoulders, but he brushed it off.

He looked exhausted. He stopped and took a breath before every move. The men waited for him patiently and held him up straight, one step at a time. "Pops," Pablo mumbled between whimpers. I held my breath.

We both ran to our father and stopped abruptly before we embraced him. It was obvious he didn't want to be touched.

"Hi, *mijos*, is okay, is okay," he said, his breath labored.

"Son, hold the door," one of the men said. "Let's get him inside, don't want him catching a cold."

A frigid winter breeze blew through the darkness as I moved out of the way and watched my father shiver in those pajamas. "Papá, Papito, what happened?" I cried.

Papá groaned. "The boiler, *mija, la jodía boila.*"

"Boiler. Burned his leg, son."

My father panted between moans and spasms. "My poor children, so small. Waiting. All alone. *¡Ay Señor Jesucristo!* help us."

He doubled over with every step as they carried him to bed, his breath so labored I was afraid he'd collapse at any moment. The two men took the bandages off, my father crying out in pain. They gave me a few bottles of pills, an ointment, and left.

Pablo and I stood there helpless, not knowing what to do. I offered him water. He didn't want water. I offered him food. He didn't want food. He couldn't lie still. He asked to sit up. We helped him sit up. He talked to us for a few minutes and then it started all over again. When it was time for his medication, he thanked the Lord and gulped down the pills. A few minutes later, he appeared calmer and then fell asleep.

Pablo and I sat at the kitchen table staring at the window rattling in the wind. He ate the cold plate of food he'd served himself earlier, and I had Corn Flakes. We cleared the table and Socorro, Uncle Felipe, Caridad, Bautista, and Perfecta walked straight into the bedroom to see Papá.

Perfecta came into the kitchen and, of course, had to take the opportunity to give me a list of everything I had to do in the kitchen. "It's time for you to take care of your father now. Cook his meals on time so he recuperates soon."

Caridad shook her head. "She can't take care of him. She's in school."

"Maybe it's time for her to stop going. Doesn't need it anyway," Perfecta said.

"Get her out of my house!" yelled my father from the next room. "Wrong, wrong, wrong. Andrea will *not* stop going to school. Understand?"

The relatives in the bedroom insisted that he calm down. I warmed up a bowl of rice with chicken, and Socorro helped him eat a few bites.

Papá's injury was serious, and it was days before he felt relief. Socorro, Caridad, and even Perfecta came in to check on him whenever they could, with soups and meals. But despite his insistence that my brother and I return to school, we didn't have the heart to leave him knowing he'd be alone for hours, and missed school instead.

The following week, we watched the kids walking home from the bus stop. Everyone waved and went into their houses, but Hannah came over.

She handed me a manila envelope. "Teachers have been asking about you guys. They sent this homework, and there's a letter for your dad."

I took the envelope. "Did you tell them about our father?"

"Yeah, I tell them every time they ask, but they said you guys have to come back to school."

Pablo and I looked at each other.

"How's your dad?" she asked.

Pablo shook his head. "Not good. I'm not going back till he's better."

Hannah nodded. "I can help you with homework if you need anything."

I hugged her, she left, and we went inside.

Papá sat up on the sofa. "Andrea, open that and tell me what it says."

I translated the letter for my father. It was from the school principal and said a social worker would be coming out to investigate why the children were missing school.

Papá looked it over. "¿Qué te parece? Those teachers are already looking for you. I want both of you on that bus on Monday morning. I can take care of myself now. You've done enough. I don't want another problem."

Pablo and I were torn. Our father could hardly walk to the bathroom. The next day we sat on the front steps and stared at the bare trees covered in snow. It was late in the afternoon when we saw a guy walking down the hill wearing an oversize coat and scruffy boots. He pulled on his scarf, as if it bothered him. It wasn't often that we saw a stranger walking into the Beehive, and less likely on a snowy day in February.

And then he placed the suitcase on the ground, and I was transported to the Isla Verde airport in Puerto Rico, muggy heat hitting me in the face, my mother leading us through a crowd. I remembered seeing those same gestures at the airport when Titi Machi pushed her chest forward and grabbed our suitcase. He wasn't a man. He was Titi. My beloved Titi Machi.

Pablo and I recognized her at the same time and bolted, screaming her name. She bent down from her waist, crying and laughing. "*Ay Dios mío*, I found you, I found you."

We pulled her arm, and she ran with us. "Do you have somewhere warm where we can go around here? *Estoy frizá*. Is this where you live? Is this your house?"

Pablo carried her suitcase and we led her into our home.

I ran into the kitchen and found my father in his underwear preparing himself a cup of coffee. "Papá, Titi Machi is here, Titi Machi, remember?"

"What do you mean she's here? Of course, I remember who she is."

"We found her walking outside. She's in the living room."

"What are you saying? Here, in my house?" He went into the bedroom, put a robe on, and came out to the living room, limping but looking excited. "*¡Muchacha!* What on earth are you doing here?"

"Don Luis, how are you, is . . . are you okay? *Dios lo bendiga*. Me here. Bothering. I hope it's not a bad moment."

"*Muchacha*, and how could that be? You're family. I'm so happy to see you, but you're the last person in the world I was expecting. What are you doing over here? Andrea, see what she wants, coffee, juice? What do we have in that refrigerator?"

I prepared her a cup of coffee while they sat at the table. Pablo cut up cheese and served crackers on a plate.

Machi shook her head, tears in her eyes, and she covered her face with both hands. "Look at that. *Ay, perdóneme*, Don Luis, it's just that I'm not used to seeing them this big and serving me."

Papá nodded. "It's been three years. More than three years that we're here all by ourselves, God by our side."

Machi laughed. "I wasn't expecting to find them so grown-up. Remember the bowls of *yautía* I fed you?"

"Oh, Papá, we loved Machi's *yautía*," Pablo said.

She told us Erasmo and Aunt Florencia had passed away within weeks of each other, shortly after we left. She wanted to build a new future for herself and spent the previous summer working in the tobacco fields in Connecticut.

"You came *emigrá*?" Papá asked.

"No. They don't take women as migrant workers. I had to pay my own ticket. I came with a friend who had a contract. He snuck me into the barracks on a farm, and that's a long story, but they hired me. After the summer, I stayed in Holyoke."

Machi told us she worked as a janitor in a community center and asked where Woronoco was, but no one knew, until a guy from Russell came around looking for someone to share a ride with him. He had dropped her off at the Woronoco Bridge and told her to turn right at the stop sign, and she'd find where the Puerto Ricans lived. "That was the coldest walk of my life and I thought, *If I don't find them, I'll freeze to death out here.*"

Papá commended her for seeking a better life, gave her his condolences for the passing of Erasmo and Florencia, and then tapped his fingers on the table as if he was searching for the correct words to use. "And what do you know of the mother of these children?"

"Raquel is in New York."

Pablo and I glanced at each other.

Papá was silent for a while. "Before she left, did that woman tell you if she has any interest in ever seeing her children again?"

"I only saw her once before she left. At Florencia's funeral. Yes, yes, of course she mentioned them and said she loves them."

"I have a sister here telling me I should send Andrea back to Puerto Rico. She's driving me crazy with that. And look. Andrea's mother isn't even there anymore." Papá looked me in the eye and smirked. "That'll shut the old lady up, won't it?"

"You don't want to send Andrea with Raquel. She's my sister, but I would say that to her face. I think she recognizes they're better off with you."

"That's one hundred percent correct, but this has not been easy. A woman who doesn't want children shouldn't get married. You get married, there will be children sooner or later."

"I understand. But you certainly can't count on her now. When she left them with me, I had no idea when she'd return," Machi said. "I guess she loves them and wishes them well, as long as she doesn't have to do what needs to be done."

Papá shook his head. "And who can understand this better than her own sister who cared for my kids? Is she with the same man?"

"She left with someone else, but that's all I know. I don't even have her address."

Our father was quiet for a while, as if he was having a hard time with her story. Then he went on to tell her everything that happened since our return from Puerto Rico. About how Pablo and I were put back a grade in school. About my bad grades. About Mr. Carter. About his injury.

Machi shook her head. "*Caramba, caramba.* If I were close, I would do anything I could to help you. I worked with them every day to help them with their Spanish class and they had good grades, am I right, Andrea?"

Pablo and I hugged Machi.

"Oh, I love these two, they know that right, *pai*?"

"And what plans do you have? Let's talk about you," Papá asked.

"I don't have any definitive plans. I don't like Holyoke. I'm not a big city person. I have money for my plane ticket to Puerto Rico, but I'd like to find work over here somewhere and stay if I could. I can't go back to that farm yet. The memories of my *viejito*, you know. He was everywhere on that farm, and his cigar shack . . . I just can't do it yet. If I could be close to these kids, I'd love that."

"I understand. That would be marvelous. Have you decided on a place?"

"Oh no. I don't know these parts."

"They don't hire women at Estrasmoar, where I work, the factory you passed on the way. But maybe you could find work in Westfield or Springfield. Those are nearby towns where there are people who speak Spanish and you might find something there. In the meantime, you could stay here."

Then he lifted his shoulders. "The only thing I don't know is how my family is going to react."

Machi stared at him. "I don't want to cause you any problems. I came prepared for a hotel."

"That won't be necessary. This is my house, and no one is going to tell me who I can have in my home. But I can't control my sister's mouth. She walks in here and sees a person, you know, how can I explain this without offending you? I don't think she's seen anyone like you her whole life."

"Yes, I perfectly understand, Don Luis. If it's going to be a problem, I'd rather stay at a hotel and return to Puerto Rico."

"No, *mija*, don't misunderstand me. Don't change your plans and my plans now because of a *vieja bruta*. I would love to help you find a job and make a life for yourself here in the United States if that's what you desire. That would be exceptional after everything you've done for these two."

"Don Luis, I see you with that injury, and I'd like to help you. I'll stay here on one condition. I take care of you every day until you're cured and back at work, and then I'll go looking for a job and carry on with my life."

"Oh, that sounds marvelous. *Magnifico*. The ways of God are so strange. The last thing on my mind was that you'd show up now when I'm in such great need!"

We all cheered, hugged, kissed, and brought her little suitcase into our bedroom. Minutes later, my father said he needed to lie down, and I went to make dinner.

"Andrea, how old are you now?"

"Twelve."

"Okay. You're old enough to help in the kitchen, but for the time being, I'll do the cooking. Just show me where everything is. Both of you need to get back to school on Monday. Your father is worried about your grades. Show me where everything is, then go do all that homework."

The next day, Pablo and I had breakfast in our pajamas while Machi did laundry and Papá instructed her how to put up ropes in the living room to hang the clothes to dry. There was scrambled eggs, toast, cheese, peanut butter, jelly, and coffee on the table.

Our father sat at the table with a big smile. *"Maravilloso, maravilloso.* Breakfast for a king."

Machi poured Papá's coffee. "I know you can't drive right now, so tell me where the *mercado* is and I'll get groceries."

"Well, that's going to be a problem. First of all, you're not on my car insurance, so you can't drive my car."

"Oh, I see. Then tell me where it is and I'll walk there. It can't be too far."

"No, *mija*, you don't understand. The closest place to do groceries here is in Westfield, a little town about seven miles away. You can't walk there and back."

Machi laughed. "Oh yes, now I remember Raquel telling me."

"This is a very isolated place. You can't get anything anywhere nearby, not even a Coca-Cola. But if you make a list of groceries, my brother Felipe will do that favor for us, and if you need to go to town for anything, I'm sure we can ask him."

There was a knock on the door, and Perfecta walked in. "How are you feeling?"

"I have a long way to go, but getting better."

"And are you two going to school on Monday?"

We nodded. Machi hung clothes on lines in the living room, and as soon as Perfecta spotted her, she looked at me.

Papá pointed to Machi. "That woman hanging up those clothes is my beloved sister-in-law. Cecilia, come over here."

Perfecta scrunched her lips. *"Mucho gusto.* Perfecta Rodríguez de Morales, at your service."

Machi walked into the kitchen. "Cecilia Vélez Martínez, *un placer.* Andrea, come get dressed and comb your hair."

"Is Andrea coming up after school on Monday?"

Papá looked surprised. "No. My sister-in law will be here to watch over both of them."

Perfecta pointed a finger at me. "You have to watch her, she's disobedient."

Machi raised her eyebrows. "You don't say? Well, she knows that doesn't work around me. Now if you'll excuse us."

Perfecta was stunned.

Machi led me to the bedroom. "Is that the one who wants you sent to Puerto Rico?"

I nodded and we giggled, covering our mouths as she combed my hair into a ponytail. Pablo came in covering his mouth, laughing.

After Perfecta left, my father yelled. "Ha! *La vieja* almost fell over backward."

But Aunt Perfecta wasn't the only one who had a problem with Machi. A few days later, Pablo and I returned with Machi from a walk to the post office when we heard Socorro yelling in our kitchen. Machi told us to sit on the steps and not intrude.

Socorro yelled at my father. "Do you think any woman in the world is going to come near you when she knows there's a *pata* that looks like a man living with you? *¿Tío, tú estás loco?*"

"Anyone listening to you might think I'm marrying her. *Por Dios,* she's looking for a job, where's your Christianity?"

"Tío, Aunt Perfecta and I are thinking of you. Aunt Perfecta is going through the roof. And what kind of an example is this woman for Andrea? Have you thought about that?"

"And who are you and Perfecta to talk about examples? You want to bring out everyone's little rags now? Perfecta's daughter was pregnant when she got married, and you're living under the same roof with a man you haven't married. I'm an invalid. And in the few days that she's been here, she's already helped more than anyone else has. That's an example right there. So, she's a little dark and maybe a little strange with her men's clothes, but those are not things to be ashamed of."

"Tío, you never ask for anything. I know I've only brought you a few meals, and I'm sorry I haven't done more, but I work, I'm not here during the day—"

"I'm not asking you or anyone to solve my problems."

"And please, let's not argue about Taylor anymore, please, we've been through this so many times. We have plans to get married, Tío, but it will be when we're ready, not before. I don't care what people say about me."

"Well, maybe it's time you apply that to others. Whether you like it or not, this woman is an aunt to my children, and my desire to help her comes from my heart, from the appreciation I have for her, because I can tell you that woman loves them more than their own mother."

"She just showed up here, Tío, don't exaggerate. She's here because she needs something from you, not because of the kids. What is she doing here? Why did she come?"

"She came for the same reason all Puerto Ricans come to this country. Same reason you came. To get a job. She wasn't planning on staying in my house, but when she saw my condition, she offered to help. And I'll tell you what you can do. Help her get a meeting with someone at Labrek."

"Aha, so it's not the love of the children that brought her here. She's looking for work. Tío, you want me to recommend someone I don't know, and someone like her?"

"She doesn't have tuberculosis, *mija*. I'm tired now. I'm going to lie down if you don't mind."

"Okay, Tío, I'm sorry. I'm not going to argue with you. All I want is for you to be well. I'll see what I can do." Socorro held the door open on her way out. "I'm not judging her, but . . . oh, *perdón*. I didn't know you were on the porch."

It was the first time I can remember feeling embarrassed for someone else's actions, when Socorro bumped into Machi and realized she'd heard all her comments. For all the love I had for Socorro, it was hard to watch Machi nod respectfully, not lift her eyes off the ground, and say a polite *"Buenas tardes."*

Pablo and I went to school and came home to find Machi and Socorro in the living room one afternoon. We looked at each other and smiled. Socorro was telling Machi how much she liked Springfield.

"It's a big city, but not like New York. It has every kind of store you'd want and big streets. That's where Taylor and I would like to live, but it's too far from Strathmore, so we'll probably move to Westfield instead."

"Whatever works out best is okay with me, as long as it's close enough that I can come see them once in a while," Machi said.

Two weeks later, Socorro and Taylor took Machi for an interview at Labrek, and when she landed the job, we had a celebration. Papá brought his *ron pitorro* out of the closet, Socorro made *pastelillos de carne*, and Taylor put a few beers in our refrigerator. They sat around the kitchen filling Machi in on the job and made plans to take her to Springfield to look for a room in a boarding house.

From then on, even though my family didn't like everything about Machi, they accepted her. Occasionally someone made fun of her behind her back. Often, they expected Pablo and me to participate in their mockery. We never did.

For the two months that Machi lived with us, we came home to warm meals, and she wouldn't allow me to do any chores until she questioned me about every class subject and made sure I had done my homework. I soon improved my grades, and we celebrated by going to Westfield for ice-cream cones. As a result of her discipline, after she left, Papá required me to do homework before we made dinner, and sometimes, when I had quizzes and tests, I didn't help in the kitchen. Papá took us to visit her every few weeks. And when she bought a car, she visited often, always loaded with gifts, and she always cooked and left a few meals in the refrigerator.

Pablo had grown used to playing outdoors without me in the neighborhood. When summer vacation started, he ran out the door after breakfast and never asked me to come along. He was eleven years old and wanted to be with "the boys" at the Woronoco Bridge, where kids swam in Salmon Falls. Pablo, Mark, and Kevin sat around listening to the older kids who came from Blandford Road and the Woronoco neighborhoods.

Hannah didn't come around, and I wondered if she was away from home somewhere. Emily went with her grandparents for the summer, and Stephanie was on vacation with her parents in Florida. Sometimes I followed my brother to the bridge and watched kids diving into the deep hole, but for the most part, I was on my own.

When Papá told me one morning that Socorro was ill, I went knocking on her door. Her tan skin had an ash color, and she looked tired and weak. I picked up her house, made the bed, and made chicken soup for her. But she couldn't keep any food down. She sat in a rocking chair and smiled, holding my hand, and assured me she'd be fine.

That night I told my father that I was concerned about Socorro.

"There's nothing to worry about. The woman is pregnant. That's all. I'm surprised it didn't happen sooner. Too bad for the poor kid, though."

"Why? What will happen to the baby?"

"That baby is going to be a bastard. A kid born out of wedlock. A kid everyone will point a finger at. People don't think of how their actions affect others. But she's been very good to us, so go over there and help her as much as you can."

Socorro visited a doctor, and it turned out Papá was right. I was ecstatic. I kept her company and helped her often. Sometimes Caridad was there with Vivian, who was now a toddler. Sometimes Perfecta visited and always complained that I wasn't going to her house for supervision.

I sat on the front porch one afternoon, watching the trains and wishing I had somewhere to go, when Nayda came over, her two long braids hanging over her shoulders. On her side were her children, Juanita, who had her same almond eyes, and María, who was smaller and had short, curly brown hair.

"How has your father been doing after the accident?" Nayda asked.

"Fine."

"Did your aunt leave?"

"She got a job at Labrek and moved to Springfield."

"So, are you alone most of the time now?"

I nodded.

"I was wondering if you might be interested in something. I'm a little worried about Juanita because she's going to kindergarten, and she doesn't know any English. I thought maybe you could teach her a few words to get her started."

"Sure I can." I looked down at Juanita. "I can teach you. And you can go to school with me on the same bus every day."

Juanita hid behind her mother's skirt while María did a cartwheel.

"See what I mean?" Nayda said. "She's too shy. What's going to happen if she has to go to the bathroom?" Nayda pulled Juanita by the shoulder and lifted her face. "You have to learn, *mijita*, otherwise you'll sit there until you pee your pants and everyone will make fun of you."

"Juanita, it's easy. I'll teach you."

"There are six more kids starting in September, let me see, Matilde has two, one for kinder, one for first grade; Elisa has one; Delia has one; and Sonia has the twins."

"The twins are starting school? Oh my God, that went fast. I remember when they moved here last summer, they were babies."

"And none of these kids know English."

"Okay, so why don't we have them all come over to the garage a few times, and I can teach them in there?" I picked up some stones from the ground. "I've written on the walls in there with these stones, it works kind of like chalk. And I can ask Papá to bring paper from the mill."

"Every kid will bring their own chair. I'll tell everyone else in case they're interested." Nayda laughed. "How old are you now?"

"I'll be thirteen next month."

"You're not even a señorita, right? Haven't even had your *quince* and already going to run your own little school."

For two days, I went to the garage after lunch and didn't see anyone there. I made lists of things I could teach the kids and made a calendar, using one my father had up on a wall as an example. I would use it to teach the days of the week and months. I circled Saturdays, Sundays, and holidays in red. I drew a Santa on Christmas Day, a pumpkin on Halloween, and a heart on Valentine's Day of the following year.

On the third day after I had seen Nayda, she knocked on my door.

"Can we start today?"

I looked over at my father's garage and saw a group of women and kids with chairs in their hands. There were Nayda's daughters, Juanita and Maria; Elisa with her daughter, Rebecca; Delia with Berti; Sylvia with Hector; and Matilde with her sons, Samuel and Heriberto. The women had brought their younger kids too.

"I'm leaving María with you too. She might as well start learning since she's going next year," Nayda said.

The other women looked excited and happy. We set up the chairs in the garage, and Nayda handed me a box of chalk.

I stood in front of the kids. "Good afternoon."

Little María giggled, her hazel eyes showing mischief. Juanita pushed her arm and scolded her sister. Samuel covered his mouth and chubby cheeks with both hands, and Heriberto laughed with hands covering his eyes.

"So you're going to school in September, and you can't speak English, right? Well, let's start speaking English."

The kids laughed with their hands over their faces. The mothers looked worried.

Nayda stood next to me, pushing her long black curls back. "Nobody gets ice cream from the truck today if Andrea tells us you misbehaved," she said in Spanish. All the mothers nodded. Then they closed the door to the garage and left. I suppose they thought the kids would take the lessons more seriously if they weren't around.

Rays of light came through the cracks in the seams of the zinc walls, and dust from the dirt floor floated in the air. I opened the door a crack to let more light in. The mothers were walking away in different directions.

I taught the children "I" and "you," and after a few rounds of practice, someone started laughing. I waited, but the laughter didn't stop. So I told them in Spanish to laugh harder, and they did. Then, I told them again and they did, but by this time, some of them were almost coughing more than laughing.

"Don't stop. Laugh harder," I said, and they laughed harder. "Harder," I repeated. Nobody seemed to like laughing by then, but I insisted that they continue laughing harder and harder.

"I want to stop," Juanita said.

"You don't like laughing anymore?" I said in Spanish.

The whole group said, "Nooooo."

"Okay, then let's stop laughing and speak English now. I'm Andrea. You are . . ." and I named each one. They all looked at me like, *Boy, is she weird,* but everyone focused.

From then on, working with them was easy. If anyone got out of line, I'd say, "Want to play the laughing game?" or "You don't want ice cream today?" And that solved the problem immediately. Birds chirped around us, dogs barked, and sometimes we heard Pablo, Mark, or Kevin talking out on the street, but we kept working.

The classes were always short, less than an hour long, but everyone showed up every day.

My father brought me stacks of writing paper, cardboard, and gray, blue, and yellow paper from the paper mill. At night, I'd write letters from the alphabet on sheets of paper and give them to each child to practice. It was always the ice-cream vendor's bell that ended the day, and all the mothers would be in the cul-de-sac waiting for us to join them.

When I gave my father details of the classes, he looked astonished. "I thought that was only going to last a few days, like a game."

"It's been over three weeks now, Papá, and they still come. Sometimes they tell me things they heard on television that they learned from me."

"Well, you're doing these women a big favor. And where's Pablo when you're in there?"

"Playing marbles and baseball."

Soon the mothers stuck around, standing at the door, and always had a sentence they wanted to learn.

"When I took Hector to the doctor, I didn't know how to tell the doctor that he had a cough, so I said, 'My baby koohoo koohoo koohoo all night,'" Sylvia said. "I felt stupid, but I had to let him know what was wrong with my son."

"It's *cough*, that's the word in English."

Every day, I worked with the children first, then the mothers. Sometimes, I drilled the kids until they were exhausted. But those kids and their mothers learned enough English that summer to dive into the language.

When the ice-cream vendor's bells rang, the kids ran out of the garage, and someone always bought one for me. I'd split it with Pablo, who showed up religiously just in time.

Stephanie, Pablo, Kevin, and the mothers of the little kids in my class showed up to celebrate my thirteenth birthday. Stephanie looked like a teenager, because she was, but it surprised me how much she had changed in only a few weeks. She was tan from her trip to Florida, wearing soft pink lipstick and white sneakers with Bermudas. She told me she was going to hang out with some kids from school at someone's house in Russell after my celebration. Steph was going to Gateway Regional High School to start ninth grade in the fall.

Nayda brought a homemade cake, and Esther brought ice cream. When I gave my father a piece of cake that evening, he said, "*Manífica, manífica,* what good neighbors we have."

I was lonely after all the kids left every day, sitting on the front stoop watching the trains until it was time to make dinner. But my English classes paid off. Toward the end of August, Nayda gave me twenty dollars from all the mothers. Just before classes started in the fall, when Machi visited, I told her I had some money and wanted new clothes. That same day, we drove to Newberry's in Westfield, and I chose an outfit. It was a polo shirt with navy blue Bermudas.

"But those are summer clothes," Machi said. "Pick something you can wear to school. You can't wear shorts to school."

That's when she helped me and Pablo buy our first set of dungarees.

When classes started in September, I took seven little Puerto Rican kids to the bus stop every day. As we passed the small hill, the dump, the paper mill, and the big hill, I kept them in a line singing, "The Ants Go Marching."

I was in homeroom getting ready for the bus line when Miss James, the kindergarten teacher, came in and called me into the hallway.

"I'm having a little problem with Rebecca and was wondering if you could come in and speak with her."

"Sure," I said.

"Grab your things for the bus line, and I'll meet you in my classroom."

When I arrived in the classroom, Rebecca was sobbing. I ran to her and asked what had happened. As I placed my arms around her, I noticed she was soaked.

"I didn't have time, I didn't have time," she cried in Spanish.

Miss James looked heartbroken. "Why is she crying?"

"She wet her pants."

"Oh, I see. Well, let's change her clothes. Her spare clothes are in this locker to the left."

Then I heard a little voice coming from the back row. It was Juanita speaking to me in Spanish. "It was Jack," she said, pointing to a tall boy sitting to her left. "He wouldn't let her in."

"What do you mean he wouldn't let her?" I asked.

"He stood at the door like this." And she put her arms up on each side.

We found out that Jack had stood at the bathroom door, frightening Rebecca, and not allowing her to pass. Before Miss James could say anything, I ran over to the boy.

"So you like to bully girls smaller than you, eh? Well let me tell you something, and I'm only going to say this once. You go near her again and I will whip your ass. Have I made that clear?"

Miss James was on my tail. "I'll take care of this, Andrea, thank you."

I stared at Jack. "I meant what I said."

Miss James sat Jack in a chair next to her desk while I helped Rebecca change into a clean set of clothes, and we were off to the bus line.

There were times at school when I was called into the cafeteria because no Puerto Rican kid would eat their lunch. It was usually macaroni and cheese, and Juanita could barely stop herself from throwing up.

"What's wrong with it, what are they going to eat?" Miss James asked.

I shrugged. "It's the hot milk and the cheese."

There were times when they were sick, like when Samuel had a fever and the nurse called his father at Strathmore. I was taken out of math class to speak with Mr. Rivera because the nurse couldn't communicate with him. From then on, no one at the school spoke with a Puerto Rican parent without calling me first.

When Delia's son Alberto, whom we all called Berti, fell off the Tarzan swing one afternoon after school, he screamed so loud that we all came out of our houses, running onto the street.

I turned off the stove before running like a maniac.

Delia had Berti in her arms like the Virgin Mary with Jesus. *"Se rompió, se rompió,"* she cried. He couldn't straighten his arm, and his screams pierced our ears.

Emily ran to her mother, and Mrs. Belanger jumped in the car and drove us to the hospital in Westfield.

As soon as she saw the doctor, Delia said, "Is broken."

The doctor smiled. "Let's see what we can do."

I was the one explaining what happened to the doctor and then telling Delia what the doctor said.

One afternoon, a girl from Hill Street knocked on my door. I knew she was a Girl Scout. "Can you help me sell cookies to the Puerto Ricans?" she asked. We went from one house to another until we'd knocked on all thirteen doors. I translated for nurses, census workers, and salesmen for Avon, Fuller Brushes, and vacuum cleaners.

When these events interrupted my cooking schedule, Papá was not happy. Sometimes I told Pablo to watch a pot of rice or a stew on the stove, but a few times, Papá came home and dinner wasn't ready.

"You can't take the clothes off one saint to dress another saint, *mija.*

You're helping others, and your own things aren't getting done. What about your schoolwork?"

"But I like helping people, Papá."

"I don't like you all over the neighborhood selling vacuum cleaners. There's a difference between selling things and helping a neighbor in need. From now on, you help the neighbors, not any *Juan del pueblo* who comes around selling *la madre de los tomates*."

When classes started again after the holiday break, I stayed at home as much as possible so my father wouldn't be upset with me. I liked having excuses to get out of the house and felt like an important, useful person when I was helping someone understand our community. But it was cold, I had a lot of homework, and Pablo never went anywhere after school. When Socorro almost had a miscarriage and the doctor ordered that she avoid walking, I knew she needed help. Her feet were swollen. She was in bed when I stopped in one day right after school, still in her pajamas.

Every day I checked in with her on my way home. And after I cooked our dinner, I prepared a plate for her and dropped it off.

"*Sopas*, that's the only thing I can eat," she said.

I made her soup after soup after soup. Sometimes, when she was feeling up to it, she cooked for all of us, and I did my homework at her house until Taylor came home and I knew she was safe.

It was March when I came home and found her door locked. I knew she had to be in the hospital.

My father walked in that evening and a cold wind blew through the house when he opened the door. "I just saw Taylor," he said. "It's a boy."

The first time I saw baby Ismael, I wanted him to be mine. I came home from school every day dying to see him. And the fun part was that Socorro loved having me over because it gave her time to shower and dress up before Taylor came home.

"You always have to look pretty for your husband. Don't ever get into the habit of looking like an everyday rag."

⌒⌒⌒

Ismael was a big chubby baby, grabbing things, mumbling, "Mamama." When I wasn't playing with him after my classes were done, I was with Vivian, who was a two-year-old holy terror.

In the summer, Caridad and Felipe announced they were moving to Springfield, and I helped her pack boxes.

"The only thing I'm going to miss about Woronoco is spending time with you. I hate leaving you here."

"I'm going to miss you and Vivi. Oh, I'm going to miss her so bad. But at least I'll still have Socorro."

Caridad made a tsk-tsking sound. "I'm sorry to tell you this, but I don't think Socorro will be here much longer."

"Oh, really?"

"Woronoco is not a place to stay forever. It's too isolated, *mija*. When I was here all by myself that time when Felipe left me in winter, all I saw was a red bird that came to my window everyday—"

"A red cardinal?"

"Well, I don't know what you call him, but he perched on the same tree every single day. So beautiful with the snow all around him. But there wasn't anything more for me here but that little bird. You were in school all day, and when all the kids were gone, this was like a cemetery."

"I wish I could live somewhere else too."

"I don't see your father going anywhere, though, so use your time to study, *mija*. Keep going until you finish high school."

"But that's so far away. I'm only starting eighth grade in the fall."

"I know. But don't lose sight of what you'll have after. You can go to college and marry a man with a good career and have your own life. Nobody can take that away from you. But stay away from the *vieja*."

Right after she said those words, we heard Perfecta calling, "Caridaaaa," in a strange voice that almost sounded like she was choking. And then there was a loud thump and glass breaking.

We both ran out of the apartment. The door to Aunt Perfecta's apartment was closed. *Was someone in there?* We scrambled out onto the back porch and through her back door.

She was stretched out on the floor with both hands on her chest, her breathing labored.

"Oh God, she can't breathe," Caridad screamed. "Tía, Tía, can you hear me?"

I opened the living room window and saw Pablo with Kevin sitting on the front stoop at Mark's house.

"Pablo, it's an emergency! It's Titi Perfecta! Run to Emily's house and call Dad, call an ambulance, call a doctor, do something, hurry up."

Pablo looked annoyed. "What? Call who?"

Kevin yelled, "It's an emergency, she said, let's go make the phone call," and they ran to Emily's house.

I ran to my aunt's side and picked up her hand. Her face looked gray, her hands were cold, she was covered in sweat, and with each breath, a groaning sound. I heard Pablo and Socorro yelling to each other outside, someone's footsteps pounding up the staircase.

Socorro walked in with Ismaelito in her arms. *"¡Santo Dios!* How long has she been there?"

Caridad didn't take her eyes off Perfecta. *"¡Ay Dios mío!* Only a few minutes. What can we do?"

Then Perfecta's eyes turned up, her face turned ashen, and the creases in her skin grew deep. I brushed her straight light-brown hair out of her face and cried for the good that I knew was somewhere in her, for the end of all her wrongdoings to me.

My art teacher, Mr. Johnson, was different from the art teachers in the rest
of the elementary grades. On the first day of class, he told us we'd have a
project that had never been done at our school and asked us to bring magazines to class.

At the same time, we were studying Homer's *Iliad* in reading class. Mr.
Johnson set boxes on a windowsill labeled with the names of colors, and
for weeks, we sat at our desks cutting out the colors we found in magazine
pages. Then we drew scenes from *The Iliad* onto a massive wall mural that
hung in a corridor at the school entrance and "colored" them by pasting the
magazine papers onto the mural.

I was pasting yellow pieces of magazine paper onto Hector's shield when
the principal came by.

"Andrea, you are so talented," she said. "When you're not singing, you're
translating, and now look at that artwork." Then she complimented the
teacher and the rest of the class.

When we arrived in the morning, parents stopped to praise how the
mural was coming along, and I remembered when I'd drawn the turkey
in third grade. Five years had passed since then. I was fourteen now, and
things had changed for me. I was no longer worried about integrating with
my community, and I no longer had my aunt's accusations to worry about.

Ever since I could remember, Pablo and I had had a conversation before
our lights were out at night. On the first day we read *The Iliad* in reading
class, I couldn't wait to come home to tell Pablo about the book. This was
no *Charlotte's Web* kind of story.

I'd go to school the following day looking forward to reading class to
find out what happened next and seek answers to the questions my brother
had. And when I told him the story of Achilles weeping at the ocean, and
how his mother, Thetis, the daughter of the sea, heard him and rose in a
cloud from the depths of the ocean to comfort her son, I wept.

"Why are you crying? It's just a story," Pablo asked.

"Because she came from so far away to help her son."

"Yeah, I still don't get why you're cryin'."

"I wish we had a mother like her."

Pablo was quiet for a few moments. "Well, we don't. But we have Papá, and Machi, and each other, though, don't we?"

"Yes, we do."

"And that's going to be forever, right?"

"Of course."

fourteen

"Beehive kids" our age outgrew the cul-de-sac. Emily went with her grandmother for the summer. Stephanie got her driver's license and was never in the Beehive. She had friends from Gateway Regional school, places to go. Kevin and Mark went to a summer day camp.

Every afternoon, Pablo waited for the bus that dropped them off at the stop sign. On their walk home, they told him they took swimming lessons, went for hikes, learned survival skills. But once they reached the Beehive, they said they were tired and hungry and went home. Pablo waited, hoping they'd come out to play, but they didn't. They had dinner and watched television and did it all over again the next day.

The street was empty. Older kids who'd played baseball in the cul-de-sac took summer jobs. Emily's brother and sister worked in stores in Westfield. Kevin's brother got married. Stephanie's brother, Charles, went somewhere up north to pick blueberries; Hannah's sister, Claire, went to Westfield, and her brother, Brian, to work on a tobacco farm. To top it off, Hannah spent the summer in Westfield with Claire.

Every now and then on the weekend, Machi showed up and asked Papá's permission to take us out. "I know you're sitting around with nothing to do, so let's go have fun," she'd say. Pablo and I would run to get dressed. When she was short on time, we went to Grandmother's Garden in Westfield and ran around with her like little kids. Sometimes she brought things like a kite or Hula-Hoop. Then she'd take us out for an ice-cream cone, and we'd go home to cook dinner.

The best times were when she took us to Mountain Park in Holyoke and bought us all-day ride stamps. The moment Pablo got stamped, he ran to the Wildcat ride. Machi drove against us in bumper cars, rode with us through the Pirate Dark House, and rode the Flying Jets like she was another kid. By

the time we did one round of our favorite rides we were starving, and she
bought us corn dogs and candy apples. Occasionally she'd spend the night
with us and leave early the next day.

On weekdays, Pablo and I watched television, and all you could hear in
the cul-de-sac was the sound of the little kids playing hopscotch. The little
Puerto Ricans played with the American kids just fine. They didn't need me
to teach them English in the garage anymore.

One day, my brother and I went to Valley View Avenue on the bikes
we'd outgrown. We didn't find anyone up there. There were little kids doing
arts and crafts in the clubhouse. We rode to the bridge and stopped. There
wasn't anyone swimming in Salmon Falls either. Everyone our age had van-
ished.

A few days later, we went to the riverbanks past Papá's old garden, which
no one tended to anymore. We climbed down to the river and sat on the water's edge. Wild white and yellow buttercup flowers beamed in the sun next
to dark green waters, quiet and still. Halfway into the river, turtles bathed
under a ray of light on a log. Butterflies went from one flower to another as
Pablo threw rocks into the water. Turtles swam away.

"I have two years to get my permit. But you can get yours after your
birthday in July."

"Hadn't even thought of that."

"You don't think Pops will let you use his car?"

"You know how he is with that car."

"Americans lend their kids the car, you know?"

I shrugged. "Yeah. He's different."

"Thinks we can live like when he was growing up in Puerto Rico. I'm
tired of not going anywhere. Aren't you? Even if you get your permit, it's not
going to make a difference. That's why sometimes I understand Mom, you
know? She wasn't the only one who left. Everyone leaves this place."

We climbed back up to the road and walked home. There were still a lot
of Puerto Ricans in the neighborhood, but they weren't our relatives. Soon
after Perfecta died, Bautista retired and left. I heard Angela and Ramón

moved to Puerto Rico. I didn't know the neighbors who moved in upstairs. The men worked at Strathmore. The women lived behind closed doors, cooking on the same stoves where my relatives had cooked for years. Pablo was right. Everyone in our family except Socorro had left.

I spent the rest of the summer with Socorro and Ismael, who was now more than a year old. One day she asked if I'd watch him while she went to Westfield with Taylor, whom she still hadn't married. There wasn't anyone to care about what Socorro did anymore, except for my father, and he'd given up on her being a "respectable" Puerto Rican woman. Socorro's relationship with my father taught me that men like him, who want to control the lives of women in the family, eventually stop if you put up a fight for long enough.

Several times a week, I'd walk with her to the mailbox, Ismael in a stroller. The sky was overcast one morning when we sat next to the rose bushes on the Strathmore lawn where she read her mail, as my mother and so many other Puerto Rican women had done in the past. Ismael played in the grass.

"Taylor and I are moving at the end of the month."

"Moving? Where?"

"We were only staying here until Taylor could save for a house in Westfield. And we found one we can afford. It's close enough for him to drive back here for work."

I didn't know what to say. Socorro was the last relative I had left, but more than that, she was like my big sister. I couldn't imagine what life would look like without her.

"I didn't know how to tell you. But at least I'm not going back to Puerto Rico. We can still see each other often. Hell, you can ride your bike over there if you want to."

"I don't have a bike anymore."

"I knew you were going to be sad, Andrea. But Woronoco isn't meant to be a place where people stay. People come and work for a while, make some money, and go to one of the towns nearby and buy a house. There's nothing here but these houses owned by the factory. Houses you will never own."

I nodded, but there wasn't anything she said that could take away my sadness.

"I want to be in a place where I don't have to wait for Taylor to come home to buy me a bottle of milk for Ismael, where I can go to a corner store or a pharmacy without someone else having to take me. Here in Woronoco, we have to rely on the men for everything. Even if you need a pair of underwear, you have to tell him and wait for him to take you. This is too far from anything."

"I know. That's why my mother left."

"That's why Caridad left too. I worry about you, *chica*. Other girls have mothers thinking ahead for them, but you don't. Your father is only thirty-four years old. I know that sounds old to you, but he's not going to be alone the rest of his life. He can still start a new family. Even Pablo will have a wife and a family one day."

I laughed.

"You think it's funny now, but life goes fast, *mija*. And when their lives take the course each one chooses, what will you have?"

I shrugged.

"The most important thing I want you to remember is to stay in school. Go as far as you can. And the other important thing is don't accept the first boy you like, *mija*, you hear me? Is there any *muchacho* you like now?"

I flushed. Of course there was. It was always Frankie Ross. But I'd never spoken to anyone about my feelings for him, because what good would that do? No one could make him like me.

Socorro smiled with mischief in her eyes. "You're not telling me. When you like a *muchacho* you have to give yourself time. Sometimes, after a while, you realize you don't like him that much and you get yourself another one."

I listened and nodded, but I couldn't imagine myself choosing between boys.

"There's going to be older kids with you in that new school."

"Gateway?"

"Yes. When you get there in the fall, it's going to be a whole new world. There are high school kids there. And you're a beautiful teenager. But don't let these American boys get the best of you, Andrea, know what I mean? You're still going to come home to Woronoco every day. All alone here, listening to those trains come and go. But you have to get through school. Understand? You can have a boyfriend when you find *un muchacho bueno*. One that doesn't interfere with your studies."

I smiled, nodded, listened, and wondered why she was so concerned.

"I don't think Tío Luis is going anywhere. But the time will come when you'll graduate from high school. And what are you going to do then?"

"I don't know."

"You need to think about that and have a plan. Haven't you always said you want to be a teacher?"

"Yes, I do. I want to be a teacher."

"Then say, 'I'm going to college.' Keep that in your mind and do whatever is necessary to get there. You'll be a great teacher. You already are. You're a smart girl. I want you to have a life different from all the women in the family who never got their diploma. Like me. I don't want that to happen to you."

I nodded and we smiled at each other. "Okay," I whispered.

"When you get lonely, just think it's one more day you cross off your calendar to reach that goal of being a teacher. Don't forget what I'm saying."

It sounded silly to hear Socorro talking about me as if one day I'd be an adult. I knew people went away to college after high school, but that seemed far into the future. I was going to ninth grade at a new school in fall. I didn't have a clear notion of what growing up meant, of moving anywhere without my father. Yet her words stayed with me.

When the neighbors heard that I babysat Ismael, they asked me to take

care of their kids. I earned a small income that summer, enough to go shopping at Newberry's with Socorro, where I bought my first bra. At first, I didn't
want to wear it because I thought it brought attention to my tiny breasts.

"It's more noticeable if you don't wear one," Socorro said. "You're growing and hunching over to cover up your chest. Stand up straight. Next time
we come, you get another one."

When Pablo saw me wearing the bra, he stared at me. "Where'd you get
that? You look like you have tits now."

"Newberry's."

"Yeah. Look like a real teenager going to Gateway now."

I was excited about going to the Gateway school in September. I prac-
ticed combing my hair into a French twist, and teasing it into a pouf, half
up, half down. With money from babysitting, I put together a small ward-
robe and could not wait to wear the clothes. I had two sweaters, Machi
bought me an empire dress, and Socorro gave me a pair of sling-back flats
and a bottle of pink nail polish.

I did my hair and nails one day to get my brother's opinion. Pablo said
I looked super cool, but the moment Papá walked through the door, he inspected me from different angles.

"You're fixed up good with that *moño* hairdo, but I haven't given you
permission to paint your nails. You're not a *señorita* yet. Take that off right
now."

"I'm a teenager, and I'll be fifteen in two weeks."

"I don't want you painting your nails until you're fifteen. Not one day
before that. Understand? I don't care what *las gringas* do. Puerto Rican girls
are *señoritas* at fifteen, not fourteen, and that's the way I want my daughter
to behave. When I get back, I want to see those nails completely clean."

"But it doesn't come off without remover."

"You put it on, now you figure out how to take it off."

My father left for the grocery store with Pablo and left me at home to
clean off my nails. It was early on a Saturday morning, and I knocked on
Socorro's door.

Taylor answered with Ismael in his arms. "She's getting dressed, come on in."

As I walked into the living room, I noticed the apartment was lined with boxes.

Taylor stood at the entry to the living room. Socorro walked in looking like a movie star, and we looked at each other without saying a word. I stared at the boxes and couldn't stop my eyes from watering.

"It's a really good house, and you're going to love it when you come over . . ." Her shaky voice trailed off.

Taylor opened his eyes wide and spoke with excitement. "Hey, it's really close to town and has an extra bedroom. You can come stay with us whenever you want. I'll pick you up when I get off work and take you with me. Anytime you want. Just have to ask your Dad."

I nodded, but I felt broken. There would be no one to turn to in Woronoco now. Socorro sat next to me, and Ismael came running over to us on the sofa.

"It's going to be better," Taylor said. "We have a backyard, no trains. We're going there now and doing some shopping. Come with us."

"I can't." I showed Socorro my nails. "Papá got mad and told me to take this off before he gets home."

Socorro shook her head. "Did he really? *Ay,* Tío." She went into the bedroom and came back with acetone and cotton balls.

A week later, there was a small pickup truck with Socorro's mattresses and furniture tied to the back in front of their apartment. Papá and Pablo hugged her, and then she hugged me with teary eyes. I kissed Ismael, and they got in the car. Taylor's brother got in the truck, and they disappeared up the little hill out of the Beehive.

Papá looked at me and my brother with resignation. "*Caramba. Se fue todo el mundo.* Everyone came and everyone left but me."

Pablo looked at me and pulled his lips to one side.

Papá headed toward our apartment. "Well, let's clean up this place. There's another day coming tomorrow."

fifteen

Once I started ninth grade in Gateway, I didn't see much of my brother. My bus arrived earlier than his, so I woke him up before leaving, then rushed out the door. There were new kids on the bus, and Hannah seemed to know everyone. Emily and I sat together, but when we arrived at school, we discovered we were in different groups.

For the first few weeks, I felt lonely and out of place. I missed my brother and the comfort of Russell Elementary. None of my former classmates were in my group. But when we were taken on a tour of the library, I knew I had found my second home. As soon as I was granted a library pass, I told the librarian that I liked *The Iliad* and wanted to learn about the ancient Greeks. Her lips curled. "Oh my, I don't get a request like that very often." She returned with a big reference book of ancient Greece and a copy of Euripides's *The Trojan Women*.

For weeks, she helped me along, and soon, I understood how plays were written. A movie played out in my mind. I imagined the chorus, the tragedy of Hecuba and the Trojan women having to serve the men who killed their husbands. The horror of Hector's child, Astyanax, being thrown off a cliff.

I was hooked on learning about ancient civilizations and asked for more passes to the library than any other kid in class. But there were two other girls who went to the library often. One of them was Barbara Kelley, a chubby girl with acne, thick black eyeglasses, and a big smile.

"I don't read those kinds of books," she said, eyeing my reference book.

"What books do you read?"

"*The Golden Name Day*," Jennifer said with a smirk. Jennifer was the tallest girl I'd ever seen, with thick eyebrows and short bushy hair.

Barbara hit her on the shoulder with a magazine. "Stop making fun of me. She says that because I've read it four times."

"If it's that good, maybe I should read it too. What's it about?" I asked.

Jennifer giggled. "Yellow roses on the wallpaper in a girl's bedroom."

I made a funny face. "Okay. I'll check it out. What do you read, Jennifer?"

"Honestly, I don't like reading. I just follow her around," Jennifer said. We all laughed.

"I can't get rid of her," Barbara said. "No, seriously. You're going to find that people are a little stuck-up in this school, and as you can see, we're not your typical cheerleaders, so we stick together."

When they asked where I was from, they were surprised to hear that English was my second language and wanted to hear more about Puerto Rico. From then on, we always met at the library and were often scolded by the school librarian for giggling.

We were looking at magazines one day when Emily walked in, speaking out loud with two other girls. They'd been with us in elementary school and were part of a cliquish group that came to school with new clothes and things no one else could afford. Their fathers didn't work at Strathmore.

The librarian placed her finger on her mouth, telling them to hush. Emily sat next to me, and the other girls joined us at the table.

"He gave Cathy a ring over the weekend," Emily whispered.

The girls huddled around Cathy, looking at a ring she wore on a chain.

I rubbed the corner pages of a book. "A going steady ring?"

"Yes. You know him from Woronoco. Frankie. Frankie Ross."

Frankie had a girlfriend? I tried to hide how surprised I was to hear this. "I thought it had to be a high school ring?"

"Oh, it doesn't matter, as long as it's a ring."

Cathy looked at me across the table and smiled. This wasn't her fault. Even though my heart was broken, I gave her a big smile.

On the way home, I was quiet.

Emily placed her hand on my arm. "I'm sorry," she whispered.

I looked at her with startled eyes. "For what?"

"I know you like him."

"When did you make friends with those girls?"

"At my grandmother's. In Russell."

After school, Pablo was surprised to see the books I'd brought home from the library and eager to share his experiences of the day. There was a new art teacher at Russell Elementary, and she didn't do the mural project based on *The Iliad* that I had so enjoyed in eighth grade. Since Pablo already knew the story, he was bored in reading class.

What he wanted to talk about was something else. He was in love with Theresa Gerou.

"She wore a plaid skirt with a white shirt and a navy blue sweater today. I like her clothes the best. I wish you had clothes like hers. Her parents must have more money than Pops. And when she saw me—Andrea, are you listening? Did you fall asleep?"

"No. I'm listening."

"Well, when she saw me, her eyes got really bright. I can tell she likes me."

Every day, almost to the exclusion of everything else, he spoke of Theresa. "She walked past me at least three times. She got up to get napkins or something. She didn't have to go that way, she went that way just to look at me. I know she'll wear my ring one day, Andrea. She's going to be my girl."

"A going steady ring?"

Pablo laughed. "Yeah, and a wedding ring after that."

"Remember Cathy Miller? Frankie gave her a ring."

"Really. I don't understand that because I know he loves you. You have to get out of that library, sis. You're going to a teenager's school but acting like a lawyer or an English teacher. You still don't have friends."

"Yes, I do."

"Who? Emily? Hannah? You already knew them. You have to start acting like a teenager and make other friends or you'll never have a boyfriend."

"I have two new girlfriends. You just don't know them because they're from Blandford."

A few weeks later, Papá brought home a Christmas tree, as he always did, and I decorated it with the bubbling lights he'd bought years earlier when we arrived from Puerto Rico. We spent Christmas Eve with Felipe,

Caridad, Socorro, and Taylor. Machi visited us on Christmas Day. But there were no festivities in the neighborhood, as we'd had for so many years when all the relatives were together, going from one house to another singing and playing Puerto Rican holiday songs in *parrandas*.

That winter, Pablo and I never went outdoors after school. We were too old for toboggans and sleds, and it was too cold to walk anywhere. We cooked dinner together, Papá came home, we ate, then we cleaned the kitchen. My father and brother watched *The Virginian*, *Gunsmoke*, and *Bonanza*, while I did homework. The only television show I never missed was *The Ed Sullivan Show*, where I'd seen the Beatles and the Rolling Stones for the first time a couple of years before.

After Papá gave me a transistor radio for Christmas, I lived to hear my favorite songs by the Righteous Brothers, the Supremes, the Four Seasons, and the Beatles. It didn't matter if I was doing dishes at the sink or homework at the kitchen table, or if a blizzard was blowing the world away outdoors—music filled my world.

The following fall, Pablo was an instant hit at Gateway. The kids in honor roll and the athletes included him in their groups, and girls swooned around him. Hannah introduced him to her friends, a group of kids I'd never paid attention to. They were four guys, all in higher grades, who were from Huntington and Chester. Stephanie knew them. Attractive and defiant, they snuck out of school through the gym's back doors and smoked cigarettes. Hannah followed them like a roadie.

When Pablo first told me about their escapades, he sounded surprised that anyone would dare sneak out of school. And then Hannah was suspended for two weeks for smoking on school premises. A few days later, I saw her on her porch and sat next to her.

"Stupid teacher came in the back way. I was just having a smoke, for Christ's sake. Not botherin' anyone. I don't even want to go back."

"What did your parents say?"

"They're pissed. I'm not even supposed to be out on the porch."

"It'll go by fast. I can bring you homework."

"Don't even bother. I don't give a shit."

"But, Hannah—"

"Hey. Forget it. If you really want to help, you can bring me a few cigarettes from those boxes your dad has on the wall. He won't notice. I can't even cop a cigarette from anyone now."

I didn't want to steal cigarettes from my father, but they were old, he'd bought them before he quit smoking. The box they were in looked like a birdhouse. Every kid in the neighborhood had seen the quirky wall hanging. The cigarettes had probably gone stale.

I shrugged. "I'll see what I can do."

I ran into the house, took a pack of cigarettes out of the box, and gave it to her.

"Now you're talking, girl. Thanks."

A few days later, I was at recess with Barbara and Jennifer. They were startled when Hannah's friends approached me. The guys asked about her, and I told them I'd seen her briefly.

One of them smirked. "Too bad she got caught, but something's wrong with that girl."

Another guy laughed. "Yeah. We both told her to come inside, and she takes another drag. I mean, duh, I'm telling you to hurry up and you act like nothin's happenin'."

"She almost got all of us in trouble."

"I'd be in a shitload of trouble with my parents if I got suspended."

I shrugged. "Maybe she doesn't care what her parents think."

The guys looked surprised.

A guy with a black jacket and a Mick Jagger face came over to me. "So, you're Pablo's sister. I'm Kirk."

"Yeah, from Puel-toe Weeko," the other guy said, and laughed.

"Hey, Pablo is a cool kid," Kirk said.

"What's your name? I'm Jeffrey, but everyone calls me Moose."

I introduced myself.

Kirk nodded. "Don't pay attention to the Moose over here. So how long have you guys been in the US?"

Jeff nodded over and over again. "Andray-ah. Andray-ah. I like the way you pronounced that. So, do you listen to Spanish music all the time? What kind of music do you like?"

I looked away from him. "No. I never listen to Spanish music. I like the Beatles. The Beach Boys. We've been here most of our lives."

Jeff smiled to one side. "Oh, I get it now, I get it. So, yeah. That's what most girls like. Have you heard The Animals?"

Kirk nodded. "The Rolling Stones? Those bands are changing the history of music."

"Yeah, their lyrics are revolutionary," Jeff said. "You should listen to them sometime and you'll see the difference. So where do you hang out?"

Kirk looked annoyed. "She's from the Beehive. That's where she hangs out. Don't you get it?"

Barbara stepped in. "Okay, Moose. See you later, guys."

She turned around and walked in the opposite direction, and I followed.

"Why'd we do that?" I asked Barbara. "I don't like them, but we didn't have to be rude."

Barbara put her arm around my shoulder. "Those guys are troublemakers. They're not interested in being friends with any of us. They just want to show off how much they know about music and all that stuff. Who cares? Plus, we like what we like, whether they think it's better or not, right?"

Jennifer looked disgusted. "Yeah, revolution. What the hell was that all about? They were high. Didn't you notice? You didn't like him, did you?"

"No. No, of course not. What do you mean, high?"

The bell rang and we hurried to get out of the cold.

Barbara came around to me, clouds coming out of her mouth as she spoke. "On drugs. Didn't they look half drunk? Talking about the history of music. Dopes."

No, they hadn't looked drunk. I thought they were intimidating but actually quite interesting. I hadn't noticed anything wrong with them.

Later that day, Emily sat next to me on the bus, as she did every day. We didn't see each other often because our groups had recess at different times, and once we got home, neither of us went out again.

"Tell Pablo he shouldn't hang out with those guys."

I laughed. "Moose?"

"Yeah. You finally met them? They got suspended today."

I was shocked. "But I saw them at recess. They were asking about Hannah."

"I don't know what you think, but . . . my mother doesn't want me around her anymore."

"Yeah. She's really changed."

"My mother says Claire is a bad influence on her."

"I feel sorry for her. She was always so sweet."

"She's pretty nasty now, though, if you ask me."

We reached the bus stop and walked as fast as we could to get out of the cold. The last train of the day came by and washed out the sounds of our goodbyes.

"I heard my friends got suspended from school today," Pablo said, his voice loud. "It's like you can't be a cool person at that school."

"Hannah got caught smoking, and I heard those guys are using drugs."

"Nah. That's not true."

"Well, they got suspended, so they must be doing something wrong. Why are you friends with them?"

"They like me. They're nice. Ever since the first day of school, they've been good to me."

"But they're troublemakers."

"No, they're not. They have good grades and they're always talking about going to college. They just do things all teenagers do. Moose drives his father's car sometimes, and they go to The Corner Store in Russell and hang out outside. You don't need money for the soda fountain, just hang out outside. Get to see the girls and meet people. And for summer, they said they'd give me a lift to go to the lake."

"What lake?"

"Woronoco Lake. The Pond? I don't know what the name is."

I didn't say anything and focused on cutting potatoes for french fries. My brother wanted to do things that I suspected our father wouldn't like.

"Who do Mark and Kevin hang out with?"

"They're square. I don't want to be like them. Plus, their parents take them places. We don't have that."

Pablo was right. Papá was trying to find someone to marry and excluded us from most of his activities. He acted more like a single guy than a parent.

"Moose and Kirk aren't the only guys with cars. Why don't you try to make friends with other kids? And try to do more things with Mark and Kevin?"

"Yeah. Okay. I know you're worried, but there's nothing to worry about, sis."

That winter, Emily's grandmother grew ill, and they moved to Russell. She had grown into a tall, breathtaking redhead. Happy, outgoing, a cheerleader, in the drama club, the most popular girl in class, she even had a boyfriend that her mother didn't know about. "I'll tell her if we ever get serious, but why get her all worked up now?" she said.

Her siblings Richard and Jessie had gone to college, and even though she was in my group, and I saw her every day in school, I missed seeing her in the Beehive. "It doesn't matter where we live, I'll always be your friend," she said, the day they moved. I really missed her when summer came around. Everyone was gone.

I had taken up baking, which I learned in Home Economics class, but didn't always have the ingredients I needed, and sometimes Papá wouldn't buy them.

Pablo wasn't interested in hiking through the forest, the way we had as children. Mark, Kevin, and Hannah were the only kids our age left in the Beehive. Hannah spent most of the time with her sister in Westfield, and

Mark and Kevin worked at a day camp and took all kinds of classes. Mark played flute and Kevin played violin. They were both in karate and their mothers took turns taking them to their activities.

I still babysat for the Puerto Rican families and made enough money to buy myself a few pieces of clothing now and then.

But Pablo had no means of making money. People in Woronoco didn't own homes. There were no lawns to mow or basements to clean. In winter, everyone shoveled their own path to the garage, and that was the extent of shoveling snow.

I once told my father that if he gave Pablo some money for clothes, I'd give my brother ten dollars to add to his budget. My father was so embarrassed that he gave Pablo all the money and wouldn't take any from me. But Pablo always chose more clothes than he could afford, and I ended up giving him money, or if we were lucky enough to go shopping with Titi Machi, she always made up for the difference and more.

That summer I bought myself a pair of plaid Bermudas, and Machi gave me a pair of white sneakers. I looked forward to seeing kids from school in my fashionable new clothes.

"You look like a *gringa* now with those clothes and that blonde hair," Machi said. "We need to take you to Puerto Rico and get you a little color in the sun."

sixteen

Pablo was getting invited to parties in Russell and asked Papá if we could go.

"It's a school party, Papá. A girl from the avenue is taking us, and Mark's mother is bringing us home."

"I don't like you two going so far, and to a lake while I'm—"

"Dad, Andrea just turned seventeen," Pablo said in English. "There isn't anything to do here. We can't spend the rest of our lives in the Beehive. You have to let us go."

Papá responded in his broken English. "Well, is okay if you go, but I no wan' your sister wearin' no bading suit."

"No one's wearing bathing suits, Pa," Pablo said. "We're just going to get together, the parents bring things to eat, and we'll come home with everyone else."

Papá didn't argue, and I couldn't contain my excitement as I washed dishes that evening.

Emily, Barbara, Jennifer, and other friends from school showed up at the pond that day, and we were catching up with each other when Frankie and his older brother, Daniel, walked in from the parking lot and lingered with a crowd of boys that were standing around a car with the trunk open. The girls went swimming, and I watched them from the sandy banks of the pond.

One kid had a radio on and sang to The Doors' "Light My Fire" when I noticed Frankie walking in my direction with a big smile on his face. I didn't want him to notice me staring at him and looked away. There wasn't anyone sitting next to me. Why was he coming this way?

Then I heard his voice. "Well, you sure look all alone over here. Mind if I sit next to you?"

I faced him, my hand shading my eyes from the sun. "Of course not. Everyone else went for a swim."

"Aren't you going in?"

I wasn't about to tell him that my father forbade me from wearing a bathing suit. "Nah, I didn't bring a swimsuit."

"I don't think I've ever seen you anywhere but at school."

I smiled, too nervous to speak.

"Or at the library," he said with a grin. "So, where do you hang out when you're not at school?"

My nose and eyes crinkled. "I don't go out much."

"My uncle works at the second Woronoco Mill. He knows all the Puerto Ricans there."

"That's where my father works."

He got really close to me, and my whole body stiffened. Then he placed his hand on my forearm as if he was accustomed to touching me.

"He says they're really, no offense . . . old-fashioned. Traditional, I mean. Is your family like that?"

"Yes, my father is."

"Is your mother like that too?"

"I don't think so, but she doesn't live with us."

"Oh. I didn't know that. Jesus, we've known each other our whole lives and barely talked before."

I nodded.

Frankie leaned toward me. "So, what was special about today? I mean, why is this the first time I've seen you here?"

"Pablo convinced him that this was a school meeting."

Frankie grinned. "In the middle of summer?"

I laughed. "It's not entirely off the wall. He used to be in honor roll, and they had summer activities."

"So, I guess you need to come up with more white lies so we can all see you more often. I see you in the library at school. What do you do in there?"

I couldn't stop myself from smiling. Frankie looked at me as if he knew why I was nervous.

I shrugged and my voice turned to a whisper. "Read."

He laughed. "Yeah. I gathered that much."

"Magazines or books. Sometimes I ask Mrs. Briar a question, she shows me articles and shelves on the subject. Don't you go to the library?"

Frankie made a face. "Not unless I have to. Are you talking about school stuff or things you like to read?"

"Mostly school stuff from history class, you know, like the project we had on the war, the race riots. That kind of stuff."

"Yeah. I did a project on Muhammad Ali last year. I like him but I don't like reading."

"What do you do for fun?"

"Well, you know I'm on the basketball team."

I only vaguely remembered.

"I'm coaching kids in my neighborhood this summer, I've been in the rifle club since grade school, I've worked at the summer Y Camp for two years now, and I go to the Y a lot."

Some of the guys hanging out around the car with the trunk open called him and he waved. He squeezed my arm. "Hey, I'm getting myself a beer, would you like one?"

I had never had alcohol before, except for a shot of Manischewitz wine my father occasionally gave me because he believed it would strengthen my blood. "No thanks."

Frankie went over to the car and returned with a can of Coke. "Elliot's brother-in-law got these for us," he said, sitting next to me. "He's twenty-one. We all chip in and he helps us out when we want to party. Sure you don't want one?"

"No thanks, I'm fine."

Frankie smiled, a sneaky look creeping into his eyes. "Everyone brings empty soda cans to pour their beers in." He held up the Coca-Cola can. "Looks legit, right?" He took a sip.

We looked around at everyone else. The girls were laughing in the water with a few guys I'd never met. It was an awkward moment—I didn't know what to say, mainly because I was too excited to think straight.

He sighed. "Yeah, Elliot's going to college in the fall."

"Oh, cool. Where's he going?"

"Holyoke Community College. He's going to commute. He really didn't want to go, but decided to so he doesn't get drafted."

"Yeah. That's a good idea. My cousins in Puerto Rico got drafted, and a couple guys I know from Springfield."

"I hope it's over by the time we graduate."

"Me too."

"Elliot's going to work part time at Strathmore to pay his way through. He hadn't planned on college, you know?"

Most of our friends were still swimming. Pablo had a Coke in his hand and was talking with Theresa and another girl. Behind Frankie, Emily had come out of the water and looked at me with a huge funny grin. She held both hands up in the air with fingers crossed.

"You really should come see me play next season."

"I . . . I'd love to."

"You have a couple months to figure out how to tell your father. Maybe Pablo can help you come up with something."

As he said that, my brother headed our way and flicked his hand at me. I knew what that meant. *Let's go.* Mark's mother was in the parking lot.

"Hey, Pablo, you and Andrea have to come see me play next season," Frankie said.

"Yeah, that would be cool," Pablo said.

Frankie's eyes met mine. "I'll see you guys at school in a few weeks."

Emily followed us to the car, whispering so loud everyone in the whole town of Russell could've heard her. "So, what just happened?"

I couldn't say a word.

"Holy shit, Andrea. Damn, I wish you guys had a phone. I'll ask my

mom for the car again this week and come over so you can tell me everything."

"I thought he had a girlfriend?"

"I don't think he's gone steady with anyone since he broke up with Cathy
years ago."

I hugged her and joined my brother in Mrs. Abbot's car.

As I greeted Mrs. Abbot and climbed into the back seat, I couldn't get
my mind off Frankie. Why had he even approached me? Did this mean he
liked me, or was he just being friendly? I couldn't wait to spend time with
Emily, because my mind was reeling, and I knew she'd help me understand
what had happened.

Papa had fixed dinner and was watching television when we walked in.
Pablo and I sat next to him, eating out of plates he'd left for us on the stove.
Since the John F. Kennedy assassination in 1963, Papá had started watching the evening news, always hoping to find an explanation for the assassination.

The news was covering the race riots that were occurring all over the
United States.

"Look at that. Forty-three people killed in Detroit. Cheap people rioting
in Boston, Philadelphia, everywhere. Now they're saying over a thousand
buildings were ruined. They have to put all those *morenos* in prison," he
said.

"They're not cheap, Papá. They just want to be treated like everyone
else," I said.

"Well, they're not going to get very far after they burn down half the
city. Johnson had to mobilize *el ejército* to control those *bandoleros*. And
look what they're saying now. Forty-three people died. Those *morenos* are
troublemakers."

Pablo cringed. "Yeah, because they're not treated right, Pops."

Papá smirked. "Kennedy would've solved the problem by now. You probably don't remember this, but he stood up to Fidel Castro and the Russians.
This Johnson guy doesn't know what he's doing."

"But those are two different situations, Papá," Pablo said.

"Well, the situation may be different, but the Russians turned those ships loaded with weapons around and went home with their tail between their legs. This Johnson can't stand up to those *morenos* in his own country."

I wanted to argue with my father but chose to be silent. Mrs. Briar, the librarian, had told me that if I was well informed, it would be easier for me to speak in favor of racial equality, but she had never met my father. He'd made up his mind that Blacks were the villains a long time before I was born. The tense racial scenes of our times only gave him more munition. I wanted to change his mind. But how? I wanted to ask Mrs. Briar how to respond to him with convincing arguments, but I wouldn't see her for another month.

That night, Pablo waited for me in our bedroom. "No use arguing with him. Get him mad about one thing, and then we can't go anywhere. You didn't tell him I had a beer, did you?"

I looked for my hairbrush in the dresser drawers. "Why would I do that? But don't you feel like we have to educate him now and then?"

"He's such a racist. Nothing you say will change him. I gave up. Don't waste your time."

I held the brush in my hands and stared at my brother. I didn't want to believe my father wouldn't change his mind, even when proven wrong, but maybe my brother was right. And if he was, what was the point of studying about the war, about racism or anything, for that matter? What was the point if you couldn't convince people to change?

Pablo looked serious. "Why are you looking so worried? What does it matter what he thinks about anything? Only thing that matters right now is that you were with Frankie and I was with Theresa today. How did that feel?"

I sat on my bed and smiled, almost embarrassed.

"I'm happy for you, sis. Now you can see why I keep telling you we need to get out of here and see the kids from school. Frankie invited us to a game. He wants to see you again."

I brushed my hair.

"I wish we could go, but we only went out today because Mark's mother gave us a ride. That doesn't happen all the time."

"We can always find a lift, sis. I'll take care of that even if I have to steal someone's car. Now, tell me about Frankie."

I put the brush down. "Pablo. Don't even joke like that."

"Andrea, thousands of people our age are going to California. They just pick up and go in vans, buses, they hitchhike, take motorcycles. They go on whatever they can find to get them there. And here we are waiting for our ole man, a *jíbaro* from the mountains in Utuado, to give us permission to do anything. You can't even wear a bathing suit! We can't stay here forever."

"You're not thinking of doing that, are you?"

"Course not, but you have to change, sis. Papá will come around eventually, but we're going to have to push him into it or we'll get stuck here. Tell me what happened today. Frankie's in love, Andrea. I can see it all over him."

"I think you're exaggerating. He just talked to me, that's all."

"There were at least twenty people there. Lots of people sitting on the banks, but he walked all the way over there to sit next to you. That says something."

"He asked where I hang out. I was so embarrassed because I didn't have anything to say."

"So, what did you tell him?"

"I said I don't go out much. What else could I've said?"

"Don't worry about it. It's the truth. Did he ask you on a date?"

"No. Dad wouldn't let me go anyway. I don't know what I'm going to do when a guy does ask."

"Just say yes, and we'll figure out a way to get you there."

"Really? But I don't know if I can lie to Pops. I'll be too nervous thinking he's going to show up and do something in front of . . . Oh my God, he'd probably show up and slap my face."

"Well, we lied to him today, didn't we?"

I nodded. "I guess so."

seventeen

Emily visited me several times in August. We'd walk all over Woronoco talking about Frankie and John, the guy she was dating. Sometimes Hannah joined us, but I noticed Emily was quiet around her, not offering any personal information. I felt bad because I knew Hannah felt the distance between them, and she'd soon be on her way home or walking in the direction of the post office.

"Where do you think she's going?" I asked Emily.

"I think she bums a ride to Westfield to see Claire."

Emily and I talked about Frankie until we'd dissected every sentence he uttered at the Russell Pond. We made plans to go to Russell. Emily would take me and Pablo. I was confident my father would allow us to go with her, but she suddenly disappeared. I later learned that when her mother found out she was secretly dating someone, she restricted Emily's use of the car for the rest of the summer.

August was sweltering, the heat sucking the life out of the Woronoco forests and every living creature under their canopies. The trees looked thirsty, their wilted leaves moving painfully in the breeze. Insects buzzed hard, and I looked forward to the ice-cream vendor, the main event of every summer day. Pablo watched television as the cul-de-sac quietly gave in to the rumbles of a distant train and I sat on our front porch.

Hannah walked over and flicked her hand in the direction of the back of the house. A train screeched at the docks as we sat next to each other on my back porch, where her mother couldn't see her smoking.

She lit a cigarette and took a deep puff. "Elliot is having a party tomorrow. Want to go to Russell?"

The thought of running into Frankie brought on nervous excitement.

But I knew Mark was on vacation in Maine, Kevin was visiting his grandparents, and Emily had disappeared, so we couldn't count on any of them
to give us a ride.

"How would we get there?"

"Isn't anyone around that can give us a ride. We could hitch, though."

"You mean hitchhike to Russell?"

Another train came by with its rattle tattle while she nodded and drew
on her cigarette. She stared at me, waiting for a response. But I was astonished.

Before the train was gone, she lifted her shoulder and hands like, *So,
what's it going to be?*

"I . . . uh, I don't know about hitchhiking, Hannah. It's kinda scary, don't
you think?"

She pulled out a switchblade and I stood up, freaking out.

She opened it. "Not scary if you have this."

"Okay, that scares me."

"Well, it shouldn't. We're not little girls anymore. Andrea, sometimes I
don't understand you. Don't you get sick of being here?" She got up, threw
the cigarette on the ground, and stomped it out. "All right, then, if you don't
want to come."

When I told Papá about Elliot being admitted to college and having a
party, he shook his head.

"Nope. I no like it," he said in English.

"But, Papá, all the other kids are going. You're treating us like
elementary-school kids. I'm seventeen. We need to see people our age."

I picked up one of the books I'd brought home from the library for summer reading and held it up.

"Other kids at school are reading this too. We talk about these things.
When we get tested at school, we all do better if we see each other and talk
about this stuff."

Papá looked at me with compassion, and for a moment I thought, *Wow,
I'm getting through to him.* But then came the letdown.

"Better you stay here in the house, where nothing bad can happen. Machi will be around soon to take you to Riverside Park."

Pablo came into the kitchen.

"Pops, we're not interested in Riverside Park. That's for little kids. Let us go to The Corner Store. Our friends go there, talk for a while, and then everyone goes home," he said.

"That Corner Store in Russell?"

"Yeah. You know where it is."

I interrupted. "If you give us a ride over there, we can get someone to bring us home."

Papá raised his shoulders and looked at Pablo as if he was out of touch with reality. "You want to go there with your sister?" he asked in Spanish. "But your sister is a *señorita*, are you crazy? She can't be standing in front of a package store with you."

Pablo raised his hands, arms, and voice. "It's not a package store. There's a soda fountain inside—"

"I don't know what *pájaro loco* might be there. No. That's not a good idea."

My brother slammed the door and sat on the porch the rest of the evening. I did the dishes and didn't bother reminding him of his chores. It kept me busy and stopped me from crying even though I was torn up inside. I was furious. We weren't asking for anything unreasonable.

I wanted to run out of the house and never return. Sleep under the bridge listening to the falls, or under an oak tree where the crickets would cleanse my soul with their constant buzz. I wanted to be anywhere but in that house.

Pablo took a dive into the worst mood I'd ever seen him go through. When I spoke to him, he didn't respond in complete sentences. It was a wave, or a flick of the hand to brush me off.

Then Hannah came over with Donnie.

When we met Donnie, he said he was spending a few weeks with his aunt on Valley View Avenue. He was a tall, skinny kid with straight blond hair. He said he was going to be, like me, a junior in high school, but I got the impression he was older than I was and had been put back a few grades.

Pablo invited him in, and that was the only time he was ever invited into our home. From then on, he invited himself. Pablo had the television on, and the kid sat on the sofa, then got up and changed the channels. Acted as if he'd known us from the day we were born. He'd say things like how much he dug my brother because he was such a "cool cat," and all I wanted was for the guy to shut up and go home.

After he left, I asked Pablo what he thought of him.

"He was really cool."

"I didn't like him at all. He's an imbecile."

The kid had no boundaries. After that day, he stayed at our house for breakfast and lunch, and if it hadn't been for our father coming home for dinner, he probably would've stayed for that too.

"Pablo, we have to tell him we can't keep giving him our food. Pops is going to get mad, you know? He's going to notice."

"I know, but if he's here playing cards with me or watching television, and I get hungry, what am I supposed to do, not offer food?"

"He's not supposed to be here all the time. You know Pops doesn't want anyone in the house when he's not here."

"I know, but I feel bad for him. I don't think his aunt treats him nice, and I feel bad telling him to leave."

"Tell him you have things to do and he can take off."

But even when Pablo told Donnie that he'd meet him outside, he stepped into the house, put his feet up on the table, and asked what I was cooking and if he could have a taste. Then he walked up to Papá's cigarette wall hanging.

"What is this thing? Are these Winston cigarettes in here?"

"Hey, leave those right there, my dad's going to get really mad if you take them," Pablo said.

"Hannah told me to bring her one or two. She said your old man doesn't smoke anymore. Why you want these on the wall getting stale? Come on, he won't even notice." Then he stuck two cigarettes behind one ear and two behind the other. "Okay, I'll see you guys tomorrow."

Pablo closed the door and came to the kitchen. "See what happened?"

"Yeah. You told him to cool it with our stuff and he took off."

"But I didn't want him to leave, Andrea."

"Nobody threw him out. We're going to get in trouble if he keeps taking things and hanging out here all day."

The next day, kids I'd never seen before showed up on our porch. Donnie asked Pablo to bring out a box of cigarettes, and he did. They sat in our living room for hours, smoking. I didn't want to start dinner and have all of them coming into the kitchen asking what I was cooking, so I stayed in my bedroom while Pablo went from watching television to card games to just hanging out doing nothing with them.

When Papá arrived and dinner had not been started, I had no excuse.

"What did you two do all day? Why didn't you start dinner?" he asked.

I looked at my brother but couldn't tell my father that Pablo was letting Donnie in the house. My father noticed an ashtray full of cigarettes.

"Who smoked all these cigarettes?" He walked over to his birdhouse cigarette holder. "Who smoked them? Pablo, are you smoking?"

"No, Papá. It's just a friend who lives on Valley View Avenue. He came over and he smokes and he took one." Papá counted the cigarette cartons. "¿Un solo muchacho? This thing was full of cigarette boxes."

I knew his suspicion index was set to high.

"Both of you are lying to me. I don't want anyone in here when I'm not home, and you know that. I'm not paying for anyone's vices either. If that kid wants to smoke cigarettes, he can pay for them himself."

"We're not lying, Papá," Pablo said.

"One person doesn't smoke all those cigarettes. That's enough. Get in here and help your sister make dinner."

But the next day, Pablo let Donnie in again.

"Don't worry, I won't be here when your old man comes," he'd say. And more than once, he jumped out of a bedroom window when Papá came home earlier than expected.

I couldn't bring myself to tell my father what was going on. I didn't want him to think I was a part of this, but I didn't want to get my brother in trouble. Donnie was taking advantage of us both. I didn't like the control he had over my brother, but whenever I touched on the topic with Pablo, it ended in an argument.

"We can't go anywhere, so at least someone visits us, Andrea. What do you want me to do, sit here watching *Captain Kangaroo* while you read books? We've been locked up our whole lives. Lay off, man."

The house was full of kids one day when Papá barged in, early in the afternoon, way before his usual time. I was afraid the whole neighborhood heard him when he yelled *sons of bitches* in his broken English. "*Saramambiches*, get, get, get outta here!" He used his jacket like a broom to sweep them out.

Some kids ran out the door, others laughed and yelled at my father. Donnie yelled, "Fuck off, you old spic," and gave my father the finger.

I'd never even heard the word *spic*, had no idea what it meant. Papá had a hand on his hip and bobbed his head up and down with a look of disgust on his face, speaking in Spanish. "And who the hell does that *pendejo* think he is, insulting me like that? Where did he come from?"

Pablo kept his eyes on the ground and responded in English. "He's my friend, Pops. He didn't mean that in a bad way."

"Well, you tell that *maricón* if he comes back to my house, I'm calling the police. Understand? I don't want him here no more. I don't want nobody here no more. And I don't like you with that kid. I don't wanna see you with him."

Donnie didn't return to the house for the rest of the summer. But Pablo wasn't there either.

eighteen

A few weeks after the incident at our house, Papá told us to get dressed and accompany him to church and Casa Hispana in Westfield. We hadn't accompanied him in years. Pablo refused to go.

Papá came out of the bathroom in a white sleeveless undershirt with suds on his face and a razor in his hands. "You complain that I don't take you anywhere, and then when I do, you don't want to go. I don't understand you. Get dressed and come with us."

"What's wrong with me staying here? I don't want to go. I don't play dominoes."

"When I was your age, I was working on a farm helping my family. Nobody was trying to understand what I wanted. Look at everything you have in life, but all you do is complain." Papá went back into the bathroom.

Pablo stood at the bathroom door while my father shaved. "I'm not asking you for anything that's a big deal, Pops. All I want is to go to Russell during the day. That's all I've ever asked. All the other kids go there to hang out. They even get money from their parents to go there, but I'm not asking for that. All I'm asking is you drop us off and pick us up on your way home. I'll take care of Andrea. But no, you go where you want to go. You don't care about us."

"Listen to that. I didn't care when I found you starving in Gurabo and brought you home, did I? Drop you off in front of that store in Russell, that's what you want. So you can stand on the street like a bum? I've told you, there's nothing but trouble on the street. If you're not coming with us, then you can stay here."

I got dressed and went along with my father without argument. That day, I found out why he visited Casa Hispana so often without us, and why he didn't have time to take us anywhere. Papá was courting a woman in

Westfield. Her name was Carmen. She'd come from Puerto Rico for her niece's wedding and would be returning after the event.

Everyone there was my father's age. The girls who'd been Hijas de María when I was a child were, like myself, high school students, and didn't go there anymore. I sat around bored, except for the days when I helped in the kitchen, where the women praised me for being a good cook.

Myrna, who was my age, walked in one day and went directly to her father, who was playing dominoes. Her eyes met mine and she smiled. She put her hand out, and he dug into his pocket and dropped a set of keys in her palm. She gave him a kiss, and he said, "Careful, princess." Minutes later, she was rolling out of the parking lot in his car.

I later learned that she had dropped out of school that year to work at J. J. Newberry. She wore a thick layer of foundation, dark eyeliner, and fishnet stockings under miniskirts. Everything about her would've been prohibited in my house, but her father was my father's friend. Sometimes she came to Casa Hispana with her older sister, María, who the women in the kitchen told me was engaged to a guy from Springfield. After a while, I figured out that these girls were Carmen's nieces.

If anyone spoke Spanish to them, they responded in English. The most important realization I had that summer was that the biggest difference between those girls and me was our parents. My father was not only from another country, he was from another century, another world.

One Sunday evening, we were pulling out of the Casa Hispana parking lot, and I waved to the girls. On the way home, I confronted my father.

"Myrna and María drive their father's car and go out by themselves. Myrna is my age. María is one year older than me, and she's engaged. Why are you so different from their father?"

He wrinkled his forehead and shook his head. "That girl that's getting married hasn't even finished high school. That's not what I want for you. You get married, and if that man treats you bad, you can't even support yourself. No. I want you to go to college so that one day, you can support yourself if you have to. Or have you changed your mind?"

"No, Papá, I haven't changed my mind. I want to go to college, but I still have two years to go in high school. Pablo has three more before he can go. We can't spend all that time locked up in the house. Nobody else does, not even other Puerto Ricans."

"But I don't understand why you have this problem now. You never had this problem before. Now all of a sudden, our home isn't enough for you and your brother. Nothing I do is enough."

"Maybe it hasn't crossed your mind that we've grown up. We used to play in the Beehive. We used to ride our bikes and sleds and do all the things kids do, but we're not kids anymore. And all the kids we know, they're doing things you don't allow us to do. You should let us go out once in a while like everyone else does, *gringos* and Puerto Ricans."

"You've been to that lake, and you've been out with Machi. That's enough for now."

"But why can't you let me get my permit and use your car once in a while? Even other Puerto Ricans do that. Look at those girls. We're not doing anything wrong, Papá. You go out. Everyone wants to go out now and then."

Papá shook his head and raised his voice. "No. I don't let anyone, not even my own family, drive my car. If you smash this car, what do I have left? Who's going to fix it? The only thing I have, and I've worked years to pay for it, is this car. If you and Pablo want a car, finish school, get a job, then go buy your own car. You're not driving mine."

"Where are we going to get jobs, Dad? How are we going to get anywhere where we can get a job if you don't take us?"

Papá didn't answer, and I could see in his eyes that he didn't want to be bothered with such concerns.

What our father didn't know was that Pablo didn't stay at the house when we went to Casa Hispana, which meant he was with Donnie every day of the week except for Saturdays. I never said a word about my brother's whereabouts to our father, because what harm would it do for him to hang out at Donnie's house for a few hours? He was seeking what all people our age sought. And what would my father have done to change my brother's behavior? Nothing. Papá was focused on finding a woman to marry. He'd been wanting this for years. And now he was pursuing Carmen. She seemed to like him, from what I could tell.

For the rest of that summer, I listened to my transistor radio and waited for one of my favorite songs to come on so I could imagine singing, "Dedicated to the One I Love" by the Mamas and the Papas to Frankie, or him singing "Never My Love" by The Association to me, or Van Morrison's "Brown-Eyed Girl." Oh, how I wished I could be that brown-eyed girl.

⸺

When classes started, Pablo stopped coming home after school. Donnie had enrolled at Gateway and we were both juniors. Luckily, he wasn't in my group. Pablo and Donnie got off the bus together and walked toward the avenue. Minutes before my father walked in, Pablo showed up to empty the rubbish bin.

Once I walked into the house, it was the same every day. The same stinking dishes, the stinking food I'd been cooking since I was ten years old, and the stinking linoleum floor that I'd scrubbed until it lost its sheen.

But I was worried about my brother. I didn't like his friends. He no longer told me where he was going or what he'd done when we spoke before bed at night if we spoke at all. When I asked where he'd been or what he'd done, he'd tell me he'd been at Donnie's on the front porch or at the club.

I knew things had gone too far when my brother didn't come home for dinner one evening. I set the table as Papá fried pork chops and grilled me with questions.

"Did he come home with you?"

"Yes, of course."

"So, he came home and left? ¿Dónde está tu hermano?"

"Out there in the cul-de-sac, probably. He sits out on Mark's back porch with him and Kevin, sometimes."

"In this cold?"

"Papá it's not even winter yet. It's not so cold. He'll be in any minute."

"Let me tell you something, *mija*. Either he's taking you for a *pendeja* or you're not telling me the truth. You know those basketball games at the club he said he was watching in the summer? I went in that club and found an old lady at a desk downstairs in the basement floor. She told me they weren't having no basketball games in there anymore. That club is closing down. Your brother is lying to us both."

We had just finished eating when we saw a red light flashing on the walls and ran to the window. My father was white as a sheet, and my whole body felt like it was flashing brighter than the lights on the police car parked in front of our house. We ran into the cold darkness with no jackets on. I could breathe again when I saw Pablo sitting in the back seat of the car.

"*Pero ¿qué pasó?*" Papá asked Pablo.

My brother had handcuffs on and hung his head low. The cop waited for him to step out and walked over to my father. When the police told him they'd found Pablo hitchhiking on the Turnpike with a Mr. Donald Watson, Papá grabbed my brother by an ear and pushed him against the police car.

"I tell you I no want you with that Donnie and you do this? You better having a good explanation for me later."

I followed Pablo into the house while Papá spoke with the police.

"You're in shit waters now, you asshole," I said.

Pablo threw his hands up in the air and walked into our bedroom. "You don't know what happened. What did you say to him?"

I followed him. "Hey, I've been covering your back the whole time. But you know what? I'm getting sick of it. What the hell were you doing in West Springfield?"

"We couldn't get a ride home. That's what happened. It's freezing out there. I was glad the police gave us a ride."

"A stupid problem and a stupid way to get a ride. But you didn't answer my question. What were you doing over there?"

"Just checking out chicks in Springfield, Andrea. Cool it, will you?"

Papá came into the house with papers the cops had given him and told Pablo he was grounded for the rest of the semester.

I was in the kitchen cleaning up when I heard my father's voice booming through the walls.

"Do you think I'm raising a bum? Get in the kitchen and help your sister, we don't have slaves in this house. Go empty the rubbish and sweep up like you do every day."

My brother walked into the kitchen without a shirt on and did as he was told. "Jesus, Pops, I was just going to take a bath and come help when she's done," Pablo said.

"That's your dinner on the stove, if you're hungry," I said.

"You can throw it out," he said, went into his bedroom, and closed the door.

Papá slammed the bedroom door open and spoke in English. "Hey, you think I working all day, *como un buey*, to buying food for this house, for you to coming home and say 'throw it out'?"

I walked up to my father and put my hand on his shoulder. "Papá, he didn't mean to offend you."

Papá went on and on in Spanish. "You hear me now. I don't want a bum here. You know what's happening to men who don't become someone of good use to society? They're sent to the army to fight that stupid war Johnson never fixed. And that's what's going to happen to you if you continue on this path you've taken. Is that what you want? To end up in Vietnam?"

My brother mumbled. "Calm down, Pops. Of course not. But that war will be over by the time I graduate."

Papá's face grew red, his voice vibrating through the walls, and he continued speaking in Spanish. "That *pendejo* Johnson isn't doing anything to end that war. You don't watch the news? You're too busy wasting your time with that *gran cosa* of a friend you found. And all those thousands of people protesting in Washington and all over the country burning those draft cards, they aren't going to change that Johnson *un carajo*."

I walked up to my father and whispered in Spanish. "Papá, *está bueno*, let's calm down."

Pablo yelled. "I still have good grades. That's not going to happen to me."

"Have you seen how those men are coming home? Men your age. They're coming back with no arms, no legs, in wheelchairs for the rest of their lives. That's what you can expect if you don't change. The only ones that have a future are the ones who are in school."

Papá went into the living room to watch television, and I knew he wasn't focusing on anything on the screen, because I was just as worried about my brother as he was. I scrubbed the pot where I'd cooked beans, the smell of fried pork chops still in the air.

That Saturday afternoon, Machi showed up with a beautiful *gringa*. She looked like my physical education teacher with strong legs, Bermuda shorts, and white sneakers. Machi escorted her out of the car, opened the door, extended an arm. Then she came in and introduced Carol Weinman.

Machi peeked around. "Where's your father?"

"In the back, washing the car."

"And *el jefe*?"

"I don't know."

Machi looked surprised, then stood behind Carol and made a sneaky face and spoke in Spanish. "My girlfriend," she said. "*¿Verdad que es bella?*" Carol smiled and I saw embarrassment all over her.

I smiled at both of them. They looked so happy. It had been more than four years since Machi had shown up in Woronoco, and I was glad to see that she had a full life. Carol stepped away from her. She was proper.

Machi stepped out to the backyard. "Don Luis! How are you?"

Machi introduced Carol, they shook hands, and Papá started on Pablo.

"That kid doesn't live here anymore. He hardly comes around," he said in Spanish.

He told Machi about Donnie and the police. Then he turned to Carol and spoke in English.

"I grounding him, and he's already gone this morning. What can I do when he disobeys? He's a grown man now. If I hitting him, he could hitting me back. *El hombre está hecho un problema.*"

"How old is he?" Carol asked.

"He's fifteen," Papá said. "Taller than me. But he's turning into a bum."

Carol nodded. "At his age, it's understandable that he wants to go out with friends, but he should let you know where he's going and when he's coming home. You should still have a say in those things."

What Carol didn't know was that Papá didn't allow us to go anywhere. There was nothing to negotiate.

A few days later, to my surprise, Machi was at the bus stop when our school bus arrived on the way home. Pablo introduced her to Donnie, and she asked if she could speak with Pablo alone. Donnie went his way to the avenue and the rest of us headed toward the Beehive. I noticed behind me, Machi put her arm around Pablo. They walked to the bridge and stood there talking.

By the time my father came home, Machi had made dinner and the table was set.

"Don Luis, Pablo has something to say to you."

My father looked at my brother with a stern face.

"I'm sorry, Pops. I didn't mean to disrespect you."

"Oh, but you disrespect me every day with your behavior. You're not stupid. You know what you're doing."

Machi stepped in. "Pablo would like to have a talk with you later, when you can, about things that are bothering him."

"Well, I don't have a problem with talking about anything, but he has to understand that in this house, no matter how tall he is and how old he is, he does what I say."

Pablo nodded.

Papá came over to the kitchen table. "Okay. Let's have dinner now. Look at the meal my sister-in-law has made for us."

That night Pablo lay awake in bed.

"Are you going to talk to him?" I asked.

"What the hell for? He ain't changing anything, Andrea. You heard him. It's obey his rules or get out. He's holding on to his cards, and you know what? I'm not waiting for his showdown."

I didn't even know what that meant, but Pablo was in no mood to explain.

nineteen

Papá told me someone was coming to the house to install a telephone.

"We're getting a phone? Oh my God, Papá, that's fabulous," I said.

"Carmen is my girlfriend now, and I want her to be able to call me whenever she wants. She decided to stay in the US a while longer to get to know me better, and if it works out, if she thinks I'm the man for her, she'll marry me."

"Are you engaged?"

"No, no, not yet, but I think I will be soon."

Sometimes Pablo was home, but often he wasn't, and even though he wasn't following Papá's rules entirely, our father let things go, probably for the sake of avoiding confrontation.

"I want you to be able to call me at any time too," Papá said. "We can't count on *el hombre* to watch over you."

I could not have been more excited when I gave my number to Emily. "Oh my God! Basketball season is coming. You have to come. You have to watch Frankie play," she said. Even before I said anything, Emily continued, "Hey, you have a phone now, all you have to do is let me know, and I'll get the car for that day and take you home after the game."

I had seen Frankie in the bus line after school several times since classes started. He'd wave before getting in his car. Frankie was one of the few students who drove a car to school.

Every time I saw him, I tried to read something more into his smile, his wave, the way he walked away, but it all seemed normal. Just a guy being friendly. I was plagued with doubt. Maybe everything I'd read into that time at the pond had been an exaggeration. Maybe Pablo and Emily were wrong.

A few days after the phone was installed, Frankie came into the school library and sat next to me. I was reading newspaper articles about the Vietnam War for a project. It was the only thing we talked about in history class.

He smiled with a twinkle in his eye. "You know you're probably the only girl in this whole school who seems to enjoy reading up on this. How've you been?"

"I'm fine, thanks. I can't be the only one reading this, because it's an assignment."

Frankie gave me a light shove, his grin going from ear to ear. "I'm teasing. I was looking at those same articles yesterday. What a mess we have in this country, don't you think? My Dad and I talk about it all the time."

"Yes, my father does too."

"I see you in the bus line but nowhere else at school. Where've you been since classes started?"

"I haven't seen you either. Nothing new. Same old thing."

"I was wondering when we can get together."

I stared at him and fumbled to open my mouth. "That . . . that would be nice."

"How about we go to Westfield?"

"Um, sure."

"Could go to Newberry's or Grandmother's Garden or maybe the movies."

I knew my father wouldn't allow me to see him or go anywhere despite having told me: *The day you find a good man in your life, you bring him here, to me, before you go anywhere with him.* But if I did follow Pablo and Emily's advice and hid this from my father, I couldn't go to Newberry's. What if Myrna, the girl from Casa Hispana, saw me? Would she tell her father? Would that guy tell Papá?

"What are you thinking? I've been meaning to ask you out since last summer, I just never saw you again. I thought you'd come to Elliot's party."

"We couldn't go."

"Oh. Hey, do you have a phone? Next time that happens just call me and I'll pick you up."

I gave Frankie my number and said I'd tell him when we could go out, but not to call me after four. "My dad might pick up the phone, and I don't know what he'll think about me talking to a guy."

Frankie squeezed my hand. "He's that strict? Wow. What can happen over the phone?" Frankie chuckled. "My uncle knows your dad. Says he's a really nice guy. Ask him if I can come to your house, then. I mean, no harm in us sitting on the porch, don't you think? I don't remember the last time I went to the Beehive, must've been seven or eight years old."

"I'll talk to Pablo and then we can decide."

"I like you, Andrea. Whatever works out best for you will be fine with me. Well, I have to go now. This isn't my reading period. I switched with Lyle Winters because I thought you'd be here. How about I see you at reading period again on Thursday?"

Reading was the last period of the day. When I returned to homeroom, I didn't get a chance to speak with my friends before we were all packing for bus lines. Frankie walked by the bus lines and waved, his eyes seeking mine. I smiled, trying to act as if it was normal for me to relate to him, but my face got warmer by the minute.

I couldn't wait to tell Pablo what had happened. I looked around for him but didn't see him anywhere. I wanted to tell him to come home early so we could talk. I needed his advice. What would I tell Papá? I got on the bus and looked at every seat. Pablo wasn't there. All the kids my age were talking about Hannah. Someone had seen her and said she'd dropped out of school. I hadn't seen her in the neighborhood either. Hannah was gone.

Just before Papá came home, Pablo walked through the door. After everything we'd been through, all the dreams we'd had and lost, all the times I'd stuck up for him, he wasn't there for me when I needed him.

"What's the matter with you? Are you okay?"

I ran to the bathroom and grabbed a piece of toilet paper to blow my nose and yelled at him. "Yes, Pablo, I'm fine."

"Okay. Hey, just asking."

"I've been waiting for you to come home for hours. I waited for you on the bus. Where were you?"

"Donnie had his aunt's car today."

"It'd be nice if you let me know. How do you think I feel when I look at every seat on that bus and you're not there?"

"What did you think, a ghost swallowed me? Andrea, come on, you know I'm with my friends. You know I'll be home before Pops gets here. Is that why you're crying?"

"Well, yes, but I'm crying because I'm dying to talk to you before he gets home."

"What happened?"

My tears turned to laughter. "Frankie asked me on a date."

Pablo looked at me almost like my father would have, with prohibition in his eyes. "Where were you?"

"At school, where'd you think I was?"

"He's not in your group."

I told my brother everything. He was quiet for a while and then shook his head.

"You can't tell Dad, Andrea. You tell him, and that will be the end of your first date in your whole life. He's never going to agree for you to see a guy until after you've graduated from high school and the guy comes and asks for your hand and he gives *la entrada* and all that fucking Puerto Rican bullshit. By that time, Frankie will be long gone. He's the most popular kid at school, are you kidding?"

I dried my hands on my apron and sat at a kitchen chair. "So you think I should lie?"

Pablo sat in front of me. "Just don't tell him. It's not a lie. Tell him you're going out somewhere and just go. Don't rot next to the fucking dump here. You're here alone most of the time. Go to the other side of the bridge or the post office and meet him. Go out with the girls from school and meet him. Dad won't have any idea."

He was right.

"And what about you? Has anything new happened with Theresa?"

"No, but I have tons of girls after me. Donnie and I get girls easy. His aunt works at a restaurant in Westfield now. So we sneak girls into the house and other kids too. She's never there. She doesn't care."

Papá walked in. As we finished making dinner, I thought of my brother's experience. He couldn't spend the rest of his high school years locked up in the Beehive. Papá was being unreasonable. Pablo's advice reminded me of Socorro's experience. I decided to listen to my brother. I would put up the fight.

The next day at school I couldn't wait to tell Barbara, Jennifer, and Emily that Frankie had asked me on a date. I wrote a note, passed it to Emily, and she passed it on to the other two. The three of them opened their mouths at the same time and before I could react, our math teacher blurted out, "And may I ask why you four young ladies are looking at each other like I have a clown mask on?" I couldn't focus until we had recess.

The moment we were out the door, Emily grabbed my shoulders. "You have nooooo problem! I'll pick you up and take you wherever you guys decide to meet."

Barbara's long silky brown hair lifted in the breeze as she looked me in the eyes. "Hey, you've been a good, obedient girl, and you're not doing anything wrong. We all go on dates."

Jennifer hugged me. "Awww, I'm so happy for you. You've got the cutest guy in school. I've been dating for two years now and never have a problem with my parents except I have to be home at a certain time."

Emily flashed her palms. "I'll talk to Frankie and tell him about your father. Everyone in the Beehive knows how strict he is. Just tell him you're going out with me."

Then I remembered Hannah. "By the way, have any of you heard from Hannah? Someone said she dropped out of school," I said.

Barbara squeezed her lips tight and then raised her shoulders. "I mean, it doesn't surprise me."

Emily stared at me with sad eyes. "I didn't know. Her sister. What a bad influence."

Barbara shook her head, her eyes wide. "It's not just her sister, it's tons of kids dropping out and going all over the place, but you know, you have to decide to make something of yourself, you know?"

"You're right. It's all over the news," Jennifer said.

By the time I saw Frankie in the library on Thursday, everything was set up for a date on Sunday morning, after my father left for church, where he'd meet with Carmen and then spend the whole afternoon with her.

Frankie walked in with the most beautiful grin I'd ever seen on a guy's face. His eyes glowed, and I thought he was nervous. I wanted to jump up and down and hug him but focused on not being awkward.

"Emily called me and said we're seeing each other on Sunday, right?"

"Yes. I mean if you still want to."

"Of course, I do. Great. So, what do you want to do?"

"I know you wanted to go to Westfield, but my father will be in Westfield, so Emily and I were thinking we could go to Russell instead, to The Corner Store."

Frankie nodded. "Okay. We're going to run into a lot of people, but if that works for you, let's do it."

"That's actually even better for me. If my father does show up, which I doubt, there won't be anything to worry about."

"That's a good point. So, this will be your first time at The Corner Store?"

"Uhum."

"So I'll pick you up at the Woronoco Post Office at ten?"

⁓

On Friday evening, Papá was getting dressed to go out and Pablo was watching television when I decided to tell my father a partial truth. He came out of the bathroom smelling of cologne, as he always did on weekends.

"Dad, remember Emily? Mr. Belanger's daughter?"

"Belanger the big boss. Yeah. What happened with Belanger?"

"Nothing, they're fine, but I just wanted to tell you Emily is picking me up on Sunday morning and taking me to Russell. She's driving her mother's car. We're working on a school project and when we're done, we're going somewhere for a hamburger."

Papá scratched his chin. "So here you come with the same problem as your brother."

"No, Papá, I'm not coming to you with a problem. I'm telling you I have to meet with kids from school, so you know where I am in case you get here and I'm not back."

"And where are you going to eat?"

"I have no idea. But you know her parents. They're pretty strict. It must be someplace nearby."

"Okay, Andrea, I trust that you know how to take care of yourself, and I expect you to be here before dark."

After Papá left, Pablo came into the kitchen and gave me a thumbs-up. "You did good, sis, you did good. I guess I should've started out that way, but too late now."

Donnie showed up in a car, and Pablo went with him. I spent hours going through my outfits, combing my hair, and putting makeup on. Later that night, Pablo came into the bedroom. "Donnie and I are going to be in the living room till Dad gets home, do you mind? It's fucking freezing out there."

"Just don't do anything he'll notice."

twenty

After our first date at The Corner Store, the awkwardness of being with a guy wore off and I was comfortable with Frankie. A lot of kids from school were there, and in front of all of them, he held my hand. Emily sat at a booth with us and swooned. From then on, when I came home from school, the phone was ringing the moment I walked through the door, and it was Frankie.

Frankie and I saw each other every Tuesday and Thursday at the library. Some days he drove me home. He picked me up on Sunday mornings and we went for lunch, sometimes as far as El Rancho on Route 20, on the way to Springfield.

Most of the time we went to the A&W in Westfield. He bought hamburgers and we ate in the car behind the restaurant because I was afraid my father, who was out with Carmen, might show up.

"I don't know that there is anyone our age in the Beehive. So who do you hang out with?"

"To be honest, I don't hang out with anyone—"

"So, what do you do after school every day?"

"You know my mother doesn't live with us, right?"

Frankie nodded. "Yes. Is that hard for you?"

"It was when it happened, but not anymore."

"So when you come home, there's no one there but you and Pablo?"

"Exactly."

"What do you guys do? I know your brother is close to Mark and Kevin. He must see them, right?"

"Not since Donnie moved to the avenue."

"Oh, that kid. Lyle said he's from Northampton and he was held back a few times. Doesn't have parents. Some really sad story. So what are you doing when Pablo isn't around?"

"Cooking or doing laundry or ironing. I just do my clothes and Pablo's, because my Dad takes his to a lady in Westfield—"

"Wait a minute, slow down. You sound like my mother. You know how to cook?"

I laughed. "Yeah. I'm seventeen. That shouldn't be a surprise."

"I don't know that any of our friends know how to cook anything but a hot dog. How did you learn?"

"Been helping in the kitchen since I was nine or ten years old, but started cooking every day at around twelve. I don't do everything. The three of us get together as a team, but I do most of it."

"You don't cease to amaze me, but that's a hard life for a kid. I wish you didn't have to do all that. And when your brother takes off, what do you do after you cook?"

"Go to my bedroom and listen to music, read books."

"Wow. That's so different from my life. I go somewhere different every day after school. When I was a kid, Mom would take me to games, classes, all the time. And then I'd come home, and she'd make dinner. I mean, it never even occurred to me where food came from until a few years ago."

I laughed. "You're a spoiled brat."

Frankie smiled. "I guess I am. I've never had to do anything but homework and sometimes mow the grass or shovel snow. But not always. So, do you ever go anywhere?"

"Not really. My dad goes out on weekends. He has a girlfriend now, and he sees her on Sundays. Saturdays he does groceries."

"Okay. So you really are the girl from the Beehive."

"I'd say more like the Puerto Rican girl from the Beehive."

"And that's one thing I've never done. An airplane. You've been on an airplane to Puerto Rico."

"We better get going, Frankie. Have to start dinner."

"Call me when you get home."

Frankie dropped me off at the post office, and I walked home.

One day, he took me home and parked the car along the street in front of the post office. Then he took my hand and pulled me, running toward Woronoco Bridge. As we approached the bridge, I was afraid my father could see us from the big windows of mill number two.

"Frankie, stop! Stop! He could be at one of those windows!"

But Frankie pulled my arm, and before we reached the bridge, he headed to the side, going under the road. He stopped at the edge of the riverbank with its huge boulders, specks of mica shining in the late October sun. He stood behind me and embraced me, and we stared at the waterfall.

Then he turned me around and we kissed for the first time. I rested my head on his chest.

He held my face in his hands. "Is it too soon for me to tell you that I want to marry you?"

I squeezed him tight. We sat on the grass, the arches of Woronoco Bridge above us.

"I've been here so many times with my brother and other kids. We've climbed all over that bridge, and some kids have dived from there into that hole under the waterfall."

"Holy shit. That takes guts." He laughed.

"But for all those years, I never thought my first kiss would be under this bridge."

Frankie paused, staring at the arches. "I've liked you for a long, long time, but didn't dare ask you on a date."

"Why?"

"Did you like me?"

I smiled and blushed. "Of course. Since the third grade."

He snickered. "Me too. I remember when you and Pablo came from Puerto Rico. I've liked you ever since you drew that turkey in art class. The one with the spirit coming off the rooftop. I thought, *That girl is different. She's really cool.* Remember when you brought those horrible crackers to the Christmas party in fourth grade?"

"Oh God. Don't remind me. My father forgot to buy me something to bring to school and just handed those to me that morning."

"I wanted to bash Danny in the face when he made fun of you. I always remember that. I know it's been hard for you, being an immigrant and all."

"Frankie, Puerto Ricans are American citizens."

"I know. But you still have another culture and a different language. I have to be honest. My mother doesn't understand this. She doesn't see Puerto Ricans as Americans."

"Have you talked to her about me?"

"No, I haven't."

"Why? You don't get along?"

"I don't think she'd want me to date a Puerto Rican, so I've kept it to myself. I feel that I have to tell you that."

I looked at him, my mouth open. "Is that why you didn't ask me out before?"

"It is. But you don't have anything to worry about. She's not the one marrying you."

"But how could you marry me if your mother disagrees?"

"I'll just marry you, that's how. And we'll live our life. She's never seen you. You don't even look Puerto Rican. She thinks all Puerto Ricans are, you know, Black, or dark-skinned, like most of the guys in the paper mill. She's probably going to change her mind when she meets you."

I'd always thought my father's racism was an embarrassing problem, but now there was this. Racism was everywhere I looked.

"But I'm . . . white," I said.

"Oh, absolutely. Whiter than me. I've told her a hundred times, you know, that some Puerto Ricans are white, and she says, if you're Puerto Rican, you're not white even if you look white."

Frankie took my face in his hands and looked into my eyes. "That doesn't matter to me, understand? And that's why I'm telling you I want us to get married when we graduate. Why drag all this out? Your father, my mother—their opinions are just opinions. We should get on with our life."

"It's funny. My father is a racist. He doesn't like Blacks. Well, I have news for him. Some people don't like him either, even though he thinks he's so white. Him and his Puerto Rican heritage."

"Andrea, we can't fix everyone around us before we decide to give each other a chance, you know?"

"Don't you think we need to know each other better, though?"

"Well, we're not getting married tomorrow. We still have two years of high school."

"Next year will be better. We'll be seniors. There will be lots of excuses I can come up with to go out."

"I'd like to get married right after graduation. What do you think?"

"And go to college together?"

"I don't know if I'm going to college yet. I might have to work at Strathmore for a year so I can pay for it."

"What? You'll get drafted if you're not in school. You have to go to college. You're one of the top kids at school, the athlete with the good grades. The guidance counselor said there are scholarships for athletes. Haven't you heard about those?"

"Yeah, I know, but I don't know if I'll qualify."

I was stunned. "She said me and Pablo could get a scholarship because we're Puerto Rican."

"Yeah, you're right. There's a chance I can get an athletic scholarship, but I don't know yet. My parents are business owners—"

"I thought your father worked at Strathmore?"

"He does. But we have a package store. Mom runs it with her brother, mostly. I don't think I can get any financial aid because of that."

"I really want you to go to college. I don't want you to get drafted."

"Oh, don't worry. We've had the biggest marches ever seen in America because of that war. People are burning draft cards all over the country. This mess will have ended by the time you and I graduate. It just can't hold up much longer, everyone's against it. You're going to have to find something else to do at the library. Mark my words."

"My father isn't so hopeful."

"What's he worried about?"

"Pablo. He doesn't want him getting drafted. And he says people in the government aren't taking the protestors seriously because of all the sex and drugs."

"That's not everybody."

"Frankie, I thought you wanted to go to law school? You can't graduate and just work at Strathmore."

"We'll see. Let's see what happens in the spring when we start filling out forms for all this stuff. But I do know one thing. I want to marry you, Andrea Inés."

⁓

Frankie drove me to the Beehive cul-de-sac, and as soon as I walked into the apartment, I called Socorro and told her everything about him.

"*¿Pero cuál es la prisa?* There's no need to be talking about marriage yet, what's the matter with him?"

"I think he just wants to know that I'm his steady girlfriend, you know, not dating anyone else."

"Andrea, you can't make a commitment to someone who is already telling you he's not going to college. College is your way out of Woronoco into a better life for you and your future family. Getting married to him isn't a way out of Woronoco. Do you want to spend the rest of your life there? With a guy working at Strathmore like your father?"

"But I love him. I've known him my whole life."

"Is he really cute?"

"He is. He has black hair and blue eyes, he's tall, and he's really smart and kind and sweet. He told me he'd come to my house and talk to Dad if he had to, just to see me."

"Like he said, you have two years to go. So don't break up with him. But Andrea. Listen to me. Do not have sex with him. *¿Me entiendes?* You have a future. Don't ruin it."

We hung up and I started dinner as fast as I could. Pablo walked in.

"Hey, I saw you in the car with Frankie, but you guys didn't see me. Better be careful the old man doesn't see you out the windows on the Tekoa Avenue side of the mill."

"Did you want a ride? Oh, I'm so sorry."

"That's okay. I just don't want you getting caught." He grabbed the broom. "Let me sweep up the kitchen."

I had rice going, and we had leftover beans and onion steak from the day before. I placed the food in pots to heat it up on the stove.

Pablo stopped in the middle of the kitchen, facing me with the broom in his hands. "Hey, how do you think those kids hitchhike all the way to California?"

"I don't know. I guess you keep taking one ride after another until you get there. You're not thinking of doing that, are you?"

"Course not. I'm curious, though, 'cause that's really far. Where do they sleep?"

"Under bridges, in their cars, I guess."

"Some kids I know are planning on going over there. I mean, it would be a cool thing to do in the summer, don't you think?"

"Those kids on the news are running away from home. I don't think they intend to return to their parents."

"I think you're right. But who pays for all the concerts? You think they're free?"

"I think so."

"A friend of mine from Chester is talking about going."

"To California?"

Pablo laughed as if I'd told him a joke. "Some of them are having second thoughts."

"What's so funny? Who's having second thoughts?"

Pablo looked surprised. "Woo hooo hoo." He laughed, his eyes looking around the room as if he was following someone. "And we want to live life too, you know? You want to get some bell-bottoms and a shag, you want the wide leather belt and the fishnet stockings, the cool cat but in a girl, not the Raggedy Ann doll type, no sir, this girl is the Puerto Rican from the Woronoke Tribe."

I tried to make sense of what Pablo had just said but I couldn't. I walked up to him and took the broom out of his hands. "What the hell did you just say? Why you talking like that?"

Pablo grabbed the broom. "Gimme that. Ole man's gonna walk in any minute."

I checked the food on the stove and got dishes out of the pantry. Pablo didn't even realize what he'd said was gibberish.

"Why are you talking about Raggedy Ann and the Woronoke Tribe?"

Pablo looked confused. "Was I?" He laughed.

It was reading period on a Tuesday afternoon around the middle of October when Pablo's teacher called me into her classroom and gave me his progress report. I was speechless when she told me he hadn't been to school in over a week.

"Is he sick?" she asked.

My face and chest grew warm as I took his report from her hand. "No."

What the fuck, Pablo? I thought.

"So why is he missing school? Is he home?"

"I honestly don't know why he's not here. He's home every day but he hasn't told me he's not coming to school."

"Do you see him on the bus?"

"He's been getting a ride from a friend."

"Donnie Watson? He hasn't been in school either. I just spoke with his teacher this morning." She shook her head and walked around her desk. "This is unfortunate, because Pablo is a good kid, and he had such good grades. But he's really changed this year. I'm sorry, but all those absences are in this report, and your parents will have to sign this. We're also going to need a parent here to see the principal before Pablo is allowed back in school."

I returned to homeroom. Emily noticed my gloomy demeanor right away and asked what had happened. I told her I'd call her when I got home. Then I remembered Frankie was waiting for me at the library and asked my teacher for my pass. There were still fifteen minutes of reading period left. I ran through the hall but when I arrived, the library was empty. Mrs. Briar was at her desk eyeing me above reading glasses, the ones with the pearls hanging down the sides of her face.

"He waited," she said, and smiled.

I smiled back. "Thank you." Well, that was one nice thing that happened that day. I felt a sense of pride in being old enough to have a boyfriend, but a wound in my soul, knowing what awaited me at home. Pablo had slipped out of our window several times before and returned at daybreak. He was never on the bus to school. What would I say to my father?

The phone was ringing when I walked into the house, and of course it was Frankie. "What happened? I waited, but you never came. Are you okay?"

I told him about my brother.

"Look," said Frankie. "I never wanted to tell you this, but those kids he's hanging out with, they're doing acid, smoking dope, skipping school. You need to tell him to stay away from those guys."

I'd never seen my father as angry at Pablo as he was that night. I stuttered when I gave him the reports. Papá read both reports and didn't say a word to me. Pablo walked in after dinner and looked at me like, *What the hell is this about?* I shrugged.

Papá didn't waste any time. "Hey. Tell me something. Where have you been? I don't remember you asking permission to go anywhere, and you walk in here like you govern your life without any respect for what I have to say. Where were you just now?"

Pablo looked at me like, *What the hell?* "I was at the avenue, Pops, where I go every day. I didn't think you had a problem with that anymore."

My father looked at me the way he did when he considered me his accomplice. "Listen to him. *Embustero*. Lying is a person's worst trait."

Papá held up the progress report and ran his finger up and down one
side. "And is that where you were on all these days marked here as absent?
Or are you going to tell me another lie now?"

Pablo hung his head low. What else could he do? He turned his head just
enough to give me a look that burned into me like a lightsaber. I looked back
at him like, *Hey, don't blame me.*

Papá pushed his chest out and tapped Pablo on the shoulder. He spoke
in Spanish, and he was *pissed*. "I know more than you think I do. That Donnie kid was arrested last week for breaking into a house. The people at the
mill tell me everything. And you think I didn't notice that you don't sleep
here anymore?"

"That's not true, Pops. It's only been a few times, and all I've done is sit
outside with my friends and after they go home, I come right back in. Right,
Andrea? Andrea?"

I nodded, but Papá wasn't looking at me or listening.

"I don't ask your sister anymore because she lies to me to protect you.
I don't blame her. But you don't deserve the sister you have. It's one thing
for you to go out now and then, but missing school? That, I'm not going
to tolerate. If you're not in school, then get a job. Understand? Let me tell
you something, and you hear me well. If you can't be a man of good, a man
that will someday become a productive citizen, good for something in this
world, then you can go right back where you came from just now."

I couldn't stand hearing those words. "Papá, please don't say that."

"Oh, I'm saying it again. This is the end of the line right here. No, *mijo*.
You're not ruining your sister's life and mine. I don't want these problems in
my house. You're not even a part of this family, off on your own doing what
you please, not cooperating with anything, and now you're obsessed with
that criminal friend you have. Well, go and become a bum like him if you
can't follow the rules of this house. I'm not feeding and supporting a bum."

Pablo didn't say a word, he just grabbed his coat and headed for the door.

I ran after him and pulled his arm. "No. No, wait. Pablo, don't go, Papá's mad, that's all."

Pablo had fire in his eyes. "I haven't done anything, Pops, just getting out of this dump once in a while. But you know what? You see all those kids on television going to California? Everyone I know is headed there. And I'm better off going with them."

Papá laughed. "It's going to be pretty cold asking for rides all the way to California in the winter."

Pablo walked out and slammed the door.

I ran after him. "Pablo, where are you going?"

He pushed me away. "Leave me alone."

I grabbed his arm. "Don't pay attention to Papá. He's mad, Pablo, he doesn't mean it. There were a bunch of absences on your report card. Even I didn't know about them."

Pablo continued walking. It was cold out, and I didn't have a coat on.

"Pablo, please, come back. Just come sit on the porch with me until he falls asleep. You know him. He'll forget about it in the morning."

I ran up the hill until I reached him and pulled on his arm again. He stripped my hands off and continued up the hill in the dark. "Go home, Andrea. Don't worry about me, I'll be a lot better off than I am here."

My brother's shadow disappeared over the little hill. When I walked into the house, Papá was in a chair in the kitchen. He looked at me as if he expected me to say Pablo was on the porch and hadn't left, but I dropped into a chair in front of him.

His eyes met mine as he shook his head. "*¿Se fue el hombre?*"

My lower lip trembled. "Yes, Papá, he's gone."

I put my pajamas on and climbed into bed, my brother's nicely kept bed across from mine. I thought he'd show up the next day. But that didn't happen. His teacher came to my classroom to inquire, and I told her what had transpired.

She covered her mouth with her hands. "Oh dear. Let's hope he returns. Please bring me the progress report card signed by your father."

At recess, I told my friends.

Jennifer shook her head and hands. "Don't worry about him. He'll be back in a few days."

"I agree," Barbara said. "Look at how cold it's gotten. Where's he going to go?"

On the way home, I remembered my brother sitting next to me for so many years and tears came to my eyes. Convinced that he'd walk into the house that day, I calmed myself. But Pablo didn't come home. The phone rang, and I knew it was Frankie, but I didn't answer his call. I couldn't.

I did the dishes and waited a while, running to the window and back, but soon grew too anxious to stay in the house. I ran to Valley View Avenue and looked for Donnie. I ran up and down the street hoping to find him sitting on a porch with my brother. Wouldn't they both be at Donnie's aunt's house? I didn't find him anywhere. It was getting dark, and I walked home.

As I passed the paper mill, I remembered when Pablo and I used to ride our bikes down the big hill, then the little hill, competing over who could let go of the handlebars longer. I passed the dump and remembered him looking through the trash for treasures.

The closer I came to the cul-de-sac, the uglier it looked. The train tracks on the left. The Tarzan swing that no one used anymore, still hanging from the big oak tree. The slope where we went sledding. The middle ground where the big kids played baseball and we dug holes to play marbles. And now I hated every corner of the Beehive. Everyone had left but me.

Mark and Kevin were the only ones around, and they didn't care for us anymore. They were two walking brains. They had plans to go to medical and engineering school. They had noticed Pablo turning in the wrong direction and steered away from him way before I had realized anything was up. The only thing left for me in the Beehive was the train.

At reading period that week, I went to the library only to tell Frankie I didn't want to talk to him or anyone about my brother.

Frankie reached for my hand. "I understand. Just stay here awhile, you don't have to say anything."

Day after day, Frankie gave me a ride home, and every day I wanted to do something to find my brother.

"Can you take me to the avenue?" I said.

"You think we might find him there?"

I nodded. As soon as we got there, I climbed out of the car and asked the first person walking by if she knew Donnie. She was a young woman with a baby in a stroller. She shook her head. A lady sitting on the stoop of her porch pointed to a house.

"A kid moved there last summer. Aunt was an alcoholic. They moved out a few days ago."

The kid fit Donnie's description. Frankie spoke with her and figured out who the aunt's husband was, and where in Strathmore he worked, while I looked through the windowpane. The house was empty.

Frankie and I sat in the car on the side of Blandford Road for a while before he took me home. I felt safe because I knew my father never came that way. Frankie caressed my hair as I lay my head on his shoulder, telling him story after story about growing up with my brother.

"You're going to have to put it to rest, babe. After going through all that hardship as a child, you deserve some happiness of your own. He's made his decision. You can't change that. You'll see him again, but only when he decides he wants to see you."

"But how could he leave me? I would never leave him."

"You're asking the wrong person, because I would never leave you."

"He knew I'd be worried about him. That I'd be lonely."

"Maybe he wasn't thinking about you. The crowd he was hanging around with, they're doing drugs. I'm not saying he was, but it's possible that's why he changed so much."

I remembered several occasions when Pablo wasn't quite with it and didn't make sense.

"He found the only way out he could. You have to think about yourself now."

That night, I told my father that friends of mine from school had taken me to every house on the avenue. I thought it was a good idea in case he'd seen me with Frankie.

He shook his head and whispered, *"El hombre desapareció."*

I nodded. "Yes, Papá. He has disappeared. My friends are going to take me to some other places and some of the streets in Russell too. But if I don't find him, we should call the police."

"No. I don't want to involve the police. And I don't like the idea of you going around looking for your brother either. What are people going to think?"

"But maybe I can find him with people from school. Someone might know someone who knows something."

"If I call the police, I turn him into a delinquent. Let things go for a while. If anything happens to him, they come here. To this house. To tell me, his father. When things get difficult out there with no money and no food, he'll come back."

twenty-one

As soon as basketball season started that fall, Frankie insisted that I go to the games. It was a Tuesday evening in November when I told my father I wouldn't be home until late on Thursday evening.

"There's a basketball game and all the kids from my school will be there. I don't want to be the only kid that doesn't show up."

"And how will you get home?'

"You could pick me up at nine."

Papá looked mortified, but he agreed. "Make sure you come out when I get there. I don't want to be out there waiting for you for an hour, I have to go to work the next day."

I promised my father I'd be at the door at nine.

Frankie was an all-star that night, the cheerleaders and his teammates all over him when I pushed my way through to kiss him. He grabbed me by the waist, pulled me in, and gave me a passionate kiss. Then he was pulled in all directions and I stepped aside. A beautiful brunette I'd never seen before pulled his arm, then there were the kids from our classes and even seniors, pulling him in other directions.

I looked at my watch. It was ten to nine. Frankie was having a great time with his fans, but I had to leave. I looked for the doors and glanced at him one last time. His eyes met mine, and then he was gone, carried away by the cheering crowd.

On the ride home, Papá told me that he was getting engaged.

"To Carmen?"

Papá laughed.

"Oh, Papá, I'm so happy for you. When is the engagement?"

"On Thanksgiving Day at Socorro's house. What do you think? I'll show you the ring when we get home."

"The ring? You bought her a ring?"

"Well, *mija*, there's no engagement without a ring."

As soon as we walked through the door he went into his bureau, brought out a small box, and handed it to me. I hugged him. "It's beautiful, Papá."

"I'm marrying her next summer. And then she's coming to live here. With us. She'll be the woman of this house."

"I'm only going to be with you and Carmen for a year, Papá. Then I'll be going to college, if I get accepted. I have a lot of activities coming up this year, and it's important that I participate like everyone else at school."

"You mean activities at school?"

"Yes. At school, and other places too. I won't be waiting for you to take me or bring me home. You've got your own things to worry about now."

"But who's going to bring you home?"

"I can find someone from my class to bring me home."

"But I have to know who that person is."

"Papá. Let me tell you something. I'm doing everything I can to live by your rules, but sometimes your rules are impossible, and I don't think it's fair that I have to choose between being a normal high schooler and following your rules. If you wanted me to grow up like a Puerto Rican, we should have moved back to Puerto Rico. But we stayed here."

Even though I made progress with my father, it wasn't enough for Frankie. On the way from school one day, we sat in his car at Blandford Road.

"Andrea, after the games, everyone is there but you."

"I know. I'm sorry. At least he's letting me go."

"But when he picks you up, the night is just getting started. Everyone goes somewhere, we hang out and have something to drink, some kids have a smoke, you know, all the guys with their girlfriends, and we just cool it, you know? But I never have you there."

"I know. And I can't imagine ever being there unless I get married."

"That's a real drag. I want you there to celebrate with me."

It was mid-November, and I hadn't been to the last two games. Barbara and Emily and I walked out into the stark cold at recess, our breath clouding as we spoke.

Barbara stared at Emily. "If you're really her friend, you'll agree with me telling her."

I looked at them both, wondering what they were talking about, when Barbara blurted out: "I went to the last two games. You weren't there. I saw Frankie in the parking lot making out with some brunette."

I walked away and sat down. The girls followed. Emily brushed her hand along the top of my head. "Geez, you didn't have to tell her like that. Maybe it was nothing. But Andrea, listen to me. This is the first guy you've ever dated. There will be more guys, you know?"

Barbara shook her head. "He thinks he's a famous athlete now, and that gives him the right to go around kissing any girl he wants? He's not worth it, Andrea. Emily is right. I'm only seventeen, and I've already dated three guys."

"Well, she's the one kissing him. I don't think he expected all this attention, but still . . ." Emily said.

Barbara raised her shoulders. "But he's kissing her back. I saw him. That's cheating any way you look at it."

On the bus, as we passed the waterfalls covered in dyes from the paper mills, I leaned against the window, hopeless. I hardly knew anyone on the bus anymore. There wasn't anything more I could lose that mattered.

When I walked through the door and heard the phone ring, I didn't pick it up. I knew it was Frankie, but what would I say? I called Socorro instead.

"You were right," I said, and burst into tears.

"¿Ah, sí? ¿El muchacho?"

I wiped my nose. "Uhum."

"What did he do?"

I told her, between blowing my nose and wiping my face.

"I know how you feel, but it will pass. There will be others, *mija*. Just wait and see what your life is like when you get out of that hole. We'll see each other in a few days for Thanksgiving. Your father's getting married, you're going to be a senior, and then off to your studies. There's a lot to look forward to."

That weekend, my father and I went to María's wedding in Westfield, and I was surprised to see her husband wearing a military uniform. Carmen was the maid of honor and I sat in a pew next to my father.

"That man you see there is going to Vietnam a few days from now. Those two get to be together for only a few days after this wedding, and then off to war, imagine that." He shook his head. "This is the worst president we've ever had. He says he hates this war, but we're still over there."

A few days before Thanksgiving, I was able to change my library reading period so mine wouldn't coincide with Frankie's. I took out some books and left as fast as I could. At home that day, I sat at the kitchen table going through my books when someone knocked on the door. Frankie's Volkswagen was outside.

"Andrea," he called. "If you don't want the whole neighborhood to know that I'm here, then open the door. I know you're there."

I opened the door. "What are you doing here? I can't let you in, you know that."

"What do you expect me to do? You've disappeared and won't answer my phone calls. What am I supposed to do?"

I put my coat on and went outside. "I can't get in that car with you, and I can't let you in."

Frankie looked around with suspicion. "Okay, I don't want to cause problems for you. So we can sit out here in the freezing cold. I don't care, long as we can talk."

We walked over to the maple tree under the Tarzan swing and sat on the roots of the tree where there wasn't any snow. Frankie stretched his arm out to bring me close, but I moved away.

He held his face in his hands between his knees. "I don't know what . . . There was a game in Chicopee and . . . and there were all these girls all over me. Is that what Jennifer and Barbara and Emily told you? 'Cause that's the only thing I can imagine someone told you that would bring this on."

"Yes, they said you were making out with a girl with dark hair."

"Andrea, that's not—"

"Frankie, this isn't going to work. It doesn't matter what you say now, so don't even try."

"Dealing with this whole thing with your father is not easy. You're never there when everyone else is together, when everyone else is with their date like it's the most normal thing in the world. All the guys on the team are celebrating, hanging out after a game, their girls there, and I can't have my girl with me."

"I know. I understand and I wish I could be there, but there isn't anything I can do about it. I can't go to your parties, so let's not talk about it anymore, Frankie. Just go ahead and enjoy your stardom and all the girls around you and be happy now. There's nothing more to this." I looked away from him. "I'm sorry."

At that moment, my father's car came into the cul-de-sac and moved around the back of the houses to our garage.

"I have to go."

"Are you going to get in trouble?"

"No. I'll just tell him this will never happen again, and after a while, he'll believe me." I got up and walked away.

"Andrea. You've got it all wrong. I love you. I mean it. I always will."

I turned around. "I will too."

I don't know how I found the strength to show up at the side of my father's car with a cheery face only a minute after breaking up with Frankie, but I did. Thankfully, he hadn't even seen us.

Papá was gung ho over his engagement to Carmen, which happened on Thanksgiving Day at Socorro's house. Machi came with Carol, and Felipe and Caridad came with their two little kids, Vivian and a new baby boy named Marcelo. I was overjoyed to see my father's happiness for the first

time in my life. Carmen served him, asked him if he wanted more of this or
that, brushed the collar of his shirt with her hands, and he was in heaven.
I'd never seen him get so much attention. When they announced their wedding date for the summer, we all cheered.

Machi whispered in my ear, "And you will come to Puerto Rico with me
and Carol."

"What?"

"Yup. *Nos vamos.* They can have the house to themselves, you know, give
them privacy, and you and I show Carol around the farm and Puerto Rico.
And when we return, you can stay with us in Springfield until your senior
year starts and then you can stay with us on weekends."

Socorro overheard us and came over. "Was thinking the same thing.
Come over to my house on weekends. Not that you'd be a bother to your
father, but you need to get out of that cave down there, anyway."

Just before Christmas, Barbara's boyfriend was drafted. I'd never met
him, but she showed me pictures. At school she spoke of nothing but the
war, and how she was afraid that he'd get killed. When I got home, she'd
call to continue the same conversation. I listened and wanted to say something positive, but I had nothing in me to give. Barbara and I were like two
ghosts going through the motions of being alive.

Carmen came over one day during Christmas vacation and set up a
Christmas tree with my father. It was his way of showing off what a nice guy
he was and doing something to cheer me up. But as I hung each Christmas
decoration, the bulbs with bubbling water, the glass ornaments, I thought
of my brother.

Snow on the rooftops and on the sides of the road created a postcard
image that people who visited us found beautiful. But for me, the scene
brought on sadness, memories of my brother, and additional worry about
his whereabouts. Did he ever get to California? Had he eaten? Or was he
freezing outdoors somewhere and starving? When tears rolled down my
face as I pulled an ornament out of a box, Carmen hugged me.

"You both have to move on with your lives."

"Why do you say 'both'? My father seems to have moved on just fine."

"He talks about your brother all the time."

"Really?"

"Yes. And he talks about you. He's so proud of you. He says he always thought your brother would be a lawyer and you'd never finish high school, but you're going to prove him wrong."

"I wish we'd both finished."

That day, she asked me where everything was in the kitchen and helped with dinner. She cooked a *carne mechada*, which I'd never made, and a vanilla flan for dessert. My father was in heaven. Then she made a wish list of all the things she wanted to buy for the apartment.

As their wedding plans progressed, boxes of new things piled up, and I saw more of her. I was eager to have her join us. We would be together for a whole year. After that, if Carol was right, I wouldn't have any problem getting admitted into college, especially being a minority. And my counselor told me there were plenty of grants available to cover my expenses and tuition. My father was transferring to the mill in Westfield and we would be moving there after my graduation. I prayed that Pablo returned home before we moved, before I went off to college. Otherwise, how would he find us?

When I returned to school, my sole attention went to Barbara. When she didn't show up to school for two days and wouldn't answer the phone, Emily and I went to her house and found her sobbing. She was pregnant and didn't know how to tell her parents.

One morning we forced her into the shower, dried her off, helped her get dressed, and dragged her to school with us. Before walking out of her bedroom, she kissed a Vietnamese doll her boyfriend had sent her. That evening, we sat on her front porch as she told her parents that she was pregnant from her boyfriend stationed in Vietnam. "Oh, my poor baby," I heard her mother cry. And through the window, we saw a silhouette of her whole family in one big hug.

Everyone at school was supportive of her, but while they were taking aptitude tests, filling out college applications, and talking about jobs, she couldn't take her mind off the fact that her boyfriend might never meet his child.

Meanwhile, the war raged around us. Images of US bombers pounding Vietnamese cities into rubble came across the television screen every night. Five young men were indicted for counseling others on how to resist the draft. I had just finished the dishes when Papá called me into the living room and we saw Walter Cronkite tell the nation that the only rational way out of the Vietnam war was "to negotiate, not as victors, but as an honorable people who lived up to their pledge to defend democracy." But the war continued.

"Even the bums are gone," Papá said. "Remember all those bums on the street corners in Westfield? You don't see a single one of them anymore."

Papá was right. They'd all been drafted. Some of them returned in caskets and others in wheelchairs. We came home to a television screen announcing music festivals, massive protests, marches, rallies, and demonstrations. There were guys fleeing the draft to Canada. There were all sorts of groups protesting: women's groups, the Black Panthers, the Young Lords, priests, nuns, even mothers.

When Martin Luther King, Jr., was assassinated that spring, Papá couldn't take his eyes off the television.

"Look at the way that man opened fire with that gun on that poor *negrito*. That poor man was Black, but he was decent, the most decent Negro I've ever heard of, and look how they killed him."

Riots surged through every major city in the United States, and we heard of cracked skulls and ribs at peaceful demonstrations in Chicago. Then came the May riots in Paris that brought France to a halt and spread like wildfire through embers that were still burning throughout this country.

"The death of that man was an atrocity," he said, one evening. "And now the *morenos* are furious, but they have reason to be. That man was a peaceful leader."

I nodded. "I agree, Papá, I agree."

"This country is for the rich. Americans don't like Blacks or Puerto Ricans. They don't like anyone who isn't pure white."

I thought perhaps my father had changed his mind about Black people, but I didn't want to press it. The reality around us was enough of an example of injustice in the world. Or maybe his own happiness was allowing the better side of him to shine through.

My father's wedding to Carmen that summer came as a relief in midst of all that commotion. She was a widow and chose a simple Catholic wedding at the Westfield church where they'd met. But they had a beautiful party in the backyard at her sister's house in Westfield. A few people came from Casa Hispana, and the men played dominoes after the bride and groom left for their honeymoon. The next day Machi, Carol, and I would be on a plane to Puerto Rico, where we'd spend the month of July.

I was helping Carmen's family pick up tables and carry plates into the kitchen when a gorgeous, tall, curly black-haired Puerto Rican walked into the backyard with one of Carmen's male relatives. The moment he saw me, his eyes lit up. I too was stunned and smiled.

I was surprised to even feel attracted to a guy other than Frankie. But it had been over six months since our breakup. And this guy was no high school kid playing basketball. He was older than me, with a penetrating look, and a seriousness about him that gave off a confident, intellectual air.

I took dishes into the kitchen and asked if they needed more help. Everyone in there told me to go outside and enjoy the party. I sat next to Carol. Machi went to an ice chest to get some beers, and the two guys approached her.

"Now, that is one smart kid," Carol said. "I know him. Let's see if he comes over and I'll introduce you. He went to Tech High School, and I got him into UMass. That's where I want you to go. I wonder what he's doing now."

And then Machi came over with him, a bottle of beer and a bottle opener in her hands. She opened the bottle and handed it to me.

"I never drink, Titi."

Machi laughed. "I know. Have a few sips anyway." Then she turned to the guy. "And what is your name?"

Carol interrupted. "Arturo is his name. Arturo, how are you?"

He wiped his hand on his pants with a surprised look on his face and shook her hand. "Ms. Weinman. How nice to see you."

Then everyone turned to me, and my heart accelerated. Carol introduced us.

"Are you still at UMass?" she asked him.

"I am. I'll be a senior this fall and probably staying there for graduate school."

I noticed he had a heavy accent, the kind that someone from Puerto Rico would have.

Carol had a big smile. "I'm so happy to hear that. Still in political science?"

He nodded. "Yes, and in this social climate, I've gotten more and more involved."

Carol glanced at me as she spoke. "Andrea is applying to UMass. She graduates next year."

He raised his eyebrows. "I hope you get admitted. What's your major?"

"English. Education."

"The education department is very good. You're going to love it. It's a great place. I look forward to seeing you there."

Machi extended her hand and told him we were leaving for Puerto Rico the next day.

"The three of you?" he asked.

I nodded.

"How lucky for you. I haven't been back in three years."

We thanked Carmen's relatives for the party and left.

twenty-two

Machi, Carol, and I rushed across the airport lobby. A small, skinny tan guy walked up to Machi and hugged her. Something about the shape of his body seemed familiar, and I thought he was a taxi driver, but when he stepped away from my aunt and I saw his face, I recognized him. It was Tito. My beloved childhood friend, all grown up, with hair on his face, had come to the airport to pick us up. Tito and I hugged and kissed each other, choked up with tears.

"I wanted to surprise you," Machi said.

"Well, you certainly did!" Tito said and hugged me again.

Titi Machi and I couldn't contain our excitement hours later when we crossed a wide cement bridge over the river to her house.

"No more jumping over stones," Tito said.

We got out of the car in front of her house, and Machi walked around in circles with tears in her eyes. I choked up again, overwhelmed by the memories brought on by the earthy scents and sounds. Carol's eyes looked wide, her mouth a big smile.

"What an amazing place this is," she said.

Tito gave Machi a set of keys. "I hope you like the new additions."

We walked in and he showed us around. There was a sink inside the kitchen, and a gas stove. "I use the *fogón* now and then, but this is what I use most of the time." He led us to a new bedroom he'd added to the house. "Andrea, you can sleep in here. Brand-new bed and sheets."

Machi looked around, her eyes wide open. "But this room is a lot bigger than I thought it would be. Did you add some money of your own?"

"No. *Ni un centavo*. It was all done with the money you sent me. That's what happens when you have people from *el barrio* helping you out."

Then he went to the old bedroom where Pablo and I had slept. "My bedroom. Same as you left it." He led us across the kitchen and opened a new door. "Bathroom. Look at the shower. Hot water. Heater is in the shack on the other side of this wall."

Machi twirled around in circles. "Hot water, oh my God. Remember how I heated pots of water to bathe you every night, *mija*?"

"Of course I remember, Titi. And you always cooked at the *fogón*."

Carol and I walked out to the porch.

She looked around, awestruck. "This is paradise. I can see why she talks about it so much. Look at all the ferns and flowers. How could you guys have ever left?" She stared at Machi. "No wonder you wanted to come back."

"I was in this house for a short period, less than a year, but I never wanted to leave," I said.

"Listen to that river," Carol said.

Machi and Tito walked out to the porch, talking about neighbors who had died, moved away, or were still around.

Tito clasped his hands together. "How about we have lunch? I have *bacalao guisado, plátanos, y yautía*."

The next day we explored Machi's farm, showing Carol all the produce. There were still chicken coops, tobacco, and workers coming by to get paid and drop off farming tools. Many of them recognized Machi and hugged her.

After a few days, we left to show Carol around our homeland. We went from El Morro Castle to the El Yunque National Forest, from the Taíno Caguana Indigenous Ceremonial Park to watching surfers in Rincón. Then Machi and Carol went off on their own for a few days to La Parguera and I stayed with Tito.

The next morning, Tito knocked on my door at sunrise. "*Vamos pa'l río*."

I rushed out of bed and got dressed. We ran to the riverbank and made a left turn at the bridge. We scurried along the bank together and then down to the boulders where crystalline waters surrounded us, the waterfall up ahead. Tito grabbed my hand and pointed to the *flamboyán* tree. The same tree we used to sit under, watching the *guaraguaos*, when we were children.

"Are they still there?"

"There were two years when they disappeared. When the bridge was being built. I thought they'd never return, but they came back."

We crawled over the boulders to the spot where we'd sat years ago and lay there next to each other, looking at the sky, the trees, flaming red petals twirling in a breeze, and the *guaraguao*, swirling above.

Tito's voice surprised me.

"Machi told me it was your mother who took you. She cried for days. Weeks."

I couldn't say anything.

"I told her I'd go with her to Gurabo, but she said it was better to find your father."

"Pablo and I missed you so much."

"I missed you too. But here we are, almost ten years later."

"We never forgot you. You taught us so many things. What year are you in now?"

"*Tercer año* in August. And you're going to be a high school senior. Hey, how's Pablo? When's he coming down?"

I told him about my brother.

"I'm sorry to hear that. We hear a lot about the hippies here. Kids leaving home and living in communes and all that. There's a commune in Caguas, so I heard."

"There aren't hippies here?"

"Not really. People listen to *el rocanrol* and there are a few Americans who come here to go surfing and live like vagabonds on the beaches in Rincón and Vega Baja, but that hippie thing hasn't really caught on here. We have other things to worry about. Have you heard about the plebiscite?"

"No. What is it?"

"Next month. The governor is holding a referendum where we vote to choose between Estado Libre Asociado, statehood, or independence."

"Really? Would we actually change?"

"I doubt it. We can vote all we want, but it would take a long time for things to change, if they ever do."

"And you're voting for statehood, right?"

"*¿Estás loca?* Why would I do that?"

"Just saying, because Papá says the *independentistas* are communists."

"With all respect, I have to tell you he's wrong."

"I don't know anything about Puerto Rico. I'm ashamed of that, but I don't get any news over there about what's happening here. Don't you believe in democracy?"

"I do, but there's no democracy here. Our relationship with the United States has never been democratic."

"What are you talking about? The United States is 'the land of the free.'"

"That's a lie, Andrea. You need to learn about your country's history."

"What is 'my country,' Tito? I've never felt that I belong here or there."

"That's the problem Nuyoricans have."

"I'm not Nuyorican."

"You still have the same problem. We didn't ask to become an American colony in 1898, it was imposed. Your father says that because he's an ignorant man, no offense. *Jíbaro. Campesino.* All the farmers and conservatives want Puerto Rico to stay the way it is because they're afraid of change. And after the Cuban Revolution, they're all scared of communism. But why do you think Machi left? No one buys local anymore. And the government doesn't provide incentives for farmers. Incentives go to the big factories coming in. And who's going to work on a farm when they can get a check every week in a factory without getting their hands dirty? We have an economic mess."

"So why don't Puerto Ricans do something about this? Look at people in the States. They don't want the war, so they protest. We should protest the lack of aid for farmers."

"We've been protesting since 1898. And before that, against the Spaniards. We've never stopped. The most recent incident is what happened to members of the *nacionalistas*. They want Puerto Rico to be a free nation.

And all the leaders have either been imprisoned or killed. We can't protest. You can get thrown in jail."

"But America is a democracy and we're American citizens—"

"You call a country that killed Martin Luther King, Jr., a few months ago and killed Bobby Kennedy right after he won the democratic primary in California a democracy? Democracy is in the streets, Andrea. That's the only way you achieve it."

"But we'd be the same as everyone else in the US if we were a state."

"The same as who? The white Americans? We're still Puerto Rican, Andrea. We're never going to be like the white people in the United States."

I remembered the conversations I'd had with Frankie and how his mother didn't think I was white. There was too much about Puerto Rico I didn't understand.

"How many Puerto Ricans and Blacks have already died in Vietnam? Think of that. This isn't just an economic war, it's a racial war. Even if we vote for statehood, it won't happen. We're too brown. And they'll never give us independence either. They want to keep us in this Estado Libre Asociado status, which is limbo, because they need us to fight their wars and work at their factories."

"So why are we even talking about this if we can't change anything?" I asked.

"I didn't say we can't change things. We have to struggle for the country we want. That's why I'm going to law school. That's going to be my way of contributing. What's yours going to be? Teaching English?"

"Maybe. I'm so proud of my Spanish, even though I know it's not perfect. I know Puerto Rican kids my age who won't even speak Spanish. Sometimes I don't know which side of myself to hide. Over there and over here, it's all the same for me."

"Stop hiding. The reality of Puerto Rico is that we're a colony, and that affects all of us in one way or another. It's not your fault. But recognize that before you talk about statehood for Puerto Rico, you need to understand our history."

That evening, we went to the Aguas Buenas plaza in front of the cathedral. Papá had given me a hundred dollars to spend, and I'd bought myself a jumpsuit in Old San Juan. It had a V-neck with wide pants and a bright-green geometric print. I wore big white plastic hoops and lime-green patent leather strappy sandals. I had glossy lipstick, green eyeshadow, and false eyelashes on.

I thought I was dressed properly for an evening event, but when we arrived at the plaza, I was shocked to see the way girls were dressed. They looked like adult Hijas de María on a Sunday morning, all dolled up in dresses with nylons and high heels. I was the only girl wearing pants. They wore very little makeup, from what I could see when they spoke behind the Spanish lace fans they held up to their faces.

The girls circled the inside of the plaza, their eyes going up and down me as we passed by, their fans hiding their whispers. I felt totally out of place.

Tito gently tapped my arm. "Everyone's going to think you're my *novia*."

I grabbed onto his arm. "So let them think I'm your girl. But why didn't you tell me to wear a dress?"

He tapped my hand to say, *No worries.*

On the outside balusters of the plaza, guys stood under lampposts and benches, watching the girls. A man selling warm roasted peanuts pushed a cart along the street surrounding the plaza, leaving the aroma behind. Tito introduced me to his friends.

One of the guys stared at me. "I remember you. You were the girl from *allá afuera* in grade school."

I shook hands with him and smiled. "I guess I'm still that girl from *allá afuera.*"

My senior year in high school was not what I'd always thought it would be. I couldn't get over the absence of my brother. Frankie became a serial dater with a new girl on his arm every week. I didn't go to any senior activities to avoid seeing him.

Barbara had a one-month-old baby called Nanette when the news came that her boyfriend had been killed in Vietnam. I brought lunch to her in homeroom class when she couldn't bear to see anyone in the cafeteria. Emily took her for a ride in the car, just to get some fresh air, when she couldn't stop crying in the middle of a science lab. Had it not been for our guidance counselor and homeroom teacher's support, Barbara might have not survived.

Carmen was devastated when her niece María's husband was killed just weeks away from the birth of their baby. Taylor's brother came home in a wheelchair. Caridad's brother was killed, and she couldn't go to Puerto Rico for the funeral because she was about to have her third child.

I never spoke about Pablo. I felt that my loss was minor compared to the tragedy everyone around me faced. At least I hadn't had to face a man in a military uniform knocking at my door to tell me my brother was dead. There was still hope, but when I lay awake at night wondering where he might be in the chaotic world I was experiencing, I waited for the DJ to play Jimi Hendrix's "All Along the Watchtower" just to hear that lyric that says: "There must be some kind of way out of here." I knew that was exactly how Pablo had felt when he left.

In February 1969, my letter of acceptance to the University of Massachusetts Amherst arrived. Carmen had given me one of the TV dinner tables to keep all my application papers at hand in my bedroom, and the first thing I did was throw them all up in the air. Then I called Titi Machi and Carol.

"We have to celebrate," Carol said.

Carmen told me to invite a few friends. Stephanie, who had gone to Boston University two years before, was in Woronoco, and I invited her over. Emily came over and surprised me with the news that she was also going to UMass.

"Maybe we can go to the same dorm," she said. We screamed.

I had gotten my driver's license in September when Papá couldn't keep up with Carmen's doctor's appointments. She was pregnant and due at the end of February. Papá left me the car, and we went wherever we wanted. Carmen and I were like sisters. We went shopping in Westfield, we cooked together, she taught me baking and I taught her how to knit, a skill I'd learned from a homeroom teacher. Carmen also calmed my father down when I didn't do exactly what he wanted.

February 18, my brother Julio was born. Carmen sat next to me that morning, while I finished rolling *pastelillo* dough. "We're all done. You're done, I should say, because I've been useless. All we need is to mince some meat and fill them up." And then she wheezed and groaned, and held on to the countertop. "Oh, *Dios mío*, Andreíta, take me to the hospital, I think the baby is coming."

I was a nervous wreck when I called Strathmore and left a message for my father. When he arrived, I was in a waiting room.

"I felt terrible leaving her all alone, but they don't let anyone in there," I said.

"Your mother had you and your brother with a midwife in the mountains of Utuado. At least Carmen is in a hospital." Papá laughed with mischief in his voice. "I'm hoping it's a boy. I had enough with one girl."

"Papá, you're talking like I was a problem for you. If anyone was a problem for you, it was your boy."

"You weren't a problem. That's the way it is, though. You always have to worry about a girl, that no one harms her. But now you're a grown woman, so I don't worry about you anymore."

"I never thought I'd hear you say that. Does that mean I get to drive the car more often?"

"No, sir, it doesn't mean that."

I looked away. "You're not being fair—"

"I'm getting you your own car."

I stared into his eyes, perplexed.

"Yeah. It was Machi and Carol's idea. Those women love you like mothers."

"Papá, what are you talking about? I don't get it."

"You're getting a car from me and Machi soon."

I flew out of my seat and clung to his neck in a hug. "Oh, Papá, that's so amazing. I can't wait. When will you buy it?"

"I can't tell you exactly right now, but soon. It's not a new car, just something *regularcito* so you can get back and forth from college. They say when kids go to college, they never come back. At least I'll have a new little bambino here to keep me busy."

"Papá, stop, I'll always want to see you."

A doctor came to the doorway and called my father. "You have an eight-pound son, sir."

"*Maravilloso, maravilloso,*" Papá whispered. He smiled and smacked his hands on his knees. "Look at that, Andrea, it's a boy."

Our neighbor Don Carlos took me home, and Papá stayed at the hospital until he could see the baby and Carmen. When Carmen came home from the Westfield hospital with my brother Julio in her arms, a new sense of purpose filled my heart.

I wanted a perfect world for my baby brother. I wanted to be there to ensure that he wouldn't need to run away from home one day in order to fulfill his dreams. I would do whatever it took to support my father's marriage so that little Julio would always have a loving home with both parents.

I rocked him to sleep at night and sang him songs I made up just for him, my little brother. While this began to fill my heart and soothe my wounds, I still missed Pablo.

twenty-three

My father and Carmen were moving to Westfield, and I spent the first part of summer helping Carmen pack and care for Julio. And then my father and Machi gave me a 1963 blue AMC Rambler for my birthday, and I was off to college with Emily.

The trees were turning colors when we arrived in September, and every spot on campus had a breathtaking view of the mountains, the town, the lake. Emily and I shared a dorm in Butterfield Hall, and we even took a few classes together.

From my seat on the SST bus to Bartlett Hall for my first class of the day, I saw groups protesting the Vietnam War and military draft. By the time I reached the classroom, I'd been given at least four or five handouts announcing a November 15 march in Washington. As we got closer to the date for the December lottery draft, the campus grew more agitated. A guerilla theater event popped up in front of the Student Union before a scheduled teach-in to discuss why the United States should withdraw from Vietnam. Handouts informed us about buses and other travel arrangements we could use to participate in the march.

It was hard to ignore these young men and women who worked through rain and snow as if their lives depended on convincing us to go to this march. But Emily and I walked by and looked the other way. Was this something we should miss classes for? I was on student aid and was afraid I'd lose my scholarship if I received lower grades. Emily had received a grant for tuition, and her parents were paying her dorm fees. We couldn't risk flunking any courses. But when half a million people marched to Washington in November, and it was hailed as the greatest march in the history of the United States, I knew we were in the midst of something greater than ourselves and felt guilty for not having been there.

Later that year, I was standing in front of the Student Union, waiting for our student representatives to announce their decision to join a national university strike. Through the crowd, I couldn't see the young man who came out with a megaphone. As he announced that the strike would start on Tuesday and listed our demands, something about his voice sounded familiar. He had a Puerto Rican accent.

"The United States of America must put an end to its expansion of the Vietnam War into Laos and Cambodia, their complicity with the war machine, and the oppression of all political dissidents!"

In the midst of cheers and antiwar slogans, he walked into the crowd, and I saw his face. It was Arturo, whom Carol had introduced me to at my father's wedding. He'd grown out his hair and beard. Soon afterward, I was with a crowd in front of Dickinson Hall when someone patted my shoulder. I turned around, and Arturo was there smiling at me. He was stunning. His dark, tan face and black beard contrasted with caramel-colored eyes. He wore black bell-bottom jeans with boots and a gray T-shirt with a black fist on it that said STOP THE WAR. His loose curls were shaped into an afro, and he had a bead necklace that pointed to his fit chest and abs.

He smiled. "Andrea, right? Ms. Weinman introduced us. How are you liking Amherst?"

I was about to start talking when three guys walked toward me, waving, with big smiles. At first, I found their faces familiar, but couldn't tell who they were. Arturo followed my eyes and smiled at them. Then I remembered. Moose and the Mick Jagger wannabe. But who was the other guy with a beard? Ah, yes, it was my childhood neighbor, Pablo's best friend, Mark.

"Oh my God, Mark? I hardly recognized you with that beard. Do you go here?"

Mark laughed. "Yeah. I jumped two grades."

I took a step back. "You what? How come I never knew?"

Mark said he was in engineering and the other two were studying music. I was about to introduce Arturo when everyone laughed.

Moose had a goofy smile. "We all know this guy, Andrea. He leads things here. To get us out of this fucking war."

Arturo smiled. "Hey, guys, there are no leaders here. It's one movement."

Mark squeezed his hands together. "So, uh . . . any news on Pablo?"

I shook my head.

"Man, that sucks. My little buddy."

Kirk looked like a hippie with long hair, bell-bottom pants, and several strands of beads. "Yeah. That stupid Donnie guy."

Jeff, the guy everyone called Moose, shook his head, and whispered, "Little piece of shit was all he was. Pablo shoulda known better. Hey, if you ever need anything, just let us know. Maybe we can share a ride or something to get back home sometime."

Mark pulled a notebook out of his book bag. "Let me know if you hear from Pablo or if you need anything or just want to get together." He wrote down his dorm number. "I'm over in engineering."

Kirk took the paper. "Yeah, let me give her my information too. Let us know, man."

They said goodbye and left.

Arturo looked at me with confusion in his eyes. "So you know those guys from high school?"

"Yes. I've known Mark my entire life. We grew up in the same neighborhood in Woronoco. And you're an organizer?"

"Yes, me and a lot of others like them. Those guys have worked their butts off this year. It hasn't been easy. If you don't inform people, you can't expect them to act, you know? So, *cuéntame*. How long were you in Woronoco?" he asked in Spanish.

When I told Papá that I had a summer job at the library, the phone grew silent.

"I have to make money for food, books, clothes."

"That means I won't see you until Thanksgiving?"

"I can see you for Father's Day."

What my father didn't know was that, for a whole semester, I'd seen Arturo every day. We were either working at the library, in meetings with student antiwar organizations, or having something to eat. Emily went home for the summer. She had a new boyfriend who'd already met her parents in Russell.

"Why don't you stay with me for the summer?" Arturo asked, parking his bike at the rack in front of the library. "You haven't even seen my apartment."

I looked at him over my sunglasses. "I haven't lost anything over there."

"You just translated that from Spanish, and it doesn't sound the same."

I laughed. "You got the message, though. We've only known each other a few months."

⌒

I couldn't have been happier when I visited my father a few weeks later for Father's Day weekend and sat in the living room playing with Julito. He was one and a half now, a whirlwind of excitement. The first thing my father said when he walked through the door was, "You should come over more often."

Later that day, I went to see Machi and Carol. They'd just bought their own home in the Springfield Forest Park area and had a backyard barbecue going when I arrived. Machi gave me an ice-cold Corona beer, we spoke about the war, and I told them about my involvement in the student movement.

"So, what's the surprise news you said you have?" Carol asked.

I smiled, my face flushing.

Machi looked worried. "Oh, I know that face. What happened?"

I didn't know how else to tell them, so I just blurted it out. "I have a boyfriend."

Machi stared at me with her mouth open, then covered her mouth with her hands. Tears filled her eyes.

Carol giggled. "Well, it was going to happen sooner or later, Titi Machi. Is it serious, or are you just dating?"

"He introduced me to his parents at his graduation, and neither one of us is dating anyone else."

Machi's eyebrows were stuck up close to her head. "*Pero, Andrea, ¿y tus estudios?*"

"It's not affecting my studies, Titi. Don't worry about that. He's also very committed to his schoolwork. But there's more to it."

Carol waved a long barbecue fork in her hands. "Spit it out before this one has a heart attack!"

"You know him, Carol. You introduced him to me at Papá's wedding."

Carol gasped. "Is it Arturo? Arturo Molina?"

I nodded.

"Ah, that is one cool kid! So responsible and smart and good. Oooh, and so handsome. I couldn't be happier for you!"

Machi smiled shyly. I hugged her.

"You worry for me, I know. Well, let me tell you something, he's not my first boyfriend. You never knew, but I had one in high school, and I survived."

Carol laughed. "Now you're surprising even me. How did you keep that a secret?"

"I mean, it wasn't much of a relationship. You know how my father is. I barely saw the guy."

Machi turned somber, her lips turned down. "I have to giving you some news."

"Okay?"

She said she'd been in touch with relatives who wrote to her from Puerto Rico.

"Your mother wants to see you and Pablo. She wants to ask your forgiveness."

My gaze met hers, then turned away.

"You don't have to see her. It's up to you."

"But give it some thought. You only have one mother," Carol said. "Maybe you should see her so you can forgive."

"Forgive? She doesn't even know that Pablo's *gone*. How dare she ask to see me. The answer is no."

C────

When I returned to Amherst after Father's Day, Arturo met me in the Butterfield Hall lobby. After we spoke about my mother's reappearance, he insisted that he wanted to meet my family on the Fourth of July weekend.

"Artu, no. I was hoping I could come up with an excuse to stay here and celebrate my birthday with you."

"Why don't we celebrate your birthday with your family? It's only an hour away. I can come back here afterward, and you stay with your family a few days."

"That's not a good idea right now."

"Why? Do you not want me to meet your family?"

"I don't want to have to deal with my father's attitudes right now. He's going to think I haven't known you long enough. And really, I haven't. Let's wait until he doesn't have excuses to go against us."

"What's the problem? I can ask for your hand if that's what you want. All Puerto Ricans are like that. I'll do whatever he wants me to do. I love you, Andrea. This is our life, our future."

I didn't know how to tell Arturo that my father was racist. Would Papá consider him *trigueño* and not have a problem with his color, or was Arturo not white enough? Maybe he'd pull out the bottle of rum, like he'd done with Taylor after a few minutes.

"I don't want any problems with my father right now. He's going to be upset because I haven't finished college. He's protective. I'm all he has left of me and Pablo."

"So, you're going there for Thanksgiving and Christmas?"

This was all so unfair to Arturo. What would he do for Thanksgiving?

True, I wasn't responsible for him, but I was his girlfriend, and his family was in Puerto Rico. It wasn't fair for him to have to spend every holiday alone.

"How about we plan on you meeting him for Thanksgiving? By then, we'll have known each other a whole year."

"I hope we won't have to wait until you finish college, but all right. It's better than nothing."

Socorro and Taylor invited the whole family for a barbecue on the Fourth of July. Uncle Felipe, Caridad, and my aunts were there when I blew out candles on a cake Socorro baked for my twentieth birthday. Papá bragged about my studies to become an English teacher, the scholarships I received, and my grade point average.

"I always thought the boy would be a doctor or a lawyer, you know, something of importance. But life brings us many surprises."

Carmen was putting Julio to bed that evening when, out of sheer spontaneity, I told my father there was a guy in college that I liked.

He nodded and stared at me. "Well, that's something you have to think about very seriously. Sometimes you like a person, but that person isn't the best choice for you. What does this man do?"

"He's a student, three years older than me. He's doing a master's degree and plans on going to law school."

"So, he's over there in Amherst? And where does he live?"

"He has his own apartment, in the little town off campus. We're just friends, Papá, but his parents are in Puerto Rico, and I was wondering if he could spend Thanksgiving with us. Remember Mark Abbot from Woronoco? He knows him too. He doesn't have to stay here. He could stay with Titi Machi."

"¿Puertorriqueño?"

"Yes, Papá. He was at your wedding." I took a picture of Arturo out of my wallet. He had his hair pulled back and was wearing a button-down shirt. "I didn't know him then, but Carol has known him for a long time. He went to school where she works, at Tech High School, in Springfield." I showed the picture to my father.

Papá stared at him and shook his head. "But this man has *pelo malo*. This man is Black." He threw the picture on the coffee table. "Of all the men at that enormous university you had to pick the one that's Black?"

"Papá, I know you think Blacks and whites shouldn't mix, but in Puerto Rico, we're all mixed."

"Other Puerto Ricans are mixed, that's true, but not me. Not my family. My family comes from Spain. That's why you have blonde hair and blue eyes. No. There are no negroes in my family, and I'd like to keep it that way."

"But that's not true. Socorro is *trigueña*. Her mother was not white, and your brother Bartolo married her. Bautista is very dark, I wouldn't even call him *trigueño*, and Perfecta married him. And what about Machi?"

"Machi doesn't count in this because she's not my family, she's your mother's family, and even that can be argued. Nobody in my family has *pelo malo*. None of those people you mentioned. They may be a little dark, but they can comb their hair. That's the difference. Understand? And I don't care what anyone else in the family has done. I'm talking about *my* daughter. My house, not theirs."

"Papá, I'm not looking at the texture of a man's hair when I meet him. I don't understand how you go to church and call yourself a Christian and then talk like this."

"I don't want you to have children that can't comb their hair, children that will be embarrassed of their father when they walk outside with their blonde, blue-eyed mother. I don't want that for you."

I was so angry, I stuttered. "Doesn't what I want even matter here? You always told me if I was in love with a man, you didn't care if he had *bembas*, don't you remember that? You said all you wanted was a hardworking man. He's a good person, Papá. You're not keeping your word."

"That was only a saying, not something literal. I wanted you to bring me a hardworking man, that's all. I never meant for you to go find the blackest man in all of Massachusetts and bring him here."

Carmen, who'd been standing at the doorway, came in and picked up the picture. "Oh, he's a good-looking *muchacho*. He's not Black, he's *trigueñito*. And his hair doesn't look *malo*. Luis, you're exaggerating."

"I wish you'd both stop it with this *pelo malo* thing," I said. "There is no good or bad hair. It's just hair. This isn't acceptable."

Papá got up from the sofa. "Well, he's not courting you in my house. I don't have anything against Black people. But Black people should marry Black people, and white people should marry white people. That's my belief, and it won't change."

I cracked my knuckles as I paced back and forth. "Papá, I've tried so hard to understand you. I get that you were brought up this way, but you have to look at reality. I'm not going to let you decide who my friends are, who I date, or who I marry. And if I fall in love with a Black man, you are not going to stop me from marrying him."

"I knew there was a reason why you were visiting Machi and Carol. That man has been coming over there all along, hasn't he? I bet that Carol was the one that found him for—"

"She did no such thing. I found him myself. I only came to know him in college. You're not even considering the fact that he already has his degree, that he's doing his master's degree? None of that matters to you more than the color of his skin?"

"That's exactly what I'm saying. I'll tell you something right now. If you marry a Black, you can forget about me."

Carmen gasped. "Luis, what are you doing? *Esto es innecesario.*"

"I'm done trying to please you, Papá. Have it your racist, cruel way, all to yourself."

I ran into the bedroom and packed my bag. Carmen ran after me. "*Ay Dios mío, mija*, don't pay attention to him. He'll regret it tomorrow, don't do anything, please, *cálmate.*"

"Those are the exact words I said to Pablo the night he left. I'm sorry to upset you, Carmen, but he'll never learn, and I can't live my life trying to please him anymore."

When I walked into Machi's house that night, I didn't have to tell her what happened. She looked at me and hugged me. She whispered calming sounds, her strong, heavy hand gliding over my head in long, gentle strokes, soothing my pain away the same way she had done when I was a child.

The next day, I left for Amherst. Arturo was surprised when I knocked at his door.

I walked in and placed my bag on the floor. "Can I stay here with you?"

He looked shocked. "Well, of course. I keep asking you to. What's wrong?"

I sat on the sofa and looked around his apartment, tears in my eyes. "Papá is so difficult."

"You told him about us?"

I put my head down on his sofa. Arturo took my shoes off and brought me a pillow. "You look . . . tired. You don't have to tell me."

twenty-four

The United States invaded Laos six months later, and our country's political climate caught on fire. This certainly showed in February 1971, when massive marches took place in every major city and college in the country, including UMass. Arturo continued to lead the student movement and often had meetings in New Haven. During the protests, helicopters flew overhead, snapping pictures of us, and thousands were arrested across the country. But after days of protesting punctuated by Arturo's graduate studies, me being a sophomore, hours of work in the library, and more hours of handing out leaflets, Arturo and I had takeout and planned our summer wedding.

It was Memorial Day weekend when Machi and Carol visited us in Amherst, and my aunt told me she had spoken to my mother again.

I didn't say anything.

"And I told her you're in college and doing well, and I mentioned Arturo and your wedding."

"Titi, I don't have a problem with you telling her whatever you want. She's your sister."

"Well, she asked if she could come to the wedding."

My mouth dropped.

"She was never there for me, and now she wants to show up on the most important day of my life?"

"I understand, I understand, but I have to tell you because she asked. So, what do you want me to say to her?"

"I don't want to see her, and especially not on that day. Please, Titi."

I sat on the sofa shaking my head, thinking, *Not this shit again*. My father, whom I adored, wouldn't be there; I hadn't seen him for almost a year, and he didn't even know that I was getting married. And Machi expected me to let this woman, who now wanted to be my mother, walk right back into my life?

Carol saw the disgust and anger on my face.

"You don't have to do anything you don't want to do—"

"Then why is she bringing this up *again*?"

Carol stared at the floor, then looked up at me. "Because this is about your mother. She's not just any old person, she's your mother. And you can choose to ignore her. But you only have one wedding day and one mother."

Arturo walked behind the sofa and massaged my shoulders gently. "Babe. Just let it go. As far as I'm concerned, whoever wants to come to the wedding is welcome. Let her come, and then we'll leave and you won't see her again."

"I don't think it works that way," I said. "After the wedding, then she's going to want to come here to visit us, see me, see our kids . . . There will be no end to this. But all right. Go ahead and tell her she can come, but I'm telling all of you right now. It's no more than a hello and goodbye from me."

"Is okay," Machi said in English.

⌒

Our wedding was far from a traditional wedding with a white gown and veil. I wore a light-pink dress made in India with a pair of strappy brown sandals. As I brushed my hair, Machi stood behind me in a light-blue pant-suit and white sandals, and placed a little crown of flowers on my head as the photographer took a picture.

"Remember when I braided your hair for school in the mornings?"

I grabbed onto her. "Oh, my Titi." My eyes blurred. "Pablo and my father aren't here, but you are."

A door creaked open. "And so am I," Socorro said. She hugged Machi and me, and we all laughed.

"I'm so fortunate to have had both of you," I said.

"Well, I was here first," Socorro said, teasing Machi.

"Um, nope, no, no, I don't think so," Machi said.

"Here in Massachusetts, I was," Socorro said.

"Okay, okay, I'll give you that, but don't forget who they lived with as children in Puerto Rico."

They pushed at each other's arms in a playful way as I put my lipstick on.

"We were a good team, Titi Machi," Socorro said.

Machi peeked out the window. "And we're not done yet."

"Is she here?" I asked, in English.

"No. Just your friend from Russell with the baby getting out of the car."

Carol walked in. "Oh, sweet darling, you look gorgeous, gorgeous. The judge is here."

"Where's Arturo?" I asked.

"He's out there looking as handsome as ever, white poet shirt and beads and bell-bottoms. You make such a perfect couple."

Machi stood at the window. "There's your friend Emily and the musicians now," she said in Spanish.

"And what about my mother? She hasn't called or anything? Are you sure she has the right address?"

"Yes. I sent it to her in writing. And we moved the wedding to the afternoon so she'd have plenty of time to get here. So she should be here any minute."

"Who's bringing her, anyway? I doubt she ever learned to drive a car."

Machi did not take her eyes off the window, the curtain in her hand. "A cousin of ours."

Carol returned. "Everyone on your list is here."

"Arturo's parents? Are they here and seated and taken care of?"

"Yes, they are," Carol said.

"So what are we waiting for?"

"We're waiting on your mother," Carol said.

I stared at myself in the mirror.

Through the laundry window, I saw Carol organizing the wedding party on the side of the house. The judge was up ahead speaking to someone who

I thought was Arturo, but I couldn't see him. I could see his best man, his friend Ernesto, the guy who'd taken him to my father's wedding, behind him. Emily, my bridesmaid, paired with Mark, behind them. Socorro and Vivian were trying to keep Ismaelito from getting his clothes dirty before their roles as flower girl and ring bearer.

I ran to the bedroom and looked in the mirror one last time. Carol came in. "Are you ready? We're all set out there."

"It's time to go," Machi said in Spanish. "If she comes, she comes, and if not, well, we gave her the opportunity she wanted. *Vámonos.*"

"I'm ready," I said and stood up.

Machi handed me a bouquet of flowers, kissed my forehead, the photographer took pictures, and we headed out the door. The minute I stepped onto the ground, I heard a child's voice calling, "Andy, Andy, Andy." At first I thought it was Ismaelito, but it was Julio running to my arms. I swept him off the floor. "Julito, my little Julito." Carmen smiled and kissed me. *"Felicidades, mija."* And there was my father up ahead of me, patting Arturo on the back, welcoming him into the family, kissing Machi, hugging Emily.

When Papá walked up to me, I almost dropped my flowers, my eyes watering when he hugged me. Machi straightened my crown of flowers. And then my father kissed me and said, in Spanish, "I'm here to *entregarte, mi hija,* you have my blessing. God bless your marriage."

Machi stepped in front of us as the maid of honor and I walked down the side of her house with my hand deep under Papá's arm, my small bouquet in my other hand as he handed me over to the love of my life on July 27, 1971.

As soon as the ceremony was over, Arturo introduced my father to his parents and sniffles came from all corners of the backyard. Most of my friends knew of the falling-out I'd had with my father and were glad to see him there.

Barbara Kelley, my friend from Gateway Regional High School, came with a new boyfriend and her toddler, Nanette, who was now nearly three. Jennifer, also from Gateway, had also brought a date. Kirk and Jeff were there, as were Artu's friends Karen and Judy. Carmen's niece María, the girl from Westfield who'd lost her husband in Vietnam, came with a baby and her sister, Myrna.

There were flowers on tables, in hanging containers, and along the side of the house leading from the driveway to the backyard. A group of Puerto Rican musicians, whom Machi had met when she was a farmworker and lived in Holyoke, played *música jíbara*. Arturo and I had paid for a Puerto Rican catering service, and his parents had paid for the beautiful cake that we'd ordered with real flowers on top. We danced and sang and rejoiced all afternoon, until it was time for us to leave for our honeymoon. Papá called Arturo over and handed him an envelope.

"For your trip," he said, and patted him on the back.

Arturo thanked him, I gave him a big hug, trying not to cry, and we jumped in the car. We stayed in a hotel in Boston that night, and were on a plane to Florida the next day, where we'd spend our honeymoon in Key West. I turned to Arturo when we got settled on the plane.

"She never showed up."

He squeezed my hand.

twenty-five

Arturo and I graduated in the spring of 1973. He was offered the teaching job he had always wanted in the political sciences department at Boston University, and we moved to the city a few weeks after graduation. I was twenty-three years old when my son, Andrés, was born during a snowstorm in Boston. We lived in a brownstone apartment in the South End with two bedrooms and a beautiful bay window in the living room.

One evening in February 1975, I had just put Andrés to bed and Arturo was doing dishes when the phone rang at nine o'clock in the evening.

Arturo answered the phone. "It's your father," he said.

I ran to the phone, startled. My father never called after seven.

"Papá? ¿*Cómo estás?* Is everything okay?"

"Everything is fine, *mija*. I have important news for you. They found your brother."

⌒

I drove from Boston to Marcy, New York, in February 1975 to see my brother. A female guard who looked as if she'd never smiled in her life patted me down, and when I asked why I had to remove my bra, she said, "This is a correctional facility, ma'am." Then a guard led me to a meeting room and closed the door.

I sat in a metal chair, shivering, and stretched my old worn-out blue sweater over my hands. But no one came. I walked to the glass-paned door, hoping to see someone. There was a corridor with paint peeling off the wall and old linoleum with grayish wax built up around the corners. On one side, the hallway continued out of sight. On the other, a sign read PSYCHI-ATRIC CENTER with an arrow pointing down the hallway. Was this a psychiatric ward or was the sign pointing to the other end of the building? My mouth dried.

A metallic clanging grew louder, and keys jingled at the door. Two guards came in, carrying Pablo by the arms.

A guard addressed me. "Miss Andrea Inés Rodríguez?"

"Yes, sir."

"Mr. Pablo Luis Rodríguez. This is a fifteen-minute meeting, ma'am."

The sight of my brother made it hard to sound positive, but I tried. "Pablo," I said, trying to smile. "I'm so happy to see you. How are you?"

Dressed in a blue prison uniform, he had difficulty standing, heavy chains around his ankles and cuffs around his wrists. The guards assisted him into a chair. He appeared half asleep, and it seemed like he was looking right through me.

"Pablo, it's been a long time. I drove from Boston to see you. What's going on?" I got up and moved toward him, my arms outstretched. But as soon as I got close, a guard stepped up, his hand coming out of nowhere, stopping in front of my face. "No physical contact, ma'am. You must remain seated at the table."

I returned to the chair. They stood behind him, next to the door, staring somewhere else. I called my brother's name repeatedly, but he didn't answer me. His black hair was cut in jagged asymmetrical strips, patches shaved off. He made only a slight gesture. A guard watched his move. "Keep your hands on the table, Mr. Rodríguez. On the table."

I feared the fifteen minutes would end without a word out of him, and I asked him to look at me. He didn't. He sat there, unresponsive, with grayish burns on his fingertips and half-shaved eyebrows.

"What happened to him?" I asked the guards. They stared into space without even a glance at me. "Sir, please, why is his hair cut like that? And his fingertips are burned. Please, tell me what happened to him."

The guards didn't move or respond.

"I'm sorry, but I'm not understanding what's going on here. Are you not allowed to speak? Look, I just want to help my brother."

"Ma'am," a guard said, "in response to your questions, he's done all that himself."

"We're only here to protect him," the other guard said.

They both stared at the walls again. But what were they protecting him from? Had someone assaulted him?

Pablo scratched his hands, his metal cuffs rolling across the table. He lifted his head and squinted. I waited, motionless, holding my breath until his gaze dissolved into a curious stare.

"Pablo, it's me, Andrea, your sister."

At first, I wasn't sure if he recognized me—until a lopsided smile appeared on his face, the same smile I'd known for as long as I could remember.

"Andrea. You found me."

"Course I found you," I said. "Papá called yesterday, and I came out here right away. What's this all about? Tell me. We only have a few minutes before these guys take you away."

"I killed him, sis. Don't be mad. Don't tell Mom either. She won't understand. But I killed him."

"What are you talking about?"

"No one understands, Andrea, nobody but you."

"No. No, I don't understand."

He looked over his shoulder. "You know who I'm talking about?"

"No. I don't."

"I lived with that fucking bully for long enough, sis. But now I'm free."

His eyes were fixed on me with a look of satisfaction. I didn't know what to do next, and I worried that time would run out and I still wouldn't have the slightest clue why he was imprisoned.

Pablo laughed, gave me a dramatic stare, laughed louder, and continued laughing. There was no way I could have a reasonable conversation with him. Our time was up, no one was giving me answers, and I had no idea what to do next. He pointed at me, faced the ceiling, and howled. Then he smiled as if he'd accomplished something. "That's my sister, Andrea."

"Rodríguez, let's go," a guard said.

I rose from the table, my whole body shaking. "Please, don't take him. Please, just a few more minutes, just a little more time, please."

"He already had several extra minutes, ma'am," a guard said.

He laughed as they dragged him out. Then they closed the door and turned the lock. The clanging of my brother's chains faded in the distance. I put my head on the table, the sound of fluorescent lights humming above, the stench of an ashtray burning my nose.

The door squeaked open. Someone walked in, pulled a chair, and sat at the table. A soft-spoken man introduced himself as Dr. Khatri.

"How much longer does my brother have to complete his sentence?"

"Your brother doesn't have a sentence."

"There are no charges against my brother?"

"I don't have his legal history, but we can put you in touch with his attorney. I've been his doctor for the past six months. He's boasted about killing someone since the first day he came a year ago, but he was never accused of murder. So he has received treatment and eventually the charges were dropped. That was before I came in."

"My brother has been here a whole year even though he's never been charged with a crime and was receiving treatment for—"

"Schizophrenia."

"He has schizophrenia?"

"Yes."

Memories of Pablo riding his bike next to me flashed through my mind, interrupted by images of his lethargic appearance and manic laughter that day.

"I don't understand. He was always a straight-A student. He never had mental problems."

"His grades and previous mental condition don't matter. The cause of this is still unknown in the scientific community. He has admitted to a history of substance abuse for the past four years, which can trigger episodes. We've been working on adjusting his medications to find the best treatment. At this point, I want to focus on what he can do with the rest of his life. Twenty-three years old makes him a very young man."

"What do you mean, 'focus on what he can do'?"

"There is no reason for him to be here once we find the right combination of medications."

"How long does that take?"

"A few days. These medications become less effective over time and have to be adjusted periodically. Once he has a doctor that he sees regularly, he will be monitored closely, and these changes won't be as noticeable."

"Where will you send him?"

"I want to send him home. But he has no home."

"He has family. We haven't seen him in years—he just got up and left one day. But he has us, and we love him."

He smiled. "We can't release him unless a relative is willing to assume his custody. He'll be on probation. It's routine."

"Why weren't we notified that he could leave?"

"We have no relatives on file."

"Dr. Khatri, he disappeared."

"I understand. I'm sure we can verify your relationship with the right paperwork. I'm sure you've missed him."

"I love my brother. When I heard he was here, I came the next day. But I don't know anything about schizophrenia. Can he live with me and my husband? My father? Does he have to see a doctor regularly? Where do I start?"

The doctor looked through my brother's file.

"He can live a relatively normal life. There are programs out there that will help you. His parole officer will assist you. Are you interested in processing his release?"

"Release to where?"

"That's a family matter. But you would have to be his legal custodian for the time he's on parole."

"You're saying he can come home? To my home?"

"Why, yes, of course."

A guard knocked at the door and asked when the room would be available for another family.

Dr. Khatri got up and led me to the door. "The paperwork takes time and it's important for you to initiate the process now so that you don't have to return before his release. In a day or two, a parole officer will contact you, and soon after, your brother will be on his way home."

I filled out the paperwork for my brother's release. Even though I didn't understand the consequences of his illness and senseless imprisonment, there was no measure for my happiness.

C

I drove to the hotel and called Arturo. "How's your brother doing?" he asked.

"Pablo will be coming home."

"Oh, wow. I bet your father will be glad to hear that. How did they decide that?"

I explained everything I'd learned. "He wasn't under arrest for anything, and he can go home. He's been in treatment, and with the right meds, he doesn't have to be in a hospital anymore."

"Have you told your father?"

"No. I wanted to tell you first."

"Don't you think you should've asked him first?"

"Asked him what? He's my brother. I was the one there. I had to make the decision."

"But if he's going to his house, don't you think he should've had some say in this?"

I was silent for a few minutes. This wasn't going the way I expected. "Arturo, honey, Pablo will come to our house. I'm sorry if you think I should've asked you first, but I didn't have time to think about this."

"Andrea, how will that work? We have a one-year-old. I'm teaching, grading papers. They expect me to be doing research to publish a book. I can't take care of Andrés and do all of this. I'm being evaluated for tenure. You don't even know what your brother will be like. And where's he going to sleep?"

"I've already thought of that. We can move the crib into our room."

"That's not a good idea. Not good for the baby. Or for us."

"It's not forever. It's just until he gets his feet on the ground. I was expecting you to be supportive. This is my brother. You know how much I've missed him and how much he means to me."

"I want to be, but there's only so much we can do. I'm just trying to be realistic here. Your brother might need a lot more help than we can provide, and we don't even have a spare room for him."

"This is only temporary. What else do you expect me to do? Leave my brother locked up in an institution when he hasn't done anything wrong and can function in society with a few meds?"

"Who's going to give your brother the time he needs? You're working now."

"Arturo, you're an only child. You don't know the love of a brother and a sister. Pablo was the only person I had in the world for most of my life—"

"Until he took off. Don't idealize him, Andrea. He took off with nothing but the clothes on his back and never even called you, not once in eight years."

"I don't know what the story is."

"So where was he for all those years?"

"Arturo. Stop. I'm not leaving my brother stranded in a prison. And if you can't or won't cooperate with me, I'll figure out a way to help him without counting on you."

"We'll do what we can, and hopefully we can get him back on his own two feet. I'm just trying to reason with you."

"I have to call my father now."

"I love you. Drive home safely in the morning, and if it starts snowing again, stay over there another night."

Arturo didn't understand that a brother and sister would live under a rock, in a cave, under a bridge, for each other. Maybe I'd expected too much from my husband, especially since he didn't have siblings. Maybe he was right about Pablo and the way he left without a care for my father or me. But Arturo didn't know what it had been like to live in Woronoco as a teenager, to meet my father's demands. I called my father and told him everything.

My father's deep breaths came through the phone. "God help you, *mija*. I wish you hadn't taken this on your shoulders; we could have found another solution. *Es. Qui. Zo. frenia. Esquizofrenia*," he whispered in Spanish. "*Dios mío*, that's the worst mental failure a person can have. *Santo Dios*, they say that the person who has that changes into another person from one moment to the next. I guess that's exactly what has happened. He's acting like someone we've never seen before."

But there was no question in my mind that I was doing the right thing by bringing my brother home. Arturo, though . . . That was going to be a struggle.

I remembered the lonely whistle of the train in Woronoco before Arturo was in my life. I didn't want to lose my husband, but Pablo needed me.

We'll work things out, Pablo. We'll work them out.

twenty-six

Pablo arrived at a bus station in Boston on a Monday afternoon in June, and we drove home with the sun shining in our faces and the radio on in my blue Honda. Arturo greeted us on the steps of our South End apartment. I had prepared dinner, made an apple pie, and bought strawberry ice cream, Pablo's favorite. He ate, went to bed, and slept through the night into midday.

For the first few days, he didn't say much. He would smile at Andrés and stroke his head. For most of the day, he sat on a wooden box on the fire escape, smoking cigarettes and gazing into the distance.

When he was silent, I didn't pressure him into a conversation. He was easily startled, stared at strangers with mistrust, and didn't want to go outdoors. I cooked Puerto Rican meals that he hadn't eaten in years and pounded spices for *sofrito* with my mortar and pestle.

One afternoon while Andrés was in a playpen next to the dining room table, he sat on the living room rug and went through a crate of records.

"You like Jackson Browne?" he asked.

"I do. You've heard him?"

"Course."

"You mean you listened to music in . . . in New York?"

"Radio. Never get to see the album covers, though."

He brought a record over. "Can you play this? 'Late for the Sky,' I've heard this song."

"You have? That just came out last year."

I covered the rice, lowered the heat on the *habichuelas guisadas,* and placed the record on the turntable. He rested his head on the wall, closed his eyes, and sang along with the song. I returned to the aromas of cilantro in my kitchen and set Andrés on the floor. Pablo changed the record and sang along to "Doctor My Eyes." He came into the kitchen. "He talks to the soul, sis, doesn't he?"

"Yes, that's why I like him."

"Sometimes you don't know how to say something, and you hear your heart in one of his songs."

"Yes, he's like a poet."

"My life has practically gone to waste. But now it's almost like all those years never happened."

I hugged him. "I have the same feeling. Like no time has passed because you're here now."

Arturo came home, kissed me, and picked up the baby. "How are you liking Boston, Pablo?"

Pablo smiled. "It's big. I'm not used to it, you know?"

"Bah, you'll find your way around in no time. And there's no rush. Just relax and enjoy yourself. You two have a lot of catching up to do."

"Thank you, *cuñao*. I really appreciate everything you and my sister are doing for me."

I sat Andrés in his high chair and fed him peas and carrots with grilled chicken.

Arturo served dinner. "Pablo, how about we go for a walk after dinner? The weather is spectacular today. It's usually unbearably hot at this time of year."

"That's a great idea," I said. "I'm dying to take him to Harvard Square, Faneuil Hall, the Charles River."

Pablo smiled. "Can we do that another day? I just don't know how I'm going to feel out there."

"We're not going on that street in the back," Arturo said. "It's kind of a rush out there, people running back and forth to the train. We'd be walking on the street out front, the one you see from the bay window in the living room. See the trees? But we can go another day if you prefer."

Pablo smiled and sighed with relief. "Okay, okay, I'll take you up on that, bro."

I served myself a piece of apple pie and ate while feeding some to Andrés. "You're free now, Pablo. You can forget everything that happened and create a whole new life any way you want it to be. Remember when we went to Faeries Meadow, and you talked about the plans you had to go to college and all that?"

Pablo smiled and stared at me for a long time, like he was reminiscing. "Faeries Meadow. Yup. I wish I could pick things up right back there."

He helped me clear off the kitchen counter and place leftovers in the fridge. "Have you heard at all from Theresa?" he asked.

"Who?"

"Theresa Gerou. Remember her?"

"Theresa Gerou? Nah, I haven't heard from anyone from grade school in years except for Emily. Oh, wait, I take that back. And Mark."

"Mark? Waaaoooooow. Mark, my little buddy. I'd like to see him."

"He's working for an engineering firm in Brazil."

Pablo nodded without taking his eyes off of me. "Always said he wanted to be an engineer, didn't he? Did you see anyone else we know at UMass?"

"I did. Remember Kirk? He's acting in LA. And Jeff, remember him? He's a music teacher in Northampton."

Pablo laughed. "Moose. Man, that guy was so cool. He holds his cards well, you know? Knew how to get in trouble without raising any waves."

"The damn nut is a poet. Published in a few magazines while we were in college."

"What about Kevin?"

"Kevin went to Philly. I'm not sure what he does now. We didn't stay in touch."

"And your friends Stephanie and Emily?"

"Emily went to school with me. She studied history and is a teacher in Springfield now. Stephanie, I lost touch with. Heard she married a guy at Strathmore and lives in Blandford."

Pablo looked tired. "Did I ever tell you I kissed her?"

"Who, Stephanie?"

"No, Theresa."

"Oh, yes, Theresa. Right. When was that, seventh grade? You dated a lot of girls afterward, though, didn't you?"

He nodded and smiled. "I'm sure she remembers. You know the way kids are—they might be kids, but they still have dreams. And I was her first love."

I felt for my brother, holding on to a childhood dream. "You'll make new dreams, Pablo. You have a whole life ahead of you."

A week after he arrived, I was scheduled to return to my part-time job as an instructor in a GED program for Hispanic migrant workers in the North End. Arturo and I lay awake the night before.

He held his hands over his head on a stack of pillows. "So how is it going with your brother?"

"Fine. I think he's fine. We have meetings with his probation officer and a psychiatrist in the next few weeks. And he's spoken with my dad over the phone."

"Has he left the house at all yet?"

"No. But he's going to have to go to those appointments, so we'll see how that goes."

"What's he going to do all day here by himself when you're back at work and Andrés is at daycare?"

"I don't know. Probably listen to the radio, listen to music. This must be like an oasis for him. I think his mind just needs to adjust."

"Have you noticed anything, you know, weird?"

"Aside from looking tired sometimes, I don't see anything wrong with him. I think he's eventually going to be close to normal. Have you noticed anything?"

"Well, he's not totally with it, Andrea. He's like, off in his own world, not here, you know. Whenever I try to have a conversation with him, he just looks at me and smiles."

"I think he's being self-aware. People probably haven't talked to him much since he went to prison."

"It's going to make it difficult for him to be in a public environment, though."

"We'll see. It hasn't even been two weeks since he got here. And the probation officer told me he'll have to attend group therapy sessions."

When I returned from work the next day, I found that Pablo had read halfway through a child psychology book he'd taken from my shelf. He'd dropped out of school, but he still had the intelligence that characterized him throughout our childhood.

Every day while I was at work, he read from that book until he finished it, and after Andrés went to sleep, we discussed what he'd read.

Pablo had become an avid reader in prison and was very informed about everything going on in the world. He read the newspaper voraciously. This added to my belief that he could obtain the college degree he'd always wanted. I could help him go through the GED test. But I didn't mention any of this to him; I didn't want him feeling unnecessary pressure. He was still fragile.

I thought a good place to start getting Pablo out of the house would be going to Westfield to visit our father. Pablo had never seen Papá's current home or met his wife, Carmen, and our six-year-old brother, Julio. But even though Papá called him every few days and told him he was eager to see him, Pablo didn't want to make the trip.

It was July when I insisted that we visit our father.

"You go ahead and leave me here. I'll be fine," Pablo said.

"But you've been in this apartment for a whole month, other than those appointments. Do you have a problem with seeing Papá?"

"Of course not."

"Then what's the matter? Didn't you ever get outdoors in New York?"

Pablo stood at the kitchen window lighting a cigarette. "It isn't the same. I knew that place like the back of my hand. I don't know anything here."

"I understand. But you were fine when we went to see the parole officer and the doctor."

"Maybe it seemed that way. I was shaking inside."

"Ah, so you were nervous. That's to be expected. That was the first time, but it will wear off. We have to get you ready for your group therapy sessions. We can take a short drive or walk for a block. Why don't you start by coming along to buy your cigarettes, then? Come on. Let's go before I pick up my boy."

We walked to the corner store. From the moment we left the building until we returned, Pablo's hands were sweating, and he kept glancing behind his back, turning around in circles to see whatever and whoever was around us. People stared at him, some even crossing the street to avoid him. I assured him this would get better in time.

One evening, he reminisced about the kids we'd gone to school with.

"Do you remember the party at the lake? Frankie and Theresa were there. All the kids thought we were so cool that day, remember?"

"What I remember was feeling out of place with everyone except Emily and Stephanie. We didn't have anything in common with the kids from Russell."

"They were nice to us."

"Emily and Steph? Yeah, but they weren't from Russell. They grew up in the Beehive, like us. Pablo, I graduated from high school with those kids. Sure, everyone was nice, but they were the Americans, and I was the Puerto Rican, or they were the kids from Russell, and I was the girl from the Beehive. Those differences never went away."

"You didn't make friends with anyone. You were a bookworm."

"I did have friends! Eventually. But let's face it. The Woronoco Beehive and Russell were worlds apart. The kids from our schools lived in homes their parents owned with carpeting and wood paneling. Their mothers served ice cream and grilled in the backyard on the weekends. They had beautiful clothes and went to the hairdresser."

"Those kids would've been our friends our whole lives if I hadn't taken off."

"It's not that simple."

"I would've stayed in touch with them. They weren't the problem. Dad and his ancient ways were the problem."

"You have a point there. But nobody knows who would've stayed in touch with who or what might've happened. We only know what happened, Pablo. You left. You didn't even stay in touch with your own family."

Pablo nodded and walked over to the bay window.

I worried that I was being too harsh. "I dated Frankie, you know."

"Oh, I knew you would. For how long? Why did you break up?"

"It was only a few months. He let basketball go to his head. He had girls all over him, and he cheated, so I stopped seeing him. Plus, his mother told him she didn't want him dating a Puerto Rican."

He chewed on his lip. "The Russell kids were what we wanted our whole life. To be friends with them. To live like them, like normal Americans."

"We already were normal Americans. We just didn't know it. Everyone came here from other countries, just like we did."

"I wanted to get married and raise a family in Russell my whole life. I wanted my ashes to be thrown into Salmon Falls. I still want that, sis."

"There's nothing wrong with that. But if all of that was so important to you, then why the hell did you leave? You and I had goals, remember? What was important enough to take that away?"

Pablo nodded like he knew I wasn't going to let him off the hook. "You kept your end of the plan, didn't you?"

"I've done my best. But you were the smart one. I still have to kill myself for an A."

"You got your BA?"

"Yes, I did."

"Good. That's good, sis. And Arturo's a prof, right?"

"At BU. When are you going to tell me where the hell you went?"

"I spent some time with Donnie, his—"

"I knew you were with that fucking asshole. Papá saw him once, and he ran. To this day, if I saw him, I'd want to spit in his face."

"He wasn't a bad person, Andrea. Just a kid with no parents. We headed to Florida in a stolen car."

"Florida? I thought you were going to California. You know how many times I saw crowds of teenagers, hippies in LA on television, and stared at the crowd, thinking maybe I'd see your face?"

Pablo sat in the recliner. "I'm sorry, sis. Never made it to California. It was too far. A lot of us went to Florida instead. Slept on the beach in Fort Lauderdale for weeks, under a bridge. Then Donnie took off, and that turned to years for me. Under bridges, looking for scraps of food. Then I was a dishwasher in a commune, and honestly, I can't remember a lot of what happened after that." Pablo lit another cigarette.

"Hey, you're smoking way too much." I opened a window. "Hold off for a few minutes, will you?"

Pablo put the cigarette out in the ashtray. "Then I headed to San Francisco with a group, must've been like two hundred. In cars. On motorcycles."

"And not once did you think of calling us?" My voice broke. "I cried for years. Socorro, Machi, we all cried and prayed for you."

Pablo looked pained and smacked the cigarette box. "Maybe those prayers are what saved me."

"Papá got so depressed. I thought he'd kill himself driving on Old Woronoco Road. He was drunk for days. You never called. Not once. You weren't there for my high school graduation. You weren't there when I got acceptance letters for college. You weren't even there for my wedding."

"I made some bad choices, sis—"

"You sure as hell did."

"I'm sorry you had to go through all of that alone. I'm so sorry, Andrea. I wish I could take it all back."

"I see you standing here now, but the pain still hasn't left me, you know."

"Don't say that. I thought of you all the time. I was taken in by a group of kids. We were all on drugs. Everyone ran out of money, and we were starving. Eventually, I got stranded somewhere in upstate New York. Spent months in a cabin with, like, twenty people. Some of them raided supermarkets, and that's how we got food, until one day we got busted. To be honest, going to prison saved my life. Bad way to get put up for the night, but it's the truth. I always missed you and Papá. I'm sorry I hurt both of you so bad."

I went into the kitchen and wiped my tears with a napkin. "You're back. That's all that matters."

"Do you forgive me?"

"There's nothing to forgive. But if you want everyone to be happy, then let's visit Papá. He's dying to see you."

"We can go from there to Russell."

"Papá lives in Westfield now, Pablo."

"Oh, that's right, he moved. That's still not far, we used to go there on our bikes. I hitchhiked there practically every day. Can we visit Russell? Maybe someone can tell me where to find Theresa."

I wanted to tell my brother to forget about our high school classmates. He was stuck in that moment eight years ago.

"Pablo, she's probably married now, with kids, living somewhere else. Even if not, I doubt she wants to see either of us." I laughed, but Pablo didn't seem to find it funny.

"All right, Pablo, we can think about it. Let's go see Papá. Let's spend the night at his house. We can go to Russell the next day if it means that much to you."

Pablo gave me a big smile and thumbs-up, walked to the fire escape, and sat on the steps. *If only he had some faith in himself,* I thought. But maybe he had to return home to find closure before he could move on.

For the next few days, Arturo made it a point to take Pablo to the corner store. I set the the clock to ring when he had to take his meds, and he did so diligently. I laid off from emotional conversations and avoided disagreements with him. Most of the time, he seemed completely normal.

I was finishing up a meeting with several other teachers one afternoon in August when I noticed a police officer standing at the door with our agency director. As soon as I looked at him, he signaled me to come over, and I knew it was about my brother. After introducing himself and confirming my identity, he said Pablo was out of control and posed a danger to the community. I grabbed my purse and rushed into his car, and he drove me a few blocks to my street.

As we neared the brownstone apartment buildings, a crowd had gathered, yelling and obstructing transit. A police officer directed traffic around it. I ran out of the car and pushed my way through. Pablo stood in the middle of the street, screaming and brandishing a wooden cane like a sword in people's faces. "Stay away from me, or I'll shove this motherfucker up your ass!"

He pointed the cane at a young man who taunted him to get closer, jumping like a chicken. "Come on, you jerk," the man said. Some people laughed while others looked afraid as Pablo tried to make his way through to the guy, screaming, "Get out of my way!"

I called out to him but couldn't get his attention, and for a moment, I feared I'd be the one he hit with the cane. I stayed as close to him as I could and continued shouting his name, the police officer stood behind me. Pablo pushed me out of his way.

At that point, I was afraid the officer would arrest him. "Pablo, Pablo, you're in Boston with me, Andrea."

The police dispersed the crowd and tried persuading my brother to give up the cane. When he saw people walking away, he stopped yelling. An older woman asked him for the cane, he smiled at her and handed it over as if there had never been a problem. As he followed me home, the woman walked next to us and told me that earlier, he'd been yelling up at the apartment buildings when a crowd surrounded him. She was the one who'd called the police and told them where I worked.

A police officer followed us home and asked for my brother's information. After speaking with me, he was kind enough not to press charges, though he assured me he'd contact Pablo's parole officer, who could seek out an orientation for me that would go over different programs for counseling, housing, and managing medications.

Once in my apartment, we had a cup of coffee. I snuck in decaf instead of regular since Pablo had been having too much coffee on a regular basis. He didn't need to be any more wired. Pablo lit a cigarette and sat on the sofa, looking content. I stood at the window. People walked away from our building, some of them pointing to me in the window.

"Was I screaming really loud?" he whispered.

Relieved to hear his normal voice again, I nodded. "You were screaming at the top of your lungs, like you were ready to kill someone with an old lady's cane. Don't you remember?"

Pablo looked away. I didn't say anything. Maybe he didn't understand his own behavior. Would trying to discuss it with him do more harm than good?

Then I remembered him fencing with that cane in the middle of the street. I tried to hold back, but I burst into laughter. I couldn't stop. Pablo stared at me, confused, but then he burst into laughter too. "That whole thing was pretty wild," I said, and grabbed my keys. "I have to go get my car and pick up Andrecito now. Can you please come with me? I don't want to leave you here and come back to you attacking people with my broomstick."

He smiled. "That's not going to happen." Then he told me that he'd gone out to buy cigarettes, and when he returned, he didn't know which building was ours because all the brownstones looked the same.

"I got lost, sis, I'm sorry. Got anxious, sis, and I freaked out. I'm anxious, that's all." He looked away.

"Okay. We have to write the number of this apartment on a paper that you'll keep in your wallet at all times, and if you're confused again, you stop and look at the number. All these buildings have a big gold number right in front. Do you think you can do that?"

"All that space swallows me, sis, and . . . I can't think when that happens."

He had beads of sweat on his forehead from talking about it. I walked over to him, knelt on the floor, and took his hands in mine.

"Space won't swallow you. I promise. Look at me, it doesn't swallow me and I'm out there every single day. Come out with me more so you get used to having no walls. You're not in prison anymore. You're free."

He rubbed his hands, and I could tell he was nervous.

"When I see someone coming at me . . . I don't know why."

"I can imagine. But nobody is coming for you. People are just walking by, that's all."

Pablo nodded, trying to convince himself. "Just normal people, walking by."

"Exactly. Just normal people, walking by."

"How far is it from here, a hundred miles?"

"To where?"

"Woronoco."

"It's pretty far. It's about a two-hour drive. Over a hundred miles, I'd guess."

"I wish I was there right now," he said.

"Let's go visit Papá soon, and maybe you can stay with him for a bit if you like it in Westfield. How does that sound?"

Pablo gave me a thumbs-up and followed me out the door. He'd finally agreed to see our father. I hoped it would help. But that night, I waited for him to go to sleep and counted his pills. Pablo had stopped taking his medications. I felt guilty. A week before, I had allowed him to take them on his own.

The next day, I got off work early and called the psychiatrist, leaving a message with his secretary. The door to Pablo's room was closed, and I didn't want to disturb him. But when he didn't come out for lunch, I became worried and opened the door a crack. He was gone.

As I headed out the main entrance, I ran into the landlord and asked if she'd seen him. "He left early this morning, right after you did."

"You mean he's been out all day?"

"I saw him walking toward the park. Yes, early."

"Did he tell you where he was going?"

"No. He didn't say a word."

I ran to the corner store and asked the cashier if she had seen him. He hadn't been there. I ran toward the park, looking down every street on my way there. I scoured the neighborhood for hours. Arturo and Andrecito were on the front stoop when I returned.

Pablo did not return that evening. The following day, I left for work, hoping I'd find him waiting on the front steps when I came back. But he didn't return.

That night, I called my father and told him what had happened.

"*Desapareció el hombre. Jesús magnífico.*"

"I didn't want to call the police. I thought I could give it some time, see if he shows up." Then I told him about the incident with the cane.

"If he does something like that again, someone could hurt him. People have no idea he's a sick man."

We waited a few days, calling each other several times a day, but there was no sign of Pablo. Machi called, Socorro called. The whole family was worried. I couldn't sleep and missed work. The moment Arturo walked through the door every evening, he asked, *Has he shown up yet?* I drove around in the car looking for my brother. I waited on my front doorstep. On the fourth day, my father called at six-thirty in the morning.

"Your brother is here. *La policía* brought him last night."

"Is he okay? Where did they find him?"

"Old Westfield Road, on his way to Woronoco."

"Are you kidding me? He told me he wanted to visit Woronoco and Russell, so I said I'd take him to see you next weekend."

"Well, it seems he couldn't wait. He says he hitchhiked from your house to Westfield and walked from there."

"*¿Qué carajo?* Papá, this is unbelievable."

"They said he was limping. They stopped and asked if he needed help and he mumbled something. And you know the police, *mija*, they keep asking questions until they think there isn't anything funny happening," Papá said. "They got his name and took him to the station. He had a piece of paper with your address and mine, and they brought him here since it was closer."

"Thank God I put that in his wallet."

"Well, they're going to be calling you today. You're the one that first signed for him."

"Okay, okay. But did he say why he did this?"

"He hasn't said why, *mija*. Carmen prepared a bath for him and fed him. That wife of mine has cried more over him in one night than his own mother has in her whole life, and she's never even seen him before."

"What now?"

"I know you tried, but there isn't anything more you can do. He can live with us for now—Carmen already fixed him a bedroom. Just get him transferred here, and we'll take care of him. It's okay."

But a few days later, Papá called me early in the evening. "*Ay, mija, qué problema.* He won't stop talking and talking and laughing with no one there, running back and forth from one end of the house to another. Poor Julito is afraid of him."

"Is he taking his medications?"

"I haven't seen any medications. Where are they?"

"They're not here, Papá, he must have taken them with him."

"Nope. He didn't bring any of that with him here."

"Papá, please call the parole officer. Tell him you need to get Pablo to a doctor as soon as possible."

That evening, Arturo got takeout from our favorite Chinese restaurant. By the time he returned I had put Andrés to bed.

He sat next to me at the table and took my hand. "How are you feeling?"

I looked into his eyes without saying a word.

"I know this isn't what you wanted, but look at the bright side of this. You found your brother. He's alive and uninjured. Couldn't it be worse?"

I nodded.

"And you did everything you could. Andrea, you have a one-year-old. There's only so much you can do for everyone else now, that's just a fact of life."

I spoke without feeling. "I know."

"Focus on your applications for grad school. You have two months to submit them. Focus on us. Let's get a babysitter and go out to a movie now and then. My colleagues have been inviting us over for dinner, and I've been shrugging off those invitations for the last three months."

I ate in silence, consumed by the thought that Pablo would never be the same again. I had to stop thinking he was the same brother who'd left eight years before, that our relationship would somehow be the same.

That night, Arturo made love to me on the sofa, and it was as if I had walked into that tiny apartment he had in Amherst for the first time all over again. We'd been married four years, and our love hadn't once wavered. Then he sat up and wrapped his robe around himself.

"Wait here," he said with a mischievous smile. He walked into our bedroom on tiptoes and returned with a box in his hands. "He's sound asleep in there, the little guy." He held the box out to me. "*Feliz aniversario, mi amor.*"

I had forgotten our anniversary back in July. "Honey, I'm so sorry. I don't even know what was going on in my head."

"It's okay. I know you've been preoccupied. That's why I decided to save it, and this moment is so much better than that day was. Go ahead, open it."

The box had a gold band with little diamonds. I put it on my finger and wrapped my arms around my husband.

"Remember this, Andrea. I will never leave you. You're stuck with me and Andrecito forever."

That night I realized I couldn't remember the last time I'd played with my baby or had a conversation with Arturo that wasn't about Pablo. I had to pay attention to my own little family before more of our milestones passed without me noticing. I had to have a life that didn't revolve around my brother.

The next day Papá called and told me Pablo was in a psychiatric hospital in Northampton.

"Oh, Papá. What happens next?"

"Oh, *mija*, you don't have to worry about that. His parole officer told me they'll keep him there for two or three weeks, and when he comes out, he'll be much better. Then he can go to a home called 'halfway,' where he lives with people like him, and they have social workers who work with him and the medications and all that. And if he can go through a period where he's stable, then they put him in his own apartment where he can live a normal life, but that depends on him. If he doesn't take his medications, he can't live alone. So, we'll see."

"That doesn't sound too bad, Papá."

"Yeah. The doctor told me he didn't understand why you didn't call the parole officer sooner."

"I was afraid of getting Pablo into trouble again."

"Andrea Inés, let's get something clear here. Pablo is the only one that has ever gotten himself in trouble. You can love someone without taking responsibility for all the things they've done."

twenty-seven

Fifteen years passed before I returned to Woronoco with my brothers, in 1990. Julio was on vacation. His resemblance to our father always stunned me, even tilting his head just so when he walked. He was a twenty-one-year-old car salesman living in Baltimore, and Pablo, now thirty-eight, wanted to show him around. We had talked about going to Woronoco at every Thanksgiving dinner for years but had never settled on a date before Papá retired and moved to Puerto Rico.

Julio wanted to see where he was born, to know where all the stories he'd heard throughout his childhood had taken place. That day, we had to get authorization from the state for Pablo to come out of the facility on a day trip with us. As we drove from his home in Agawam to Westfield on Route 20, he looked so handsome, a tall, mature guy, his straight black hair cut in perfect symmetry with a stylish mustache and beard, and a heavy two-toned watch wrapped around his hairy wrist. I was concerned he might react poorly to flickering emotions as we took Julio back in time, but Pablo seemed content in his big-brother role.

As soon as we turned from Old Westfield Road onto Bridge Street, Julio stopped, and we got out of the car. He was wide-eyed in his stylish jeans and button-down shirt.

"Man, this is really out in the boondocks. I'm glad I wasn't here as a teenager."

Pablo grinned. "Yeah, you're a big-city boy. But this was nice when we were kids. There were lots of houses here, lots of other families."

Julio looked around at the trees. "Even the air's different here. Mr. Luis Rodríguez must've thought this was the closest he could get to Puerto Rico."

That's the thing about Woronoco. It's its own little world. There's nothing quite like the expansive canopy of trees, their leaves rustling in the wind, and the flow of Salmon Falls beneath the Woronoco Bridge. The gleeful waters welcomed us home as they slid over smooth silver slates and unyielding white boulders.

From a distance, we recognized the old paper mill, its doors closed and its smokestack boasting the company name. Julio looked around. "Not much here, huh?" He laughed. "Nothing but Strathmore. I could not have dealt with this."

I knew I could never fully convey our memories to him. How could you transform an abandoned paper mill in a solitary wilderness into a vivid community through words alone? I didn't know how to describe our intimate relationship with the forest around us, with the river and its giant shimmering slabs of stone.

I pointed past the boulders on the riverbank. "Those white stone slabs aren't slippery, but they're on a dreadful incline, steep enough for you to slip and land in the river. We used to spend hours crawling over them, lying on them, taking in their warmth."

Julio's brown eyes widened in surprise. "Down there on those huge slates? Holy shit, Andrea, that's pretty steep. Dad had no idea you guys were hanging out down there, right? He woulda been pissed."

Pablo laughed. "Papá didn't know anything we did while he was working."

We walked to the paper mill where our father had spent so many years of his life. Julio looked around, his dark brown hair blowing in his face. He asked if we knew which door Papá used to get in the building, and I showed him the big blue one on the side.

Julio had only been a child when men in blue uniforms walked in and out of the mill carrying their aluminum lunch boxes. He wasn't there when our father had worked at the flats, pulling tons of blocks of paper on a cart, or standing at huge boilers that cooked rags into mush used to make the finest linen papers, the boilers that had once sprayed him, scalding his leg.

Pablo and I looked at each other, a familiar hint of tar drifting up from the steaming road. For a second, I savored its aroma, as warm and familiar as morning coffee brewing in the kitchen.

An eagle swirled above the smoke pipe as two young men carrying fishing poles approached us.

Julio tapped my arm and laughed. "American *jíbaros* from around here."

They'd come from the Beehive, walked toward Bridge Street. I didn't hesitate to pounce on them for information they might offer about anyone from Tekoa Avenue. The two men said they'd been fishing "down there." I mentioned we'd lived in that cul-de-sac many years ago, but they said they'd never heard of anyone except for the one family there now.

"There was a whole community down there, about ten four-family houses," I said. "We were part of the big wave of Puerto Ricans in the 1950s."

They looked surprised by this, as if they'd never heard of it. How could someone live two streets from the Beehive and not know that years ago, a whole community had lived on the Tekoa Avenue cul-de-sac? We'd expected to find changes here, but not to have been forgotten, as if we'd never existed.

After a few minutes, the two guys left, eventually disappearing on the other side of the bridge. Pablo and I walked on the lawn in front of the paper mill in silence. The thick hedges of crimson roses that had lined the front lawn of the mill no longer existed; there was a hypnotic, lush sweetness to the flowers and vines lining the building that reminded me of those scarlet bushes bursting with blossoms. A few old rusty wires of the fence that had kept us out was all that was left of the garden, separating us from nothing but weeds.

We climbed into Julio's car and headed down Tekoa Avenue toward the Beehive.

"Is there anything else here?" Julio asked. "Maybe a Dairy Queen?"

Pablo snickered. "Nope. All we had was penny candy next to the post office and a candy bar machine at the club, which got torn down."

On the right-hand side of the road, at the top of the big hill, I caught a glimpse of the poison sumac trees, their pointed, wine-hued flowerets standing in bold salutation, still showing us the path.

We headed down the two hills, passing the paper mill and the dump. When Julio stopped the car, all I could see was a huge, empty cul-de-sac. On the left-hand side of the street, railroad tracks skimmed along the top of the hill, and I recalled the resonant, crackling wagons gliding along. But no trains passed through there now.

My brothers and I got out of the car and stared at the one remaining house. We noticed several vehicles parked in the area.

"Is this it? Man oh man, I don't think Mamá Carmen would've liked this," Julio said.

"None of the women did," I said. "But she was here for little over a year and never complained," I said.

Julio smirked. "Probably 'cause they already had plans to move to Westfield."

The memory of the tart scent of buckets full of apples on our autumn doorstep flooded my senses. I looked for the big peach tree next to Papá's garage to smell its sweet flowerets but didn't find it. In its place, a birch tree stood tall. It's surprising how much a tree can grow in just a few years.

Above the cul-de-sac, spreading its branches over the left-hand side of the road, we found the big oak tree. Pablo and I walked through overgrown brush and thickets until we reached it, our favorite place in Woronoco. Rubbing its thick, large roots, I remembered the castles, faraway cities, and fantastical worlds I'd visited between the roots of that tree, playing with Hannah and Emily. Julio walked over to the lots where the homes had been, camera in hand.

Pablo and I stood under the railroad tracks looking at the cul-de-sac. "Last time I saw you in Woronoco, you were walking down this road in the dark."

Pablo looked down. "The night I left."

"I promise not to cry anymore," I said, wiping my eyes. "But it's hard to come here and not think about it. I wish I could understand why."

"I was already doing drugs back then, sis. There was nothing you could do."

"I was the one who'd been put through so much. So why were you the one that ran away?"

He took out a pack of cigarettes and smacked the bottom. "We had it rough. That hag aunt of ours and then the old bastard, Mr. Carter. I remember exactly where I was when it happened. At home, watching TV. I should've been with you, watching out for you." He pounded his chest with his fist. "Everything that's happened to you, it's all happened to me, too, sis." Pablo's voice shook. "I felt it."

"It wasn't your fault."

"I found the peach trees!" Julio yelled. "They're loaded with peaches."

"He's a good kid," Pablo said, and we both waved at Julio. "You want to know what made me sick to my heart? I couldn't do a thing. I heard Perfecta criticizing you all the time. And then you were almost killed, because I wasn't looking out for you. Don't you remember what Papá used to tell me? He said my job was to take care of you."

"You were just a kid, Pablo. There wasn't anything you could have done to stop that from happening."

"I know that now. But I didn't then. I wanted to beat the shit out of them." Pablo wiped a tear away. "It's because of them you never had a childhood."

"It's okay. It all made me stronger in the end."

He laughed. "It's true. Look at you, with those beautiful Hollywood sandals and your hair all styled. You got all the diplomas and one lucky kid. And look at me! I got myself my own apartment with an L-shaped kitchen, all my meals cooked for me, and a pretty girlfriend. You're right. There ain't no reason to be unhappy. Look at us. We made it."

As my two brothers walked to the car, I noticed that I was standing on the sidewalk where I had my First Communion picture taken in 1960.

Julio winked at Pablo. "This was a good day, Bro. Now, let's get some food and get you back to the program."

Pablo nodded.

The car pulled out of the cul-de-sac, and as I looked out at the sidewalk, I was suddenly back on my bicycle, Pablo on his beside me. We passed the big tree, where kids were yelling and jumping off the Tarzan swing, their voices muffled by a passing train. We pedaled past Strathmore, its smoke-stack exhaling gray clouds into the sky. We pedaled harder to make it up the big hill, turned left at the red rose garden, and crossed the Woronoco Bridge over Salmon Falls, leaving all the poison sumac trees behind.

A warm breeze brushed through my hair as I looked back through the rearview window to the place where we always stopped by the post office on Old Woronoco Road. The farthest we were allowed to go. Pablo and I were there on our bikes, in the middle of the road, watching cars turn onto Route 20. We would wave to them, then turn our bikes around to go home. But not this time. Pablo was right: we'd made it.

As Julio and Pablo sat in the front seats, debating where to have lunch, what was left of the town faded into the horizon behind us, and I said a silent goodbye to the Woronoco Beehive.

Acknowledgments

It's a great honor to have my work chosen by Simon and Schuster's Gallery Books team and publisher Jennifer Bergstrom as the winner of their Books Like Us First Novel Contest. Thank you, editorial director Aimee Bell, for your excitement and commitment to this project that provides a new opportunity for underrepresented writers to tell our stories.

My first editor, Aliya King Neil, and editing assistant Andrew Nguyen turned the editing process into a fascinating journey. Editor Amara Hoshijo's meticulous insight enhanced my manuscript and always left me with a desire to continue working.

I'm also thankful for the collaboration of Rebecca Kaplan for handling contracts and for the enthusiasm of senior publicist Sydney Morris, senior marketing manager Bianca Ducasse, and assistant marketing manager Anabel Jimenez.

Many thanks to managing editor Caroline Pallotta, production editor Sarah Wright, copy editor Cecilia Molinari, proofreader Janet Rosenberg, interior designer Yvonne Taylor, and publishing assistant Kimberly Laws. Thanks to cover designer Grace Han for capturing the entire book in one gorgeous image.

I'm privileged to be represented by Laurie Liss of Sterling Lord Literistic, who has given me extraordinary counsel and always cares about me first. My sincere appreciation also extends to assistant Mary Krienke.

My greatest debt is to my early readers. I'm immensely thankful to my sister, Elizabeth, for believing I could write this story, for reading every single draft, and for her lasting, unwavering encouragement. To my dear son,

Edgar A. Vega, for asking questions and reminding me to embellish every scene with descriptions of the senses, for good conversation, and for playing relaxing tunes on his guitar. To my lifelong friend and colleague Elsa Luciano Feal, without whom I would not have had the confidence to write anything. I'm thankful for her generosity in taking on the arduous task of reading many drafts. To dear friend Patrick D. Collins for reading my first stories and offering penetrating comments and encouragement.

I have sincere appreciation for editor Marcela Landres, who led me to the UCLA Extension Writers' Program. For professors Harry Youtt and Judith Prager for a generous, enthusiastic, and critical reading of my work. And for editor and author Chuck Sambuchino, who critiqued my submissions draft.

I thank Sheryl Willey Pearce for filling me in on what it was like to live in Woronoco as a teenager during the 1970s; Beth Miller and Sue Maxwell, members of the Russell Elementary School Facebook page; the Russell Historic Commission for their enthusiasm and for providing me with historical details; senior physical planner Niels La Cour; Allan Byam and Glenn Barrington from the University of Massachusetts; and my dear cousin, William Montañez, for helping me figure out what the campus was like in the mid-1970s. And I thank Dr. Delia Glissette Toledo for sharing her expertise pertaining to the rights of psychiatric patients during that decade.

I could not have possibly written this novel without the memory of my father, Juan Antonio Pérez Vergara, who moved our family from Puerto Rico to Woronoco, Massachusetts, in the 1950s. I like to think he would have enjoyed the tapestry of characters and events I wove together as a testimony of gratitude.

My siblings, extended family, and many friends have awaited the publication of this novel with excitement, and I thank all of them for every reassuring word. I'm especially grateful to my brother Johnny, who took my brother Tony and me to Woronoco years after all the houses in the Beehive were torn down. It was after I heard the rumble of Salmon Falls and stood under the canopy of trees in the Beehive that I decided to write this novel.

I'm thankful for my friends Edgardo Pérez Montijo and Nelson Rivera Agosto, who listened to those first stories even before they were written. I'm also grateful to have an angel for a daughter: Isaura Elena Vega often pulled me out of my office to celebrate and so we could spend quality time together. I have the infinite support of my husband, Gregory Carlson, who listened to every story, offered critical perspective, honored my need for time alone, and lifted many weights off my shoulders. Last but not least, I'm thankful to my boy Ozzy the yorkie, who has seen me through every draft.

About the Author

Elba Iris Pérez is from Aguas Buenas, Puerto Rico, spent her early childhood in Woronoco, Massachusetts, taught theater and history at the University of Puerto Rico in Arecibo, and now lives in Houston. She is also the author of *El teatro como bandera*, a history of street theater in Puerto Rico.

BOOK
CLUB
FAVORITES

READER'S
GUIDE

The
Things
We Didn't
Know

Elba Iris Pérez

This *reading group guide for* The Things We Didn't Know *includes an introduction, discussion questions, ideas for enhancing your book club, and a conversation with Elba Iris Pérez. The suggested questions are intended to help your reading group find new and interesting angles and topics for your discussion. We hope that these ideas will enrich your conversation and increase your enjoyment of the book.*

Introduction

The inaugural winner of Simon & Schuster's Books Like Us First Novel Contest, Elba Iris Pérez's lyrical, cross-cultural coming-of-age debut novel explores a young girl's childhood between 1960s Puerto Rico and a small Massachusetts factory town.

Andrea Rodríguez is nine years old when her mother whisks her and her brother, Pablo, away from Woronoco, the tiny Massachusetts factory town that is the only home they've known. With no plan and no money, she leaves them with family in the mountainside villages of Puerto Rico and promises to return.

Months later, when Andrea and Pablo are brought back to Massachusetts, they find their hometown significantly changed. As they navigate the rifts between their family's values and all-American culture, and face the harsh realities of growing up, they must embrace both the triumphs and heartache that mark the journey to adulthood.

A heartfelt, evocative portrait of another side of life in 1960s America, *The Things We Didn't Know* establishes Elba Iris Pérez as a sensational new literary voice.

Topics & Questions for Discussion

1. *The Things We Didn't Know* is inspired by the author's own experiences growing up between Woronoco, Massachusetts, and Puerto Rico. How do you predict that her connection will impact your reading experience? As you read, reflect on how the author writes about these places that are extremely meaningful to her.

2. The book opens with a conflict between Andrea and Pablo's parents, as their mother hopes to return to Puerto Rico and their father wants to stay in Woronoco. How do these opposing viewpoints affect Andrea and her brother?

3. On page 16, Andrea explains that her father permitted bike-riding and playing after school, a monumental difference from their previous isolation. What do you think this shift felt like for Andrea and Pablo? How does the author show these emotions in the text?

4. We meet Aunt Cecilia at the airport on page 23. Raquel is taken aback by her appearance, but Andrea and Pablo watch their interaction with confusion, since they "couldn't imagine her being any other way" (27). How does the children's point of view impact your experience of this

scene? What might it suggest about how people can be more inclusive in real life?

5. Many dishes are written in Spanish with English descriptions, such as "*viandas con bacalao*, a codfish stew with root vegetables" (37). Why do you think the author chose to use language in this way, and how does this affect your impression of the food?

6. On page 42, Andrea proclaims that Tito is her hero. Who was your hero when you were growing up? Was it a family member, neighborhood friend, book character, or someone else?

7. Andrea describes her excitement to wear her school uniform with complete exhilaration: "*The hours couldn't go by fast enough. All I could think of was wearing my uniform on Monday. Life was the best it had ever been*" (61). What were some of the simple pleasures you were excited about as a child (such as, Halloween candy, new school supplies, jumping into piles of leaves)?

8. Pause on page 93, when Andrea and Pablo are about to return to Woronoco with their father. What do you think will await them back in the Beehive? How would you feel if you were Andrea and Pablo?

9. On page 101, Andrea learns some upsetting news. How has the author written this scene to embody the mind of a child? Are there any specific words or phrases that stick out to you as being particularly good examples of how this news affects Andrea?

10. Two characters experience a delightful reunion on page 251. How has time changed their relationship, and what aspects have endured despite the distance?

11. How do you think Julio's childhood compares to Andrea's and Pablo's experience growing up? How do all three compare to your own experiences?

12. At the end of the book, Andrea and Pablo have been on quite a journey. Which twists and turns did you predict, and which surprised you?

Enhance Your Book Club

1. When Andrea and Pablo first meet Tito, he teaches them how to help with chores around Titi Machi's farm. Andrea and Pablo absorb these lessons with wonder and delight. Create a schedule of your own childhood chores, then describe them to your book club. Refer to page 38 for inspiration. How does your perception of these tasks change after teaching them to someone else? After learning about them, does your book club's perspective on them differ from your own?

2. The beginning of Chapter 9 describes Andrea and Pablo living out a perfect summer day, from cartoons to baseball and beyond. Design your own perfect day! What activities do you incorporate, what foods do you eat, and who do you spend it with? As you share with your book club, think about how this current perfect day compares and contrasts what your childhood perfect day may have been.

3. Two characters discuss the importance of music on page 284, with one saying the following: "*Sometimes you don't know how to say something, and you hear your heart in one of his songs.*" Create a playlist of songs that evoke this feeling in you and play it on shuffle in the background of your next book club meeting.

A Conversation with Elba Iris Pérez

Q: **What inspired you to submit this book for the Books Like Us First Novel Contest? What does it mean to you to be the inaugural winner?**

A: When I came across the announcement for the Books Like Us First Novel Contest, I felt a renewed sense of possibility. Up until that point, I had submitted my manuscript to agents seeking diverse voices but had yet to find the right fit, even after working with a professional editor. I saw this contest as an opportunity where my story would truly be seen and given a fair chance.

To be the inaugural winner of this contest is deeply meaningful to me. It's not just a personal achievement, but a step forward in the broader movement to amplify diverse voices in American literature. As a Puerto Rican writer, being part of this history feels groundbreaking. It's a sign that the stories of people like me are being recognized, and I'm hopeful that this contest will continue to create a space for more authors from underrepresented backgrounds to share their unique perspectives.

Q: We'd love to know about your writing process for this book. How long did it take to get the story on the page?

A: It took over ten years to turn my idea into a manuscript ready for submission. Originally, I set out to write a historical account of the Puerto Rican workers who came to Woronoco, but the research proved more challenging than I anticipated. After struggling to find the facts I needed, I eventually had to abandon the project—a difficult decision after investing so much time.

Years later, something unexpected sparked a new direction. I began to imagine Andrea, Socorro, and Perfecta sitting in front of a TV, watching Elvis Presley perform. This scene felt so vivid that I turned it into a short story, which received overwhelming praise. Inspired by that response, I decided to expand the story into a novel. Going from writing history to writing fiction was liberating, exhilarating.

When I finished the first draft, I sought feedback from Marcela Landres, an editor who suggested I take some writing courses. I enrolled in the UCLA Extension Writer's Program, and after completing the courses, I returned to my manuscript with fresh eyes. I rewrote it from beginning to end, and shortly after, it was ready for submission.

Q: When you started writing, did you know how the story would end?

A: When I first started writing, I had an idea of where the story might go, but the journey to the ending wasn't fully clear. In the initial draft, I began the story with Pablo's conflicts, diving straight into the action. While my beta readers enjoyed those early scenes, several agents told me they struggled to connect with a character they hadn't yet gotten to know.

After taking courses at UCLA, I realized the importance of building a deeper connection between the reader and the characters before introducing major conflicts. That's when I restructured the story, shifting to a chronological approach. This allowed me to develop the characters' backstories and relationships first, so by the time the main conflicts arose, readers were more invested in their journeys.

Rewriting the structure made me see the story in a new light, and though I didn't know the exact ending when I started, the process of letting the characters grow naturally helped shape the resolution in a way that felt authentic and earned.

Q: **Do you find that there are themes that recur in your writing?**

A: Yes, several themes consistently recur in my writing. One of the most important is my love for Puerto Rico and the desire to challenge the stereotypes that often define us in the United States. Often, stereotypes end up replacing the reality of who people are. There's a richness and diversity to Puerto Rican identity that goes far beyond the common portrayals, and I see my writing as a way to showcase the depth of our culture, our history, and our complex relationship with the U.S. I want to tell stories that more closely reflect who we are, in all our diversity and nuance.

I'm also drawn to stories about women, children, and others from underrepresented groups who face significant obstacles in pursuing their dreams. These characters often struggle against societal barriers—whether it's poverty, discrimination, or cultural expectations—and I find it important to highlight their resilience and strength. For me, writing is about giving voice to those who are often silenced and showing the complexities of their experiences as they strive to overcome challenges and achieve their goals.

Q: How did you enter the mind of a child while writing a coming-of-age journey?

A: I don't know how I entered the mind of a child to write this story. Tapping into the mind of a child wasn't something I consciously planned. My background in theater, however, may have played a big role in helping me approach this task. As an actor and theater instructor, I've spent years learning how to bring scripts to life by fully embodying the emotions and thoughts of a character. Writing feels similar. I imagine a scene vividly and then work backward, thinking about what actions or thoughts would naturally express a child's emotions in that moment. The most difficult task is finding the perfect word to show the action and feeling.

At times, I would close my eyes, trying to clear my mind of adult worries and concerns. I found that there are two main areas of concern for a child: being accepted by other children and pleasing their parents. It's not about recreating childhood exactly, but about capturing the feeling of being young—whether it's the joy, confusion, obedience, or vulnerability that comes with growing up.

In many ways, writing from a child's perspective is an exercise in empathy. Just as an actor steps into a role, I stepped into the emotional world of my characters and let their experiences guide me through their journey. It was about letting go of my adult mindset and immersing myself in the feelings and challenges unique to childhood.

Q: Tell us about some of your favorite moments in the novel.

A: One of my favorite moments in the novel is when Andrea finally finds her brother, Pablo. The emotional complexity of that scene was challenging to capture, and I rewrote it many times to get it right. Andrea's mix of relief, fear, and hope is overwhelming, and I wanted to convey how deeply this reunion impacts her. It's a turning point in her journey, where she faces both the joy of finding her brother and the pain of everything that has changed between them.

Another favorite scene is when Andrea and Pablo meet Titi Machi for the first time. In this moment, I wanted to explore the surprise and confusion they feel about her gender identity, while also showing Titi Machi's vulnerability and her need for acceptance by her family. It's a scene full of tension and tenderness, as each character grapples with their own emotions while trying to navigate this new dynamic.

Both of these scenes are favorites because they represent major emotional and plot shifts. Writing them felt like a significant accomplishment—they are filled with the kind of raw, complex emotions that I strive to bring to my work. When I finished these scenes, I felt like I had truly captured something important about the characters and their relationships.

Q: **What parts of the novel did you find the most difficult to write?**

A: One of the most difficult scenes to write was when Andrea finds her brother, Pablo. This scene hit close to home for me, as I've experienced similar moments in my own life. Drawing upon those personal feelings to bring the scene to life was heartbreaking, and there were times when I had to stop writing because the emotions became overwhelming. I even found myself in tears, needing to regain my composure before continuing.

I struggled with deciding where to take the scene. Would Pablo die of a drug overdose? Would he disappear forever? Imagining losing a loved one in either of those ways was devastating, but I knew I had to confront these possibilities to tell the story authentically. I learned that, as a writer, you must live through your characters' experiences, if only for a brief moment, to capture their emotions in an honest way. That process can be painful, but it's necessary to create something real and true.

Another difficult scene to write was when Andrea leaves Woronoco. I lived there until I was twelve, and Woronoco is the place my mind goes to when I need solace. Writing that scene felt like I was saying goodbye to it forever, which left me heartbroken. But eventually, I realized that it wasn't me saying goodbye—it was Andrea. That realization gave me the distance I needed to finish the story, and I was able to complete the scene with a sense of closure, both for her and for myself.

Q: What are your reading tastes? What are you reading right now? Do you have a particular author you admire?

A: My favorite books are literary fiction, romantic fantasy, and Latin American literature. Before writing *The Things We Didn't Know* I wrote history and academic papers. Reading these books liberated my mind and taught me that all I need to write stories is my imagination. Blending the fantastical with the real showed me that storytelling has no boundaries, and it gave me the confidence to explore my own creative voice.

At the moment, I'm reading Barbara Kingsolver's extraordinary *Demon Copperhead*. Her powerful storytelling and deep connection to character are incredibly inspiring.

Q: What do you think happens to the characters after the end of the book?

A: Andrea and Arturo have a daughter, named Sofia. Andrea secures a job at a local community college and takes up piano lessons.

Pablo and Andrea remain close, both emotionally and physically, choosing to stay in Massachusetts. Pablo works as a delivery truck driver, marries a social worker whom he met at a halfway house, and they have a daughter, named Amanda.

Luis eventually retires from the Strathmore Paper Company, just before it shuts down, and returns to Utuado, Puerto Rico. For him, going back to his roots offers a sense of peace and closure after years of hard work and sacrifice.

Socorro also returns to Puerto Rico, never marrying but finding contentment in her independence and connection to her homeland.

Machi and Carol continue to live in Massachusetts, maintaining a close relationship with Andrea and Pablo. Machi's relationship with Carol creates a new family dynamic, one based on love and acceptance that brings everyone closer together.

At Pablo's insistence, Andrea eventually travels with him to visit their mother in the Bronx. Although their relationship remains distant, this step represents a reconciliation and closure, allowing both siblings to move forward while maintaining a cautious connection with her.

Q: **What's next for you? Are you working on anything new?**

A: I'm currently working on a new project that delves into magical realism, a genre that allows me to explore the boundary between the real and the extraordinary. I plan to continue writing stories with characters from underrepresented groups, drawing inspiration from Caribbean histories, myths, and folklore. My goal is to weave together the rich cultural heritage of the Caribbean with contemporary themes, giving voice to stories that often go untold.